BENEATH A BURNING SKY

JENNY ASHCROFT

sphere

SPHERE

First published in Great Britain in 2016 by Sphere
Paperback edition published in 2017 by Sphere

3 5 7 9 11 13 12 10 8 6 4

A CIP catalogue record for this book
is available from the British Library.

ISBN 978-0-7515-6503-4

Typeset in Baskerville by M Rules
Printed and bound in Great Britain by Clays Ltd, Elcograf S.p.A.

Papers used by Sphere are from well-managed forests
and other responsible sources.

Sphere
An imprint of
Little, Brown Book Group
Carmelite House
50 Victoria Embankment
London EC4Y 0DZ

An Hachette UK Company
www.hachette.co.uk

www.littlebrown.co.uk

Jenny Ashcroft lives in Brighton with her husband and three children. Before that, she spent many years living and working in Australia and Asia – a time which gave her an enduring passion for stories set in exotic places. She has a degree in history, and has always been fascinated by the past – in particular the way that extraordinary events can transform the lives of normal people. Keep in touch with Jenny by following her on Twitter (@Jenny_Ashcroft)

For Matt, Molly and Jonah

Central Alexandria, 30 June 1891

She reached for a wall, furniture, anything that might stop her falling. But there was nothing, and she fell, knees first, landing painfully on floorboards thick with dust. She pushed herself up, snapping her head this way, that way, disoriented by the speed with which everything was happening, straining to see. But after the fierce sunlight outside, the darkness swam and she could make out nothing but shadows and luminous spots.

She started to scream. A hand came over her mouth: strong, rough, forcing the sounds back into her. Men filled the room; three of them, no, four. Her breath came quick and short through her nose. She smelt sweat, garlic, a trace of hashish. Outside, she could hear the distant noise of the street: horses' hooves, the trundle of a tram. The men talked in Arabic around her, so calm. It terrified her, how in control they sounded.

The hand on her mouth dropped.

'What do you want?' Her own voice was high, too strained, and unnaturally English. 'I want to go. Let me go.' She blinked, her eyes becoming used to the darkness. The room was all but empty; just a pile of crates in one corner, a table of glass bottles in another. The men were dressed in the white robes of locals. Their faces were concealed by rags.

Footsteps clicked in the cobbled alleyway outside; the scrape of what sounded like a handcart. She opened her mouth, screaming again, calling for help. The man before her looked down, his eyes dark, wholly empty. Bored, almost. He shook his head, and reached

1

for one of the cloths covering his own face. Seeing what he intended, she arched her body away. 'No. No, no, no.' She scrambled to stand. Someone forced her down, the other shoved fabric covered in sweat and grime into her mouth. She gagged, choking, as more cloth was tied around her face.

Barely able to breathe, with tears pouring down her face, she looked to the door. White cracks of daylight shone through it. The packed Rue Cherif Pasha was only a moment's walk away. She lunged, making a break, but they jammed her back down to the floor. Her gown spread around her. Her head cracked. *Why are you doing this to me?* It came out as nothing but moans through the cloth.

She thought about her sister outside, still on the busy street. Perhaps in Draycott's restaurant by now. The soldier, Fadil, too. Did he know? Would he come? Her mind moved to her home, all of them waiting. Especially him. Would *he* sense she was in trouble? Oh God, she couldn't be here. This couldn't be.

A man crossed to the centre of the room. He opened a trapdoor. Noxious smells rose up. She felt herself being hauled along. She shook her head, kicking. It was a useless protest. They reached the hole in the floor. She saw stone stairs, gaping black, and pulled away, thrashing, filled with new terror. *Where are you?* The question to her sister and Fadil screamed in her mind. *Why aren't you coming?*

The first man disappeared into the floor. He seized her by her boots and pulled. Another pinned her arms to her side, heaving her along. As they carried her down, her body twisting and scraping along the rough brickwork, the others followed.

Find me. The trapdoor shut over her. *Please, please. Find me.*

BEFORE

Chapter One

Ramleh, Alexandria, March 1891

Olivia looked out across the bay. Sweat prickled on her forehead, down her spine. Her bathing pantaloons and tunic stuck to her skin. It was baking for March; everyone kept telling her so. *You didn't bring Blighty's weather out with you then.* (Really, how could she have?) The sun, even at just a little after nine, was biting; the kind of hot that after years of freezing English winters and disappointing summers she didn't think she would ever become accustomed to. She rolled her tight shoulders. Her woollen costume moved with them, across her bruises, catching painfully on her cuts. She tensed her jaw on the urge to wince.

She never winced.

The Mediterranean lapped the rocks beneath her, a turquoise blanket that stretched out to the horizon and made home seem so far away. Around the headland, towards the city, long-tail boats scudded back to the harbour, sails full as fishermen returned to Alexandria's morning markets, the waiting steam trains and donkey carts that would deliver their catch to Cairo, Luxor, a hundred other desert towns. The water flashed gold, speckled with light, inviting Olivia in.

She glanced back at the house. Her new husband, Alistair, stood on the veranda, ready for the office in his three-piece, the skin of his savagely elegant face as white as the veranda fencing surrounding

5

him. He held a cup and saucer in hand, lingering over his morning tea: imported Ceylon leaves, a dash of milk from the kitchen cow, half a level spoon of sugar. ('Level, Olivia, not heaped. *Level*.') His gaze was fixed on her, watching. Always watching.

Olivia took a step. She felt rather than saw Alistair pause mid-sip, saucer held aloft, cup of Ceylon's finest suspended. She flung herself forward and held her breath as first steaming air then cool water rushed through her layers, a balm to her burning skin. She dived deeper, lungs filling, fit to burst. For a sweet, submerged moment, she was invisible.

She broke the surface with a gasp, and swam out with swooping strokes. She was a confident swimmer, she'd learnt in the Solent as a child thanks to the icy dawn immersions that the mother superior at her boarding school had insisted on (*excellent for your constitutions, girls, and your wicked souls*). The distance between her and the shore quickly grew. It was only when her arms would take her no further that she rolled onto her back and let herself drift. Occasionally she turned her head towards the house, straining to make out Alistair's ramrod form, imagining the tick of irritation in his eye.

It was a familiar routine by now. She'd been coming to this bay at the bottom of their garden every morning since Alistair had brought her to Alexandria three weeks ago; the fact that Alistair hated her doing it ('I won't descend to drag you out in front of the servants, but you should be in the house. With me. It's improper, this gadding around in the water. Your skin is turning quite native.') gave her reason enough to carry on. He made her suffer come nightfall, of course. With words first ('What's going on in your mind, Olivia? Have I not made myself clear?'), and then all the rest of it. But she wasn't fool enough to believe that if she stopped, he would. He'd been finding reasons to punish her ever since the sodden winter's day two months ago that she'd finally relented, given up on her hopeless search for an alternative, and married him. It wasn't as though she'd swum the frozen Thames back then. No, it had been her melancholy at the ceremony that he'd taken her to account for that night. After that, it was the clothes she'd brought

6

in her trunk for the P&O voyage to Alexandria (totally unsuitable, far too thick, for God's sake. Was she listening? Was she?), then her laugh at the captain's joke over dinner (frankly flirtatious), and so it went on.

Olivia closed her eyes, pushing the memories away. She floated, hair loose around her. The water muffled everything but her own breathing in her ears. The sun moved higher in the sky; she felt the tell-tale tightening of freckles cropping on her cheekbones and sighed inwardly, knowing her lady's maid would insist on doses of lemon juice for nights to come.

She glanced again at the terrace and, seeing only space where Alistair had been, exhaled. She waited a few minutes more, enough time to ensure he'd really left for the day, off to the headquarters of his cotton export business in the city, then made her way back in. As she sliced through the soft swell, her unhappiness weighing bluntly inside her, she consoled herself with the thought that her older sister, Clara, would be calling soon. She came every morning, riding over by carriage from her own home up the coast. Sometimes she was alone, more often than not she brought her sons, Ralph and little Gus. Olivia still got a jolt, seeing them all. Clara especially. Real again, at last. For fifteen long years, ever since the two of them had been forced to leave their childhood home of Cairo for England following the death of their parents, they'd been kept apart. They'd had no communication – their grandmother had made sure of that: not a letter, not a word. Olivia hadn't even known Clara was living back in Egypt, the land they'd been born in, until Alistair had arrived on her doorstep in London and told her. Clara had been little more than a shadow to her; that dull ache of knowing she existed somewhere in the world, but with no clue as to where. And a memory, just one, of the day their grandmother – full of hate towards their dead mother and determined to exact her revenge, as though death wasn't enough – had torn them apart: that freezing January morning at Tyneside docks, back when Olivia was eight, Clara fourteen, and which Olivia tried, very hard, never to think about.

She didn't think about it now as she pulled herself from the sea, clambering out of the water. Wrapping herself in her bath sheet, she turned, picking her way over the rocks and into the garden. As she padded up the lawn towards the house, grass stuck to her toes. Water evaporated from her skin, leaving salty snail-trails on the unladylike tan of her forearms. The villa loomed large before her, a palm-fringed palace. Its terracotta walls were laced with jasmine, the shutters flung open in every room revealing the shadows of servants moving within. Olivia passed into its stultifying shade.

On the way to the stairs, she paused at the door to the boarder's room – a cavalry officer by the name of Captain Edward Bertram. He'd been staying with Alistair, a business associate of his father's, for years. It wasn't an unusual arrangement – all British officers rented private rooms in Alex, there was no great garrison here as there was in Cairo – but Olivia had yet to meet this houseguest. He'd been away ever since she arrived.

Today, though, the door to his room was ajar and two maids chattered within. Olivia asked what they were doing, and they replied that Sir Sheldon (they all called Alistair so, even though he wasn't a 'Sir' anything; it was the way of Egyptian servants with their masters) had asked for the room to be readied for the captain's return. Word had come that he'd be back that night.

Olivia shrugged, unsurprised by Alistair not bothering to mention it to her, and only mildly curious to meet this captain at last. Her life was so full of strangers these days, what difference would one more make?

She carried on upstairs, her thoughts fixed on getting ready for Clara. By the time she reached her bedroom she'd all but forgotten Captain Edward Bertram was on his way home.

Edward dropped down into his seat as the Alexandria Express creaked into motion, steam filling the air beneath the vaulted iron roof of Cairo's central station. He pulled his case of cigarettes from his jacket and lit one, inhaling slowly as the train chugged out to the fierce daylight beyond. As it picked up speed, funnel blowing, the beggar children who lived in the surrounding slums – blackened urchins with round eyes and mouths that were too big for their faces – swarmed alongside the carriages, hands outstretched. Edward stood, throwing what coins he had for them, then winced as one leapt for a window and was pushed from within, landing, a ball of scrawny limbs, in the rocks and dirt. He came to a halt just shy of the rails, but was up within the instant, ready for more.

Edward shook his head, staring after him.

'Serves him right,' came a bored voice from opposite; a sunburnt man in a top hat and three-piece suit. 'You shouldn't have encouraged them, you know.'

'Yes.' Edward smiled tightly, reclaiming his seat. 'Lazy buggers.'

'Just so.'

'Perhaps you have a factory somewhere you could put them to work in? Some sixteen-hour shifts would do them the power of good.'

The man narrowed his eyes. 'I'm in the civil service.'

Edward laughed shortly. 'Of course you are.' He took another drag on his cigarette, stretching his legs out before him, and turned to stare at the flat-roofed slums of Cairo passing by, letting the man know the conversation was closed.

The past weeks at the garrison training recruits had been hellish. He would have been pleased to be getting away from it – those baking days in the fly-infested boardroom, the lectures on the basics of the men's role (desert reconnaissance, border patrols, self-important circuits around town to remind everyone who was boss, and so on) – had he not been so depressed at the prospect of returning to Alexandria.

He'd asked for the month in Cairo as a favour from his colonel, Tom Carter, to get him out of town; he'd been disgusted by the callous way Alistair had gone off to England to fetch Clara's sister for his wife, incredulous that – more than a decade on from Clara's humiliation of Alistair, during that London season only ever spoken

9

of in whispers – Alistair should have redressed the balance with such calculated determination. For Edward had no doubt that's what it was all about, that Alistair's choice of wife had far more to do with Clara than with Clara's sister. But even he, who'd observed Alistair's fixation with Clara many times in the three years he'd been living with him – wondering how the hell Clara tolerated his pale eyes on her at parties, the curl in his lip whenever she spoke – had never imagined it would cause him to stoop so low. He simply hadn't trusted himself to be present when Alistair returned from London, dragging the new Mrs Sheldon with him. And the time away in Cairo had made him see just how sick he'd become of life in Egypt; not just his role – the drills, the endless drills, the desert trips and constant monitoring of locals who'd never asked to be governed in the first place – but living with Alistair too.

He'd wired Tom. *Any chance of my getting out and going home before my commission is up?*

None, Tom had replied. *Everything all right, old man?*

Not really, wrote Edward. *How about a transfer?*

Tom had set the process in motion: a promotion to major, in Jaipur. It would take a while, but it was going through. Edward wasn't a fool, he knew that in the end life in India would be more of the same. But since he apparently had no choice but to serve out his time in the cavalry, he might as well do it somewhere new. After all these years in Egypt, he needed a change of scene. Jaipur would *feel* different. For a while at least.

He turned to the window, watching as the city gave way to desert, the dunes rolling past. He drew on his cigarette, paper crackling, and exhaled; smoke spiralled through the open window, mixing with the white haze of the desert beyond.

He was right to go.

Really, when all was said and done, what was there to keep him in Egypt?

'Livvy!' Clara called out from beneath the fig tree. 'I hope you don't mind us making ourselves at home?' She smiled, cheeks dimpling.

She'd laid out a tartan rug in the shade and was sitting, lace skirts cushioned around her, with baby Gus gurgling on her lap. Clara's older boy, eight-year-old Ralph, was on the lawn beside them, freckled face serious, stockinged legs braced, hammering hoopla pegs into the lawn. He looked up at Olivia and waved his hammer. 'Hello, Aunt Livvy.'

Olivia waved back. As she crossed the grass towards them all, Clara gestured at a wicker basket. 'Oranges,' she said. 'I brought them from my garden, they're out early this year. All the warm weather. Try one, Livvy, they're positively bursting with sunshine.'

Olivia said she was fine, thank you, she'd never really liked oranges.

Clara's brow creased. 'You used to . . .'

'I don't think so.'

'Yes,' Clara said, 'Mama grew them too. I remember you eating them when you were little.'

'Really?' Olivia frowned, trying to recall ever doing such a thing. But there was nothing there, just a blank. All of her childhood before she and Clara were separated was just that. The morning they arrived in England after their parents died, those freezing London docks, Clara's sobbing face, her own desperate fear as her grandmother told her where she must go; there was a wall in her mind, blocking out everything behind it: her early years back in Cairo, Clara as a child, their parents' faces, the sound of their voices . . . Gone. It was Clara who held all the memories; she was passing them on to Olivia one by one. *Your education.*

'I used to peel the white bits for you,' Clara said now, staring down at an orange. 'You liked it, I promise.'

Olivia sighed, said she was sure she had. She dropped down onto the blanket, landing with a soft thud. She leant over Gus, tickling him under the chin. He squirmed, rustling against Clara's gown. Leaves cast shadows on his face. So dark, this little man, as though he'd sun-baked in the womb. He eyed Olivia warily. 'Don't worry,' she said, 'I'm not going to try and take you from your mama.' She tickled him again. 'I wouldn't dare.' He screamed blue murder with everyone except Clara.

Clara stroked the curve of his olive cheek. 'Little monster,' she said softly.

A maid came out with a jug of minted water, some pistachio biscuits. They drank and nibbled whilst Ralph played. Clara peeled an orange, dripping juice into Gus's mouth. Every time Ralph landed a hoop on a peg, he'd turn, and Clara would exclaim, making him beam.

The longer Clara watched him though, her own expression shifted, became heavy.

'Are you all right?' Olivia asked.

'Yes,' she said distractedly, 'of course.'

'You look sad.'

'No, no, not at all. I'm splendid.'

'You're not.' Olivia nudged her. 'You turn ever so British when you're only pretending to be all right.'

'Do I?' Clara laughed at that.

'So?' Olivia prompted her.

She shrugged, eyes on Ralph. 'I was just thinking of him going off to school in England, that's all. July seems too soon.'

'Have you told him yet that he's going?'

'No. I can't do it. Jeremy doesn't seem to want to either. He's obviously hoping I'll give in first.' A dent formed on her brow. 'Foul man.'

It was hardly unusual for Clara to speak of her husband so. She might have told Olivia that she'd felt differently once, years ago, back when she first met Jeremy during that London season – Jeremy, a joint partner in Alistair's vast network of cotton plantations, had been in England with Alistair on business, and Clara, introduced to them both at a debutante ball, had (to Alistair's lasting chagrin) fallen for Jeremy's charms instantly – but these days she was always calling him foul. Olivia struggled to see it herself. Jeremy was so kind to her, stopping to chat whenever he called at the house, enquiring as to whether she was bearing up

12

with the homesickness, not finding the damned heat too intolerable, the loneliness too hard. Olivia always assured him that she was well (a lie that came like breathing; a legacy of the nuns who'd beaten the habit of betraying upset from her long ago. *Self-pity is a sin. And what do sinners need? Yes, that's right …*) but she could tell from Jeremy's grimace that he knew she wasn't, that she hadn't been ever since Alistair had convinced her grandmother to exercise her legal rights as guardian, cut her off from her inheritance, leave her destitute if she didn't agree to marry him. That or send her back to the convent as a nun. She couldn't help but be grateful to Jeremy for his understanding; if they'd lived in a world where thoughts really were all that counted, his silent empathy would have meant a great deal.

He could be distant with Clara though, she supposed; the two of them rarely seemed to talk, other than about the children.

Still, Olivia would take distance over the alternative any day of the week.

'I want to keep Ralphy back another year,' said Clara. 'He's still such a baby. My baby.' She paused, frown deepening. 'I'd keep him with me for ever.'

'Then why don't you?'

'Because Jeremy won't have it. He says it's not fair on him, that we've already held him up, and it will be harder on Ralph in the long run if we do it again.'

Ralph collected his hoops, threading them onto his chubby arm. He caught Olivia's eye and smiled. She, thinking of the brutal loneliness awaiting him, managed barely a grimace in response.

Clara said, 'Grandmama's written. She wants to come over at the start of July, take Ralphy back herself. She's booked the voyage.'

Olivia turned, aghast.

'I know,' said Clara, looking as desolate as Olivia felt at the prospect. 'I've written to say she mustn't, but I'm not sure she'll have any of it.' She raised her face to the sky, eyes scrunched with the effort of her thoughts. 'I'd take Ralph myself, but Gus is so little for the journey, and I can't leave him here, it's too hard.'

'Why?' Olivia asked. 'Why is it hard?'

Clara didn't answer.

Olivia said, 'You have to do something, Clara. You can't let that witch take Ralph.'

Still, nothing.

Olivia filled her cheeks with air and let the breath out. Even the thought of Mildred made her feel ill. It wasn't just the way she'd helped Alistair blackmail her into marriage, the delight with which she'd reminded Olivia that given her parents had left no will, she'd won complete control of Olivia's person, her money, until she wed. *I mean it, Olivia, I'll see you back in that convent, don't think I won't. Who else can you go to for help? Your friends have no means. You haven't seen your sister in years, I expect she's forgotten all about you.* It was everything else Mildred had done, back when Olivia and Clara were children. Olivia could picture her even now at those docks, dressed in black taffeta, waiting at the foot of the gangplank when she and Clara got off the ship after their journey from Cairo. She could see the fog blowing from her mouth, hear the satisfaction in her thin voice as she told Clara that if Mildred was taking her home to Mayfair, young Olivia here had somewhere else to be, a convent school in fact. *Say goodbye quickly now. The nuns are waiting, Olivia . . .* And then, what had happened next . . . No. Olivia drew breath.

She returned her attention to Clara. 'You can't let her come,' she said again. 'I can't face it.'

'Nor can I.'

Neither of them spoke for a while after that. Clara fiddled at Gus's frock, then peeled another orange, only to let it sit, uneaten, by her side. Ralph threw more hoops. Olivia batted at the flies.

At length Clara asked Olivia, as she always did, how things had been with Alistair since yesterday. Olivia lied, as she always did, and said fine, or fair at any rate, and received the usual small smile: pained, disbelieving.

Olivia picked at a blade of grass. She could feel Clara watching her, waiting for her to say more. But Olivia didn't know how to begin to put words to her marriage. And really, what was the point? What could Clara do? It wasn't as though Alistair would ever let her leave; he reminded her nightly that he'd track her down if she ever tried it, that he'd have her in the madhouse as a lunatic before he released her from her vows.

Olivia pulled at the grass, making it snap. Ralph, giving up on his hoops, loped over and dropped down by her side. She tried for a smile, ruffled his tawny hair.

Clara reached over, taking hold of her fingers, squeezing. 'I'm so sorry,' she said, for the hundredth time. 'If I'd only known what he was planning when he left for England, I could have sent money, helped. Simply *forced* Grandmama to tell me where you were. But he never breathed a word of it, not to me, not to Jeremy . . .'

'It's not your fault,' said Olivia.

'I feel as if it is. What I did to him all those years ago, Jeremy too. His friend. He's never let it go, and now you're paying for it.'

Olivia looked down the lawn towards the bay. 'I don't want to be here when he comes home tonight.' She heard the words before she realised she was going to speak them. She gave a self-conscious laugh, awkward even at this small honesty.

Clara tightened her hand. 'Leave a note,' she said. 'Tell Alistair you're meeting me for dinner. Jeremy mentioned they have a big contract on, they'll be working late. If you get away from here by seven you'll miss him. I'll book a table in the Greek Quarter, you haven't been to Sabia's yet. I might be a little late, I have an errand to run, but you can always have a drink whilst you wait.'

Olivia nodded, relieved.

Edward's man, Fadil, was waiting outside Alex station, wiry in his oversized khaki, bald head glinting in the late afternoon sun. He had both their horses with him. Edward took his own stallion, patting his silky flank, then shook Fadil's hand, pleased to see him after these weeks away. It wasn't often they were parted. Fadil had been working for Edward ever since he'd come to Egypt, back when the British Protectorate was first established in '82. He was an excellent batman as well as soldier, and Edward normally took him everywhere. But he'd insisted he'd cope alone in Cairo on this occasion. Lines were rigidly drawn at the garrison there, the quarters for native soldiers were rank; Edward wouldn't stable his horse in them, let alone subject Fadil to the filth.

He hadn't written to tell Fadil that he was going to India. He was ashamed of the secrecy, but he couldn't face it, not yet. He'd asked Tom to keep the news from the rest of the men too. He hated goodbyes; until his date for going was locked, he wouldn't start them.

He asked Fadil how life had been this past month. Fadil said fine, normal. Edward enquired after each of his lieutenants, Fadil told him they were well, drilling every day.

'Naturally,' said Edward.

Fadil held out a note. 'From the colonel, sayed.'

Edward took it, stifling a yawn. It was the stuffy carriage, it had jaded him. His eyes moved over Tom's scrawled hand.

Immy's furious about your transfer, all my fault apparently. She says I'm to take you both to dinner tonight to apologise for arranging it. Meet us at ʿahīd's at seven. It'll be good to see you, old man.

Edward smiled, pleased in spite of his tiredness, at the prospect of spending the evening with Tom and his wife. He decided to go to the parade ground to change; his tails had been freshly pressed back in Cairo, he had everything he needed with him. He couldn't stomach returning to Alistair's just yet.

He swung into the saddle and rode from the station with Fadil by his side. As they clopped through the stuccoed city centre, Edward stared at the odd remnant of a shattered wall, the broken ruins where offices had once stood. Even a decade on, the rubble still made him stop, pause: these lingering marks of the damage done by the Royal Navy's guns, back when they'd had to pound Alex with cannons before the ruling khedive would allow them in to set up British rule. A reluctant intervention, so the story went, when political unrest in the country ran out of all control – government coups, riots, and so on. Everyone knew it had been as much to do with the allure of Egypt's rich cotton fields, cheap labour and easy access to the East.

It wouldn't do to speak of that, of course.

Edward kicked his horse on, down into winding streets that led to the harbour. They were packed, even at this late hour, the cobbles hemmed in by stone dwellings, market stalls, fruit shops and bakeries. The air was rich with the tang of ripe fruit, spices and onions sweating in oil. Edward wove this way and that, avoiding the crowds. As he and Fadil reached the coast road, though, Edward spurred them both on into a gallop, relieved to be in the open, moving. He gave his horse the reins and drank in the deep blue of the Mediterranean, its colour such a contrast to Cairo's dust. He kicked. *Faster.* A warm wind rushed around him, raw with salt. Desert blossom spread over the sandbanks lining the road. Edward breathed deep on the scent, the fresh air, relishing it: a short burst of life before Alex crackled and withered in the deadening summer heat.

He arrived at the restaurant early and lingered outside, looking down the wide avenue. It was a rich part of town, full of the villas of wealthy Greek families who'd moved across the sea to make Alex their home over the centuries. The pavements had more than one well-dressed couple strolling along them. Cypress trees swayed lazily in the balmy air; the sun was only just setting. Edward, legs still twitching from being on the train for so long, decided on a walk himself.

It was then that he saw her, crossing the road from where several carriages were parked. She was dressed in a sleeveless blue gown, and she was tanned; unusually so.

It was the first thing he noticed.

She looked up at the restaurant sign, eyes registering its name. She pressed her tooth to her bottom lip.

'Are you all right?' he asked, since he had to say something. 'Not lost?'

'Not lost,' she said. 'Just making sure I'm in the right place.'

Her voice was the second thing he noticed: soft, warm; nothing like the cut-glass tones he was used to.

She carried on in.

And he stared after her.

He could hardly stop himself looking.

Chapter Two

He followed her in, of course. He didn't feel as if he had any choice. He watched through the haze of cigar smoke and champagne vapour as she was shown to her table, all thoughts of Tom, the dinner ahead – leaving Egypt – gone. He saw the way her lips moved as she spoke to the waiter, her nod at whatever he said. (The third thing, the fourth thing.) His gaze settled on the cut of her cheekbones, her coy, slanting eyes. There was something familiar about her, but he couldn't place it.

She looked up at him, then away just as quickly. Too quickly. He was certain her disinterest was considered. There was a tension in her bare shoulders. He felt a beat of triumph, observing it.

She flicked another glance in his direction; he arched his eyebrow. She flushed, appearing to fight a smile, losing. She dropped her head, brown curls bouncing. Enjoyment pulled on his cheeks; he'd known that he'd like her smile.

He was almost at her table before she saw him coming. Her eyes, that were neither blue nor grey nor green, widened in surprise. He noticed that the neck of her gown was loose, as though she had recently lost weight. For some reason, the idea unsettled him.

'Are you sitting down?' she asked as he pulled out the chair opposite her. 'You can't. I'm meeting my sister.'

'Yet here I am.' He smiled across at her, willing her to smile back again. 'And it's not really improper at all, because I'm almost certain I know you. I've been trying to work it out.'

'You have?'

'I have.'

'Oh.' She nodded; she appeared to be thinking about what to say next. Her eyes moved over him, taking in his evening dress. 'You're ever so smartly dressed for a man with your accent.'

He burst out laughing.

So did she.

He liked her more.

'My da runs a textile business in Derbyshire,' he said. 'We're *new money*. I have five older sisters who all refused to marry a title.'

'A shame.'

'Yes, for me. I got put into Sandhurst as a result. An army officer in the family's the second best thing to a lord.' He grinned, held out his hand. 'I'm Captain Edward Bertram.'

What happened next, happened very slowly. Her expression remained fixed, but the light in her features, the one he'd been so enjoying, ebbed from her. It was like watching someone fall. He didn't immediately understand what was happening, but he reached for water, poured her a glass, asked if she was all right.

'I've just remembered who I am,' she said. 'I'd forgotten there for a moment.' She stared over at him. 'You're not in uniform. I might have guessed you were you if you had been.'

'What are you talking about?' He was baffled by her speaking so strangely, but sure already that whatever she said next, it couldn't be enough to put him off.

'I'm Olivia Sheldon.'

It should have been enough to put him off.

They looked at one another mutely. He realised that neither of them was trying to pretend it didn't matter. She picked up her glass of water and then set it down again. She frowned, eyes lowered so her lashes shadowed her cheeks. It was then that he realised why she'd seemed so familiar. She looked like Clara, of course. A slighter version, different colouring, but unmistakably her sister.

She said, 'So you're moving back into the house.'

'Yes.' He should tell her now that he'd be leaving Egypt within months. 'I'm sorry to have been away.' *Look up at me, please.* 'How have you found it here, in Alex?'

Her face moved in a twisted kind of smile; she raised her head, met his stare. And the hopelessness in her gaze made him wish, as he felt he'd never wished for anything before, that Alistair Sheldon, who had so infamously courted and been rejected by Clara for his business partner all those years ago, had just left her younger sister alone.

Everyone arrived all at once. Clara, exclaiming in delight ('Livvy, you never said Teddy was on his way'), and the Carters, all smiles at Olivia and Clara being in the restaurant. ('What a treat,' said Imogen, her face alight with a happiness that made her look much younger than her forty-odd years. She was always so delighted to see them; an old friend of their mother's, she had known them both too as babes. 'Let's sit together, why don't we?') Olivia felt at once present and strangely removed. She must have stood as the tables were shifted, chairs arranged, because she found herself standing. She kept looking at him, distracted by his face. His skin, so dark above the collar of his evening shirt; a hint of golden stubble. His brown hair had flecks of light in it. The sun, of course. And his eyes; they didn't dance any more, not at all. But they were weighted with something she'd never seen in Alistair's blue stare: warmth; compassion.

She'd known him less than fifteen minutes, and she felt safer than she had in months.

She thought, *So this is what it's like.*

And then, *What a shame.*

Menus were brought, handed out. Wine ordered. ('Champagne I think,' said Tom.) Olivia tried to keep her gaze on the table, her cutlery, the grains in the wood . . . But it kept moving to Edward's leg, just inches from her own. She could feel him in her skin, her muscles. *You are married. Married. He'll kill you before he lets you go.*

She picked up her menu, thought how impossible it would be to eat, and without knowing she was going to, stood.

He did too.

'Are you all right?' Clara and Imogen spoke together, all concern. They too were on their feet.

'You look hot,' said Clara. 'Are you faint?'

'She's very flushed,' said Imogen. 'Tom, get her water.'

'Please,' she said. He took a step towards her. 'I'll be fine.' She looked to the restaurant door, her carriage beneath the trees in the street beyond; the horses that would take her home, the last place she wanted to be and the only place she could go. She picked up her bag, turning.

'I'll take you,' said Edward.

'Yes,' said Imogen, 'that's a good idea.'

It was an *awful* idea.

'No,' said Clara, already gathering her things, 'I'll see Livvy home.'

It was almost as bad an alternative. Olivia needed to be alone, make sense of her own mind before she saw Alistair. *You are married. Married.* She told Clara to stay, she'd be fine by herself. Really. No need for such fuss, for goodness' sake.

She made to leave. Clara protested again, but Olivia insisted. As she passed through the restaurant door, hand shaking as she pushed it wide, she felt his eyes on her. Heat spread up her neck.

Out on the pavement, she forced herself to exhale. She tipped back her head, looking to the now starry sky, and attempted relief at being out of the crowded dining room, away. She refused to feel despondent. She wasn't. No. Not that.

She set off for her carriage. She didn't look back at the restaurant window behind her, she didn't try to glimpse him at the table. *Enough*, she told herself, *that must be that.*

Alistair was home when she got there. A candle burned in their bedroom, she could see it from the driveway; a disjointed flicker of light, taunting her. She pursed her lips, blowing her breath out slowly. Alistair would be angry. He hated her going out without him, especially with Clara. It had felt easier to pretend his rage didn't matter earlier, when Clara had suggested the meal and night was still hours away.

She placed her hand to her silken waist, feeling the bruises – fresh from the night before. Her punishment for not being Clara. And that slight to Alistair's ego, perhaps his heart too, that Clara had so carelessly inflicted on him back when she chose Jeremy instead.

Alistair's shadow moved behind the glass panes of the window; waiting, always watching. Olivia took another deep breath, bracing herself for what was to come. Strange how it seemed harder than ever tonight. She reminded herself that she'd fight, she always did. She wouldn't just give in. She had that at least.

He'd win in the end of course. She knew that too.

But since there was nothing else for her to do, she took a step forward on the gravel, went into the house and walked slowly up the stairs.

She didn't swim the next morning. Alistair left for the office, a smile thinning his lips. *I didn't not go because of you*, she wanted to scream.

She stayed in her room for breakfast, picking at a loose thread on the armchair, listening to Edward in the dining room below. His deep voice travelled up; she thought he might be speaking in Arabic, even though Alistair had banned it in the house, and found she liked that idea. *No, don't like it. You can't. You know what Alistair will do to you if he suspects.* There was a laugh, more words, the scrape of a chair, footsteps in the hallway.

A pause.

She held her breath.

No sound.

She pictured him, waiting there, at the foot of the stairs, sun-darkened face looking up. Her legs itched to run to the landing to see. She pulled herself further into the armchair.

Footsteps on the tiles, the front door opened, closed. And this time she couldn't stop herself standing, crossing to the window, craning her neck to see him go around to the stables, come back out again with his horse. She watched the easy way he swung into the saddle, then rode away down the driveway, reins in one hand, the other resting by his side. She noticed his navy uniform, how it made him look taller somehow than the night before, full of lean strength. He paused at the gate. She found herself gripping the window sill. Then he turned, looked up, met her eyes with his brown ones and tipped his hand in a small salute.

And even as she told herself that she was married, *married*, she raised her hand and waved back.

'You're still looking sickly,' Clara said as they sat down to morning tea on the terrace. 'Did you not sleep? I've been worried.'

'I'm fine.'

'I don't think you are.'

'I'm just under the weather, that's all. It's nothing.'

'Perhaps you're ...'

'No, I'm not.' Olivia shuddered, distracted momentarily from thoughts of Edward by the hideous idea of carrying Alistair's flesh and blood within her for anything longer than the seven to nine minutes he forced on her each night. She'd gone to see a gynaecologist before she left England; she had a contraption that she used secretly to make sure it never happened. God only knew what Alistair would do if he discovered her using it. She grew hot, just thinking about it.

Clara said, 'It might help things, you know, if you were.'

'I doubt it.'

'Children, they make things worth it.'

'Clara.'

'Without Ralph and Gus I'm not sure what I'd do.'

'*Clara!*' Olivia shouted it. 'I don't want to have Alistair's child. I couldn't stand it.' She raised her hand to her mouth, shocked at herself for speaking so openly.

Clara stared. 'Oh, Livvy.'

'Let's not talk about it.'

'I think we should.' Clara reached out, took her hand. 'You might feel better.'

Olivia instinctively opened her mouth to say, no, she wouldn't, but hesitated, feeling the warmth of Clara's touch, the temptation to let go some of what she'd been bottling up. Why did it have to be so hard? She'd been told by Clara that she'd been such a gabbler as a child, impossible to keep quiet. *Always, always, your little heart on your sleeve.* She couldn't imagine now what it must have felt like to be so free. To not keep a barrier within you, one which caught every urge to talk, censoring, checking. How happy the nuns would be to know the barrier was still with her; they'd worked so hard to instil it. Allergic to tears, they'd patrolled the dormitory at night, smacking girls who cried, anyone fool enough to hug another. *No touching.* ('Suck on your fist,' Olivia's best friend, Beatrice, had told her that first awful night. 'They'll be even crosser if they come back and you're still crying ... ') The fist hadn't worked for Olivia (and the nuns had been crosser, very much so). Over time, she supposed she'd taught herself to pretend none of the awfulness was real, not speak of it ... Refuse to accept it was there. It had helped her live with it. In a way.

It had been helping here.

Until last night. Now she simply couldn't go on pretending. She didn't want to. Not any more.

'Livvy ... '

'I can't escape him,' she said, and just like that, the words were out. Free. They left a hollow in her chest. 'I hate him for that, but me even more ... '

'Don't hate yourself, Livvy. Not that.' Clara held her hand tighter. 'I simply won't allow it. Hate him, just him.'

'I don't know what to do, Clara.'

Clara continued to stare. 'Livvy,' she said slowly, 'it's just words, the way he is, isn't it? You'd tell me if it was more.'

Olivia swallowed, gave a nod, unable still, even with Clara, to admit the mortifying truth. 'Just words.'

The look of relief on Clara's face made her glad she had lied. 'Hard enough though,' Clara said. 'I want to help you, tell me how I can.'

'I don't know what you can do. I married him. I made that choice.'

25

'It wasn't much of a choice.'

'But I *did* make it. I should have been stronger. Found another way.'

'What other way? Where would you have gone? With what money?'

'I don't know.' Olivia's brow creased as she searched for the umpteenth time for an escape she might have taken. She and Beatrice had turned it over and over between them; Olivia had been staying with her and her aunt when Alistair came. Beatrice had been about to leave England herself, for her parents' home in India; missionaries, they had little money, but Olivia had been planning to use her own allowance to travel out too, live there. Until Mildred put a stop to it. She'd threatened to alert the ports if Olivia tried to borrow the fare and defy her. She'd said she'd inform them Olivia was her ward, travelling without permission, take her direct to the convent, sign her over and good riddance. Desperate, Olivia had visited solicitors, several of them, determined to discover that Mildred had less power than she claimed. But they all told her the same thing – that the terms of Mildred's guardianship were beyond dispute; so long as a court deemed Mildred to be acting in Olivia's best interest, Mildred could do with Olivia as she pleased. *Best to accept it, my dear. You are so young, a woman without independent means. No judge will take you seriously. Even if we could find one who would, you cannot afford the legal fees.* 'I tried to tell myself I could make the best of it,' she said now. 'I didn't know Alistair, I thought . . . I don't know, that perhaps I could try to like him. And then he told me, well, that you were living here. That I'd see you again.' She fixed her eyes on Clara's pained gaze. 'That made things feel easier.'

'Oh, Livvy.'

'It's done,' Olivia said, 'and I'm his. He reminds me all the time. He'll never give me a divorce.'

Clara flinched. 'Would you want that?' Her voice was hushed, as though the words themselves were dangerous. 'Think what it would do to you. No one *does* it.'

'No,' said Olivia, 'I don't suppose they do.'

26

'Where would you even live? I'm not sure Jeremy would . . . Well, that he'd have you with us. The boys, the scandal.'

'Really, Clara. I wouldn't ask that of you.'

'You could, Livvy, if it was in my power to give it. But,' she widened her eyes helplessly, 'your life, it would be . . .'

'Over. Yes.' Olivia bowed her head. *It is anyway.* 'As I said, it's pointless talking about it. Alistair would need to grant it, and he never will.' She sighed. 'Let's leave this, shall we? I'd rather leave it.'

Clara hesitated.

'Please, Clara.'

'All right,' she said. 'But I'm here, Livvy. I want you to remember that. I always will be. You aren't alone.'

'Yes.' It was something.

Clara let go of her hand, reached up, touched her cheek. 'You need to eat more.' She gave a sad smile. 'Let's start with cake.'

She turned her attention to the currant loaf in front of them. As she pushed the blade down, crumbs spilling on the plate, her smile dropped. Olivia, noticing the shadows beneath her eyes, a pallor just beneath the surface of her skin, was reminded of the way she'd been as she watched Ralph the day before.

She asked her if she was thinking about him.

Clara looked up, clearly startled by the question, said, 'No, no.'

'Then what's wrong?'

'With me, Livvy? Nothing. I'm top-drawer.'

It was the 'top-drawer'. A strangled kind of laugh burst from Olivia. She didn't know where it had come from. She was very upset – about a great deal. But it came again, cutting through the tension in the air. She couldn't stop it.

And Clara, knife in hand, laughed too. Her eyes sparkled with it. She didn't seem able to stop either. The more she laughed, the more Olivia did. She had no idea what they were both still laughing about.

At length, Clara wiped her eyes with the heel of her hand. 'Oh, Livvy,' she said, catching her breath, 'what's wrong with us?'

'I don't know,' said Olivia, 'I really don't.'

Clara sighed, and shook her head. 'I'm glad that Teddy's back at any rate,' she said, reminding Olivia that he was. 'I feel better knowing he's here, giving you some company too. I met him not long after he moved to Alex, three years ago now. I found myself chatting to him one night at a party, and he's been a great friend to me ever since. I rather count on him these days. You'll like him, once you get to know him.'

'Yes,' said Olivia, 'yes.' She picked up the pot in front of her. 'Tea?'

'That's the milk.'

Olivia looked down at the container in her hand. So it was.

For the next three days, Clara was Olivia's only company. They stayed in. Clara tried to drag Olivia out, but she resisted; it wasn't that she didn't want to leave. She did. Normally she relied on getting out somewhere – if not to the city, at least to the Sporting Club for a drink, or to Ramleh's public beach, Stanley Bay, for a walk. Even the suburb's shops – that cluster of delicatessen, baker and grocer that all the British residents in Ramleh frequented – were a welcome change of scene. But she couldn't bring herself to do it. After the way Alistair had been that night she'd gone to Sabia's, she was shamefully afraid of angering him again. She'd gird her loins eventually, she was sure, but not just yet.

'Fine then,' said Clara, 'we'll have to amuse ourselves here. How about bridge?'

There were times, as they played, when Clara fell quiet, her face weighted; whenever Olivia asked what was worrying her, she'd give a quick smile, say it was nothing, she was splendid.

'No you're not,' Olivia said. Then, thinking of the discord Clara often alluded to between her and her husband, she asked, 'Is it Jeremy? Has he upset you?'

'No more than usual,' said Clara, 'and I can't have you worrying about me, Livvy. Absolutely not.'

She'd move the conversation on, distracting Olivia with stories of the boys (*You should have seen Gus this morning . . .*), or plans for things she and Olivia might do together. (*I'd like to go to Cairo, I've never been, not since Mama and Papa died and you and I had to leave. But it might be nice to go back together now. We could stay at Shepheard's, a little holiday, perhaps even go and see our old house.*)

Neither of them mentioned Alistair. Olivia felt freer though, now she'd admitted how she hated him. She was glad she'd told Clara that. She sensed Clara would ask her to talk again, that she was biding her time, just as Olivia was biding hers in getting Clara to admit whatever was nagging at her. They were treading a careful path, the two of them, still learning how to know one another better. Olivia told herself they would get there, of course they would. They were together, they had time.

For her own part, she thought she might be more honest next time Clara asked about Alistair. *It's just words, isn't it, Livvy?* She needed to find the courage, her voice, and put Clara's look of relief when she'd lied from her mind.

Perhaps.

She never spoke of Edward. Clara asked after him, though. *Teddy.* 'He hasn't called,' Clara said. 'I'm very cross. Tell him that. Tell him to call on me, please.'

'All right,' said Olivia.

She didn't.

She forced herself to avoid him entirely when he was in the house. For how could Alistair detect anything was wrong – how could there *be* anything wrong – if she never went near him?

She breakfasted in her room, waited until he had left for the morning before she swam, and then made sure she was upstairs well in advance of him returning in the evening.

Dinners were hard. They sat opposite one another at the table, Alistair between them at the head. Edward asked her so many questions, his northern voice soft, probing: what had she done with her day? Where had she visited so far in Alex? Did she swim – yes? Where had she learned? She, conscious, so conscious, of Alistair, never once allowed herself to meet Edward's eye. And even as she yearned for him to go on talking, asking, if only to know he was looking at her, wanting to know more, she said very little in response, hoping her coldness would be enough to put him off, terrified in case it should.

It was after dinner on the fourth night that Alistair went to the club and Olivia, assuming from the silence in the house that Edward had gone somewhere too, went to the drawing room, grateful not to be in her bedroom for once.

As she sat down at the piano, fingers tracing over the keys, she started at a sound on the terrace. It was Edward, coming up the stairs. He stopped short, looked in at her through the open doors.

'I thought you were out,' she said, surprise making her forget she wasn't supposed to be speaking to him.

'I was.' He nodded in the direction of the outhouses where his man kept a room. 'I went to see Fadil. My horse threw a shoe.'

'Oh.' Olivia couldn't think what else to say. She tensed her body, preparing to get up.

He came into the room. He sat opposite her in the candlelight, took out a cigarette, offered her one.

She shook her head.

For a few moments, there was silence. In the distance, the sea rolled. He struck a match, inhaled.

'Well,' she said, 'I'd better—'

'Stay,' he said. 'Please.'

'I shouldn't.'

'You should,' he said. 'This is your home. I hate seeing you like this.' He leant towards her, arms resting on his leg, cigarette in hand. 'Talk to me, Olly.' His brow creased, surprised. 'Can I call you that?'

'If you like.' And then, since Alistair wasn't home, and because the past few days had been really unutterably *long*, and she'd never wanted to do anything more than, as Edward said, stay, talk – to let him have something of her – she added, 'My friend, Beatrice, at home called me that.'

'A good friend?'

'The best.'

'You must miss her.'

'I try not to think about her actually.'

'Because it's too hard?'

'Yes,' she said, pleased that he understood, 'exactly.'

He drew again on his cigarette, let the smoke go. 'I used to be the same,' he said. 'I've got five sisters.'

'I remember.'

He smiled. He seemed to like that she'd done that. 'They write, every week. They never miss. They've got hundreds of children between them.'

'Hundreds?'

He laughed. 'Quite a few. God knows how they find the time to write.'

'But they do.'

'Yes, they do. And they tell me these stories: the ice-skating trips, the point-to-points. I'm missing it all, and I hate it, I can't tell you how much, but it helps, you know, to think of it all going on.' He looked over at Olivia, eyes appraising her. She sat quite still on the piano stool. He tapped his cigarette in the ashtray. 'Sometimes it's better to hold on to the things you've left behind. It keeps you who you are.'

'Does it?' Olivia traced her fingers over the piano keys, thinking about it, about him. She pressed one, then another; the hollow notes filled the room. 'The first day I arrived in Alex, Clara came to meet me here at the house.' She spoke without knowing she was going to. 'I hadn't seen her since I was eight years old. There were no letters, I had no address to write to, our grandmother never gave Clara mine.' She paused briefly, thinking of all the notes she'd penned then thrown away. The awful loneliness. 'I was desperate to see her again,' she said. 'I never thought I would. But I was so nervous too. I didn't know if she'd even want to know me. My grandmother told me she never asked after me . . .'

'She did,' said Edward softly.

'Yes,' said Olivia, 'Clara's told me that now. But when I arrived here, I had no idea what to expect. And then there Clara was,

31

waiting in the driveway. I can't tell you what it was like, that moment I saw her. She looked so . . . different to how I'd imagined her. I think I'd half expected a fourteen-year-old.' Olivia broke off as the dislocation of that moment struck her afresh. 'She had a suet pudding with her,' she said. 'She told me it was my favourite as a child, but I couldn't remember ever eating such a thing. I was too . . . shocked, I suppose, at her caring so much, and being there, real, to pretend I could.' She frowned. 'You should have seen her face when she realised I'd forgotten. She tried to make out that it didn't matter, lots of "absolutely understandables" and "not to worry a jots".'

'I can picture it.'

She shook her head. 'All these years, she remembered my favourite dessert. She held on to it, to everything. And I've just let it all go.' She thought of Clara's recent silences, the shadows on her face. 'It must hurt her,' she said, 'the way I've been. I hate the fact that I've done that to her. I think she's got enough to upset her as it is.' She looked down at her fingers. 'I don't know why I'm saying all of this.' She gave a small self-conscious smile.

He studied her, appearing to think. His eyes were full of the candles' soft light. He said, 'Clara's worried about you for as long as I've known her. It was one of the first things we ever spoke about when I moved here. She tried so hard to find you.'

'I know.'

'No one understands all that happened to you better than her.'

'I know,' Olivia said again. The words came out taut. A strange mass was building in her throat. She swallowed, hard, pushing it down.

'I asked Clara once,' he said, 'why your grandmother did it to you. Separated you like that.'

'Did she tell you?'

'She said it was because of your mother. That your grandmother hated her.'

Olivia nodded slowly. 'I think she always will.' Her mind moved over all she'd been told about her parents. She didn't normally like

32

to think of them – having no memories for herself, it always made her feel horribly detached, as though they were characters in a story – but tonight, with Edward looking at her, she felt more able to. 'Father was an archaeologist,' she said, 'he came out to Egypt on a dig. Mama was already here, she grew up in Alex. They met, married, moved to Cairo, and Father never went home.'

'But your grandmother wanted him to?'

'She tried to convince him, many times apparently, especially after Clara was born. She kept on at him for years. She even came out, when Clara was six; she'd arranged for him to be offered a post in London. But, well,' Olivia gave a small shrug, 'my mother fell pregnant with me, she didn't want to leave Egypt. My fault too, I suppose.' She dipped her head, thinking of how completely Mildred had exacted her revenge in the years since. 'I just wish,' she said, 'so much that I had something of my parents still. If I could just remember one thing.'

He squashed his cigarette into the ashtray. 'Do you know why you've forgotten?'

She didn't answer straight away. She was disoriented by how much she was saying, the strange way it was making her feel – light somehow, like when the laces of her corset came undone, able to breathe, yet dizzy with it.

He didn't rush her. Just kept his eyes on her.

'It was the day Clara and I arrived back in England, after our parents died,' she said at length. 'It was so awful, freezing cold rain.' She looked to the ceiling, seeing that grey morning briefly, the image shouldering itself in: a young Clara, screaming at the foot of the gangplank, face twisted, restrained by their grandmother. And herself, thrashing in her black mourning dress, being carried away by nuns she'd never met, sobbing and choking in panicked terror. 'It was such a long carriage ride, with those nuns. They didn't speak to me at all. The school, when we got there, it was huge. Dark. I can't tell you how cold. I got lost in the corridors. I was trying to find the latrine, you see.' She drew breath, seeing herself running along, remembering how she'd not got there in time; the way Sister

Agnes had told all the other girls she was dirty. 'I stayed awake all night, I was afraid . . .'

'Of the dark?'

'No,' she shook her head, 'of Clara coming to get me and not being able to find the way to where I was.' She looked over at him with eyes so dry they hurt. 'Please don't tell Clara that. She'd hate it if she knew.'

'Of course I won't,' he said.

'Thank you.' She placed her hand to her throat. The lump there seemed to have eased. She gestured at his cigarettes. 'I might have one of those after all.'

'Yes?' When he smiled, the air seemed to loosen around them.

He lit a cigarette in his own mouth and passed it over to her. Their fingers brushed.

She inhaled, coughing.

He gave her another crooked smile. 'Don't do it if you don't like it.'

'I just need to get used to it.'

'I hate those nuns,' he said.

'So do I.'

There was a short silence.

'Tell me about Beatrice,' he said.

So she did.

She didn't know how long they talked after that. Only that the hours passed and the candles turned to puddles in their holders.

Eventually, thinking reluctantly of Alistair on his way back, Olivia said she must go to bed.

Edward stood as she rose. 'I can't stand to think of you, you know, here all day. You must be going mad.'

'Clara comes. I swim.'

'But don't you want to get out?'

'Alistair doesn't like it if I take the carriage.'

Edward frowned. 'That's no good.'

She made to leave.

'Olly,' he called after her.

She turned.

'Did you see what we did?' His tone was serious, but his eyes were alight. 'We talked. And it wasn't so bad, was it?'

'No,' she smiled, 'not so bad.'

The next morning, she watched him leave the house. He saluted her, like he had that first morning. She waved back.

She ate breakfast, sat at the piano for some time, reliving their conversation the night before, biting her lip on her smile of shock that it should have happened at all.

She was married, m— She squashed the voice within her. She didn't want to hear it.

Deciding she needed air, she went swimming. Afterwards, she sat on the rocks, drip-drying, bath sheet spread out beneath her. Her shoulders baked under the warm morning sky. The sun was getting fiercer with every day. She could feel her skin growing taut, crisp with the heat. She raised her face to the sky, eyes closed, wondering where he was.

'Hello, Olly.'

Behind her, apparently.

Her head jerked around to see him. She grinned before she could stop herself, too delighted at the surprise of his being there to even attempt to hide it. He was several feet away, on the lawn at the foot of the rocks, tunic undone, a white shirt beneath it, long boots. He held his hands to his eyes, shielding them from the sun's glare.

'What are you doing home?' she asked, only remembering as she spoke how little she was wearing. She tried to pull her bath sheet up, but it was caught beneath her, and she couldn't stand without exposing herself. 'You went, I saw you.'

'Now I'm back.'

'Clearly.'

He laughed.

She pulled again at the bath sheet. '*Edward.*'

He held up his hands and turned away so his back was to her.

'I've had an idea.'

'An idea?' She stood quickly, scrambling to wrap herself in her towel.

'I've brought you a present.'

'Really?' Her heart tripped. 'What is it?'

'Would you like to see?'

'Can I get changed first?'

He laughed again. 'I think you better had.'

He told her, on the way back to the house, to try and find something loose-skirted to wear.

'Why?' she asked.

'You'll see.'

He was waiting for her in the porch when she came downstairs, her body still damp beneath her cotton day dress.

'Will this do?' she asked.

His eyes shone as they took her in. 'I think so.' He held out his hand, gestured towards the front door. 'After you.'

He led her into the stables; the air there was dusty and sweet, full of the sound of the carriage ponies shuffling on the hay. He came to a halt at a stall with a chestnut horse inside.

'Yours,' he said, opening the gate.

'Mine?'

'Yes.'

'But,' she said, 'Alistair—'

'We don't need to tell him. I'll say I bought her for myself, that I took pity on her. A brood mare, past her prime, that you're welcome to borrow.'

Olivia stepped into the stall, stroking the horse's silken skin, feeling the muscles beneath. 'She's not though, is she? Past her prime.'

'I wanted you to have her,' he said, not answering the question.

She shook her head. 'I don't know how to ride.'

'I'll teach you. I'd like to do that. We can do it when Alistair's at work if it will make you feel more comfortable; tell him you learnt back in England, if he asks. Riding will be something for *you*. You'll be able to get out, away.'

Olivia's hand moved over the horse's neck, around its head; it nuzzled into her palm, nostrils expelling damp, warm air. She thought, *He's done this. For me. Thought about it, planned it.* She looked at him from the corner of her eye. He was watching her, a dent in his forehead, still waiting to find out if he'd done the right thing. *Alistair will kill me if he guesses what this means.*

'Olly?'

'Away,' she said slowly. 'I like that idea.'

His face broke into a grin. 'Then let's go.'

Her eyes widened. 'Now?'

'Now.'

She hesitated, but only for a moment. 'All right.'

'What will you call her?' he asked as they walked back out into the sunlight.

'Bea, I think,' she said impulsively.

'For your friend?'

'Yes.'

'Good. It's a good name.'

He took her to a nearby field to teach her, kneeling and offering his hand to give her a leg up. He'd tacked Bea up with a man's saddle. She hesitated, eyeing it dubiously; for the first time, it occurred to her to wonder how she was going to get her legs either side of it.

She looked down at Edward, still kneeling on the ground. 'Now I see why I had to wear something loose,' she said.

He smiled ruefully. He said he was afraid that he had no idea how to teach side saddle. He hoped she wasn't scandalised.

'No,' she said, resolving not to be. She placed her foot in his palm. 'Of course not.'

Even so, heat filled her face as he hoisted her up and she struggled to get herself into position without revealing her undergarments. She spread her gown around her, covering her legs, and vowed silently to use her small allowance to procure one of the split-skirted riding habits she'd seen advertised back in London, as soon as possible.

He helped her with her stirrups. She tried not to notice the way his hands moved as he adjusted the leather, his arm just skimming her stocking.

He held Bea's reins, walking them both on. The trees were thick with spring blossom, sheltering them from the roadside, from view. The flowers carried a fresh, sweet scent that mixed with the tang of the dew-dampened earth. After a while, Olivia forgot how nervous she was; she began to relax into her seat.

He left her to it, moving to the centre of the field to watch her, and called out to her to go faster. 'Give her a kick. You won't hurt her.'

Olivia gave Bea's belly a gentle nudge with the sides of her feet, but Bea just kept on plodding. She tried again. 'Come on, do come on.' Nothing. She felt suddenly clumsy. 'Giddy up.' It didn't sound at all right. She raised her voice to Edward. 'What am I doing wrong?'

He was standing, tunic off, sleeves rolled up, arms folded. It was so bright, she couldn't quite make out his face. Was he laughing?

'Edward . . . ?'

'A little harder with the kick perhaps.'

'Like this?'

'No, harder.'

'This?'

'A bit more.'

For goodness' sake. She jammed her feet in.

'Yes, that's it, very good. Now just drop your heels.'

'I am.'

'Not quite, actually. Pull your toes up. No, your toes not your heels . . . Heels down. No, they're further up now. Olly, your feet are sliding on the stirrups, just put them . . . no, that's not it. Don't worry. You'd better stop, I'll show you.'

She squinted, watching as he approached across the grass. He mock-shook his head at her. Her legs, they trembled. She tensed her muscles, trying to get them under control. *Calm down.* He drew closer. She fiddled at Bea's reins, running the leather across her forefinger, under her thumb, trying to distract herself from the colour she could feel spreading through her cheeks.

'Are you all right?' he asked. 'Not too tired?'

'No,' she said. Then, 'I'm afraid I'm not being a very good pupil.'

'You're doing very well. Much better than my lieutenants when they started.'

She couldn't help but laugh at that.

He laughed too. 'Here.' He reached for her boot, brushing back her skirts. As he did, his smile dropped. 'All these petticoats,' he said under his breath. His tanned face, tipped forward, became creased in concentration. He looked almost stern.

She felt his fingers skim her calf, their warmth through her stocking. He clasped her ankle, looked up, met her eye. For a heartbeat, she believed neither of them breathed.

Then he tilted her foot, placed the stirrup on her toe. 'Like that,' he said.

'Yes.' She managed a small smile. 'Yes. I see.'

He took her riding every morning after that. He'd leave the house as normal, always stopping to look up at her window, giving her that salute – a proper one for her, a two-fingered one at her sodding husband – then he'd check in at the ground, start the men on their drills ('Excellent work, you don't need me here for this.') and head back.

Olly told Alistair that she'd taken to riding Bea – she said it was better that he found out from her – and that she used her for short trips around Ramleh, for fresh air and exercise. When Alistair remarked to Edward that he imagined he didn't want Olivia tiring his horse, Edward said no, on the contrary, he was more than happy for Olly to borrow Bea. Really, he had had no intention of telling her she mustn't.

They stuck to the story of Olly having learnt to ride in England.

Olly bought herself new riding clothes; she twirled as she came to meet Edward in the stables one day, making a show of the hidden trousers in the skirt. 'The seamstress was appalled,' she said, laughing.

Edward, absorbing her delight, had to take a moment before answering. When he could speak, he told her he thought she looked grand.

'Good,' she said, beaming.

'What does Alistair think of them?'

Her face clouded. 'He was less convinced.' She forced a shrug. 'It was nothing.'

It was clear it hadn't been nothing. He was about to press her to tell him more, but before he could, she made for Bea. 'Shall we go?' she asked.

Seeing she didn't want to discuss it, he gave in.

As the days, then weeks, passed, she got better at riding. A lot better. He taught her to trot, canter, and then to jump; he loved how her face lit up when she cleared the sticks, the way she'd forget for just a few blessed moments how unhappy she was.

They found other ways to see one another: stolen half-hours in the drawing room before Alistair returned home, snatched evenings whenever he went out to the club. They spoke of so many things, the two of them ... It would never be enough. But she started chattering; no more pauses before each word. She stopped apologising for confiding in him.

He liked the fact that she'd stopped doing that.

She told him more about her school, about the nuns. The way her grandmother had behaved over the years, how it was Mildred who'd helped Alistair find Olivia in the first place. ('She gave him my address, the only person she ever told where I was.') Edward despised Mildred, despised them all, and himself too – for being here, doing nothing, when he could have been helping her.

He told her stories of his own childhood, more to see her laugh than because he had any desire to recollect the way his sisters had dressed him up in their frocks. And when she did it, laughed, he laughed too, loving that he'd made her do it.

At the end of April, he went to see Tom. He asked if there was any way of getting out of his transfer to Jaipur.

Tom sank his head into his hands. 'Dare I ask what's brought this on?'

'It doesn't matter.'

'I suspect it does.' Tom ran his hand down his lean face, brushing over his moustache. 'Doesn't have anything to do with your riding lessons, does it?'

'My . . . How do you know about those?'

'Imogen told me.'

'Imogen? How does . . . ?'

'Imogen knows everything, old man.'

Edward looked to the ceiling. Cloth punkahs swayed back and forth, batting the heat.

'Don't worry,' said Tom, not unkindly, 'her maid saw you once, that's all. You know how Imogen worries over those girls.'

Edward sighed, nodding. Imogen had told him herself how close she'd been to Olly's mother, Grace. The years she'd spent trying to find out what had happened to Olly. *I wrote, so many times, to that woman, Mildred. She refused to say a word of what she'd done, where Olivia was.*

'I'll offer you a word of advice if I may,' said Tom. 'Best not to try and change the unchangeable. Accept what's what.'

'Are you speaking about India?'

'Not exclusively.'

'Can I get out of it or not?'

'Not.'

'Right.' *Shit.* 'Don't tell Olly I'm going.'

'I didn't want to hear that.'

Edward, already on his way out of the office, didn't reply.

'She's married, Bertram. To an unutterable bastard. She'll be the one who pays in the end. Leave well alone, old man.'

It wasn't advice Edward was prepared to take.

He longed to ask her to go with him, leave Alistair, leave it all. But then he'd see her talking with Clara at the house, at parties, their heads tilted towards one another, fair against brown – so much more at ease together than apart. He'd watch Ralph run towards Olly whenever Clara brought him over, breaking away from his mama's hand, *Aunt Livvy*, legs pumping, up, down, Olly opening her arms. And he knew it would be unspeakably selfish to break them all apart. He didn't think he could do it, not now they'd found one another again.

Every night he went to sleep imagining her sleeping above him. He didn't let himself think of the man by her side. He longed to touch her for himself, hold her; his need sharpened with every day. He thought perhaps she wanted him to – the way, at times, her whole body would go still where she stood, the careful rhythm of her breath. But he forced himself to hold back. Until she gave him some cue, he'd have to be content with simply knowing her. She'd already had so much to contend with in life. What kind of a boor would it make him to ask adultery of her? *She's married, Bertram, to an unutterable bastard.*

No, she had to be the first to cross that line.

Chapter Three

'I need you to go to Montazah.'

Edward turned at the voice behind him. It was Jeremy, framed in the timber doorway of the parade ground stables, hands in the pockets of his expensively cut three-piece. His face, as he looked across at Edward, was pensive. The golden May rays oozing through the slatted roof highlighted his ashen skin, the puddles beneath his grey eyes. There'd been a ball at the house of Imogen's brother, the famous hotelier Benjamin Pasha, the night before. Benjamin, like Alistair and Jeremy, was one of the wealthiest men in Alex, and he'd thrown a lavish celebration for the queen's seventy-second (Happy Birthday, old Victoria). If Jeremy had slept at all in the hours since, it clearly hadn't been for long.

'Can you go?' Jeremy asked. 'Now?'

'Good morning,' Edward said, returning his attention to tacking up his stallion. 'I believe that's the traditional mode of greeting someone you want a favour from.'

'Yes, of course.' Jeremy's smile only just managed to reach his bloodshot eyes. 'Morning.'

Edward adjusted the girth.

Jeremy said, 'So will you go to Montazah?'

Edward sighed. He was on his way to take Olly for a lesson and had absolutely no intention of changing his plans for the morning, certainly not to ride back up the coast. 'What's in Montazah?' he asked. 'Other than some sore heads at Benjamin and Amélie Pasha's?'

43

'A worker of mine,' said Jeremy. 'Tabia's her name. It's bloody awful. She's been killed. A peasant's horse, apparently, mowed her down sometime around dawn.'

Edward looked up. 'Jesus.'

'She's no husband, two children. The man whose horse trampled her turned himself in at the Pashas' first thing. Benjamin came, told me . . . ' Jeremy broke off, drew breath. 'I want to see that her children are all right, but you know I can't be seen to be helping. Favouritism and all that. Will you help?'

Edward hesitated before answering, uneasy somehow. It wasn't the request in itself that bothered him. He knew Jeremy liked to look after the worst-off of his employees, on the quiet of course so Alistair didn't get wind of it. Edward wished Jeremy would give as much thought to his own family's well-being once in a while – Clara's specifically – but over the years he'd passed on more than one package of money on Jeremy's behalf, made arrangements for medical care following a mill accident. Still, there was something in Jeremy's eye this morning that needled at him, a shadow of something hiding.

'Please, Bertram,' said Jeremy. 'They're alone.'

Edward ran his hand over his face. 'Where can I find them?'

Jeremy's face relaxed, he gave Edward the directions.

Edward nodded, resigning himself to not seeing Olly for another couple of hours at least.

'Make sure they have whatever they need,' said Jeremy. 'Just pass the bills on.'

'Yes, yes.' Edward knew the drill. 'I'll take Fadil with me, the children will be scared when they see a British soldier coming.'

'Thank you, Bertram. And if you can keep it quiet.'

'I always do.'

'It's more important than ever this time.'

Edward frowned. 'Why?'

Jeremy gave him an awkward look. 'I just can't have anyone knowing about it,' he said, then turned to go.

Edward stared after him. Certain by now that there was

something amiss, he called for him to come back. 'Gray? Gray, wait . . .'

But Jeremy was already gone.

Edward and Fadil had to scout around for some time before they found Tabia's hut. It was a tiny ramshackle affair, visible from neither the road nor the beach, hidden as it was within the mile-long dunes behind Montazah Bay. The air around it was silent, the surrounding sandbanks deserted. A crooked fence outside the mud hut protected a gaggle of chickens. To the right were children's play-things: a dusty red ball; a truck, rusted, its paintwork faded. One of the wheels was broken.

The day was clear, but out in the distance, somewhere at sea, thunder rolled.

'Like your navy's guns,' said Fadil.

Edward nodded, remembering.

They drew closer to the hut.

'Is anyone there?' Edward called in Arabic. His voice echoed all around.

Silence.

'Hello?' Edward called again.

This time there was movement within. Edward took a step for-ward, hand moving instinctively to his pistol; Fadil did the same. But then a girl stepped out from the hut's doorway, and Edward's hand relaxed.

She was twenty, or thereabouts, with the dark colouring of the locals. Her black hair was tied at the nape of her neck. She wore a maid's uniform: navy dress, white apron. Edward noticed how her eyes refused to meet his, but darted around him, taking in everything but his stare. She held a child to her, a boy of perhaps three or four. His head was a strange shape, and it lolled against her chest – he wasn't able to control it.

A much younger girl stuck her head out from behind the maid's skirt, peering up at Edward and Fadil. She was a startlingly pretty child.

45

'Go inside, Cleo,' the maid said to her.

The little girl didn't move.

Edward asked the maid her name. She told him it was Nailah. He asked her what relation she was to the children, and she replied that she was just their minder, helping for now.

'I'm very sorry to hear about their mother,' Edward said.

Nailah looked to her toes, shifting awkwardly on the spot. Her face was set, no sign of grief.

Edward thought, *Perhaps she didn't know Tabia well.* And then, *So what is she doing here?*

He was aware of Fadil staring at the girl, as though he too was trying to work her out.

A wind wisped over the sand. The chickens clucked.

Edward told Nailah why they were there, that he wanted to help in any way he could. He asked her if she needed anything. No? Nothing at all? 'What about the child?' he said, nodding at the boy in her arms.

'Babu?' she asked.

'Yes, he looks very ill.'

'He is,' she said, 'but he always has been. If that's all . . . ?' She began to back away.

'Wait.' Edward brought out a notebook, scribbled an address on it. Sensing Nailah didn't want him to get any closer, he tore the paper off and placed it on the sand, weighting it with a stone. 'It's the details of a good doctor,' he said. 'Take Babu to him. Socrates might be able to help. Go, don't worry about a thing.'

Nailah thanked him again. 'I really should get on.'

'Are you sure there's nothing else?'

'Nothing,' Nailah said. She turned, making it clear she wanted them away.

Edward felt a strange pull to stay. But, since he couldn't see any good reason to do so, he nodded to Fadil. As they led their horses on, back over the sand to the road, Edward looked over his shoulder at the hut. But Nailah and the children had already disappeared inside. He could feel them, though, watching from behind the door.

'What was that?' he said to Fadil.

'Fear,' said Fadil. 'She was afraid.'

'Of what? Us?'

'I don't know, sayed.' Fadil paused. 'I don't think just us.' He scratched his bald head, then looked down the road, frowned. 'Is that . . . ?'

Edward turned, following Fadil's gaze. There was a figure, about two hundred yards distant, hunched on the sandbanks, staring out to sea. 'What the . . . ?' She was still in the same gown she'd worn for the Pashas' party. Her hair was loose, in disarray, blowing in the building wind.

'I'll go on shall I, sayed?'

'Yes,' Edward said, 'yes. I'd better see if she's all right.'

As Fadil galloped off, he led his horse over to where she sat.

She raised her eyes to his as he approached. Her face was pale, blotchy. Her expression didn't move. She didn't appear especially surprised to see him. She didn't look as though anything could surprise her at all.

'Clara?' he said. 'What are you doing here?'

'Oh, Teddy,' she said. Then her face folded, her voice broke. 'What am I going to do? What on earth am I going to do?'

Olivia waited in for him all morning, but he didn't come. Clara didn't call either, and when Olivia saddled Bea up and rode over to her house, it was to discover she'd come back not an hour before and was sleeping.

For want of anything else to do, Olivia returned home, cantering to beat the rain. A wind had blown up, clouds clotted the horizon; rather a pain for the committee who were organising the Sporting Club's party that night: yet another do in celebration of the queen's birthday. Olivia barely had the energy for it after the Pashas' ball. She'd cry off were it not for the prospect of seeing Edward there, Clara too. She wanted to talk to Clara. She'd been in such a strained mood the night before, very distracted, not a hint of her usual smile. Olivia had tried to engage her in conversation several times, practically chasing her around the ballroom with any excuse to talk. But Clara had given little more than nondescript murmurs in response. Her eyes had darted around the dance floor constantly, only to settle from time to time, but on what – or whom – Olivia couldn't make out. It was only Alistair watching Clara too, his own eyes like slits, that had stopped Olivia taking her sister by the hand then and there and insisting she finally open up and admit what was wrong.

She frowned, her worry a weight in her chest. She came to a halt in the driveway and dismounted, sliding down to the gravel, leading Bea on.

Edward's stallion wasn't in the stables. Olivia's heart sank. She'd been so hoping he'd be home. She stood for a moment, forehead pressed against Bea's warm leather saddle, absorbing the disappointment.

Just one morning not seeing him, and she was a mess, an anxious, hollow mess. She drew a ragged breath.

What on earth were they going to do, the two of them? What *could* they do?

When she returned to the house it was to find that Alistair, for no reason that he was prepared to explain, had fired her lady's maid. The poor girl was already packed and gone. There wasn't a thing Olivia could do to try and help her.

'I can't believe you've done this. She was *my* maid.'

'Did you pay her, Olivia? No, precisely.'

A new woman was to arrive on the morrow: a Londoner by the name of Ada. Alistair claimed she'd worked for an acquaintance of his in England and needed a job over here. He didn't answer when Olivia asked what Ada was doing in Egypt in the first place; he refused to be held to account for whatever Olivia's now unemployed maid was going to do next. He didn't want to be bothered with any further questions, he had a great deal on his mind.

'What?' Olivia asked. 'What do you have on your mind?'

'That's none of your concern.'

A kitchen maid drew Olivia's bath. Olivia was in it, sponging herself down with angry movements, when she heard Edward return (footsteps on the tiles, that northern voice; the opening and shutting of his door). Olivia pulled herself from the bath and dressed as quickly as she might, but it took so long: her stays, her stockings, the buttons on her petticoats, her gown. He was gone already by the time she raced downstairs.

She was twitching with impatience, and still fuming over Alistair's dismissal of her maid, when she and Alistair arrived at the Sporting Club for the evening's party. Alistair set off towards the bar, muscling in on a conversation between Jeremy, Tom, and Tom's brother-in-law, Benjamin Pasha. None of them seemed especially pleased to see him. Tom and Benjamin particularly didn't trouble to hide their frowns, but then they'd never been friendly with Alistair; perhaps with the Pasha fortune behind them – Benjamin with the charge of all those hotels, and Tom married to Imogen's trust fund – they weren't blinded by his wealth in the way everyone else in Alex apparently was. Olivia moved her gaze on, looking around the already bursting seams of the club's pavilion, straining to catch a glimpse of Edward or Clara amidst the silk frocks and top hats. But neither of them was within sight. She blew air over her hot face. With the winds even stronger, still threatening rain, the balcony was off limits, and there were far too many people crammed inside beneath the lazy ceiling fans.

Her toe tapped in a discordant rhythm with the piano music. She began to feel silly, standing alone, and scanned the room again, this time for someone to talk to. She thought to look for Imogen, but it was Imogen's sister-in-law, Amélie Pasha, who caught her eye and waved her over. Olivia went, without much excitement. Clara might be friendly with Amélie, but although Olivia called on her from time to time with Clara – and had been to several of the Pashas' parties – she never sought Amélie out for herself. It was her vapid manner, the way she gossiped about who was wearing what, dining in which restaurant, not speaking to whom. Olivia struggled to understand why Clara had so much time for her. Still, perhaps Amélie would know where Clara was now.

Amélie didn't. She was entirely concerned with the recent departure of her own lady's maid, a girl by the name of Nailah. She went on and on about it in her thick French accent. 'She just left, first zing zis morning, not a word as to where. Gone,' she flounced her hands as though doing a magic trick, 'like zat . . .'

'Have mine,' said Olivia, looking around once again for Clara's yellow curls, Edward's dark face. 'I have a spare as of about five hours ago.'

Amélie sighed, said it was fine. 'One of ze under-maids 'as already taken Nailah's place. Such an inconvenience though, all of eet.'

More chatter followed. A great deal more. Olivia despaired of either Edward or Clara turning up. She thought she might just make her excuses after all and go home.

It was then that she spotted Clara, heading determinedly towards her and Amélie, evening gown swishing, glass of wine in hand. Olivia frowned at the purposeful, almost manic, look in her eye. What had got into her?

She took a step forward to find out. But then there was Edward, finally, coming in through the club doors on the far side of the room. He removed his hat, ran his hand through his hair, and looked around the room. Olivia thought he might be searching for her. But his eyes found Clara first. He frowned, set off towards her.

Olivia froze, statue-like, at what happened next. Edward intercepted Clara, quite smoothly, and took her by the arm. Clara's shoulders slackened in defeat. Her eyes lost that glint. She let Edward lead her away, through the sweaty throng, out onto the stormy terrace.

Amélie, apparently oblivious to them leaving, or indeed to Olivia staring, strangely unable to move, talked on. 'I was so sorry to miss so much of ze party last night. My migraines, you know. Eet sounds like it was quite ze night. The 'ousekeeper told me she found a lady's shawl in the garden zis morning.' She laughed. 'I wonder what eet could 'ave been doing there.'

Olivia barely listened. Her eyes were locked on the swinging balcony doors. The moment Amélie paused for breath, she mumbled something about the powder room and headed straight for the terrace herself.

The wooden deck was empty. The wind swept her gown around her, rippling through the silk. She held her hand to her head, keeping her loosely pinned curls from her face. The air was hot, not at all fresh, and damp with unbroken humidity. There was no moon, and only two hurricane lamps burned in the blackness, just by the stairs down to the polo lawn. Olivia's eyes watered, straining as she tried to see where Edward and Clara could be.

She found them finally on the far side of the deck, standing close. Clara was speaking, face raised to Edward's. Edward was talking too, over her. Olivia moved towards them, ear cocked, but they were speaking in urgent whispers, voices blocked out by the wind. Clara shook her head, and Edward put the heel of his hands to his temple, flexing his fingers, obviously frustrated.

Olivia was almost upon them when he turned, saw her. He took a step towards her, tried to smile. 'Hello, Olly.'

Clara's head swivelled, but she turned away just as quickly. 'I'm going to go,' she said. 'I'm very tired.'

'Clara,' Edward said, 'wait.'

'Don't worry, Teddy. You've made your point.' She walked from him, body bent against the weather, towards the steps that would take her out around the back to the carriages. As she passed Olivia, she said, 'I'm sorry to leave, Livvy. We'll talk tomorrow.'

'I'll come with you now.'

'No,' said Clara, still walking. 'Please.'

'Wait,' Olivia said.

But she was already gone, into the night, arms hugging her satin-clad body, skirts flapping. She looked so alone.

Olivia turned back to Edward, her gaze questioning.

He said, 'Please, don't ask me.'

She was about to anyway when the terrace doors opened, flying against the club walls. Noisy chatter and light spilt out into the darkness.

Tom was there. He shook his head as his eyes settled on Olivia

51

and Edward. Raising his voice above the wind, he said, 'It's no night to be out here.' Then, 'Bertram, I need you, old man.'

'What is it?' asked Edward.

'Something rather strange has come up. Come, let's to the stables. I'll tell you as we walk.'

Edward hesitated, his eyes on Olivia. But Tom didn't move from the door. It was obvious he was intent on waiting.

'All right,' said Edward. 'All right.' He smiled briefly at Olivia. 'We'll speak later.'

'Yes,' she said, 'we will.'

But later didn't come. Olivia had barely set foot back in the club before Alistair appeared quite suddenly at her side, like a sadistic conjuror's trick, and told her they were going home. Now.

And the next morning, when she woke, intent on speaking to Edward or Clara, and ideally both, it was to find a hastily scribbled note from Clara on the morning tea tray. Olivia sat up in bed, reading, eyes widening in disbelief; Clara had left Alex, the whole Gray family had, gone to Constantinople. Just like that.

I have no idea how long we'll be away, Clara wrote. *Jeremy's just announced that there's a ship in dock and we have to be on it. I'm so sorry, Livvy, I hate leaving you like this, especially after last night. You mustn't worry about me though, please. I'll write again as soon as I can.*

Olivia turned to Alistair, coming in from his dressing room. She asked him what it was all about, why Jeremy had taken the family away so suddenly. He told her something urgent had come up, to do with the business. Gray had to attend to it.

'But Jeremy never takes Clara and the boys when he travels.'

'And yet,' said Alistair, 'he has. Oh,' he continued in a tone that was trying to be careless, 'don't plan dinner for Bertram tonight. He's away too. He'll be gone for some weeks.'

'What?' The news landed like a glancing blow to her stomach. 'Where?'

52

'The desert.'

'Why?'

'There's some nationalist activity hotting up. He's gone with Fadil to investigate. I don't want *you* going out on your own any more. I mean it, Olivia. Not even to plod around on that horse. I've told you how I hate it. Stay in. These are dangerous times.'

'No they're not,' she said, too distraught at everything unfolding to bite her tongue. Besides, the lie was so blatant she couldn't help herself. Tension might exist under the surface in Alex – she'd heard countless tales of the riots in the streets when Britain seized power in '82, the chants of 'Egypt for Egyptians'; that kind of thing didn't just disappear – but it was firmly buried. No one *worried* over it. All anyone spoke about was how safe things were now the Empire had Egypt in hand. *Good old Blighty.* 'You're trying to scare me,' she said. 'You want to keep me here like a prisoner with this rot. What the hell is going on?'

'Rot?' He came and leant over her, his face so close she could see his greying stubble, the ticking muscle in his cheek. 'Rot?'

And then he taught her never to say the word 'rot' again.

A family of Bedouin arrived that afternoon, a mother and two boys, and set up their canvas home at the front gate. It was hardly an unusual arrangement. Many Bedouin pitched their homesteads outside British villas in Ramleh; the villa owners let them make use of their water pumps, their well-irrigated grass to graze their goats, and in return the Bedouin were pleasingly humble and grateful.

This mother and her boys were different, though. There was a guardedness to them, the mother especially. And the way they stared . . .

'Give them nothing,' said Alistair over dinner, 'not even a sip of water. They'll move on soon enough.'

They stayed, a welcome diversion in the lonely days that followed. Alistair grew gradually more enraged by their presence, and Olivia warmed to it in equal measure.

She gave them the odd sip of water.

She watched the mother from her window, taking in her sad smile as she talked with her sons, the graceful way she moved: shelling peas, stirring stews on the fire, gathering sticks. She wondered what her story was, what had brought her to Ramleh in the first place. If she had any Arabic, she might have asked.

But since she didn't, she kept quiet.

The hours blurred into endless mornings, boiling afternoons, and tortuous nights. May slipped into June, and not a word came from Edward, only a short wire from Clara confirming they'd arrived safely in Turkey. (*Staying at the Grand Jumeirah STOP Hope you are keeping well STOP*). Olivia was hurt, almost more than she could believe, by them both disappearing so suddenly. She didn't know whose absence upset her more: Edward's or Clara's. Clara who she had truly started to believe she could rely on again.

She had no idea how to reach Edward, but she wrote to Clara. *Why did Jeremy take you all away? What were you and Edward talking about at the Sporting Club? What's wrong?* She riffled through the post, brought each morning on a silver tray, searching amidst the calling cards and dinner invitations for Clara's looping hand. Eventually a letter arrived, its envelope coloured with exotic postage stamps. Olivia tore it open with impatient hands, eyes moving down the page eagerly. But as she read, her face grew heavy and the hope went out of her. For although Clara had written at some length – about the chaos of Constantinople, how sorely she missed Olivia, her own desire to return to Alex – she shed no light on why Jeremy had taken her away in the first place (*I've asked of course, but he's not giving me straight answers – apparently, we'd both be better keeping out of it. In all honesty, Livvy, he's in such an odious mood I'm happy not to push him more for now. You must stop fretting too, about everything. You have enough to contend with, and I'm fine, absolutely I am. Now I must just tell you about what Ralphy said this morning . . .*); there was no mention of Edward in the letter. Olivia read it over and over, desperate to spot some hidden reference to him, a few lines explaining what had happened at the Sporting Club. A small clue she'd somehow missed. When she knew the paragraphs by heart and was still none the wiser, she wrote again to Clara. *Won't you please trust me? What were you both discussing?* Clara's response – a short but sweetly worded missive telling Olivia how desperate she was to return, that she hoped Olivia wasn't too lonely, was looking after herself, getting out and about – once again ignored the question.

The unknowns tortured Olivia, sharper with every day. *What was Clara hiding? What did Edward know of it?*

When were they ever going to send word of their return?

Tomorrow, she told herself, *word will come tomorrow.*

She swam, but she no longer went alone. Her new maid, Ada, perched on the rocks, the brim of her sunhat just failing to conceal the staring tilt of her eyes. As Olivia made her way back to the house, Ada would trail her steps, helping her bathe, dress. Then she'd follow Olivia downstairs, ask her what the plans were for the day. Everywhere Olivia went, *everywhere,* Ada went too: an unshakeable five-foot shadow, an ever-vigilant, brown stuff-skirted gnome. Olivia became nauseatingly sure that Alistair had hired her as a spy.

Tomorrow, she told herself, *one of them will send word they're returning tomorrow.*

Imogen started calling. She'd arrive after lunch, a flurry of bright silk and coffee-coloured skin, filling the emptiness left by Clara. She told Olivia stories of her mother, how the two of them had grown up together: Olivia's mother, Grace, the daughter of a British archaeologist, and Imogen and her younger brother, Benjamin Pasha, the children of an Egyptian general and an Anglo-French lady. 'We spent all our days together. Grace even came to live with us after her poor parents, your other grandparents, died of typhus. I think Benjy fell in love with her a little. He was only thirteen.' Imogen sighed. 'But then your papa arrived from London and swept Grace off to Cairo to go digging for treasure. It was years more before Tom came and whisked little old me off my feet. I almost gave up hope of ever finding anyone. And I missed Grace terribly. I used to visit all the time. Oh, how she adored you two, *her girls.* The way you used to be, Olivia. You would give away smiles, you know. And you were never seen before you were heard. I was so worried after you left for England . . .'

Olivia was quiet with Imogen at first, listening much more than she talked; in the nearly three months she'd been in Alex, she'd only ever spoken to Imogen at parties and dinners, mostly with Clara, Tom or Edward there too. She'd known – from Imogen's gentle enquiries into her health, how she was finding life in Alex – that she worried; Edward had told her that Imogen had tried as hard as Clara to find her after she was sent to the nuns. Olivia wasn't sure why she'd kept her distance all this time, never taking Imogen up on her invitations to come around to lunch or dinner, always fielding her questions with caution.

Perhaps it was the idea of how much Imogen cared and all she knew, when she, Olivia, remembered not a bit.

In any case, as the afternoons passed, and Imogen talked on in that lilting way of hers, Olivia found herself relaxing, chatting more. Never about Alistair of course (she'd gone back to it being easier to pretend nothing was real); and she didn't trust herself to mention Edward either, or her confusion over the strange closeness she'd witnessed between him and Clara at the Sporting Club. But she did enjoy talking about life back in England, the good bits at least: the couple of years when she and Beatrice had lived with Beatrice's aunt in London – walks in Regent's Park, boating on the Serpentine, toasted buns for tea, all of that. She liked reliving it.

Edward had been right about that.

And when Imogen listened, laughed, Olivia almost forgot he was gone, Clara too. Then she'd remember with a thud.

'Why did Jeremy take her away, Imogen?' Olivia asked it time and again. 'What is all this secrecy?'

'I don't know, I really don't. I keep wondering why Edward's gone too. I've asked Tom, but he's being very vague.'

Tomorrow, Olivia told herself, *one of them will come back tomorrow.*

She kept riding, in spite of Alistair telling her not to. She went to the same field Edward had taken her. Ada stood awkwardly on the grass, brown skirt as stiff as a board in the breeze. Olivia felt empty, seeing her tiny figure there where Edward should be. She rode harder, faster, trying to race the feeling away.

'A little slower, why don't you, Mrs Sheldon?'

'I'm not going to fall.'

'You might, Mrs Sheldon. I don't want you hurting yourself.'

Olivia kicked her heels in.

Tomorrow. One of them will come back tomorrow.

The second week of June became the third, then the fourth. She wrote again to Clara: the same questions, but this time no letter came in response. The heat built, Olivia swam, Ada watched, the Bedouin mother tended to her sons, Imogen called.

'Nearly a month they've been gone,' Alistair said as Olivia undressed for bed one night at the end of June. 'A month, when Gray and I agreed a fortnight was all that was necessary.'

'Are *you* ever going to tell me what made that fortnight so necessary?' Olivia asked it without any hope.

And when Alistair stared over at her, his blue gaze incensed in the soft light, and he flexed his fingers, she bit her lip, wishing she could scrape the words back in.

Tomorrow, she told herself as he took her face in his hands, *one of them will send word they're coming tomorrow.*

And then finally, on the last day of June, one of them did.

THE FIRST DAY

Chapter Four

Ramleh, Alexandria, 30 June 1891

The morning the Gray family returned, Alistair was especially insistent that Olivia not leave the house, not even to gad over to see Clara. Especially not that. He gave Olivia her orders over breakfast, just after he'd finished reprimanding her for allowing the marmalade to run out. (Was it too much to ask that she stay on top of the household management? Was it? She had precious little else to think about, after all.) He strode out to the office saying he'd be very late. He had a great deal to catch up on with Jeremy. Obviously.

Olivia didn't bid him goodbye. Obviously.

'I mean it, Olivia,' Alistair called from the front door. 'You're to stay in. I'll know about it if you go against me on this.'

She raised her eyebrows. *Will you?*

She waited until she heard his hooves crunching gravel, then rose and went upstairs to change into a nicer gown. Clara's note was clenched in her hand.

I'm so sorry, Livvy, for being gone so long, I can't tell you how much. I'm going to make it up to you. Let's start with lunch, I'm taking you to Draycott's. Be ready at eleven. I've missed you.

Eleven was less than an hour away, Olivia didn't have much time.

*

She had just finished dressing when she heard the clock chiming eleven and Clara's carriage in the driveway below. She went to her window and, even in spite of her confusion and frustration, felt a lurch of happiness as she took in Clara's blonde curls and the curve of her heat-rouged cheeks beneath her parasol. *At last.* But still . . . Olivia narrowed her eyes; there was something about the disjointed way Clara was twirling her parasol, the jerky tap of her gloved hand on her skirts. She was undoubtedly on edge. Whatever it was that had upset her so badly before she left, it clearly hadn't gone away.

Olivia turned to Ada. 'I'll go down to see my sister alone.'

'Mrs Sheldon.' Ada's flat London voice was pregnant with protest.

'No, let me be, for once. For goodness' sake.' Before Ada could resist, she brushed past her, through the bedroom door and down the stairs; her heels clicked on the tiles to the rhythm of her breaths. She paused at the porch to fix her hat in place, then passed out into the fragrant front garden.

Clara climbed down from the carriage as she approached, and reached forward, grasping her hands. 'Oh, Livvy, I can't tell you how marvellous it is to see you. Really, just splendid.'

Olivia hung back, examining the lines around Clara's wary eyes, the even deeper shadows beneath them, hearing again her *marvellous*, the *just splendid*, those oh-so-English turns of phrase, confirmation – as if any were needed – that Clara was anything but top drawer. 'What's wrong?' she asked her. 'All these weeks, you kept ignoring my questions.' Her voice slipped, betraying her hurt. 'I've been so worried.'

'I'm sorry.' Clara's shoulders slumped, she dropped her hand. 'I wasn't ignoring you . . . I *want* to talk to you. I just . . . ' She looked to the floor, moving gravel with the toe of her slipper; her bonnet cast shadows on her furrowed face. 'I didn't . . . Well, letters . . . Nothing came out right . . . and . . . Oh, I don't know.' She looked up, her expression at once sad and rueful. 'I hated being away like that. I've missed you terribly.'

Olivia felt her own face soften. 'Do you still not know why Jeremy took you?'

'No,' said Clara, 'not really.'

'He's told you nothing?'

'Nothing that makes sense. He's been so strange. Actually, he's been awful, wanting to know what I'm doing all the time, where I am, not sleeping, drinking far too much. He's even angry at Alistair over something.' She frowned. 'Frankly, I don't think he was particularly keen on coming back, but Alistair's been sending rather a lot of wires. And of course we need to get Ralphy ready for school. He's off to England so soon.'

'Have you told him he's going?'

'Yes, this morning.' Clara's frown deepened. 'You should have seen his face, Livvy, the way he tried to be brave and not cry.' She closed her eyes briefly. 'I feel as if I'm letting him down. I can't even *think* about Grandmama arriving so soon.'

'What?' Dread slithered down Olivia's spine. 'You said you wrote to stop her.'

'I *did*. But you know what she's like. And now Jeremy's making noises about me going to England with them after all, taking Gus.'

Olivia's already heavy heart sank further at the prospect of Clara leaving again. 'Why?'

'I don't know. Jeremy's a closed book.'

'Perhaps you should try harder to open him, make him tell you what it's all about.'

'I'd rather not push him.'

'Why not?'

Clara shrugged; her shoulders were tight, defensive.

Olivia studied her for a moment. A thought occurred to her. 'Does all of this have anything to do with Edward?' Her voice strained on his name. She swallowed hard, terrified she would give herself away. 'You were so upset when I saw you both talking at the Sporting Club.'

'Livvy—'

'Has something happened? Something to upset Jeremy that Edward knows about?'

'No, absolutely not.' Clara bit her lip, then, speaking as though

63

she wouldn't if she could help herself, asked, 'Why do you ask that? What has Teddy said?'

'He hasn't said anything. I told you in my letters, he left the same day you did, he's been gone ever since.'

'And you don't know why?'

Olivia ignored the question. 'What were the two of you talking about?'

'I wish you wouldn't ask.'

'Why not? You're always telling me to talk to you, Clara, that I can trust you.'

'You can ...'

'But then why can't you trust me? Talk to *me*.'

'It was nothing,' said Clara, 'really. Just some silly naughtiness.' She flinched the moment the word left her.

Olivia recoiled. 'Naughtiness? What do you mean, naughtiness?'

The horses shied at her raised voice. The driver clicked his tongue, quietening them. Clara's eyes flicked to him; she coloured. 'We should get on.'

'Tell me what this naughtiness is first.'

Clara's eyes remained fixed on her driver. 'Not now.'

'Yes, now.'

'No.' Clara widened her eyes meaningfully at the driver's back, then pointed her lace-clad thumb at the swarthy footman on the carriage's rear step. 'Let's get on. We can talk properly over lunch.'

Olivia stared. She felt like a punctured balloon, and not at all like lunching anywhere. But since it was obvious Clara would say no more here ... She looked up at the bedroom window, unsurprised to see Ada's pointy face peering down from behind the shutters. She sighed. 'Let's go then, before my maid insists on joining us. Alistair has her following me everywhere, he keeps saying it's dangerous.'

'Dangerous?' Clara frowned. 'Not him as well. It's like I've been telling Jeremy, it's as safe now in Alex as it's ever been.'

'Jeremy says it's dangerous too?' It surprised Olivia. She'd been so certain Alistair was alone in trying to keep her in the house, his words about the nationalists nothing but oily lies, spun to frighten her. But if Jeremy had warned Clara too, and was making these noises about her going to England, perhaps there was something in it.

Clara said, 'Jeremy's just trying to make life harder for me than it needs to be.' She climbed back into her seat, silk skirts rustling around her. She leant towards Olivia and mock-whispered, 'I didn't tell him we were going into town,' then gave a small smile. 'Don't you look anxious though, Livvy, we'll be fine. Come on.' She patted the leather beside her. 'Our reservation's for twelve, if we don't hurry we'll miss it.'

Olivia hesitated.

'Livvy, *please*.'

She gave in, climbed into the carriage. Clara gave her arm a quick squeeze and called for the driver to ride on.

As they left the grounds, Clara pointed at the Bedouins' tent at the gates and said, 'I see you have guests.'

'Yes. They arrived just as you left. They're driving Alistair mad.'

'Good,' said Clara. 'Good for them.'

The long, bare strip of road that connected the white enclave of Ramleh to the city was dry with dust, framed by the glinting sea on one side, steep sandbanks on the other. The spring flowers which had once covered the dunes were gone; nothing but shrivelled vines remained, varying shades of yellow and brown swaying stiffly in the hot, lazy air. A lone camel stared from the roadside as the carriage trundled past, jaw working on a bunch of roots. Its owner plonked a saddle between its humps, thwacking its bones with leather. Poor camel.

Clara chattered quietly, more to fill the silence, Olivia felt, than anything else. She spoke mainly of Ralph and Gus, dimples forming on her pink cheeks as she related Ralph's rapid progress in reading, his obsession with the new Sherlock Holmes stories, Gus cutting his first tooth on the voyage home.

She didn't mention the naughtiness. Olivia didn't press her. There

65

seemed little point with the servants in such close proximity. She would just have to wait for lunch to find out what it was all about. She waved her hand, flicking away the ever-present flies.

Eventually Clara fell silent and turned to stare at the sea. Olivia watched as she pulled at the beribboned handle of her expensive parasol, slowly ruining it. With her shoulders bowed and snub nose wrinkled, she reminded Olivia of the way she'd looked that night at the club, disappearing off into the windy darkness: like a vulnerable girl rather than a twenty-nine-year-old mother of two. Not happy, no not at all.

Olivia shifted in her seat. She felt a near-overwhelming urge to reach out and take Clara in her arms. But she didn't move. It was Clara's evasiveness these past weeks that held her back; all the secrecy.

She couldn't get past it.

She sighed.

'Penny for them,' said Clara.

'I'm not sure they're worth it.'

It took them another twenty minutes to reach the city. The driver steered them away from the shore and into the cobbled market streets, the stalls bursting with fresh fruits, fish and vegetables. They passed a bakery, great baskets of flatbreads at its doors; cinnamon and yeast wafted out from within, mixing with the scent of peaches and onions, heat and sweat. The noisy pavements teemed with as many Mediterranean faces as Egyptian: Greek merchants, Turkish tradesmen, veiled women, cap-wearing Jews. A patchwork of cultures. Edward had told Olivia how this city, founded by Greeks and grown by Egyptians, had been ruled over by the tolerant Ottomans throughout the Middle-Ages; a haven for the persecuted. Even now, mosques stood alongside churches and synagogues, tongues slipped easily from Arabic to Syrian to Hebrew to Greek. Everyone spoke one another's language. (Except the British, of course. For the most part *they* stuck to English. And lived in Ramleh.)

Olivia chewed her lip as dark, expressionless eyes came to rest on her and Clara's fine carriage, their silken skirts and frilly parasols.

They were strangers, the both of them: a race apart in this cosmopolitan land.

They left the carriage in Alex's centre square, the palm-fringed Place Mohammed Ali, and set off to Draycott's on foot. It was as they joined the crowds coursing down the main shopping thoroughfare, the elegant Rue Cherif Pasha, that Olivia felt the straining atmosphere of the day dip and darken. She looked to the heavens to see if a storm was coming, but the sky was pure blue.

They carried on walking. Olivia tried to shrug off her ill-ease, but she couldn't ignore the feeling that she was being watched. Her skin tightened, a curiously insubstantial weight pressed into her back. She looked over her shoulder, eyes watering in the sunlight as she examined the shoppers around them: men in pill-box hats and white robes, others in top hats and tails, the odd pairing of gowned women, wilting, like her and Clara, in the growing heat of the day. No one appeared to be watching them, though. Why then were her senses prickling?

'We should hurry,' said Clara as Olivia narrowed her eyes down the distance of the avenue. 'They won't hold our table for much longer.'

'Just wait a moment.' The people around them seemed to be moving too carefully, dancing a precisely choreographed routine. It was as though the windows in the surrounding buildings were trained on them. Olivia's own gaze felt sluggish, clumsy, like it kept missing things that she was meant to see. 'I feel so strange.'

'Are you getting ill?' Clara eyed her worriedly.

'I'm fine.'

'No you're not. I can see it. Is it Alistair?'

'Not now, Clara, please.'

'But there's so much I want to say, about you, about him.' Clara shook her head, trying to find the words. 'We're not so different, you know.'

'How do you mean?'

Clara gave her a long look. 'Did Teddy really say nothing about me before he left?'

'No.' Olivia frowned at the apparent non sequitur. 'Why? What would he have said?'

Clara opened her mouth to reply, then stopped short and squinted at the opposite pavement. 'Isn't that his man over there?'

'What?' Olivia turned, following Clara's stare.

'Look.' Clara pointed at a wiry, middle-aged Egyptian soldier walking along the opposite side of the road. His khaki shirt was rolled up at the sleeves, his trousers were drawn tight around his waist. Every inch of him appeared dusty with sand.

Olivia would know his sinewy strength and dark features anywhere. 'It's Fadil,' she said. If he was back, Edward must be too. The realisation sparked within her, squashing thoughts of all else. She looked around but couldn't see him. She had to find out where he was. She told Clara she was going to ask Fadil, just so she could send word back to have Edward's rooms ready, of course. She kept her face set as she spoke, containing her excitement by an effort of will.

'All right,' said Clara. 'I'll wait here.'

'No,' said Olivia, 'honestly, you go on.' She wanted a moment free of Clara's presence to compose herself. She nodded at the pillared façade of Draycott's in the distance. 'I'll meet you there.'

'Don't be silly. I'll stay.'

'No, really. You should make sure they keep our table.'

Clara frowned. 'All right,' she said at length. 'I am rather gasping for a drink. Don't be long, will you?'

Olivia promised she would be there directly. Clara nodded and walked away. Olivia watched her as she left, waiting until the sashay of her lace skirts had been swallowed by the crowd, then returned her attention to where Fadil had been.

She cursed as she realised he was gone.

She tried for close to a quarter of an hour to find him. It was only when she got all the way back to the Place Mohammed Ali without any success that, with a sigh of exasperation, she admitted defeat and set off again for Draycott's.

'I'm here to meet Mrs Gray,' she told the maître d'.

'It's lovely to see you, Mrs Sheldon.' He bowed his head,

practically scraping the lectern in front of him. 'Your table is ready. Would you like a cool drink whilst you wait for Mrs Gray?'

'She's already here.'

'I'm afraid you're mistaken, Mrs Sheldon.'

'No I'm not.'

He grimaced apologetically. Olivia rolled her eyes and took herself across the marble foyer to find Clara herself. She paused at the dining-room door and looked around. The place was full. Ceiling fans whirred, spun into action by boys operating rope pulleys; waiters stalked the floor, silver trays held high; the air hummed with the conversation of over a hundred occupied tables, only one of which remained empty, the best in the house, overlooking the sun-drenched terrace and laid for two. Olivia went to it and peered into the garden, seeing sumptuous flower beds, lounging cigar-smokers, a depressed-looking parakeet in the corner, but no Clara. She made her way to the powder room. Still nothing.

'What time is it?' she asked, returning to the maître d'.

'It's half past the hour of midday.'

'She should be here.'

'Would she have gone to attend to an errand first?' His hand fluttered in the direction of the street. 'Shopping, perhaps?'

Olivia doubted it, but went back out into the steaming day to check. She spent well over an hour ducking in and out of shop doorways, back to Draycott's, then out to the shops again, eyes wide for Clara's lemon bonnet, her pale blue dress. She lost track of the number of assistants she approached, the shaken heads she received in response to her enquiries.

'She's the same height as me, same build, fairer hair ...' Her voice was breathless with hurrying as she addressed the aproned proprietor of the Imported Delicacies Emporium.

'I know her, of course I know Mrs Gray,' the man replied with a sniff from behind jars of piccalilli and mustard, 'but we haven't had her here in weeks. I'm sorry.'

'You're certain there's been no mishap? No accident on the pavements that could have taken her away?'

'No, not that I've heard.' He shrugged. 'I can't think what else to tell you.'

Baffled, Olivia retraced her steps to the restaurant, and conducted another tour of its grounds.

'Would she have gone home?' asked the maître d', following her.

'I don't think so,' said Olivia. 'She wouldn't leave me in town like this.' Surely not. Even so, Olivia set off to find their carriage in the square, sweat trickling down her back. Clara's driver was leaning against the carriage door, the footman was slouched on the dusty floor. They assured Olivia that they had been there the whole time, that no, they'd seen no sign of Ma'am Gray. Did Ma'am Sheldon wish them to help look for her?

Olivia said no, better they stayed where they were; Clara would undoubtedly reappear any second. Of course she would. She ran her hand through her hair, realising she had somehow lost her hat, and made off again for Draycott's. She more jogged than walked along the thronging pavements, trying to ignore how white and so very *female* she felt in this city of smiling men. She attempted to talk herself out of her growing panic, repeating again and again that there were any number of places Clara might have got to, all manner of explanations for her going. But still, her earlier sense that she and Clara were being watched knocked in her chest, sharpened by the echo of Alistair's suddenly plausible warnings about nationalists.

Olivia stopped off again in every store, asking the same questions, receiving the same responses (no accidents, no ambulance bells, no sign of a woman in a blue dress); by the time she arrived back in Draycott's cavernous foyer, her gown was sticking to her body, and her hair, loose from tugging, was curling on her sweaty forehead.

'Mrs Sheldon?' said the maître d' from behind her. 'If you would just . . . ?'

Ignoring him, she made for the entrance to the dining room and pushed the double doors wide. Only a handful of diners remained at their luncheon. Clara was nowhere to be seen. Treading a now familiar route, Olivia set off in the direction of the terrace, skirts rustling against the tables as she wove her way through them. The maître d' was still behind her, calling her name. 'Mrs Sheldon, please ...' but she didn't stop.

She broke out into the gardens and held her arm to her eyes to shield them from the sunlight. It was still busy here, with men lounging in wicker chairs. They turned to look at her. It might have been funny, the way their idle gazes transformed into embarrassed recognition. *She's back then*, she could hear them thinking. *Silly girl's got herself into a bit of a state. Where's her husband? Please don't let it fall to us to sort her out.*

'Mrs Sheldon?'

She turned to face the maître d'. 'I can't think where she is,' she said. 'I can't think.'

'She must have been called away.'

'But her carriage is still here.'

He opened his arms helplessly.

'What time is it now?' she asked.

'It's nearing three.'

'*Three?* How can it be three?' She took a deep breath. *Pull yourself together*, she told herself. *Don't be a fool, falling apart like this.* 'I'd better go to her house,' she said. 'Make sure she didn't go back by another means.'

'It's a good idea.' The maître d' nodded vehemently, doubtless relieved to be rid of her, of the situation. Still, as he reached for his kerchief to blot his brow, hand jerking, it was clear he'd grown more than a little worried himself.

It tipped Olivia into resolution. 'Get word to Commissioner Wilkins,' she said, impulsively naming the most senior man in the police that she knew of. 'Send him on to Ramleh. If Clara's not home, we'll need him to help find her.'

Chapter Five

Hopeless as Olivia suspected it was, she asked Clara's footman to wait in the square in case Clara should return, whilst the driver, Hassan, drove her back to Ramleh. Olivia sat in tight-lipped anxiety as the carriage rocked down the narrow streets to the harbour, then along the dusty coast road. It unsettled her that the camel was already back in its field, hungry flies clustered around its eyes, at the end of its day's work. The sunlight reflecting off the sea had the golden tint of high afternoon. So much time had passed.

She tried to imagine where Clara could be. She thought, *Please be at home, please just do be at home.* She fixed her eyes on the impossibly long stretch of road ahead and silently entreated Hassan to hurry up and get them there.

Eventually the yellow curve of Ramleh's beach came into view. White and pink villas arced around it. The Grays' house, a terracotta mansion that, like Alistair's, befitted Jeremy's status as one of the wealthiest men in Alex, was further inland, on the very outskirts of the suburb. By the time Hassan pulled the horses around and onto the road that approached it, Olivia had made herself nauseous with nerves.

'Try not to worry.' Hassan's low voice cut into Olivia's thoughts and made her start. 'Picture Ma'am Gray well and sound.'

'Why?'

'Faith, Ma'am Sheldon.' He frowned. 'Faith. Think and so it shall be.'

It seemed a tenuous strategy, but Olivia gave it a try anyway, imagining her relief at finding Clara playing on the lawn with Ralph, or holding Gus tight in her arms. She willed it into happening with every part of her being.

Much good it did. Clara's home was empty of everyone save her sons and staff.

Olivia wasted no time in sending a servant off to ensure Wilkins was on his way, then to fetch Jeremy from the office. She asked another to call in at all the places Clara might have gone: the Sporting Club, Ramleh Surgery, Amélie Pasha's house, Olivia's own home (just in case) . . . He returned an hour later with several messages of concern, but no word of Clara.

Olivia waited anxiously for Wilkins and Jeremy. She sat with the boys in the nursery, holding Gus on her lap, stroking his chubby cheeks. She told him that all was well, his Mama was just running late, nothing more. *Don't fret, little man, she'll be home soon.*

'She never misses bedtime,' said Ralph. 'Never.'

Olivia held him closer. In her mind, she searched the events of the day for anything that could help the police. She kept coming back to her earlier suspicion that she and Clara were being followed. She doubted though that Wilkins, a self-important personality who'd come from Calcutta to kick the Egyptian police into shipshape form, would be inclined to deal in the currency of her senses.

Sure enough, 'It's a little insubstantial for me,' he said when she accosted him with her conviction the instant he finally walked through the door. He rested his hand on his waistcoat-straining gut and rocked back on his heels. 'Let's see if we can't find something more tangible to go on.' He sighed. 'No word at the hospitals though, I'm afraid – I had my men ride around before I came over. Not to worry, we'll get to the bottom of it. You're lucky I'm here actually. I've been away in Cairo, our Egyptian man there needs a deal of help. Still,' another sigh, 'that's what the Protectorate's about: education. *Education.*'

Olivia said she wasn't much sure she wanted to talk about the Protectorate, given everything else going on. Wilkins fixed her with a narrowed-eyed look, then asked where Mr Gray was.

'I hope on his way.'

'He's not at home?' Wilkins' tone was affronted. Of course it wasn't often that he, a not particularly popular member of the civil service – no matter how high-ranking – would be invited to a mansion like this, let alone to speak to Jeremy. He'd come to a show expecting the star, only to be told the understudy was playing instead. He huffed, settling himself into one of the hall chairs, then ordered Olivia up to Clara's room to check all of her things were in order, no clothes missing and so on.

'She hasn't run away,' said Olivia. 'She'd never leave her boys, apart from anything else.'

'In my experience, women do all sorts of things we mightn't expect them to.'

'Really?'

'Yes, really. So if you would be so good as to go up and check. No stone unturned and all that.'

Olivia had the distinct sense she was being got rid of. But, if only to prove how wrong Wilkins was, she did as he asked.

She paused outside Clara's door, fingers on the handle. She'd never been in before, she didn't know what to expect. She eased the door open and took in the blue and white walls, the sash windows. The room was large and airy, shadowed by dusk, and immaculately tidy. There was no sign of Clara's trunks from Constantinople, the servants had obviously finished the unpacking. A four-poster bed stood in the centre of the tiled floor; Clara's nightclothes were folded at the foot of it, waiting for her. Olivia crossed over to them, she touched her fingers to the soft fabric and drew breath.

As she went on to search through Clara's things, a dull weight grew in her chest. Nothing, so far as she could make out, was missing, but it was the sweetly scented potpourri amidst Clara's silk stockings, the spilt powder on her vanity, the blonde hairs in her comb that all made her seem at once close and so horribly absent. On the desk there was an open parcel of gramophone records: music-hall recordings from London. The paper around it was ripped, as though torn in haste. Olivia let out a slow breath as she pictured Clara pulling at it, her excitement at this package from England. She had probably been looking forward to listening to the songs that evening.

Olivia closed her eyes at the painful thought.

When she opened them again, her gaze settled on a framed daguerreotype on the bedside drawers. She went and picked it up, studying the sepia image in the day's fading light. She'd seen it before, Clara had brought it to show to her once. It was of the two of them as children, back in Cairo: Clara grinning and gangly in a dress that skimmed her calves; Olivia a little girl in a pinafore, chubby face creased in laughter.

'You see there, Livvy,' Clara had said, pointing at Olivia's tummy, 'that hand clutching you? That was Mama tickling you to make you laugh. Do you really not remember it, Livvy, remember her? Not at all?'

Olivia tried again now, eyes scrunched. She held her breath, waiting.

Nothing came. It left her feeling even emptier than before.

But it moved her that Clara kept this picture so close, that it was the last thing she looked at each night. And all of a sudden she wished she hadn't stopped herself, back in the carriage, when she'd felt that urge to hug her.

Since Jeremy still wasn't home by the time she returned downstairs, Wilkins declared (with a resigned air) that they had better get on with some questions. Olivia took a moment to gather her frayed emotions, then showed him into the drawing room. He sat opposite her in a high-backed chair. The candlelight flickered in the breeze from the open shutters, casting his florid complexion in and out of shadow. He breathed heavily through his nose, a notepad rested on his broad knee. As Olivia tried to convince him to take her suspicions about her and Clara being trailed seriously, he wrote not a thing down.

'But did you *see* anyone acting suspiciously, Mrs Sheldon?' Wilkins spoke condescendingly, as if to a little girl. His gaze kept flicking to the door, checking for Jeremy. His irritation at being left alone with Olivia, when he could be ingratiating himself with the great cotton magnate, seemed to be growing by the minute. 'Really try and think now, you might remember something.'

'I assure you I have been trying very hard to think,' replied Olivia. Wilkins gave her a tight smile. She frowned, remembering Clara's strained mood. 'Something was weighing on her mind. She hadn't wanted to go to Constantinople; she didn't know why Jeremy had taken her, but she mentioned he wanted to send her away again, to England with Ralph. I think he might have thought her in danger.'

Wilkins shook his head. 'You ladies, always fretting.'

'You should ask him about it.'

'Let me worry about that.'

'Really, he might be able to tell you something.'

Wilkins took a long breath, gathering his patience. A fleck of sunburnt skin flapped on his nostril. 'Since he's not here, Mrs Sheldon, shall we stick to what you can tell me?' Another tight smile. 'Would that be acceptable to you?'

Olivia didn't return his smile. 'Perfectly,' she said.

'Good.'

She said, 'There was Fadil, of course.'

'Fadil?'

'Captain Bertram's batman. He was in the street when I last saw Clara.'

'And you think he's had something to do with her going?' Wilkins raised his eyebrows. 'Shall I arrest him?'

'That's hardly what I'm saying.'

'What *are* you saying, Mrs Sheldon?'

'You should talk to Fadil. He might have seen something.'

'Mrs Sheldon. Are you telling me how to do my job?'

Someone has to, Olivia nearly snapped. *Get on, won't you, find Clara, for goodness' sake.* She swallowed the urge. Wilkins was clearly intent on dancing to his own tune. Any attempt by her, a mere woman, to hurry him would probably do nothing but slow him down. 'I'm just trying to help,' she said. 'Fadil might have an idea about who was trailing us. I'm certain someone was.' Still Wilkins wrote nothing down. 'Why aren't you taking me seriously?' she asked. 'Why don't you believe me?'

'You're becoming overwrought,' he said, and finally scribbled something on his pad.

'No I'm not.' She craned to see his paper. 'What did you write?'

Wilkins tapped his pencil on his chin.

Olivia took a deep breath. 'Alistair told me there's been a rise in nationalist activity,' she said. 'I didn't believe him, but I don't know . . . Is it possible they've taken Clara?'

'Let's not leap to conclusions.' Wilkins frowned, his chin forming three. 'I certainly don't want those views being bandied around town. We're all trying to live harmoniously these days.' He clicked his tongue, for all the world as though he might be doing such a thing as thinking. '*If* she's been taken . . .'

'I'm sure she has.'

'*If*, Mrs Sheldon, then it's just as likely your everyday criminal at play. The Jews can be tricky.'

'Oh for goodness' sake. The *Jews*? It sounds to me like you're clutching at straws.'

Wilkins stared. Inexplicably, he made another note.

The door opened. Wilkins jumped, Jeremy strode in. He threw his top hat and gloves on the side table. In contrast to Wilkins' complacent calm, his face was drawn, the skin around his grey eyes waxy. For all Clara's talk of awfulness, he certainly seemed anxious enough about her now.

It didn't make Olivia feel any better.

Wilkins shook Jeremy's hand. He told him how glad he was to be of service. His manner, so patronising before, was verging on the obsequious now.

'I got here as soon as I could.' Jeremy turned to Olivia. 'I'm sorry it took so long.'

Olivia was just about to ask him why it had, when another set of footsteps sounded in the hallway. Seconds later, Alistair appeared. She might have known he would come. She didn't greet him, just stared coldly. He met her gaze with clear, blue eyes. She held herself rigid as he crossed the room, pulled her to her feet, and hugged her tight to his empty chest. 'Don't ever run off like that again,' he said. 'Silly little fool.' Somehow his hands found the exact spots on her waist that hurt. Her cheeks worked with the effort of not giving her pain away.

At last, he released her and sat her back down. Like a puppeteer.

A short silence followed. Olivia pressed her hands to the back of her neck. Her pumping pulse felt horribly audible.

'Wilkins,' said Jeremy, 'we'd like a word in the study, if you please.'

Olivia made to stand. Alistair told her to stay where she was.

'What?' she said. 'No. Clara's my sister. You can't leave me out of this.'

'I told you to stay,' said Alistair.

'Just for now, Livvy,' said Jeremy, more kindly.

'Yes,' said Wilkins, following them both out, his ample being inflated with importance at being included in this little tête-à-tête. 'You must trust us.'

'Wait, please.'

But they were already gone. Alistair shut the door behind him with a cold click.

Olivia stood mute, furious at the dismissal, even more so at herself for accepting it. Her mouth opened and closed like a fish. The hysteria she had been staving off all day rose dangerously in her throat. She was perilously close to the edge and knew if she stayed where she was a moment longer she'd lose control.

So she began pacing Clara's dark house instead. Her skin beneath her bodice felt stale with dry sweat, her mind was an inarticulate jumble of thoughts (Clara, Edward, naughtiness, Clara). She trailed her fingers along the walls, her heels echoed through candelabra-lit corridors, until, without meaning to, she arrived at the nursery.

She peeked in at Ralph and Angus, both asleep beneath their tented mosquito nets. She drank them in, the pure fact of their being helping her to believe that Clara was breathing somewhere, thinking of her sons. That she might yet be returning to them.

They needed her so, these boys. Gus, arms flung wide in his cot, was still only seven months old. A baby; *Clara's* baby. He'd never know her if she didn't come back. (No, no. Don't think like that.) And Ralph had been so upset earlier. 'What if she's hurt?' he'd asked. 'I can't go to sleep not knowing.' Olivia had tried to placate him, but her arms had shaken around him. In the end his nurse-maid, Sofia, the same Greek nanny who'd once cared for Olivia and Clara in Cairo, had taken over, comforting him with her ample bosom, promises of cocoa before bedtime, and an assurance that he would see his mama the next day. It was a balm, a bandage, nothing more.

Olivia was sure Sofia had said much the same sort of thing to her when her parents had first disappeared. Not that she could recall, of course. She remembered Sofia not at all. (Sofia said the memories would come, that Olivia had to be patient. 'They're all waiting for you, *agapi mou*,' she would tell her, using the Greek endearment, my little love. 'You'll see.')

Clara said Olivia should listen, Sofia was very wise after all, she always had been; it was why Clara had hired her, back when Jeremy first brought her to Alex with Ralph growing in her tummy. 'She's just the same,' she'd told Olivia. 'She still pretend-spits on the floor to keep the evil eye away, and says forks and knives instead of knives and forks, just like when we were children. Isn't it splendid?'

She was there now, smoking one of her sweet-smelling cigarettes as she creaked on a rocking chair between the boys' beds. The mound of her starched apron moved up and down as she inhaled, exhaled. Her peppery hair was arranged in a caterpillar roll. Beneath it, she had the same olive skin and hooked nose that so many Greeks in Egypt shared. She had lived here her whole life, her grandparents having fled to Alex during the Greek War of Independence. Olivia didn't know how old that made her, forty, maybe fifty. Sofia said it was rude to ask anyone with grey hairs for a number.

Her eyes certainly looked old enough now. Swollen too, and full of worry. For all her brave words to Ralph earlier, it was clear she had been crying. Olivia wanted to say something to console her, but for the life of her couldn't think what. Instead, as Angus let out a small cough, she looked dubiously at the smoke coiling over his cot.

'Should you be . . . ?'

'Don't worry.' Sofia waved her hand distractedly. 'I'm batting it away.'

Another cough.

'You might want to bat a bit harder.'

'He's fine.'

'He's not fine.' Olivia didn't know why she snapped. It wasn't poor old Sofia she was angry with, not at all. But still, she couldn't help herself. 'He's not.' Her voice came out strangled, halfway between a whisper and a shout. 'He's fit to choke. As if he didn't have enough to be contending with already *with his mother missing*. Put it out.'

Sofia's eyes widened. She reached for her ashtray and stubbed her cigarette into it.

Olivia took a breath. 'I'm sorry,' she said. 'I shouldn't have . . . '

'No.' Sofia gave her a sad smile. 'That's the sparky little miss I remember. It's done me good to see you again.'

Olivia shook her head, then raised her eyes to the dark ceiling. 'Are the boys all right?'

'The little lambs are fine. I've told them their mama's on her way home to us.' Sofia reached under her apron and pulled out a handkerchief. She blew her nose. 'I'm glad you're here, *agapi mou*. I was going to come and find you. I couldn't talk earlier in front of the littlies . . . ' She paused, pressed her teeth to her lip. She was clearly fretting, deciding whether to go on.

Olivia frowned, confused. What could be so hard for Sofia to say?

'Sofia?' she prompted. 'What is it?'

Sofia sighed, nodded. 'You need to do something for your sister, just in case she isn't back as soon as we're praying. I saw her writing something this morning in the study that she tucked away when she spotted me looking. Go and get it, Mrs Livvy. I don't think Mrs Clara would want Mr Jeremy to find it.'

Slowly, Olivia digested this new piece of strangeness. So Clara *was* keeping secrets from Jeremy. It came as disturbingly unshocking.

Nothing seemed to make proper sense any more – it was the only thing that made sense. Olivia felt as though she had fallen headlong into an upside-down wonderland; like Carroll's Alice, she now wanted very much to go home. But unlike Alice, she didn't have her sister by her side ready to wake her just at this point of her nightmare becoming overwhelming. No, she had absolutely no idea where Clara was, and was grimly certain of being wide awake already.

'Can't you fetch the letter yourself?' she asked Sofia.

'What if someone saw me? No, you have to do it.'

'I can't get in the study now, Jeremy's in there with Alistair and Commissioner Wilkins.' Whatever it was they were discussing.

'Go tomorrow. Mr Jeremy won't find it so quickly anyway. You need to know where to look.'

'And you know?'

'Second to top shelf, third book along.'

'Did you read it yourself?'

'No, *agapi mou*.'

'You know what's in it though. I can tell.'

Sofia didn't deny it. 'Take my advice, Mrs Livvy, just get rid of it. If Mrs Clara wanted you to know what she was writing, she'd have told you.'

Before Olivia could answer that Clara might well have been about to, Alistair's voice calling, 'Olivia, we're going,' echoed down the corridor and cooled her veins with dread.

Reluctantly, she went off to find him.

Chapter Six

As Olivia followed Alistair out to fetch his horse, she asked him what he'd been speaking about with Wilkins. 'Why were *you* even talking to him?' She lifted her skirts from the hardened mud path, jogging to keep up. 'What does this all have to do with you? Tell me, I won't go home until you do.'

'Don't be petulant.' Alistair pushed the stable doors open. 'It doesn't suit you. As for what we were discussing, there's absolutely nothing to tell. We were just … encouraging … Wilkins to take what's happened seriously.'

'Why? What do you know that he doesn't?'

'Leave this now.'

'No.' Olivia's voice rang through the night air, bouncing off the haystacks; the horses shied in their stalls. Clara's driver, Hassan, looked up from shovelling straw, curiosity writ large across his dark features.

Alistair stopped. His square shoulders rose and fell in a breath. He turned and crossed back over to her. She jerked away as he made to touch her face. His blue eyes snapped. 'Come now,' he said in that quiet way of his, 'you've had a long day.'

'Stop talking to me like I'm a child.'

'Stop behaving like one.'

She flinched at his steely tone; it maddened her that she'd done so, and her anger pushed her on. 'Clara's been upset lately, although I never found out why. I think you might know though.'

'How on earth would I?'

'She said Jeremy's angry at you, that he didn't even want to come back.'

'Oh, for God's sake. Stop this.'

A small voice told Olivia to listen, do as he says, *don't go too far*. 'Clara loathes you, you know.' The words were out before she could swallow them. 'She always has, even when you were trying to convince her to marry you instead of Jeremy.'

'That's more than enough.'

'Don't tell me when enough is—'

'*Olivia*.'

The word cracked. Olivia's determination withered in her mouth. Alistair's lips turned in a smile; he knew he'd won. She watched, eyes smarting with humiliation and frustration, as he strode from her, past Hassan, to the furthest stall. He untethered his hunter and pulled himself into the saddle.

As she waited for him to ride over, she tried to steady herself with thoughts of Edward. For once it didn't work. All she could conjure when she tried to picture him was the way he'd been the last time she saw him, head to head with Clara. She couldn't let the image go. And he wasn't here to help her. For all she knew, he might not even be home.

She took a step back as Alistair came alongside her and held out his hand. She stared at his symmetrical face, his near-transparent skin, feeling her own cheeks flame. Ignoring his offer of help, she fetched a nearby crate to stand on, gripped his horse's mane and hoisted herself up. She levered herself so hard that she lost her balance and nearly fell over the other side of the horse's flank, headlong to the floor. She struggled to right herself, scrambling in a mess of petticoats and stockings to reach back and grab the girth. Alistair pulled her into place in front of him. 'Be careful,' he said.

'I'm fine.' She flicked her hair from her hot face.

Alistair laughed quietly and kicked them into motion.

Hassan stared after them as they left, his rake motionless in his hand.

They rode in silence along the moonlit road. Olivia, tight in

Alistair's hold, took in the glinting sea, the swaying palms, and wondered whether she felt even worse because everything around them was so beautiful.

The Bedouin were already asleep when they got home, their canvas home silent. The villa was swathed in darkness, the creeping jasmine nothing but sweetly scented shadows on its walls. There were no servants to be seen. The only noise came from Olivia and Alistair's heels on the staircase, the crackling candle in Alistair's hand, and the screech of cicadas outside.

Alistair didn't speak as Olivia undressed, just watched. She swallowed against the shivers of anxiety building in her. Not tonight, surely? All she wanted was to lie silent, untouched; hold her fears for Clara close to her – a melancholy kind of company. *Where are you?* The question repeated itself over and over in her mind.

As she crossed over to the bed, she'd never felt more scared, or more alone. She pulled back the gossamer folds of the mosquito nets, and climbed onto the mattress. She rolled onto her side, away from him. Her chest rose, fell. She heard a stealthy padding as, step by step, he came and leant over her, one hand either side of her body almost, but not quite touching her.

'Roll over,' he said. 'Look at me.'

When she didn't do as he asked, he rolled her himself. He had the candle in his hand.

'Why did you speak to me like that earlier, Olivia?' The candle dipped, a line of wax ran down its side. 'Why did you go off on your own today?' He shook his head. The flame shook with it. 'What were you thinking? I wish I could hear your thoughts.' He kissed her neck. 'If I could, I'd know everything about you.' He kissed her again. The wick crackled. 'You can't lock me out.' His hand ran down her body. 'You mustn't.'

'No, Alistair. I can't stand it, not with Clara ...'

'Shhhh.' He tightened his grip on her thigh, gathering her night-dress up. His fingers pressed into her. And even though she knew that it was futile, that it probably made things worse, still she struggled. Her limbs filled with panicked energy as she tried to push him away. He laughed shortly, as though the sport had just started. He brought his hand from beneath her gown, he raised it above her. Her eyes widened, and before she could move, or even beg him not to, he jerked his elbow sharply into her stomach, taking the breath and the words from her. She gasped, immobile with pain. Her eyes locked on the nets, a dead mosquito, anywhere but on him. The candle sizzling into the raw burn on her pelvis wasn't a surprise, but it was a shock, and she must have screamed, because the pillow came down heavy on her face.

He pushed her legs apart. She clenched her eyes shut.

Edward saw their light go out from where he was standing in the front garden and thought, *Let him be comforting her. Let her sleep now.* It killed him to be back, so close at last that he could shout and she would hear, and not be able to hold her in his arms himself.

He ran his hand down his face. With a sigh, he pulled his horse's reins, leading him towards the stables at the back of the house. He opened the neck of his shirt as he walked, letting the cool night air onto his skin. He was exhausted, he couldn't remember the last time he'd been so tired. He'd been up since dawn, riding at pace across the dunes: the final stretch of a three-day journey triggered by that message. *Give it up, you've searched long enough. The Grays are on their way back from Constantinople, you're needed here now.* All he'd wanted to do when he finally reached home was wash the sand from him, see Olly, then get to Tom to find out some more about why he and Fadil had been sent on that bloody wild goose chase into the desert in the first place. But when they got to the house, no one had known where Olly was, just that she had gone out with Clara.

Edward had been furious; after the month he'd had, it beggared belief that Clara should swan around in such a way. He and Fadil had left in search of her and Olly: Fadil to the city centre whilst Edward hunted everywhere else. Edward shook his head, thinking of the futile hours he'd spent trawling Alex's cafés and parks, how incandescent with rage he was by the time he gave up and went to find Tom at the parade ground. He'd had the words ready to berate him in his head. *Do you think perhaps we might ask Clara that in future she informs someone of her plans before she goes off gallivanting around God knows where? That she has a care before dragging her sister along with her? I'm not a sodding babysitter.* Stripes or no stripes, no matter his respect for Tom, he was ready to go for him. He was too angry, and too shattered, not to.

But as soon as he'd entered Tom's office and seen the shock on Tom's face, the words had died on his lips. He'd listened in grim silence as Tom told him how Alistair and Jeremy had just left: the worst had happened, Clara was missing. 'She didn't know,' said Tom. 'They didn't tell her how much danger she was in, even though they assured me they would. Just fed her some claptrap about nationalism in general being on the up. Sheldon claimed it should have been enough to keep her on her guard, said they didn't want to worry her with the truth of it – or risk the gossip if she mentioned it all to anyone else.' Tom's tone was incredulous, full of as much anger as Edward felt. Grief too. Tom had known Clara even longer than Edward had, ever since she'd come to Alex as a newly-wed. As for Imogen . . . Tom would be dreading telling her what had happened. 'Damned arrogance,' Tom said. 'The two of them are on their way to talk with that arsehole Wilkins now. Olivia called for him.'

'Olly's safe?' Edward had managed to ask.

'She is, thank God. For the moment.'

For the moment. Never had three words turned Edward's stomach with such force.

He'd turned to leave, intent on getting to the Grays' house, just to see Olly there. Tom had tried to keep him back, said they needed to speak of India, the papers had come through, Edward's passage was in less than a fortnight; he needed to get ready, tell the men. Edward hadn't wanted to hear it. He'd strode from the room, ridden hard for the Grays'. But he'd found the place empty, the drawing room dark, the study too. A servant had told him that everyone had left, Sir Gray was on the terrace if Captain Bertram wished to join him.

Edward hadn't. He'd come straight home. To where she was.

He flexed his fingers now on the reins, examining them in the moonlight. They were trembling. His whole body was jumpy with fear. He clenched his hand, tight. He needed to get hold of himself. He'd never been scared like this before, not during his brutal training at Sandhurst, the early days in Egypt, those desert patrols into hostile territory during the Sudanese war . . . The emotion shocked him.

He led his stallion into the stables, past the empty stall where Fadil's hunter should be. Not back, then. Edward hadn't seen him since they'd separated that morning. He hoped to God he was out chasing a lead.

He paused by Olly's horse. He ran his hand around her silky neck, clicking his tongue as she nestled into him. He breathed deep, thinking of all those riding lessons, the hours in that field. The memories had kept him company whilst he'd been away. Olly's smile, her laugh, the guiding touches to her calf, her waist.

He closed his eyes. Get a grip, man.

He went to the terrace from the stables. There was no point going to bed, he wouldn't be able to rest until he had spoken to Fadil. He climbed the wooden steps, struck a match on a cigarette, and turned to look out at the sea. His lips shuddered as he inhaled.

He thought about Olly asleep upstairs, her body curled beneath the sheets. He thought about Clara too: where she was, what she might be enduring, and how they might begin to find her.

He hated that the last time they'd spoken she had been so upset. He'd been sharp, too sharp with her, that night on the club's terrace. *How could you be that selfish, Clara? What use would telling do now? Think about someone other than yourself.* God, but she'd looked crestfallen.

He took another drag on his cigarette. His legs twitched. He couldn't just stand here as he was, doing nothing. Where the hell had Fadil got to? He decided to go out in search of him. He was just about to, when the click of the terrace doors opening stopped him in his tracks.

He turned. The instant he saw her, the tension in his muscles eased. He realised that until that moment, he hadn't quite been able to accept that she was safe.

She didn't notice him straight away. Her expression, as she stared out across the garden, was distant. He watched the way her brown curls moved in the breeze, how she wrapped her arms around her body, gathering her nightgown close. She started, as if in pain, and seeing it, knowing how she must be thinking of Clara, Edward took a step towards her. A floorboard creaked.

Her whole body went still. She held her breath.

'Hello, Olly.'

Her smile nearly ripped him in two. So sad, so relieved. 'You're back.'

'Yes,' he said, 'I'm here.'

'Thank goodness.'

They stood for a moment, looking at one another. By an effort of will Edward kept his arms by his side. *It has to come from her.* 'I'm so sorry,' he said, 'for the way I went. I'd have written, but we were in villages. It was hard. And I didn't want Alistair seeing.'

She nodded slowly, then made her way across the terrace, stopping just short of where he stood. He could smell lavender on her skin.

He offered her his cigarette.

She took it and inhaled. It crackled, tip glowing.

Their arms rested on the rail, inches away from one another.

She asked if he knew about Clara. He confirmed that he did.

'I saw Fadil in the street,' she said, 'just before Clara went.'

'You did?' Edward frowned, taken aback. 'Did you speak to him?'

'No. I tried to find him. I sent Clara away on her own so I could.' Her voice cracked. 'She might still be here had I not.'

'Olly . . .'

'Why was Fadil there, Edward? Why did you both go away?' She turned to him. 'And why are you back, on today of all days?'

He hesitated before answering, unsure how much to reveal. It wasn't that he agreed with Jeremy and Alistair concealing the threats that had been made (if ever there was proof that forewarned

88

was forearmed, today was it), but their secrecy unsettled him. Tom said they'd never even shown *him* the blackmail letter Jeremy had received before he'd gone to Constantinople, just told him that men were after company money, planning to hurt Clara or the children if Jeremy didn't pay up, and could well target Alistair next. ('We'll do what we can whilst the Grays are away,' Tom had said to Edward that night at the Sporting Club, 'interview the usual suspects, search the desert villages, find out who's playing foul. But I wish Sheldon hadn't ripped up that damned blackmail note, however insulting he found it. It might have given us some clues.') Edward couldn't help but wonder why Alistair, a considered bastard if ever there was one, had done something so stupid. Tom said the same conundrum was bothering him.

Then there was that favour Jeremy had pleaded of Edward, the very morning before those torn-up threats had arrived: that deserted hut he'd sent him to in Montazah. Those silent children; the wary way that maid-girl, Nailah, had stared. Edward couldn't shake it from his mind.

It all meant something, he was sure. But until he worked out what, he didn't want to burden Olly with half-cut suspicions.

She looked up at him, gaze questioning, impatient.

'I don't know what to tell you,' he said truthfully. 'I'm back because I was ordered back.'

She narrowed her eyes.

He drew on his cigarette, lips touching the imprint hers had left on the paper.

She asked, 'Have nationalists taken Clara?'

'I don't know.'

'But you believe she's been taken?'

'Yes,' he frowned, 'I'm sorry.'

'Do you think you can get her back?'

'I hope so.'

'What were the two of you talking about, at the Sporting Club?'

'Olly,' he grimaced. 'Don't.'

She stared. 'Edward, what the hell has happened?'

He said nothing. Her beautiful face, just inches from his, was miserable. Abruptly, he could take it no more. Being here with her, watching her become less and less like the person he'd first met, more and more unhappy. 'I don't know how much longer this can go on,' he said. 'I can't stay.'

She inhaled sharply. She looked as if he had struck her: the very last thing he could do.

'So I'm losing you too,' she said.

'Olly, no. That's not what I meant.' He took a step towards her, she took a step back. There was so much he wanted to say to her now. But if ever there *was* a time to talk of India, it wasn't tonight. He should never have raised it. 'You must stay here until we find out what's happened to Clara,' he said. 'No going off on your own. God knows if you're in danger now too.'

'Why should I be?'

'Just promise me, Olly.'

She made no reply. She neither promised nor refused to before she turned, shoulders heavy, and walked away.

'Olly, wait.'

She didn't. She didn't even look back.

He cursed. He scrunched the burning end of his cigarette into a ball, and threw it into the darkness. *Idiot*. He leant the heels of his hands on the terrace rail, breathing deep.

'Sayed?'

He started, looked around.

It was Fadil, at the foot of the terrace stairs. Returned, at last. His black eyes looked every bit as gritty with tiredness as Edward's felt.

With an effort, Edward pushed Olly from his mind. He asked Fadil for an account of his day.

Fadil gave it. As he talked, Edward dropped his head, frowning, trying to make sense of all Fadil said.

When Fadil was finished, Edward asked, 'Why didn't you come and find help sooner?'

'I didn't want to waste time, sayed.'

Edward nodded, accepting it. He stood silent, thinking. 'Whoever has Clara,' he said at length, 'they know this city like the back of their hand.'

'Yes, sayed.'

Edward looked to the sea. Light was seeping from the horizon. The day would break soon. The mosques around the city would be opening their doors for dawn prayers. In less than an hour, the streets would be full of locals. The police would be all over them, of course, asking questions. As though anyone who knew anything would admit it to them.

Edward stood straighter, an idea taking root. Why hadn't he thought of it before? He needed to go into town. Now. Sleep would have to wait for later.

He couldn't waste time if they were to have a hope of finding Clara.

THE SECOND DAY

Chapter Seven

The low melodic notes of the muezzin's call to worship rang through the narrow streets of Alexandria's old Ottoman heart, the Turkish Quarter, and entered into Nailah's dreams of whispers amidst jacaranda trees, slowly drawing her from them. She opened her eyes in the watery dawn light, taking in the dusty, sparsely furnished room, and remembered with a jolt that it was where she lived now. It felt even meaner for the beauty of the sleep-world she'd just left.

She shifted her weight on the straw mattress. Her hip ached from where it had pressed against the floor all night. Her ten-year-old cousin, Cleo, lay beside her, still dreaming. Her hand was resting on Nailah's arm, just as it had been when they fell asleep. Three-year-old Babu nestled between the two of them, bottom wedged in Cleo's tummy, head tucked under Nailah's chest. They had become like three pieces of a puzzle this past month, slotting together in this hovel.

A door slammed. Then another. Footsteps sounded in the stairwell as the men leasing the other rooms in their terraced dwelling set off for mosque. Their murmured greetings to one another, 'Sabah el-kheir', drifted upwards. The floorboards vibrated as one after another they left. Nailah waited for the front door to swing shut for a final time, and, with all the men now safely out of the house, she eased herself away from her cousins, moving carefully so as not to wake them. She picked up the pail of last night's urine, and went down to the yard to empty it into the latrine. She held her breath, as she always did, and squatted over the hole in the floor herself, nightgown clutched high above the rank puddles at her feet. Her eyes watered in the stench of the men's waste. She tried to blank her mind of where she was, the humiliating filth. She hurried to finish and scrambled back outside, then upstairs to dress.

Her body was grimy with sweat, she yearned for a bath, but since there was none in the house, she made do with a flannel and bucket. She rubbed herself brusquely, clenching her jaw against the discomfort of the cold water. With the sound of the children's steady breathing in her ear, she reflected habitually, longingly, on her life before their mother had died. Back when she had worked as a maid for the Anglo-Egyptian Benjamin Pasha and his wife, Amélie, up near Montazah on the Aboukir Peninsula. She sighed, remembering the sun-filled starts breakfasting on platters of fruit with the other maids, the ease of the week's work caring for Amélie's beautiful clothes, arranging her hair, sympathising with her worries over who should be sitting with whom at a dinner. And every Sunday spent at her Aunt Tabia's hut, barely ten minutes' walk away, cooking and talking, playing with the children. Nailah squeezed her eyes shut. It hurt too much to think of Tabia. As for the rest of it, it was becoming harder and harder to recall: her life back then, the old version of herself. The one who was never hungry, who didn't fret, but who had always had one ear cocked for the sound of that voice, his voice . . . No.

Nailah's eyes flipped open.

She looked around at the scrubbed floor, the lopsided table, the rising sun through the one grimy window. *Don't torture yourself. This is your life now.* With a nod of resolution, she reached for her brush and went to the mottled looking-glass.

As she coiled her greasy hair into a bun, she stared into her own dark eyes. She turned her head, tucking in a pin here, a flyaway strand there. She was one of the few not to wear a headscarf in these tight Muslim streets. Most of the women here wore full hijab, as much, Nailah thought, to protest against the British rule banning it as anything else. But it hadn't been part of the uniform at the Pashas'. Before that, Nailah had never been expected to wear one;

her mother, Isa, who earnt her living as a singer and dancer, was hardly one to bother with such matters, whilst Nailah's father had died before she was even born. Isa swore blind he'd married her first; she could go on for hours about the wedding ceremony: fellow actors who'd come to celebrate, the way she'd done her hair … But still, there was gossip. (*Marry Isa? Why would he have bothered? She's anyone's for a penny when she's on tour, never mind the example she's setting to that daughter of hers. Oh, but the way she leaves her here, all alone, weeks on end. She's entertaining the army in Luxor this month, you know, and not just with singing, I'd wager. The bare-faced shame of it.*)

'Don't listen to them,' Isa would say on the rare occasions she could be coaxed off stage to visit home. She'd press Nailah's school fees into her hand. 'Study hard, escape, we're better than this, my love. You should have seen them cheer for me at the encore …'

Nailah had used to believe that she could be better. But for all she'd slogged at school to perfect her English, her French, and haunted the steps of the city's grand salons, offering to sweep, clean, anything to watch the women there work, learn, make herself skilled enough to be employed by a woman like Amélie Pasha, she was right back where she had started: in the neighbourhood she'd killed herself to leave. Only this time she had dragged her cousins down with her.

She looked at their sleeping forms; lips parted, cheeks flushed with the night. So vulnerable. She hadn't wanted to bring them back here from Montazah after they'd lost their mother, dear Aunt Tabia, five weeks before, but she hadn't known where else to go. *I'm sorry*, she told them silently. She bent to kiss their olive skin. She frowned as her lips touched Babu. He had another fever. She crooned endearments to him, hoping the words might soak into his sleepy thoughts as the call to prayer had done into hers, and that he might manage to understand them, mute as he was. He stirred and rolled over, stretching arms that had grown too lean around his oddly proportioned head. She ran her hand over his tufty hair, the lines of his distorted skull, and willed away the burning in his skin. She felt the familiar pull of grief that he, with his soul full of smiles

97

and sloppy kisses, should suffer so. God had surely been looking in the other direction the day he was born.

'You look sad.'

Nailah started at the high childish notes of Cleo's voice. She watched as Cleo pushed herself to sitting, legs crossed beneath her. Her hair fell in silken folds around her shoulders. Her face was soft and round, her oversized eyes the colour of syrupy coffee. The image of Tabia. As she yawned, her little mouth opened reluctantly, as though fighting her greedy instinct to breathe.

Nailah said, 'You mustn't worry about me, habibi,' then winced. Habibi, my beloved, was what Tabia had used to call them all. Suddenly, she was there; an invisible shadow in the air. From the way Cleo dropped her head, she felt her too.

Nailah searched the room, trying to come up with a distraction, for her as well as Cleo.

Her eyes settled on the fruit bowl. 'Will you help me with breakfast?' They made it each morning for the men in the house. They washed the sheets too. In exchange, the landlord took a couple of pennies off their rent. Cleo always seemed to like popping the pomegranate seeds, stirring them through the yoghurt, gap-teeth pressed to her lip in the effort not to make a mess. Nailah went to the bowl, tossing one of the fruits to her cousin.

Cleo caught it, smiling in a way that barely moved her pretty cheeks, then set to work.

By the time the men returned, Babu was awake, heavy on Nailah's hip, and Cleo had laid out the meal: goat's yoghurt, fruit, nuts and day-old bread. Nailah and the children stared as the men fell upon the spread. Nailah's stomach pinched in hunger. But she didn't move to eat, none of them did. They waited silently to satisfy themselves with whatever the men left.

It was only once the meal was done, the room cleared, and the first of the day's linen scrubbed and hanging in the yard, that Nailah said she had better go to market. She thought she might drop into the baths too; the morning's work had added a new layer of sweat to her grimy skin, she was longing for a proper wash. 'Will you mind Babu?' she asked Cleo. She touched her fingers dubiously to his forehead. 'He's hot, I don't want to make him worse by taking him out. Will you be all right?'

Cleo told her they'd be fine. 'I used to watch him all the time for Umi, remember? I watched him all that night . . .'

'All right,' said Nailah, interrupting. It came out shorter than she'd intended, but she didn't want to talk about that night. She patted Cleo's shoulder to take the sting from her words. 'Thank you.'

Steam filled the cavernous rooms of the public baths, the sound of women's chatter and cackling laughter echoed off the tiled walls, bouncing from shiny surfaces dripping with condensation. Nailah handed her coin to the attendant and murmured her thanks as the lady gave her a brush and soap in exchange. For the second time that day, she slipped from her clothes and slid quickly, self-consciously, into the hot water, hiding her skinny frame. She kept her eyes averted from the brazenly exposed flesh around her, the careless way the black-toothed matrons lounged, flabby arms stretched behind them, revealing thick clumps of damp hair. Clenching her soap in her cracked, work-roughened hand, Nailah set about making herself clean for the first time in a week. She unbound her hair, poured water over her head, and rubbed at her scalp until she was swathed in lather and could smell nothing but citrus-tinged carbolic.

The voices of the other women trickled through to her: conversations about the birth of daughters where sons had been hoped for, miscarriages, marriages. Police visiting homes that morning enquiring about a missing British woman.

Nailah's head jerked up. 'What's that?' she asked. 'Who are they asking about?'

'Ha,' said Sana, a woman not much older than Nailah's twenty years, but married to a fisherman and with two screaming brats already. 'She honours us, ladies, by speaking. God is good this morning, we must thank Him.'

Nailah didn't rise to the taunt; she was used to Sana's sharp tongue by now, and besides, it wasn't the time for a sparring match. She repeated her question, 'Who are the police asking about?'

'A Madame Gray,' Sana said, pronouncing the name in a mocking accent that made her disdain for the moneyed British clear. 'Why?' She snorted. 'Do you know her, Miss Hoity-toity?'

Nailah knew Ma'am Gray, of course she did, but she was hardly likely to tell Sana that. 'What do they think's happened to her?'

'They don't know,' said Sana. 'She disappeared yesterday. The police are trying to find her. The army too. I saw an officer outside mosque this morning. He was talking to some men.'

'What were they saying?'

Sana shrugged. 'Whatever it was, they're fools to be speaking to that officer at all.' She narrowed her black eyes. 'You get between an onion and its peel, all you end up with is a bad smell. You watch, anyone who gets dragged into this around here will find themselves in the shit.' She laughed humourlessly. 'The way the British leave us to rot, then come scuttling over when they need our help. Pathetic. They'll never find her, you watch. Useless, the lot of them.'

'I'm not so sure they are,' said another woman uneasily. 'I saw that soldier too, and he looked as if he knew what he was about, I wouldn't want to mess with him. I don't like it, them all coming here. They must think someone in the quarter was involved.'

'Why would they think that?' asked Nailah.

'Because they always think it's us, stupid,' said Sana. 'Anything goes wrong, what do they do? They blame us natives. Look at what happened to that poor man after your Aunt Tabia copped it.'

Nailah flinched at the thought of the Bedouin peasant who'd been arrested for allowing his horse to escape, then punished with twenty lashes for the horse mowing Tabia down. He'd died in jail afterwards.

Sana laughed again. 'You've forgotten what it's like here, that's your problem, cocooning yourself in that palace of infidels in Aboukir. You need to get used to how things are. You're back in the slums now.' Sana folded her arms over her sagging chest and looked at Nailah challengingly.

Nailah summoned up a tight smile. 'As you've said, God is good.'

'I hope he is,' said another lady, 'and that they find the poor lady. It's said she has five sons.'

'I heard six,' said someone else.

Try two, Nailah corrected them silently.

'They won't find her,' said Sana. 'A white woman, alone, missing. She'll be dead already, mark my words.'

Chapter Eight

Sana's proclamation plagued Nailah as she left the baths, damp hair dripping down her neck. She tried to shake it from her mind as she wove her way through the narrow, baking streets to the market and immersed herself in her shopping. She concentrated as she never had before on rooting amongst the cages of pigeons for a skinny one to barter for, sniffing the herbs, tapping the watermelons for ripeness. But as she looked despondently at the cost of fever medicine, her thoughts returned stubbornly to Ma'am Gray. Ma'am Gray who had been such a frequent visitor at the Pashas'. Ma'am Gray who played so carelessly with fire.

Distracted as she was, it was mid-morning by the time she completed her shopping and set off, lopsided with the weight of her basket, towards home. She paused to gather her breath, pressing the heel of her free hand to her sweaty forehead, then stopped short as she caught sight of the man staring at her across the crowds: oiled hair impatient to escape, eyes the shape of almonds, slight body taut beneath his well-laundered business suit. Sweet Mother. She swallowed hard. His amber gaze met hers. Could it be?

He nodded, as though he'd heard her silent question. He took a step towards her.

Nailah looked around her at the shouting stallholders, the veiled women haggling, arms raised, coins glinting in the sun. One reached into a cage and grabbed a chicken, breaking its neck with a snap.

Nailah stepped back.

He moved forward again. A dance.

With a new urgency she turned on her heel and rounded the corner into the first of the criss-crossed streets that led to the house. Voices carried down through open windows: scolding words, barked orders, laughter. The tones leeched into the hot air, mixing with the tang of cooking and dung. Nailah stole a glance over her shoulder. It was him. It really was. Her heart knocked. It had been so long . . . so, so long. Her sandals thwacked, his smart heels clicked in alternate rhythm.

She reached the alley behind her street and hurried into it, her legs moving under a momentum of their own. And then she stopped. She turned.

'Nailah.'

Her stomach rippled at the sound of her name. His voice, so rich and insistent. She backed towards the wall. The two of them were hidden in the shadows of the tenements, and so close that if Nailah moved, she could touch him. Her eyes moved over his smart clothes, his aquiline nose, the diagonal cut of his jaw; she watched as he threw a look from left to right, squinting at the crowds moving to and fro at either end of the alleyway, assessing, judging.

'No one will see us,' she said breathlessly, 'no one comes here.' It was a mean corridor, all but forgotten by even its nearest neighbours. It was why she'd chosen it. 'It's just rubbish and rats here.'

'You're wrong,' he said.

'No . . .'

His lips curved cheekily. 'I meant about the rubbish and rats. Me?' He placed his hand on his heart. 'I've been called worse. But I can't allow such an insult to you to pass.'

A laugh bubbled in Nailah; it loosened her shoulders for the first time in weeks.

Kafele grinned. And suddenly he was no longer a businessman in fancy tailoring, but a boy from the streets. Her boy. The one who'd grown up in the same crumbling house as her, each of them in rented rooms much like the one Nailah was in now. Kafele had lived with his ailing grandfather back then, supporting him until the day he died, running errands for stallholders, buying from and selling to farmers, earning, always earning. But he'd come to Nailah every night, no matter how long his day, and would lift her from loneliness with his stories, his ambition. They'd sit for hours on the floorboards, plotting their future together: the grand house they'd live in, the places they'd travel, the things they would see. The two of them had been building plans for a better life ever since they'd been old enough to dream.

He took her basket and set it on the floor. 'I've been wanting to do that since you bought that watermelon. It's nearly as big as you.'

'How long have you been watching me?'

'Since you left the baths.'

'Were you waiting for me?'

'Yes.'

Nailah's smile grew.

'Tell me,' he said, 'why were you going so fast? You weren't running away from me, were you?'

She lowered her head, eyeing him through her lashes in just the way the other maids at the Pashas' had used to practise. '*To* you.'

He exhaled noisily. 'Good.'

'Ohmm.'

He chuckled. The warmth of the sound washed through Nailah, and the long weeks since she'd last heard it, hidden beneath the swaying shade of the Pashas' jacaranda trees, almost disappeared. *Almost.* 'I've missed you,' she said.

His smile became sad. 'I called in at the Pashas' yesterday,' he said, 'after I got back from Cairo. I had to talk to Benjamin about suppliers for his hotel there.'

Nailah nodded. She knew how important the Pashas' business was to Kafele. He was building up his trade as a middleman, selling produce from farmers on to ever-bigger hotels and restaurants. Benjamin Pasha had been buying from him for his Alexandria establishments for some time, but Cairo was a new opportunity. One day, Kafele hoped to supply all of the Pashas' hotels, beyond Egypt and into the rest of Africa.

'When I finished with Benjamin,' Kafele said, 'I went into the garden, even though I knew you wouldn't be there.' He laughed ruefully. 'I waited for you.'

'You waited for me?'

'I did.'

'Oh.' Nailah's heart ballooned. She pictured him on the lawn, bursting with energy after an hour in Benjamin Pasha's study, jacket slung over his arm. She imagined the shadow of leaves on his white shoulders, herself coming towards him, smart in uniform instead of the stained, rough robe she wore now, hugging the trees so no one from the house would see her. His joy when he spotted her, as wide and open as it had ever been when they were children playing in the street, back before anyone could have known he'd grow up to be so very successful, she nothing more than a drudge stuck in the slums.

She sighed and looked down at her toes, dusty again already. Fleas hopped around her feet; she moved instinctively, squashing one, then cursed herself for the unnecessary death.

'I'm so sorry,' Kafele said, 'about Tabia. I came back from Cairo as soon as I could . . .'

She pressed her lips together, she didn't want to talk about it.

But Kafele persisted. His voice was soft with regret as he said, 'I shouldn't have stayed away. It's just there was so much to do, and Benjamin gave me contacts for some new customers . . .' He grimaced apologetically. 'Has anyone been helping? Your mother?'

'Not her,' said Nailah. Isa hadn't even come home to pay her respects when Tabia was killed. Her own sister. *I'm in the middle of a tour of the backwaters,* she had written. *We have shows every night. My voice isn't as strong as it used to be and I've been finding it harder to find dancing work lately, when a tour like this comes along I have to take it. We'll need the money more than ever with Cleo and Babu to look after . . . don't be cross with me, my love.* Her letters had been as infrequent as a desert rainstorm in summer ever since. Nailah had learnt to expect nothing more.

'Someone else then?' said Kafele.

'Who else is there?' asked Nailah. 'Tabia's parents are dead, and as for the children's father . . .' She broke off. She wouldn't waste words on him, that coward who had abandoned Tabia in childbed and run back to his village within an hour of seeing the shape of Babu's head.

Kafele said, 'I wish I could take it all from you.'

'I wish she hadn't died.' Nailah's voice cracked. She took a breath, then another, trying to get herself under control. But under Kafele's pained stare, the fight went out of her. The thoughts she normally struggled so hard to mute, rose up. All she could see was Tabia: her aunt, her warm, beautiful aunt. 'You're here, habibi,' Tabia would say whenever Nailah called in on her free time from the Pashas', as though it were the greatest gift. She'd rise from whatever she was doing – cooking, or washing, or massaging Babu's head – and take Nailah in her arms. Even now, Nailah could smell her sweet scent, see the curve of her lips. She could almost hear her throaty laugh. She could almost . . . 'Oh.' She pressed her knuckles into her eyes.

Kafele took a step towards her.

'I'm fine,' Nailah said, 'please. Ignore me. You mustn't worry, please, I don't want you to.'

Kafele held out his fingers. She wanted for him to drop them as he always did, but instead he stroked her face. At the shock of his skin on hers, she closed her eyes, losing herself, for just a few short breaths, in his touch. But much as she'd dreamed of this moment, as she wanted it to go on, a tear slid from her at its coming. For Kafele had sworn that he wouldn't do her the dishonour of coming near her until they were married, once he had made enough money that they wouldn't have to raise their family in these slums. He'd told her a thousand times that he wanted to wait to feel her; she was worth waiting for. And now he had broken his word.

It felt like the ending of a dream.

She reached up and squeezed his hand with her shaking one, removing it from her face. She felt anger replace her sadness. It was the way that life, which just a few short weeks ago had been so blessed, had turned so wrong.

And now this news of Ma'am Gray.

Nailah met Kafele's pained gaze, wondering if he'd heard

anything of her fate, or the questions that were being asked around town.

She told him what the women in the bathhouse had been saying about the police, the officer at the mosque.

He said he knew nothing of it. 'Why are you worried? What do you care about Clara Gray?'

Nailah studied a nick in her big toenail. 'I just don't like to think of her coming to harm.'

'There's something else bothering you, I can tell.'

Nailah kept her eyes cast down, fighting the urge to confide. It was the first time she'd done such a thing with Kafele, and it hurt. But she swallowed her secrets, her fears; tempted as she was, she didn't even tell him about the soldiers who'd come to Tabia's hut, the day after Tabia was killed. She couldn't. Once she started talking, she wouldn't be able to stop.

She shifted uncomfortably, though, remembering the soldiers' visit; they'd come just as she and the children were packing to leave. She'd recognised the tall handsome officer, *the captain*, instantly – he'd often been at the Pashas' dinners, their balls, all the maids had used to spy on him – although he hadn't seemed to know her. He had told her such a strange story about Tabia being a cotton worker he wished to help. Tabia, who had never worked a mill in her life, but made her money from selling eggs. Nailah hadn't had the nerve to confront him on his lie. And when he'd enquired after what had brought the children into her care, she'd fibbed herself, letting him think she was just an acquaintance of Tabia's. She had been too wary, with everything going on, to admit how she was related to Tabia, or where she was taking the children to live. She'd sensed, from the considered look the captain gave her, that he knew she was holding things back. As for the other soldier, the bald-headed Egyptian, he had stared at Nailah, as though he'd read her mind if he could.

'Nailah?' said Kafele, pulling her back into the moment. 'What's wrong?'

She said it was nothing. 'I just want to know who that officer was at the mosque.' If it was the same captain who'd been at Tabia's, then he might have started to guess . . .

Kafele said, 'You can talk to me, Nailah, you know that, don't you? Tell me anything, no matter what.'

Nailah made no reply. Kafele kept his eyes on her, clearly waiting for her to speak. As the silence lengthened, he sighed and said, 'I'll ask around, find out what I can.'

Nailah exhaled. 'Thank you.'

He smiled, the most troubled one Nailah had ever seen on his face. Then his eyes flicked towards the end of the alleyway. 'Son of a dog.' He darted away, flattening himself against the far wall. 'I don't think he saw me.'

'Who?'

'Sweet Mother, Nailah, who d'you think?'

Nailah turned to peer down the passage's grimy light. Her mouth turned to dust at the unmistakable silhouette of her mother and Tabia's brother, Uncle Jahi, in the street beyond.

'He hasn't seen us.' Kafele exhaled. 'He'd be here already if he had. We're safe.'

'Yes,' said Nailah. Even so, as she reached down for her basket to leave, her body was heavy with foreboding.

'I wish you didn't have to go,' said Kafele. 'I want to keep you here with me.'

'I want you to, too,' she said, eyes locked on Jahi's solidity. 'But you can't.' *Not until we're married.* If they ever would be, now. If only Kafele hadn't touched her. She longed to ask him if it meant what she feared, but was afraid that if she said another word, she'd weep. So she left the words unspoken. And with them, all those things that Jahi knew of her and which he, Kafele, could never be allowed to discover.

Moving before Jahi could spot her or Kafele, she left, feet dragging as she made her way to the opposite end of the alleyway from where Jahi stood. She cast one final look back at Kafele, so worried and smart and completely motionless as he stared after her, then carried on, up and around through the crowded parallel street, sidestepping the mounds of donkey dung, fingers tight on her basket. By the time she had circled around to her front door, Jahi was walking towards it himself, one finger held to his closely cropped beard, apparently lost in thought.

'As-salaam,' she said, dipping her head as he approached. Tall and broad, he towered above her in the sunlight: her uncle who held such secrets.

'Ah, Nailah.' He bit his lip as he studied her, revealing his crooked front tooth, the only weakness in his swarthy face. Half the women in the neighbourhood were in love with him, Sana most of all, despite her husband, and two brats. She was on the street corner now, watching him through her veil with hungry eyes. 'You've been to the market I see,' Jahi said, with a nod at Nailah's shopping.

Nailah glanced down at the watermelon, balanced precariously on the top of the other groceries, ready to topple.

'You look troubled.' Jahi's face shadowed with a look Nailah could almost think was concern. 'Are you?'

Nailah made no answer. She didn't need to. Her uncle knew all too well how she felt.

He sighed. 'We'd better go inside. We have a deal to discuss, you and I.'

109

Chapter Nine

Over in Ramleh, Olivia woke late, groggy from a disjointed slumber, and too warm after turning restlessly all night. She squinted at the light filling the room, and put her hand to her temple, wincing as recollection of the previous day's events washed through her with sickening speed. She closed her eyes, trying to block the reality for even a few moments more. But her mind filled with Clara: her pink face, so concerned yesterday, on the Rue Cherif Pasha; the swing of her skirt as she disappeared into the crowds. *I am rather gasping for a drink.* Had she even had one? *Would she still be here if Olivia hadn't insisted she go on ahead?* Olivia drew a sharp breath; the question hurt too much. And as for thoughts of Edward . . . *I don't know how much longer this can go on.* She pulled her sheet over her face, as though the linen could do a thing to block out her fear of his leaving. To think how relieved she'd felt to see him standing there, so sure he'd be able to make things better, since he always did. She'd never expected him to be so guarded. She knew she should be trying to work out what his secrecy meant; yet all she could grasp was that she might be about to lose him too, and that a life absent of him felt even more impossible than one together. She didn't know how she might begin to stand it.

Her face grew damp with sweat. It was so bloody hot. She threw the sheet from her. Paper rustled. Alistair had left a message. It echoed, in somewhat brusquer tones, Edward's request that Olivia under no circumstances leave the house; Alistair would be back for dinner. *Wait for me to eat. Make sure it's something light, I imagine I'll be late*. She scrunched up the embossed paper and threw it at the wastepaper basket, missing. As if she was just going to sit here all day. No, she would go to Clara's, find that letter in the study. She swung herself to standing, then held out her hands to steady herself as her head swam from the sudden movement. Her clock told her it was almost noon, even later than she'd thought.

Intent on escaping the house unseen, she got herself into her riding habit alone. She held her breath as she forced the buttons of her navy skirt into place, then the clasps on her double-breasted jacket. She skulked out to the stables and saddled up Bea. As she mounted, she thanked Edward silently for his lessons, trying to ignore her guilt at using them to go against him now.

As she rode away, Ada ran out of the house, a laundered petticoat in her hand. The fluttering linen might have looked like a flag of surrender had Ada's tiny body not been moving so quickly, her cockney voice yelling, 'Stop,' so loudly. Olivia shouted back that she was going for a long ride, she would be quite some time. Ada's stare was incredulous, but short of tackling Olivia to the ground, what could she do? Olivia dug her heels into Bea's side and cantered away.

There were two Egyptian police at the gate of Clara's mansion, stiff and uniformed, their set-faced presence a horrible reminder, as if Olivia needed it, of what had happened. She nodded at them and carried on into the driveway. In contrast to the arid landscape outside, Clara's front garden was filled with colour. The lawn glistened smugly from its morning watering. Flower beds overflowed with purple and pink agapanthus and the white roses Clara was so proud of cultivating. (*See, I can be clever when I try. Sugar water, that's the key; it's a trick I stole from the Pashas. Although, small sigh, I suppose that makes me a thief, and not really clever at all.*) Orange trees clustered by the stable side of the veranda, lush with tangy fruit. (*'Try one, Livvy, they're positively bursting with sunshine.*') Olivia couldn't look at them.

Instead, her gaze settled on Clara's driver, Hassan, washing the carriage. His dark head was bare, hair shining, the sleeves of his white tunic were rolled up to reveal muscular arms; so exotic it was almost obscene. The footman who had stayed in town yesterday appeared from one of the outhouses. He stalked over to the carriage, threw his tarboosh on the ground, wiped sweat from his forehead, then took up a cloth. He said not a word to Hassan. Olivia wondered if he was angry about the wasted hours he'd spent in the square. His sulky face, observed from the corner of her eye, gave nothing away.

She dismounted clumsily, limbs stiff with self-consciousness in front of Hassan after the scene he'd witnessed between her and Alistair the night before. She set her sights on the stables and pulled on Bea's reins. Bea stuck her hooves into the gravel. Olivia yanked again. Ordinarily Bea was a compliant horse, but today something had unsettled her.

'Do you need help, Ma'am Sheldon?' Hassan called.

'Thank you, I'm fine,' Olivia replied, eyes fixed on Bea. 'Come on, *now*.' She thwacked her with her crop and nearly keeled backwards as Bea started into motion.

She took her time in the stables; she brushed Bea down, mulled her own jacket and fanned inside the of her clammy bodice, then forelock onto for Bea to munch. Even so, Hassan was still damned well in the driveway when she came out again.

He looked at her, squeezing his rag free of soapy water. His slender limbs moved with such quiet dignity Olivia became even more conscious of her own agitated state. She shifted her weight. She should say something to him, stop being so rude. It wasn't his fault he'd overheard her and Alistair after all. 'I'm sorry if my husband and I embarrassed you last night,' she blurted, then gaped as she heard her own, entirely inappropriate, words. Colour rushed into Hassan's cheeks, turning them mahogany. Olivia hurried to talk away his discomfort with garbled expressions of gratitude for his help yesterday. 'You were really rather kind ... Meant a lot ...' She trailed off.

Hassan looked to the floor.

Olivia tried to think of something to fill the silence. Perhaps she should address the surly footman, make Hassan feel less singled out.

She turned to him. 'Thank you too . . . ' She broke off, realising she didn't know his name.

He stood, waiting.

What was his name? She wasn't sure she'd ever known it. Beads of awkwardness prickled in her armpits.

The footman raised an eyebrow. Finally, he said, 'It's El Masri, Ma'am Sheldon.'

'Yes, of course.' She squinted apologetically in the sunlight. 'Well, I'd best get on.'

'Has there been any word of Ma'am Gray?' El Masri asked as she set off. 'We're not being told anything.'

'Neither am I,' said Olivia.

'We were all questioned first thing,' El Masri said.

'I'm sorry I could not help,' said Hassan quietly. 'I feel I have let Ma'am Gray down.' He swilled his cloth in the bucket. 'I wanted to ask, Ma'am Sheldon, did you manage to speak to the soldier you were looking for?'

'No.' Olivia frowned at the mention of Fadil, remembering Edward's surprise when she'd told him he'd been in the street. She wondered if he'd found out yet what Fadil had been doing there. 'I hope someone will speak to him. As I've said, no one's talking much to me.'

El Masri raised an eyebrow in a way that suggested he wasn't surprised. It was an insolent gesture, his observation all the more vexing for being right on the mark, and Olivia was tempted to give him a jolly good dressing-down. She would have, but her silent 'jolly good' distracted her, reminding her of Clara. Was her tendency for extreme Britishness in times of stress catching? Or hereditary? Had their mother done it? Or maybe it came from their father's side, although Olivia couldn't imagine her witch of a grandmother saying jolly anything . . .

Oh *God*. Her chin dropped as remembrance struck her.

There was a rapping at the upstairs window. She turned towards it, mouth agape. Jeremy opened the glass and asked her what she was hanging around outside for.

'Never mind that,' she said, 'when's my grandmother's ship due?' With everything else going on, she had all but forgotten Mildred was coming.

Jeremy blanched, grey eyes widening; it had clearly slipped his mind too. He shut the window and disappeared. Olivia arrived at the front door just as he opened it.

'She'sh docking the day after tomorrow,' he said. He was swaying on his feet, his waistcoat buttons were mismatched in their holes, and he had a fleck of what looked like butter on his cheek. Ralph stood moon-eyed by his side. From somewhere deep in the house, Angus was screaming. 'I told Clara I didn't want her.' He frowned. 'Can't she shtay with you?'

Olivia stared. She'd never seen Jeremy in such a state. She was used to watching him stride into functions in pristine tailoring, head high, eyes sharp; a magnet for attention. (Much more so than Alistair, whose best attempts at charisma always fell short of convincing. Olivia was certain Jeremy's popularity irritated him, the veritable salt in the wound after Clara chose Jeremy in̶s̶t̶e̶a̶d̶ ̶o̶f̶ ̶h̶i̶m̶. She'd noticed he was e̶s̶p̶e̶c̶i̶a̶l̶l̶y̶ ̶v̶i̶o̶l̶e̶n̶t̶ after time in Jeremy and C̶l̶a̶r̶a̶'s̶ ̶c̶o̶m̶p̶a̶n̶y̶.) Still, no one would want to know Jeremy now – he had unravelled overnight. The extremity of it shocked Olivia, especially given the discord Clara spoke of between them. But then she *had* said things were different once . . .

'Olivia?'

'What?'

'Mildred. Can't you take her?'

'Absolutely not.' Olivia had no intention of even speaking to her. 'Jeremy, have you been up all night?'

Jeremy sighed. 'Hard to shay.' He beckoned Olivia in. 'Drink? Brandy? Gin and it?'

She ignored the offer, tempted as she was to accept. And much as she yearned to seize the moment and press Jeremy on why he'd taken the family to Constantinople, what it was that had had him so afraid for Clara, she didn't. She'd clearly get no sense out of him, and besides, Ralph was there; she didn't want to upset him further by bringing it all up. 'Who's with Angus?' she asked instead.

'The nanny,' said Jeremy. 'Whashecalled? Whashecalled? Whashecalled?' He clicked his fingers in time with the words.

'Sofia,' said Ralph.

Jeremy ruffled Ralph's hair. 'That'sh my boy,' he said. 'I tried to quieten Gus earlier, but he gives me sh . . . sh . . . short shrift. Looks at me like he wants to punch me in the fasche.'

'All right,' said Olivia, taking Ralph's chubby fingers in hers. 'Let's go to the nursery.'

'That hushband of yoursh said anything more about Clara?' Jeremy asked as they left.

'Not a thing,' said Olivia.

Jeremy let go of an expletive. Olivia pulled Ralph's hand, picking up her pace.

Sofia was changing Angus's napkin when they arrived at the nursery. Her glasses were balanced on her nose, her bosom strained against her apron as she gripped thrashing legs with one hand and fastened the safety pin with the other. She had another of her cigarettes in her mouth, the glowing end of which teetered above Angus's raging form. 'I'm watching the ash,' she said to Olivia through the side of her mouth.

Olivia took the cigarette and stubbed it out.

Sofia continued dressing Angus, apparently oblivious (or possibly just immune) to the cacophony of his wails. 'There we go,' she said, finishing. She picked him up and held him out to Olivia. 'Hold him a while, *agapi mou*. You could both do with a cuddle. And I could do with a rest.'

'Oh no.' Olivia took a step back. 'I don't think so.' She wasn't used to holding babies. No one she knew back in England had had them, and Gus wasn't exactly one for being passed around.

'Don't be silly,' said Sofia, bundling Angus into Olivia's arms.

She nearly dropped him. His screams became even more incensed. 'Hush,' she said, since that was what women were supposed to say

115

to crying babies. He stared up at her, brown eyes helpless with fury. She rocked up and down, every muscle in her body tense. 'Do please hush.'

He didn't.

She asked Sofia what she was doing wrong.

'Worrying.' Sofia collapsed into a chair. 'Although we're all doing that.' She pinched her hooked nose and shook her head. 'You need to relax, Mrs Livvy,' she said at length. 'Babies are like animals, they sense our fear.'

'I'm not sure what I can do about that,' said Olivia. Even so, she tried to force herself loose. It seemed a small enough thing that she could give Clara, this effort to comfort her son. 'Shhh, Gus.' Awkwardly, she kissed his head. He smelt sweet, his dark curls were soft. 'Hush now,' she said, more quietly.

It took a minute more, but slowly Angus's crying subsided. He rested his head on her chest and closed his eyes. A sigh shuddered through his hot little body.

'There,' said Olivia.

'There,' echoed Sofia. She smiled softly. 'I think he must like your arm. You and Mrs Clara wear the same scent. It was your mama's, you know.'

Olivia nodded slowly. She'd bought it on an impulse at Fortnum's just before she left London, thinking to make herself feel better. It was Clara who'd told her it was their mother's favourite.

'It was a bad business,' said Sofia, 'the way your mama and papa went, what that woman did to you after . . . ' She took off her glasses and tipped her head back. 'I can't stop thinking of it all, how we hoped your mama and papa would come back. The waiting.'

'I remember it,' said Olivia. 'The hope, at least.' It had taken her years to accept that there was no point. That her parents, who'd ridden out from Cairo on an archaeological dig, never to return – killed, so it was supposed, in a sandstorm – weren't going to miraculously reappear and whisk her away from her cold stone school.

Sofia sighed. Then, gathering herself, she replaced her glasses and sat up straight. She nodded at Ralph, who was sitting motionless and

116

staring next to the toy box. 'This will be different though. I've told Ralphy here that his mama will be back before he knows it, maybe even as soon as tonight. Isn't that right, Ralphy?'

He nodded silently.

Sofia asked Olivia if she'd been to the bookshelves yet.

'No,' said Olivia, eyes on Ralph's sad face. 'I was about to go.'

'Will you stay with us for a while?' asked Ralph. He reached into the toy box for the Holmes book Clara had mentioned him liking. 'We could read, or if you think that might be dull, we could do something else?' He widened his eyes imploringly. 'Anything you want to do, we can do it.'

'All right.' Olivia smiled down at him. 'Book first.'

Sherlock Holmes became snap, which became Holmes again, which became lunch in the garden, which became just stay until Gus goes to bed since he's so happy in your arms. It was dusk by the time Olivia finally extracted herself from her nephews with promises to return the next day. She was trying to believe Sofia's continued assurances that Clara might be back by then, but there had been no word from anyone all day; it was getting harder and harder to hold faith. As for thoughts of where Clara might be, what she might be going through . . . it hurt too much to wonder.

Before going to the study, Olivia went in search of Jeremy. Since the last she'd seen of him was several hours ago, wandering aimlessly around the rose beds with a bottle in his hand, she doubted he'd be in a fit state to interrupt her, but even so, she wanted to check. He was stretched out on the veranda floor, no more than a foot away from a comfortable-looking chair, mouth open, dribble snaking down his chin. Olivia sighed at the thought that he'd already given up.

She was exhausted from her strained day in the nursery, her ever-rising fear, and nervous as to what she might be about to find amongst the bookshelves. Her hand trembled as she eased the study door open and approached the shelves of expensively bound volumes. She scanned the second to top shelf and pulled out the books at either end. She flicked through each one impatiently, then turned to the next.

Nothing.

Curiouser and curiouser.

Slowly now, taking her time, she went through the volumes again. She turned each one upside down and shook it rigorously. Still, nothing. She went through them once more. Nothing. She was still pondering the meaning of it when she heard footsteps coming down the corridor. The door handle turned. Thinking fast, Olivia dropped into Jeremy's chair and began thumbing through one of the books she had scattered over the desk. Chest tight, she raised her eyes as the door jostled open and Jeremy fell through it.

'Whatsch are yoush doing in here?' His mouth stuck as he spoke.

'I want something to read to keep my mind off things,' said Olivia, hoping Jeremy was too far gone to hear the breathlessness in her voice. Jeremy glanced down at the book in her hand and frowned in confusion. It was a copy of Mrs Beeton's tome on household management. She pushed it to one side. 'I'd best get on,' she said, rising.

Jeremy caught her arm as she walked past. His touch was surprisingly strong. 'I like you, Livvy, I always have. I told Alistair, you know, that he should never have brought you here.' He shook his head, trying to push the haze of inebriation away. 'Don't meddle. For your own shake, shtay the hell out of it.'

Chapter Ten

Fadil was in the front garden when Olivia returned home. He was dressed in the same oversized khaki trousers that he always wore, a cracked leather belt holding them up; his withered arms were sinewy with muscle beneath his shirt sleeves, and his wrinkled face was coated with a sheen of sweat to match Olivia's own, as though he too had just been galloping. He took Bea's reins whilst Olivia dismounted. Olivia looked around for Edward, assuming he must be home too. But the leafy grounds were still, quiet; only the sad singing of the Bedouin mother preparing supper at the gate could be heard. Olivia and Fadil were alone in the dusk.

Olivia ran her handkerchief across her forehead, staining the white linen ruddy with dust. 'Have you been following me, Fadil?'

He tilted his bald head to the side.

Olivia asked, 'Does that mean yes or no?'

Another head tilt.

She narrowed her eyes. 'I saw you there yesterday,' she said, 'on the Rue Cherif Pasha, just before Clara went.'

'Sayed Bertram has told me, Ma'am Sheldon.'

'Did you see Clara being taken?'

'No.'

'Did you see anything?'

'No.'

'Nothing at all that might be useful?'

'No, Ma'am Sheldon. I am sorry.'

Olivia gave him another long look. He met it without waver, but then he was hardly one to be cowed by the force of a stare. He'd been a soldier longer than Olivia had been alive, first with the Egyptians, then the British ever since the '82 invasion. Edward had told Olivia that Fadil could have stayed on with the Egyptian Army if he'd wanted to, it had been kept running by the Protectorate, just with British officers in charge. But, *He never wants to serve with Egyptians again. A band of nationalist soldiers took against him in the early eighties, when he refused to help them in an uprising. The men locked his wife and children in a hut and set fire to it. I tell you, Olly, there's evil on every side . . .*

Fadil had been Edward's man for years, first during the war to extend the Sudanese border, then in Cairo, now here. Edward said he was a great soldier, indispensable in a crisis. There was one story in particular that had stuck in Olivia's mind, about Fadil guiding Edward's company past a hostile troop of Sudanese, just feet beneath them in the dunes. It had turned her rigid with fear to hear it. She'd wanted to beg Edward never to go into the desert again (she hadn't, they'd been at dinner, Alistair with them; all she could was, 'Oh for goodness' sake'). She knew Edward relied on Fadil, she supposed she was touched by him giving his right-hand man over to her guard, but the covertness of how he'd gone about it unsettled her, as did Edward's believing such a babysitter necessary. Did he really think she was next?

She took a deep breath, inhaling the emptiness of the garden, her terror for Clara, the unknowns crowding her mind, so noisy they made her want to scream. When she swallowed, her throat felt sore and tight. If she hadn't been so sure she never cried, she might have been afraid of bursting into tears. She wanted to go somewhere, but she didn't know where. In the absence of a place to move to, she stayed still and it was lunacy, madness, that she was where she was, standing in the shadow of a house she despised, in Egypt, *Egypt*, the home of a man to whom she'd pledged her life out of cowardice, the place he did the things he did night after night. And Clara vanished, Jeremy making his slurred threats, Mildred coming the day after tomorrow, and Edward, Edward, not hers, never hers . . .

'I'm not all right,' she said, even though Fadil hadn't asked if she was. 'I have to go inside, you see,' she said, giving him another explanation he hadn't asked for. 'There's nowhere else. I can't stand it.'

Fadil's eyes crinkled in an expression that might have been compassion.

'Am I being overfamiliar? I am, aren't I? I'll be telling you about the nuns next.'

'The nuns?'

'At the convent.'

Fadil nodded as though she was making perfect sense.

She laughed, not nicely, a jarring, strangely pitched, gasping sound. In a matter of moments, without realising it was happening, without *allowing* it, Olivia was crying. Sobbing. She stared at Fadil, horrified, snorting and wailing, the tears pouring from her. It had been years since she'd last cried; she barely understood what was happening to her: the gasps in her throat, the release in her eyes. She shook her head helplessly, trying to get herself under control, but she couldn't, and the frustrated attempt just made her cry even harder.

'Come,' said Fadil. 'I'll take the horses. Why don't you go and sit in the garden, watch the sea. You like it, I think, our beautiful Mediterranean.'

She sniffed and wiped her nose with her gloved hand, horsehair sticking to her damp skin. 'I'm not going into the garden,' she said, and as a single calming breath shuddered through her, she knew where she needed to be.

She'd known all along, of course.

Edward stood in the parade ground's furthermost paddock, his five best lieutenants before him. He clenched his jaw as, one by one, they ran through their fruitless day's search for Clara: their trawl of taverns and boarding houses, the miles of farmland stretching up the coast. He nodded tightly, feeling his impatience grow with every passing minute. As the last man tailed off, silence descended. The lieutenants eyed one another. Edward bit down the urge to tell them what a bloody useless lot they all were. He looked to the rapidly darkening sky, calming himself. They'd slogged all day, his men, they were trying their best. Edward could hardly blame them for coming up with nothing; his own search of the desert border hadn't been any more successful.

He'd spent hours riding between settlements, interviewing the local fellahin. His scorched skin was tight from the sun. But no one had seen anything. The dunes were so damned vast, that was the problem, and the coastline and city so full of hiding places. They had no idea if they were even searching in the right places. Were they looking for a captive – in which case they should focus on spots with access to shelter and fresh water – or a body? They needed a lead. Edward's only hope was that one would come from the Turkish Quarter. He'd tracked down an informer of his, a merchant by the name of Garai Aziz, at dawn. Garai had proven himself adept at sniffing out all sorts of things in the past: potential agitators, murmurs of ill-feeling. Edward had left him in no doubt that this was his most important job yet, and that the reward for his help would reflect that. *If* he could help.

Edward took a swig from his water flask, swilling the water around his gritty, sand-lined mouth. If they could just work out how the hell Clara had been taken so fast, without a murmur. Fadil had told Edward it had been just past noon when he'd spotted Olly, alone and panicked in the street, and realised what had happened. He had followed her, thinking that the kidnappers might target her next and lead him to Clara. It was a bold move – one which Edward would never have dared to play himself – and, it transpired, a dud one. No one had gone for Olly. So after Fadil had seen her safely into the Grays' carriage, he had carried on combing the hidden alleyways of central Alex, well into the night. Another of Edward's men had been at it all day. But they'd found nothing. Clara had vanished.

No. Not vanished. People didn't just disappear; she was *somewhere*, they just had to find where. They *had* to. Edward owed her as much. He needed to get her back for Olly too. The way she'd looked last night, hugging herself in her nightgown. Bereft. Alone.

God, he hoped she'd been all right today.

He sucked in his breath and returned his attention to his men, barking instructions on where to continue their hunt in the morning. As he dismissed them and they led their horses away, he snapped, 'Straighten up, soldier,' at no one in particular, out of pure frustration. All five of them lengthened their spines. In any other circumstances, it might have made Edward laugh.

He pelted the sand with his boot. He stared across the paddock, towards the corrugated roofs of the stables and offices in the distance, and saw Tom crossing the ground towards him, head down, hands clasped behind his back. Edward narrowed his eyes. Alistair sodding Sheldon and Commissioner Wilkins were behind Tom, leading their horses. What were they doing here?

They met him at the paddock gate. Tom told Edward that a ransom note had been left at the Sheldon-Gray offices, marked for the attention of Jeremy, demanding a colossal amount of money for Clara's release. 'At least we know that she's alive,' Tom said, with no little relief.

'Yes,' said Alistair, 'so you have to find her. There's no question of Gray paying the ransom.'

'Absolutely not,' said Wilkins. 'We can't be seen to give in.'

'Gray wouldn't want to.' Alistair brushed dust from his tailored arm. 'He's not a coward.'

They spoke so smoothly; it was like they'd had the words prepared. Edward caught Tom's eye, he shook his head. He'd clearly heard it all already.

Edward returned his attention to Alistair. 'Have you even asked Gray what he wants?'

'I haven't.'

'You might want to, Clara being his wife and all that. He could well surprise you.' If it was Olly gone, Edward would do anything to get her back, he didn't care how weak that made him.

'He's in no fit state to discuss anything,' said Alistair. 'I saw him first thing, drunk as a bloody skunk.' He smiled, as though to say, *What can you do?*

Edward's lip curled in distaste. Alistair never missed an opportunity to score points on Jeremy. Edward had been observing it ever since he'd been transferred to Alex from Cairo three years ago and given into his da's entreaties to accept Alistair's invitation to board (*I know his reputation, son, but he's written to me here, says you can be two bachelors together. He's an important supplier, it will be awkward if you refuse . . .*). All the snide comments about expendable employees Jeremy insisted on keeping on (*You're a soft touch, they walk all over you*), export deals he might have got a better price on, the oh so concerned questions about Clara's upsetting aloofness . . . how very unlike Jeremy the new baby, Angus, was (*Is he the postman's boy, old pal?*). Alistair was jealous, it was obvious. But even knowing that, it seemed incomprehensibly sadistic of him to take enjoyment out of Jeremy's worry now.

'I gave him a talking to, of course,' said Alistair. 'Told him to pull himself together, be British.'

'I'm sure he appreciated that,' said Edward. He ran his hand through his hair. Sand stuck to his fingers. 'Where's this note? I'd like to see it.'

'It's in my office,' said Wilkins. He put his thumbs in his pockets and puffed his stomach out. 'I have the care of it.'

Edward stared. 'Do you? And you didn't think to bring it now?'

'Apparently not,' said Tom wearily.

'I didn't see the point,' said Wilkins. 'We've told you what's in it.'

Edward's brow creased at this, yet another note he and Tom hadn't seen. He looked from Alistair's set face to Wilkins' self-satisfied one. He felt that tingling in the nape of his neck he got when danger was near. 'Is there something you're not telling us?' he asked.

'Don't be ridiculous,' said Alistair, too smoothly.

It was all Edward could do not to seize him by his pristinely pressed collar and shake the truth from him. He wanted to hurt him, get under that sickly pale skin of his somehow. 'I stopped by on the Bedouin at your gate this morning,' he said. 'They don't think too highly of you.'

'Don't they?' said Alistair. 'I wouldn't know. I've never talked to them myself, I don't speak native.'

'Well I do,' said Edward. 'The woman thinks you're a bad man.' She'd muttered it under her breath as she'd hugged her boys. 'She wouldn't tell me why.'

'She's probably not all there,' said Wilkins with a snort.

'Oh, I think she is.' Her dislike for Alistair had disturbed Edward. He'd wanted to press her further on what had caused it, but had held off. She had a sadness about her; he'd felt sorry for her, alone as she was with her sons. 'Have you done something to upset them?' he asked Alistair now.

Alistair's blue eyes hardened. 'Such as what?'

Edward didn't answer. He left the notion that there were any number of things Alistair might be capable of unspoken.

Alistair ground his teeth.

Wilkins' heavy breathing went in, out.

The silence lengthened.

'It's late.' Tom's voice sliced through the tension in the air. 'I want to get home, Immy's very worried, and there's a lot to do tomorrow.'

Wilkins said indeed there was. He patted his stomach and nodded, but gave no indication of his plans for the day, or, indeed, of leaving.

Alistair held out his hand to him. 'I'll be by in the morning,' he said.

Wilkins looked surprised, clearly taken aback at being dismissed. 'Of course,' he said, 'of course.' He turned to his horse and made to mount. He struggled to get his foot into the stirrup without the aid of a mounting block. In the end, Tom gave him a leg-up. They all watched as Wilkins dragged his clumsy bulk into the saddle and adjusted his buttocks. 'Till tomorrow then,' he said to Alistair.

'You know,' said Edward, 'I think I might well call by too.' He gave Wilkins a measured smile. 'I really do want to see that note.'

Olivia had ridden past the security posts of the parade ground many times before, peering in for a glimpse of Edward training his men, ears strained to catch the bass of his northern voice. She'd never been in though and she looked around, swollen eyes curious, as Fadil led her through the rows of huts and stables. Late as it was, there was still a lot going on: stable hands lugging wheelbarrows of feed and hay, soldiers drilling in the sand paddocks, a few more idling outside a hut marked 'Mess'. Off duty. Olivia was so busy taking it all in that she didn't notice Wilkins' fuming face approaching until he had ridden past.

She turned, wanting to make sure it was really him. His jacket-straining back was unmistakable, his lolling shoulders full of such utter pomposity they could hardly have belonged to anyone else. She called out to him, but he either didn't hear her or affected not to, and carried on towards the gate. She was about to go after him when Fadil signalled at the perimeter of the furthermost paddock. Edward was there with his colonel, Tom Carter. Oddly, Alistair was with them, a Savile-Row-suited fish out of water in this world of uniformed men. He looked so squat and brutish next to Edward and Tom; so sickly pale beside their sun-darkened complexions. His expression was motionless as he talked. He was the only one of the three of them not folding his arms.

Olivia dismounted, handing her reins to Fadil, and made off towards them.

'I don't know why you're being so difficult, Bertram,' Alistair was saying as she approached. She hung back, heart pattering, to hear what came next. 'All I'm saying is that it's best to keep it as quiet as we can for now. Keep the force on it small, hush-hush. There's no sense causing a scare, or alerting the bastards doing this to our movements. And neither Gray nor I want this in the papers. Wilkins agrees . . . '

'Wilkins is a fucking arsehole,' said Edward.

'An irrefutable fact,' said Tom. He ran his finger along the edge of his greying moustache, eyebrows turned in on a frown. Fine-featured his aristocratic face might be, but there was a toughness in him as he said, 'I don't know if he can be trusted . . . '

'Of course he can,' said Alistair. 'He's the British commissioner, for God's sake. What are you insinuating?'

Tom was about to answer, then he spotted Olivia. His smile was tired, but as kind as ever as he said, 'Hello, my dear.'

Edward and Alistair's heads swivelled. Edward's brown eyes widened in surprise, then warmed instantly with affection, albeit a baffled kind, as he met Olivia's gaze.

Unlike Alistair's pale stare, which became – if such a thing was possible – a degree cooler than normal as he snapped, 'What are you doing here?'

'What are *you* doing here?' asked Olivia, taking the age-old best form of defence. She looked around her, playing for time. 'Has Jeremy come too?' There was no sign of him.

'Let me ask again,' said Alistair, voice straining with control. 'Why have you come?'

Olivia frowned, looking for an explanation, a fictionalised excuse eluding her.

'Sayed Bertram sent for her,' said Fadil, fibbing seamlessly (wasn't he good at it?) as he approached with the horses. 'To answer some questions.'

'You should have got my permission first, Bertram,' said Alistair.

'Should I?' Edward's jaw ticked. 'And there was me thinking I only needed hers.'

Alistair's eyes narrowed. For an awful moment, Olivia thought he might have started to suspect what was felt. But then he sighed impatiently and told them to hurry up and get on with it, he wanted to fetch water for his horse anyway, would Tom take him? He strode off behind Tom without a backward look, apparently too arrogant after all to imagine that Olivia might look to another, or that any man could covet what was his.

Edward spoke briefly to Fadil in Arabic. Olivia watched him talk, the absent way he ruffled his thick hair, and felt, in spite of her fears, relief at being near him again. Safe.

I can't let you leave, she thought, *I can't.*

He took Bea's reins from Fadil, sent him off, and crossed to Olivia's side. His expression softened as he looked down at her. 'You've been crying,' he said. 'What happened at the Grays'?'

'Fadil told you I went?' She gave him a despairing look. 'For goodness' sake, Edward, you don't need to spy on me.'

'Olly, I'm trying to look after you. I'm frightened for you. I've never been so scared in my life.' He sighed. 'You have to stop running around as though you're living in bloody Hampshire. It's too dangerous.' His lips twitched. 'For goodness' sake.'

Olivia's own mouth moved reflexively. She could see her sad smile in the hazel flecks of his eyes. She could smell his curious mix of soap, cigarettes ... something else. Moving instinctively, she took a step towards him.

'Stay at home from now on,' said Edward softly, 'please.'

'I can't accept doing nothing, knowing nothing. I shan't.'

'You shan't?'

'No.'

'So there?' Another small smile, quickly dropped, dragged down by the gravity of it all. 'Have you considered that whoever took Clara might decide they want you too?'

'But why would they?'

Edward hesitated, then told her about the ransom letter. She listened, horrified, as he related Alistair's determination not to pay. 'You're Clara's sister,' Edward said, 'married to her husband's business partner, there's every chance whoever has her will come after you next.' He broke off, frowning over Olivia's shoulder. Alistair was coming back towards them, he was just a hundred or so yards away. 'Stay where the staff can see you from now on,' he said. 'Don't be alone if you can help it. I can't be everywhere all the time.'

'You said last night you were going to go away.'

'I didn't mean without you.'

'But I can't leave, you know that.'

His rigid jaw suggested he didn't know any such thing. Something had changed in him since he'd returned; he'd lost patience with the impossibility of it all, and it scared Olivia, because it *was* impossible. She was married to Alistair, she knew too well there was no changing that; the only variable was whether Edward stayed or left. She glanced again at Alistair, almost upon them now, and turned back to Edward.

'Promise me you won't disappear like you did last month,' she said. 'I don't want to not know when it's the last time I'm seeing you. I've had too much of that.' Her eyes welled for the second time that night. She rubbed them impatiently with the heel of her hand. 'I couldn't stand it. Not with you.'

'And you won't have to.'

She wanted to ask what that meant; whether it was that he'd say goodbye or wouldn't go after all. She hoped desperately that he would not go. She knew how unhappy being here made him, she'd have to be blind not to see it. It would be a selfish kind of relief to have him promise to stay, but a comfort nonetheless.

As it was, she didn't have the chance to find out, nor to tell Edward, as she'd meant to, about Clara's missing letter. Alistair was upon them. All she had time to do was hurriedly ask Edward if he'd be at dinner. When he replied no, he needed to go to Tom and Imogen's, talk to Tom some more, she said, 'Meet me later then, in the garden?'

Before Edward could answer, Alistair barked at them both to get a move on; his horse stomped on the spot, hoof turning the ground. With a sigh, Olivia turned to Bea, pulling herself into the saddle. And much as she yearned to seek Edward's eye for his silent response, she dared not look at him. Not with Alistair there.

She simply had to hope he'd come.

Alistair took his time that night, it was as though he could sense Olivia's desperation to be away. As she lay in bed, she could think of little else but when Edward would be back from Tom's, or if he was home already, out waiting in the garden. Her legs twitched with her need to find out. But Alistair sat by the dressing table, silhouetted by candlelight, talking, talking; his finger moved back and forth through the flame of a candle, stroking it. He'd had several brandies at dinner; he spoke mainly of Clara. 'She was very beautiful,' he said, 'still is, of course. Back then though, that season Jeremy and I met her, every man in London was mad for her. Jeremy most of all,

I think. I used to see the way he looked at her, how he held her when they danced. I danced with her too, naturally. But,' he flicked the flame, 'she was too wilful, you see. Stubborn. Not the right woman. Not for me. I let Jeremy have her in the end. It was my choice, of that I assure you . . .'

Olivia stopped listening.

At length, Alistair fell silent. He cocked his head to one side, and smiled slowly at her across the room. Rising, he came to stand by her side. 'You do look like her,' he tipped the candle, 'in certain lights. If you put on some weight, coloured your hair yellow . . .'

'Stop it, Alistair. Please.'

He raised an eyebrow, entertained by the request. But he didn't stop.

In the end, she ceased fighting to make him, and hated herself for it.

It was approaching midnight by the time he finally fell asleep. Moving carefully, gritting her teeth against the fresh pain, Olivia went to the bathroom to wash him from her. She averted her eyes as she rubbed lavender on her burns. She had no wish to see Alistair's handiwork pockmarking her body. Gingerly, she pulled a loose cotton gown over her head.

She was half afraid, as she crept outside, that Edward wouldn't have been able to come. Or that, late as it was, he would have given up on her. But he was there at the bottom of the lawn, standing on the rocks. He cast a lean shadow in the darkness as he stared out across the sea, towards the bobbing lanterns of night fishermen. He had his hands in his pockets; his shirt rippled in the cool wind blowing in from the desert. Olivia thought, *He could be anywhere else, any place at all. But he's here for me. He's waiting for me.*

Her mind moved to Alistair upstairs, so peacefully asleep; the things he did . . . She stared across at Edward, *Edward*, who gave her more than she'd ever imagined possible, yet who she might be about to lose – and who she'd convinced herself she could never be with in the way she wanted because of fear, and vows, forced vows, to a rotten man.

130

Suddenly, it made no sense. *None.*

She set off towards him. The grass crunched beneath her bare feet.

He turned as she approached, and took her hand, helping her step up. He made to release her, but she held on to him. He looked questioningly down at her. She met his gaze: her eyes in his eyes. The sea lapped the rocks. He took a step towards her, raised his hand, the one not holding hers, and tentatively, as though she could do such a thing as protest, reached out and cupped her face.

She closed her eyes, let her cheek sink against his palm. *Finally.* He released her hand, and ran his arm around her waist. For a second, she felt pure warmth spread through her.

But then he pulled her close. She wanted it not to hurt – she held her breath with the effort of pushing the pain away; but her burns were raw, her bruises too fresh beneath the thin fabric of her nightdress. And he didn't know, she hadn't told him . . .

She bit her lip. She would not let Alistair ruin this. She would not. She moved towards Edward. He exhaled, clasped her tighter. It was then that she felt her skin fracture beneath his hand, weep. And it was too much. Against every other instinct, she pulled away.

'Olly?'

'I'm sorry.'

His face creased with concern. 'Olly, what's wrong?'

'I must go,' she said taking a step back.

'Wait.'

'I can't.' She closed her hand over the waist of her gown. It was damp, already staining. Edward stared, eyes full of confusion, worry; she knew he'd be thinking he'd done something wrong, pushed her. 'It's not you,' she said, barely managing to keep the pain from her voice. 'I swear it. I just . . . I'm not feeling well suddenly.' How weak that sounded. She wished she had the words in her to tell him the truth. 'I'll see you in the morning,' she said, then turned.

She heard him call after her, but she didn't respond. Her thoughts were fixed on getting to the bathroom, pressing a cold cloth to her skin and leaving it there for as long as it took her skin to numb. As for everything she still needed to say to Edward, about him leaving, Clara, she left the words unspoken in the chaos of her mind, promising herself she'd give them voice on the morrow.

THE THIRD DAY

Chapter Eleven

By the time the bite had entered the early morning sun, Nailah had been walking for close to an hour, across the city to the beautiful tree-lined avenues of the Quartier Grec. The houses of some of Alexandria's oldest families lay there, nestled in gardens behind cast-iron gates. One of them belonged to the doctor the captain had told Nailah about, but she was struggling to find which it was. She came to a halt on the wide pavement, the sea of pedestrians jostling past her. She pulled out the scribbled address the captain had given her all those weeks ago. She said, 'Excuse me,' to a smartly dressed lady. The lady kept her eyes fixed ahead and strode on. Nailah swallowed on her dry mouth, shifting Babu's weight in the sling. Her skin was moist with sweat.

A pair of nattering old ladies in black satin approached. Nailah placed herself in front of them, addressing them in English. 'I'm trying to find Socrates' office.' She gestured at Babu, head lolling against her, breaths like shallow sighs. His body was as warm as the ceramic hot water bottles Ma'am Amélie used in winter. 'My cousin needs him.'

The women's eyes moved in unison to Babu. One spat superstitiously over her shoulder. 'What's wrong with his head?'

'For shame, Athina,' said the other. She lay her gnarled hand on Babu's forehead. 'Keep going,' she said, 'second left, then third right. I should warn you, Socrates isn't cheap.'

'I have the fee,' said Nailah. Jahi had given her the pouch of coins yesterday, just before he left to return to his job up the coast.

Her stomach turned at the memory of everything he'd said before handing the money over. By force of will, she banished him from her mind. 'Soon be there, little one,' she whispered to Babu as she set off. She stroked his burning head. 'The captain's doctor will make you better.'

It was a few minutes more before she reached Socrates' establishment. She stared at the large villa, its lush lawns, and then down at her own faded dress, the damp circles beneath her arms, the frayed fabric of Babu's sling. She chewed her lip. Babu coughed like a cat on a hairball, then wailed pitifully. Nailah could almost hear Tabia in her ear. *Be strong, habibi. For him, please.* With a deep breath she pushed the gate open. Before she could change her mind, she put one trembling foot in front of the other, up the gravel path, and followed the signs around the house to the surgery.

Her courage nearly left her when she peeked into the waiting room. Even this early, it was full, packed with the kind of finery that had used to fill the Pashas' salon: feathered bonnets, silken skirts rippling beneath tiny waists; a flower bed of couture. Children sat in cushioned chairs, kicking polished shoes, hair thick and shiny, cheeks rounded and clean. All eyes turned to Nailah. She curled her toes, trying to hide the dirt coating them. But before she could scuttle off like the street rat she felt, the woman at the desk in the far corner stood.

'Is this Babu Rayoud we have here?' she asked briskly, crossing the room. 'You must be his minder, Nailah?' She didn't wait for Nailah to reply. 'Captain Bertram told us to expect you,' she looked Nailah up and down, 'although he didn't mention how you came to be acquainted.'

Nailah coloured. 'I used to work for friends of his,' she said, using her job at the Pashas' as an excuse, even though she was as sure as sun meant day that whatever the reason for the captain's interest in Babu, it had nothing to do with her prior employment. She doubted he even knew she'd worked at the Pashas'; she and the other maids had used to stay well hidden when they watched him: smoking, talking, so relaxed. Although that was before Ma'am

Gray's sister had arrived. He'd changed after that. Nailah remembered the first night she'd ever seen them together, at a party in early spring, long before that big May ball; she'd found herself studying Ma'am Sheldon: skin as smooth as yoghurt, wavy brown hair, and cheekbones that looked like they could slice meat. Her husband had stared at her, half like he was afraid she would break, and half as though he wanted to break her himself. Ma'am Sheldon had ignored him, stuck to the captain's side instead, slanting eyes flicking up at him, his down at her. Nailah had thought, *What is he doing? What can he be thinking?* She was sure she wasn't the only one wondering it: Benjamin Pasha's steel-witted older sister, Imogen Carter, had had watchful eyes on them both too.

'And now he's sent you to us,' said Socrates' assistant, bringing Nailah back into the moment. 'I'm Maria. Tell me what's finally brought you.'

Nailah explained Babu's malaise, his high fever, the constant vomiting.

Maria nodded sagely and led Nailah into a room with a bed, desk and chair in it. The curious stares of the other patients followed them. 'I'll send Socrates in,' said Maria, pouring water from a jug. 'You must drink,' she said, handing Nailah the glass, 'we don't want you passing out.'

Nailah wasn't sure she'd dare.

Maria made to go.

'The payment,' said Nailah, then flinched at the bluntness of her words. Maria turned, obviously confused. 'I just want to check the cost,' said Nailah. 'I'm sure I have enough, but—'

'No. No payment.'

'What?'

'Captain Bertram is seeing to your account.'

'He's paying?'

'No,' said Maria, 'someone else, although the captain didn't give a name. I must say Babu's a lucky boy, to have such attention.' She shook her head, as though it were beyond her, and left.

Nailah was too stunned to call after her, to ask more. She reached for her water with a shaking hand, swallowing hard on each sip. Who was this person funding Babu's care? Why were they doing it?

What did they know?

Ignorance prickled her palms with moisture.

The door opened. A middle-aged man with a pointy beard and round spectacles strode in. '*Yassas*,' he said wearily. He looked at Nailah. 'Or should I say, as-salaam? Bertram has told me to take special care of you, so let me see what I can do.'

For the next half-hour Nailah did her best to answer Socrates' probing on Babu's health, the regularity of his fevers. As the minutes ticked by she felt herself begin to relax, soothed by Socrates' unalarmed approach, the assured way in which he prescribed Babu's treatment.

'He'll get better?' she asked, clutching a bag of bottled medicine and a herbal fever balm. 'He'll be well?'

'He'll never be like you or me,' said Socrates, head tilted to one side as he studied Babu from the doorway. 'Whoever delivered him went to work on his skull. I suspect he was also starved of oxygen.' He sighed. 'There are some wrongs that even medicine can't right. But we'll help him live as good a life as he can. Come fortnightly, we'll see how he gets on.'

'Thank you,' said Nailah, tears of relief filling her throat.

'Now, now.' Socrates reached out awkwardly and then dropped his hand, obviously thinking better of it. 'I'll see you soon.'

'I hope so.' Nailah couldn't take it for granted. But whatever the roots of this strange generosity, however long it might last, she could only be grateful for it. *What was done was done. The past was dead.* For the time being, little Babu at least could benefit.

The soles of her feet stung as she walked them both home. She crooned over Babu, stroking him with the hand not holding Socrates' bag of bottles. He began to cry, weak mews, and she picked up her pace, anxious to get him into their room, the first of his medicine into him, a cold compress on his head.

As they drew closer to their quarter, the broad streets narrowed, cracks appeared in the houses, rust on the balcony railings; the air soured with sewage. Nearly there. Nailah hurried through the marketplace, deaf to the vendors calling the bargain prices of bruised onions and overripe tomatoes. She crossed the road, dodging donkey-drawn carts, and picked up her skirts as she stepped over a fetid puddle. Her heart lurched as she saw Kafele coming towards her, a crate balanced heavily on his shoulder. He was in shirtsleeves and waistcoat, the same grey one he'd been in yesterday and which she'd saved a year's pin money to buy. He only had two suits; seeing him in them always made Nailah ache for how high he was reaching.

He brushed past her. 'Meet me at Eastern Harbour after dark,' he said. 'Get Cleo to watch the baby. I have news.'

Nailah carried on walking. Her blood thundered within her.

Chapter Twelve

A world away from the Turkish Quarter, Olivia watched from her window as Edward left the house that morning, her thoughts full of the night before. She wasn't sure how long after she'd run from him her regret had set in; all she knew was that by the time she'd found herself slumped on the tiled bathroom floor, flannel pressed to her, she had wished she wasn't alone. That he was there to help her.

She should have let him be.

And she should have told him about Clara's missing letter. She had been wondering, through her sleepless night, if its contents could have anything to do with the naughtiness Clara had spoken of. She pressed her forehead against the warm pane, half-tempted to run down in her nightclothes now and talk to Edward about it. But it wasn't the time, not with Alistair still munching his marmaladeless bread in the breakfast room.

She ran her fingers along the shutter, picked at a fleck of paint. Edward stopped to talk to the Bedouin mother and her boys, all gathering figs at the gate. Olivia wondered whether he was questioning them about Clara. She hoped not, they seemed ill-equipped to be sucked into the whole sorry mess. The boys were little more than children; aside from their – astutely conceived – dislike for Alistair, they behaved like sun-baked innocents, running around in frayed trousers, fishing and diving in the sea. Their mother, meanwhile, carried a grief in her cloaked features that made her . . . fragile. Olivia wished they shared a language, she was more and more curious to talk to her. As it was, the pair of them communicated only in gestures.

She waited. At length Edward turned his horse, caught her eye, and touched his fingers to his cap. Olivia raised hers in a wave. The mornings had felt empty without their small ritual these past weeks. She'd been annoyed at herself for sleeping through the moment yesterday; she was relieved they'd carried on today, that neither of them had tried to forget it was what they did. In spite of everything.

He disappeared onto the road, leaving nothing but a cloud of dust behind him. Olivia turned to dress. Whatever Edward might say about danger, she was intent on getting out of the house again without alerting anyone to her movements. She had to talk to Sofia, find out what she knew about the contents of that letter.

Before long, though, the sharp rat-a-tat-tat of Ada's knuckles sounded on the bedroom door.

'I'm fine,' Olivia called.

The door opened purposefully and Ada's beady eyes appeared around it. She shook her head at Olivia's riding habit. 'No, no, no,' she said.

'Yes, yes, yes.'

'You ain't riding today, Mrs Sheldon, Mr Sheldon said so.'

'Did he indeed?'

''E did,' said Ada. 'I've pressed your violet two-piece.'

'I wish you hadn't.' Olivia buttoned her skirt, fingers stumbling in her haste, and pushed her toes into her boot, hopping on one foot as she pulled it on. 'If only you'd mentioned you were planning to do that, *as most lady's maids would*, I could have stopped you.'

'You're expected at Mrs Carter's,' said Ada.

Olivia shook her head. 'I have other plans.'

'No, tea at nine, Mr Sheldon said.'

'Nine?' said Olivia. 'Who has tea at nine? Rest assured, not me.' She frowned. 'And this will have been Edward's idea, not Alistair's. Edward had dinner with Imogen and Tom last night, he obviously worked it all out then. Alistair's just making sure I go.' She ground her teeth. It wasn't the prospect of seeing Imogen that displeased her. In fact, it would be good to talk to her; she felt she might go mad if she didn't get everything off her chest. But she didn't like the way she was being managed into the meeting, or Edward and Alistair working in cahoots to control her movements. Frankly, she loathed the thought of Edward speaking to Alistair at all. Out of all the potential men involved in Clara's disappearance, Alistair was riding high on Olivia's list of suspects, right alongside the nationalists, perhaps Jeremy, great-girthed Wilkins at a shot, everyone, in fact, except Edward. Edward was bottom. Olivia wanted to keep him there. But it was bloody hard to peg him and Alistair at opposite ends of the spectrum when they plotted together like this. 'I'll drop by on Imogen later,' she said.

'No,' said Ada, her voice as firm as Sister Agnes', Olivia's old headmistress. 'If you don't go straight to Mrs Carter's, I shall 'ave to send word to Mr Sheldon. We don't want that.'

'You'll *tell* on me?'

'If I 'ave to.' Ada squared her slight shoulders. She actually looked as if she was preparing to get into a fight. 'You're going to Mrs Carter's, Mrs Sheldon.'

'I beg to differ,' said Olivia, even as Ada crossed the room and began unbuttoning her skirt. Olivia wrenched herself away, tussling with Ada in an unseemly fashion, one foot still half in her boot. 'Get off, Ada, for goodness' sake. What's come over you?'

'I'm sorry, Mrs Sheldon. I don't like it no more than you do, but these are bad times and I've 'ad my orders. We can do it the easy way or the 'ard. Which one's it to be?'

Olivia sat in stony silence as the carriage trundled towards the Carters' home. Ada's set expression bumped around opposite her.

'It's better this way,' said Ada across the silence. 'Mr Sheldon would've been ever so angry.'

'Oh do be quiet,' said Olivia. Then, silently, *He'll be angry whatever I do.*

The Carters' grounds weren't manicured like Clara's, although the wildness had a beauty of its own. The villa glowed white in the sunlight, beds of wild jasmine and desert flowers surrounded it. Imogen waited on the lawn like an exotic butterfly, dressed in a lemon gown that set off her coffee skin and glossy hair perfectly. There was barely a whisper of grey in its blackness, but today there *was* a new heaviness in her beautiful face, and shadows of fatigue beneath her sphinx-like eyes.

'Oh, my darling,' she called, as the carriage pulled to a halt. 'I've been so worried. I called on you yesterday, but you weren't home. I thought you must be at Clara's, but it didn't feel right to go there.'

Olivia climbed down from the carriage. Imogen gave her a pained look, then said, 'Come here, do,' and pulled her into her arms.

Olivia stiffened reflexively at the unexpected intimacy, but then relaxed within the instant as another instinct took over, one which made her sink into the sweetly scented embrace, lean her cheek on Imogen's silken shoulder, and close her eyes. Warmth seeped through her. And although Imogen's clasp made her torso ache, even through the protective padding of her gown and stays, she didn't pull away. And nor did Imogen. It had been months since Olivia had been held so close, for so long. Not since she had said goodbye to her friend Beatrice on the damp, blustery morning she'd married Alistair. She had been dressed in thick ivory silks then, veil whipping around her bonnet. Her gown had crushed against Beatrice's black one as they embraced and Alistair tapped his foot impatiently by the carriage. 'Don't let him change you,' Beatrice had whispered in Olivia's ear.

It felt like something that had happened to another person.

In Imogen's arms, though, as Olivia relived that goodbye, suddenly, out of nowhere, another recollection came prodding: half-formed, more like a shadow . . . Olivia held her breath. She couldn't quite grasp it. A warm chest, that scent, a kiss . . . She clenched her eyes. She could nearly *feel* it.

But then Imogen let her go, and the almost-memory retreated. But it didn't disappear, not quite. It nestled deep in the cage of Olivia's ribs, waiting: a friend.

'Are you all right?' Imogen's brow creased. 'You've gone very pale.'

'I'm fine,' said Olivia, reorienting herself. 'Fine.'

'Of course you're not. How could you be? But I won't go on about how sad this all is. Sympathy only ever makes us feel worse than we already do. For now we must concentrate on finding Clara.'

'You believe we will?'

'We have to. Now let's go through, I have breakfast ready on the veranda. I'm sorry about dragging you here at this hideous hour.'

'Did Edward ask you to?'

Imogen nodded. 'I take it you had other plans.'

'I did rather.' Even so, Olivia was glad, after all, that Edward had arranged the call. She saw now how alone she'd been feeling.

'Come,' said Imogen. 'Your maid can wait in the kitchen.'

Ordinarily Olivia would have bid Ada goodbye, checked she knew where she was going, but today she followed Imogen into the house without a word. If Ada couldn't look after herself, the devil would surely take care of her.

'I went to the Sporting Club yesterday,' said Imogen as they climbed the front steps, 'just to see what people are saying. Tom claims they're trying to keep what's happened to Clara quiet, but everyone's whispering about why she's been taken, who's done it, enjoying the drama far too much.' She inhaled sharply. 'Horrible. Some of them have decided Edward's to blame because of him going off just as Clara did, then returning as she disappeared.' Imogen's voice echoed through the marble hallway as they passed out onto the back veranda. The lawn swept before them, framed by lofty palms. A table was set with a jug of minted juice, glasses, and a plate of cinnamon-dusted pastries. Imogen gestured at Olivia to sit down. 'A reporter from *The Times* was there, Morgan, Morton . . . ?' She frowned. 'Anyway, he was most interested in it all. Most of the ladies are *horrified* at the idea of Edward being a baddy, of course.'

'I hope this reporter isn't going to print anything,' Olivia said. 'It'd be slanderous.'

'I'd like to see what Edward would do to him if he did. But no, I think he's just snooping at the moment.' Imogen waved absently at a fly hovering by the pastries. 'Everyone's all het up, wondering

144

who's going to be next, and yet,' she frowned again, 'you're the only one anyone seems to be taking especial care over. The Gray house is the only one being guarded. Tom's told me now that it's to do with your husband's money being targeted but, I don't know. There are other wealthy men in Egypt. Plenty, in fact. My brother, for instance ... Tom.' Imogen pressed her lace-clad fingers to her temples. 'There's more to it than someone just going after Jeremy's money, I'm certain.'

Olivia nodded slowly, then proceeded to tell Imogen of all the strangeness curdling her mind, leaving nothing out – not Clara's moods before she went to Constantinople, her elusiveness whilst she was away, the strained meeting she'd stumbled across at the parade ground last night, not even Clara and Edward's covert discussion at the Sporting Club.

When she'd finished, Imogen sighed deeply, obviously digesting everything, then said, 'I hate to suggest it, but do you think Clara could have landed herself in some kind of a mess?'

'How do you mean?'

'As you've said, she hasn't been herself. I've noticed it too. She's stopped calling on me, she's never at home when I go there, and so withdrawn when we're out. Not,' Imogen held up her hand, 'that I'm worried for myself. But I really think she might be in trouble, something she's afraid to talk about. Perhaps Edward knows about it and was having it out with her at the Sporting Club. Maybe Jeremy took her away because of it.'

'She said she didn't know why Jeremy took her away.'

'Still,' said Imogen, 'I do think it's possible she's become embroiled in something against her will.' She reached for the juice, was about to pour, then paused. She leant under the table and pulled out a bottle. 'Shall we have a nip of gin?' She bit her lip. 'Or is it a glug? A glug of gin. How medicinal.' She poured a generous measure into the carafe, mint leaves swimming as the liquids mixed, and filled the two glasses, holding one out to Olivia. 'Go on, it'll make you feel better.'

Olivia took the glass, barely looking at it. 'None of this is Clara's doing,' she said, 'although I agree it isn't as straightforward as we're being told. There are just too many secrets.' She took a gulp of her drink to quench her throat, only remembering how much alcohol was in it as the inside of her mouth turned to fire. 'Willyouhelpmewithsomething?' It came out like a dragon's gasp. She reached for the plate of pastries and bit into a filo parcel; flakes of icing sugar stuck to her lips, custard soothed her tongue. She swallowed, breathed, and, when she was confident she could talk normally again, said, 'I need to go to Clara's house and find out what Sofia thinks was in Clara's letter, who might have taken it. I can't do that unless you help me avoid Ada.'

Imogen leant back in her chair. Her neck arched beneath her sapphire choker as she stared at the beating sky. 'I don't know,' she said. 'I'm worried about exposing you to risk.'

'What could possibly happen to me at Clara's? The police are guarding it.'

'These are strange times. I never would have imagined Clara could disappear from one of the busiest streets in Alex in broad daylight, but she has.' Imogen's brow creased. 'I'm scared for her, so very scared.'

'Then help me. Please.'

'Darling . . .'

'*Please*, Imogen.'

Imogen sighed. At length she said, 'I have a condition.'

'Fine. Anything.' Olivia sat straighter in her chair, blood pumping at Imogen stepping up, being her ally.

'From now on, you go nowhere alone. If you need something, come to me first. I feel terribly responsible for you. You're still so young.'

'Not that young.'

'To me you are. I've lived here my whole life, it's a long time, darling. I was here for the riots of '82, the invasion. The most sinister things can seem innocent, and you won't sniff them out as easily as I do. So, please, tell me everything. Agreed?'

'Agreed.'

Imogen clicked her tongue.

Olivia held her breath.

Imogen nodded. 'All right,' she said. She raised her glass. 'To finding Clara, and getting her home, safe again. For God's sake.'

With Ada being taken care of by Imogen's staff, it was easy enough for Olivia and Imogen to slip out to the pony and trap one of the servants had ready on the road.

'I feel like a thief,' Imogen said, hooking her arm through Olivia's as they clattered away. 'It's awful to be happy about anything, but I am pleased that we're doing this. I can't stand just sitting around, waiting.'

Clara's house was less than a mile from the Carters'; it took them barely ten minutes to reach it. Clara's driver, Hassan, and the footman, El Masri, met their trap. Hassan took hold of the pony. He smiled at Olivia, eyes like chocolate puddles, so deep she had to look away. She took El Masri's hand, leaning on it as she climbed to the ground. His darkly handsome face was as brooding as ever. And there was something unsettling about the way he was studying her.

'I can hear Angus,' said Imogen, distracting Olivia. She nodded towards the house, where Gus could, most certainly, be heard wailing. 'He misses Clara, I think.' Imogen, who had no children of her own and said it was probably for the best (*Really, I'm not good with little ones. Honestly I'm not. Much worse as I get older. It's all for the best I was never given one. Really.*), wrinkled her nose. 'The poor little mite sounds quite furious. Let's get on, get this over with.'

They let themselves into the house. A maid was in the hallway, a footman too, arranging a tray of crystal glassware. Another maid was in the corridor, polishing the tiles. Servants, servants, always everywhere.

Olivia led the way towards the stairs. Imogen nodded at the open door of the study. 'Why not go in? Double-check Clara's letter isn't there.'

'Aren't *you* good at this?' said Olivia.

'Just go. I'll keep watch.'

147

Olivia moved quickly, one eye on the door, thumbing the pages of the same books she had yesterday. A breeze blew on her neck through the open shutters. There was nothing there. She replaced the volumes on the shelves, and caught her breath at the sound of a stick cracking outside. She put her hand on her chest and exhaled. It was just surly El Masri loping towards the stables. He glanced over, but gave no sign that he'd seen her.

'Olivia,' hissed Imogen, poking her head around the door. 'Anything?'

'No. Let's go, before someone comes.'

As they made their way to the nursery, Olivia's chest tightened in the air voided of Clara's chatter, the swish of her sashaying skirts. Gus's screams, which had escalated to an almost impossible pitch, reverberated off the walls. Olivia drew breath, then opened the door marked with a wooden duck.

She was barely in the room before Sofia bundled Gus into her arms and then collapsed into her rocking chair. She placed the back of her plump hand against her forehead and shook her head. One of her tortoiseshell combs came loose in the motion, although she appeared not to notice. 'I'm glad to see you, *agapi mou*,' she said. 'Are you all right?'

'Are *you*?' asked Olivia, rearranging Gus's rigid body so she could rock him. She caught sight of Ralph, sitting cross-legged on the floor, just beneath Imogen's skirts. Imogen crouched awkwardly beside him, apologising for not bringing any sweets. Ralph said, in a grave little voice, that that was really the least of his worries.

'Where's your father?' Olivia asked him.

'He's gone to the office,' said Ralph.

'The office?'

'He said he's being British.'

Olivia frowned. 'What's that supposed to mean?'

Ralph shrugged.

Imogen shook her head. Turning to Sofia, she ran through the conundrum of Clara's letter.

'I swear it was still there when Mrs Clara went out,' said Sofia, once Imogen had finished. 'She hid it just before she left. I don't know who would have taken it.'

'You're certain?' asked Imogen. 'Because whoever did obviously has something to hide.'

'Anything you can tell us,' said Olivia, still swaying from foot to foot with Gus's tense body, 'would help.'

'You don't think *I* took it, do you?' Sofia's bosom heaved beneath her apron. 'Why would I have told you it was there if I was planning on stealing it?'

'I don't think you took it,' Olivia assured her, 'but I think you know what was in it.'

'Just tell us,' said Imogen, 'and then we won't have to go to the police.'

Sofia flushed, a glow that seeped into her grey-flecked hairline. Olivia felt awful for putting her on the spot as they were. Sofia was clearly struggling enough with everything going on, she hardly needed them grilling her on top of it all, especially in front of Ralph, who was listening, mouth open at his nanny's unease. If the matter hadn't been so important, if finding another opportunity to speak to Sofia didn't feel so challenging, Olivia would have called a halt, said they would discuss it all another time when tiny ears weren't so close by.

However, since it was what it was, she said, 'You have to talk to us, Sofia.'

Sofia cast a glance at Ralph. 'What can I say that he can hear?' She opened her arms helplessly. 'I don't know how to put it.'

'Just try,' said Imogen.

Sofia sighed and gave Olivia a worried look. What was she so concerned about? Not just Ralph, of that Olivia was becoming uncomfortably aware. Her back prickled in the uncomfortable suspicion that something bad was about to come her way.

'I never saw that letter,' said Sofia, her laboured tone making it clear how little she wanted to be speaking of it all, 'other than Mrs Clara hiding it. But yes, I *think* I know what was in it.' She shot Ralph another frown, eased herself up from her chair and beckoned Olivia and Imogen into the adjoining bedroom. She pushed the door to behind them. 'Mrs Clara,' she said, her tone hushed, 'used to go out at funny hours. A lot. Often, when I'd go to fetch her in the middle of the night, if Gus wouldn't settle, or Ralphy had had a bad dream, her bed was empty, just lots of pillows where her body should have been. She and Mr Jeremy have different rooms, they have done for a long time.' Sofia glared meaningfully at Gus in Olivia's arms. 'For *years*.' Olivia looked down at Gus's black hair, his tan complexion, so different to Clara and Jeremy's fairness.

'You think Mrs Gray has been meeting someone illicitly?' Imogen's voice seemed to come from a long way away. 'That she was writing her letter to whoever he is?'

'It would be a fair guess, yes.'

'Let me get this absolutely straight,' said Imogen. 'You're saying that our Clara was involved in an affair? That Angus here . . .'

'Oh God.' Olivia looked again at Gus's wavy curls, so dark. She felt a weight settle on her; it spread through her limbs, beating within her to the rhythm of the word 'naught-ee-ness'. 'Oh no.' She didn't even attempt to hide her alarm. She couldn't. It was too shocking. She closed her eyes. 'Who was Clara meeting, Sofia?'

'I don't know for sure. On my honour, *agapi mou*, I don't.'

'But you suspect. Was it . . . ?' Olivia broke off. She wouldn't say it, couldn't think it, she refused to speak his name.

'What are you talking about?' asked Imogen. 'Why . . . ?' She tailed off. Her eyes widened. 'Edward?'

Sofia nodded slowly. 'Mrs Clara's been so upset lately. "Teddy's so cross with me," she kept saying whilst we were away. "I wish he wasn't cross with me."'

'Teddy.' The word was cold on Olivia's lips. She turned to Imogen, far past any pretence now. 'Clara's always called Edward Teddy.'

'It doesn't mean anything,' Imogen said uncertainly. Couldn't she at least try to sound convinced?

'I could be wrong,' Sofia said.

Olivia's mind raced to draw evidence from the recent past that

150

Sofia was wrong. Edward belonged to her, *her*, just as she belonged to him. It was the only thing she had to be sure of. She couldn't let that go.

She bundled Gus into Sofia's arms before she dropped him. She didn't look at him, she was too terrified of what she might see in his features.

Without any idea of where she was going, only that she had to be gone, she ran from the room.

Chapter Thirteen

Imogen caught up with Olivia as she reached the front door. 'Wait, darling, wait and listen. I can see you don't want to hear it, God knows I don't want to believe it, but we at least have to consider Sofia might be right.'

'No, I won't.' Olivia's voice shook. 'Edward hasn't been involved with Clara. I'm certain.'

'But what about this "naughtiness"?'

Olivia dragged her mind for another explanation as to what it could be about. 'Fine,' she conceded at length, 'Clara was probably referring to her affair. But it doesn't necessarily follow that she was taken because of it, or that she was having it with Edward. Maybe he'd simply found out about it and, I don't know . . . was talking to her about it at the Sporting Club.'

'Or maybe he was trying to break it off with her, convince her not to tell anyone anything. He's not infallible, darling. He's handsome, a cavalry officer, I have to tell you he's had liaisons before now.'

'I don't want to talk about this.'

'I think we must. He and Clara have always been friends, good friends, ever since he moved here. I've often seen them talking.'

'Clara could have been dallying with anyone.'

'Well, whoever he was, he's certainly been very skilful about covering his tracks.' Imogen sighed. 'Don't you want to know for certain it wasn't Edward?'

Olivia covered her face with her hands. She did, of course she did. Whatever she might claim, her doubt was growing by the second.

She kept combing through the months since she'd arrived, looking for an action, or a word, to confirm that something had been going on between him and Clara, that yet another man had moved from her older sister on to her. But there was nothing. *Nothing*.

'I don't know what to think,' she admitted. 'I only know I don't want to believe it.'

Imogen stared, her lovely face softened by sympathy. 'I know it must hurt,' she said. 'You have ... Well, you have feelings for him, don't you? I've seen that. Even before today.'

Olivia flushed. 'Have I been that obvious?'

'No, darling. It's only because I watch you as I do. And you're so like your mama, I find I can read you better than most.'

'You must think me brazen, a harlot.'

'No,' said Imogen sadly, 'not that.'

'Nothing's happened between us, Imogen. Nothing.'

'I know, I see that too. But I'm not sure I'd judge you if it had. You have no idea the way it upsets me, how unhappy you've become.' She bit her bottom lip, frowning. 'Alistair,' she said, 'he's not a nice man.'

'No,' said Olivia, 'I don't suppose he is.'

Imogen's eyes glistened sadly. Olivia felt the temptation to tell her just how not nice Alistair was.

Imogen spoke before she could give into it. 'I hate this for you,' she said, 'the hopelessness of it. But whatever went on between Edward and Clara—'

'If something went on.'

'If.' Imogen's small nod felt like an indulgence. 'Then it won't have been anything next to what he feels for you. I remember the way he looked at you when you left Sabia's, that night you first met. It broke my heart. The pair of you break my heart.' She sighed. 'Will you ask him for the truth?'

'I don't think I can, not whilst there's a chance I'm wrong. I don't know if I could forgive myself for putting that doubt between us.'

'I can understand that.'

'I know it's hopeless. I know that I'm married to Alistair. I don't want you to think I'm being naive about that. But at least for now it's only Alistair keeping us apart. I don't want another wedge. I don't want Clara to be a wedge.' Olivia's eyes swelled, her throat tightened with tears. She swallowed them. She would not cry again. She would *not*.

'Let's go back to my house,' said Imogen, taking her arm. 'We'll have another drink, and try and find a way to get to the bottom of this hideous mess. Take a breath, darling, we'll make this well.'

Olivia stayed with Imogen most of the day. The two of them decided, over several drinks, that Imogen would make enquiries amongst her servants and ferret out any gossip that might pertain to Clara's liaison. 'They see all sorts of things we don't want them to, darling. You wait, one of them will know something.'

'All right,' said Olivia, taking another glug of gin. 'But remember she could have been seeing another man entirely. And make sure you listen for other information too. I really don't think Clara was abducted because of this adultery.'

'Have another drink,' said Imogen.

Olivia was half-cut by the time she finally left. Her head swam as she climbed into the carriage beside Ada. Imogen told her to come over any time; for herself, she'd call when she had news. Olivia sat silent for the carriage drive home, eyes heavy on the irregularly spaced villas and peasant lean-tos lining the road; the palms, the dust-coated pistachio trees, the donkeys grazing on sun-crisped grass. Ada said nothing either, until they pulled into their driveway, at which point she volunteered to draw Olivia a bath, and Olivia told her she could go to hell for all she cared (it was the gin, it had loosened her tongue).

A headache had come on her by the time Alistair and Edward got home, a pinched pain between her eyes that she was doing her best to overcome by lying in the garden with a cool compress on her head. She kept quite still as she listened to the distant bass of Edward's voice in the stables, tense, waiting to see if he would come out to her or stay away, unclear, given her inner angst, which even-tuality she'd like less. It was only when the silence lengthened with no footfall padding on the grass that she realised there'd never been any doubt about what she wanted. Why was she stopping herself from going to see him? It was like when she and Beatrice had used to draw cards back in London, deciding what dress to wear, book to read, café to visit (spades and clubs, the corner tearooms, diamonds and hearts, Lyons) and been disappointed at the outcome, yet gone along with the whim of the pack anyway. Life wasn't long enough to waste with unhappy decisions.

It was Fadil who came to fetch her for dinner. He hadn't said another word about her crying fit, but he'd been home again when she returned. It was he who had brought her the compress, asking no questions, face crinkled with concern. She managed a small smile up at him, then dropped it, remembering all the hidden truths he might know.

It was just she and Alistair in the dining room, Edward obviously having decided he'd had his fill of loaded silences and long looks served with each course, *a Sheldon speciality*. They ate at either end of the table built to seat fourteen, candles crackling in the silence; Olivia heard every slurp from her spoon as though it were echoing through a concert hall, every crack of her bread reverberated, each clang of her knife and fork was deafening. She managed to finish her stew but gave up on dessert. She threw her napkin on the lemon pudding, watched the syrup soak into the linen, knowing she should feel guilty at the extra laundry she had caused yet finding she didn't particularly care.

Alistair said something. She had to ask him to repeat it since she hadn't been listening.

He folded his own (pristine) napkin and gave her a level look. 'I asked, Olivia, if you're planning to meet your grandmother's boat tomorrow. Jeremy's told me the *Excelsior*'s due in port at noon.'

'Has he? Did he happen to mention any plans to pay for Clara's release whilst he was at it?'

'Don't talk about things you don't understand.'

Olivia bit down a riposte. What was the point in arguing? 'In answer to your question,' she said, 'no, I won't be going to meet the

Excelsior. And since Mildred is staying at the Grays', I have every intention of avoiding her entirely.'

'That's a little childish.'

'Is it?'

Alistair's left eye twitched.

Olivia pushed her chair out, she said she might go to bed.

'I'll join you shortly,' said Alistair, lips thinning in a smile.

'Please don't hurry,' she said, and left the room.

She found Edward in the hallway, sitting at the bottom of the stairwell, smoking. His shirt hung loose over his trousers.

'Were you watching for me to come out?' she asked.

'Yes.'

She wouldn't ask him about Clara, whether he'd taken her letter from the study. The questions punched in her throat, trying to force themselves out. 'Imogen got me drunk,' she said, since she had to say something.

He laughed sadly. 'I'm glad to hear it.'

'It wasn't a good day, Edward. It was another not good one.'

He ran his hand through his hair, His dark, thick hair. He shook his head and sighed. 'I had one of those myself. I couldn't get hold of Wilkins.'

'Do you think he's hiding something?'

'Perhaps. But I have no idea what.'

'No,' said Olivia. She stared down at him. He looked so tired. His handsome face was drawn with anxiety. 'You're desperate to find Clara, aren't you?' she said.

His forehead creased. 'Of course I am, Olly.'

She nodded, made to pass.

'Olly,' he said, 'about last night, in the garden . . .'

'Please,' she said, 'I can't talk about that.'

His frown deepened, but he didn't push her. He swivelled his legs to let her go, not taking his eyes from her.

Her skirt brushed his knee. She caught her breath.

Chapter Fourteen

Out on the horizon, the moon sprayed the Mediterranean with light, but the water lapping the walls of the Eastern Harbour was inky, shaded by the city buildings. Kafele cut a lone figure in the distance; slight and lithe, and dressed as he was in wide trousers and a cloth shirt, legs dangling in the sea, he could have been mistaken for a fisherman. It was the way he was staring out across the bobbing long-tail boats, towards his beloved Constantinople, that gave him away as something else. *Ambitious.* Nailah could hear his thoughts, see the pictures he was painting of the palaces and churches they both yearned to visit.

She hung back, smoothing her hair with trembling hands. She'd been able to think of little else all day but seeing him, finding out what it was he'd discovered. But now the moment had finally arrived, she was nervous to know. *Be strong, habibi. For you.* Nailah set off. As she approached Kafele, he jumped to his feet on the cobbles, quick as a gecko. His slim chest was hard beneath his loose shirt; all that lifting of crates. She realised she preferred him in his street clothes, reachable and part of her world. It made the idea of their future seem a little less improbable.

'How are you?' he asked. 'How's Babu? I couldn't stand to see you like that earlier, you both looked so beaten.'

'I'm not beaten.' Nailah gave a determined laugh, as much for her benefit as Kafele's. He didn't laugh back. In fact he frowned. 'I'm not,' she said, 'not yet. And nor is Babu. He took some bread and milk earlier.'

'What about Jahi?' Kafele stepped closer. 'What was he doing at your house yesterday? He should have been at work. What did he want?'

Nailah didn't answer. 'What have you found out about Ma'am Gray?' she asked instead.

Kafele's frown deepened. 'Nailah, has Jahi had . . . ?'

'Please,' Nailah interrupted. 'I don't want to talk about Jahi.'

Kafele sighed. At length he nodded, said they should sit.

Nailah dropped down on the wall beside him. She took off her sandals and placed her feet with his in the water. The water rippled darkly around their toes. She stared down at their bare skin, so close. She could hear her own breath going in, out. Kafele took her hand. At his touch, she felt an echo of the worry she'd experienced in the alleyway yesterday, but it was a quieter emotion than what had gone before; the shiver of content which ran through her was stronger. She did her best to focus on that, push her lingering unease away – for what could she do about it anyway – and slowly, tentatively, she dropped her head on his shoulder. Their reflections spread out before them; her exhausted features mercifully obscured by the aquatic mirror, Kafele's fine face somehow enhanced. If she could have, she would have stayed with him like that all night.

But before a minute passed, Kafele broke the spell. 'What did Jahi want?' he asked again. 'I've never seen him in town during the day before. What's happened?'

Nailah moved her foot in a watery circle, feeling the dirt lift from her, the nibble of a fish. There was so much she might have told Kafele now. But in the end, all she confided was Jahi's threats to send her away.

Kafele's shoulder tensed. 'Where does he want you to go?'

'He didn't say, I don't think he even knows yet.' She swallowed hard. 'He says he might take the children.'

'Why?'

'I don't know.' It was a lie, and it hurt to speak it, but the truth would have been harder. 'I can't go, Kafele, and I can't lose the children. I don't think I could stand it.'

'You won't have to.' Kafele inhaled sharply. 'What's Jahi thinking? You belong with me, and they with you.'

'I saw Sana this afternoon. She said she's seen you talking to Greta Sarafaglou.' Nailah hadn't intended mentioning it, she'd tried to brush Sana's taunts off. 'Greta's father's rich, of course, she could go with you wherever you want.'

'Nailah, hush.'

'I could understand.'

'Nailah.' Before Nailah realised what was happening, Kafele pressed his lips against hers. She turned rigid with shock. She very nearly wrenched away. It was too much. *I need to believe we should have something left to wait for.* But then he moved closer, saying that he was hers, and that was all there ever would be, and her bones seemed to soften within her, her worries retreated. His lips found hers again, and her feet became liquid in the sea, seeping into it. She no longer wanted to tell him to stop. In that moment, she couldn't think why she should.

In the end, it was him who pulled away. Nailah stayed where she was, leaning towards him, mouth ajar.

'Never speak like that again.' Kafele's amber eyes bored into her. She could see nothing but them. 'Greta was passing a bill on from her father, she means nothing. She never could. My life's with you. Jahi can go hang before I'll have it any other way.'

He seemed to mean it. But Jahi had been so determined the morning before, Nailah had no doubt he'd meant it too. She scrunched her forehead, her thoughts a mess. Her skin was firing from Kafele's touch. 'Sometimes,' she said, 'when I'm with Jahi, I feel as if I'm losing who I am.'

'You can't. I would never let you.'

She nodded slowly.

'Look.' Kafele spread his arm, the one not holding her, out to encompass the sea. 'There's a whole world waiting for us. We'll leave this place one day and go to it. You'll forget Jahi and Sana and all of this, I promise. You'll be too busy to remember, visiting museums, staying in fine hotels.' He took a deep breath and exhaled. 'We'll make it happen yet. We'll see sights, you and I, they'll make our eyes burn with wonder.'

Nailah could feel the burning even now, but it had nothing to do with wonder. She blinked the tears away; she had enjoyed Kafele's story, she liked the fiction, and she didn't want to crack the warmth created by his hold with her melancholy. She gave him her best attempt at a smile. And as they sat in silence, feet floating, she tried to imagine herself in rich clothes, holding his hand as they explored the Parthenon, the Champs Élysées, the Tower of London.

But her thoughts pulled her back to Ma'am Gray. It was no use, she couldn't wait any longer, she had to know what Kafele had found out. Gently, not wishing to pull him from his fantasies too quickly, she asked him to tell her.

He sighed, coming back to join her on the rough stone wall. 'People aren't keen to talk, they're afraid to get involved. A British woman, missing.' A shadow crossed his face. 'It's safer, Nailah, to stay out of it.'

Nailah knew that he was warning her for her own sake. But for the first time she considered the risks she might have exposed him to by drawing him into it all. She was about to say as much, apologise, when he carried on talking, silencing her.

The officer outside the mosque had been Captain Bertram. He'd been asking after a man by the name of Garai Aziz. 'Garai's a supplier of mine,' said Kafele. 'I've spoken to him myself now.' He sighed. 'It seems he works as an informer, although he's asked me to keep *that* to myself. He's been on British pay for years, tells them about any discontent, brawls, all the insolent things us nationals get up to.' An unfamiliar note of bitterness crept into voice. 'They pay well, apparently. Garai says the captain's asked him to help find Clara Gray, that he's certain someone from the city has her.'

'How does the captain know that?'

Kafele shrugged. 'Garai might have found a lead, though.'

'What? What kind of lead?'

'Garai didn't say very much. He wants to look into it before he goes to Bertram, make sure it's real. It's so strange, you see.'

As Kafele talked on, Nailah studied their submerged feet, mind snapping to piece together the implications of all he said. He fell silent; it took her a moment to realise he had.

'Nailah,' he said, 'you have to tell me. Why do you care so much about all of this?'

'I ... I'm scared about Ma'am Gray.' She thought of Ma'am Gray's smile, her yellow hair. The way she used to hold her baby so tight, one arm around the older one, like they were her only friends. Nailah had heard her weeping one day in the drawing room, she supposed with Ma'am Amélie, although she hadn't been able to see. It had been a rainy February afternoon just before Ma'am Sheldon arrived. 'I can't stand what Alistair's done to her,' Ma'am Gray had said, her voice echoing out into the hallway, 'but I suppose I'm glad, in a strange way, too. Because now she's coming, and I'll see her again. I've been so alone, you see.' She'd taken a shuddering breath. Nailah had backed away from the door, unseen. 'So desperately, horribly alone.'

Nailah looked up at the stars, imagining Ma'am Gray's God looking down. Were his eyes pointed on her? What could he see? She said, 'I want to know if there's a chance she'll be found.'

'You swear there's no more to it than that?' asked Kafele.

'I swear.'

Kafele studied her a moment more. She strained her cheeks, just managing to keep her expression level.

He nodded. 'Well,' he said, 'all we can do now is hope. If this lead of Garai's comes to something, perhaps it will be enough to get Clara Gray home.'

THE FOURTH
AND FIFTH DAYS

Chapter Fifteen

The next morning, Olivia waited in her bedroom until Edward left. He turned his horse, tipped his hat. She tried not to wave.

She waved.

She stayed in and drifted around the stifling house; she couldn't summon the energy to fight Alistair and overcome Ada to go out. She knew too that Mildred's ship was due to arrive within hours, that Mildred would be at the Grays' house by lunchtime – she didn't want to risk running into her. Images of naughtiness, Gus's features, and Clara's horribly broken body plagued her. At times it was as though they were pressing into her soul, slowing her mind, and it was all she could do to breathe.

She wondered if she was becoming hysterical. Imogen, who dropped by despite saying she wouldn't until she had news, said Olivia should try to stop worrying, she must hold on to hope. Clara had been gone so little time, it hadn't been a week, not even close. Imogen was going to call at her brother Benjamin's house, see if someone there knew something about Clara's affair. Clara was always visiting, after all.

That evening Edward sat on the veranda whilst Olivia lay on the lawn. She heard the crackle of his cigarette, the creak of his chair. She sensed he knew she'd withdrawn from him, she wondered if he'd pull her up on it, ask her what she suspected. She thought, *He will if he's got nothing to hide.*

He didn't pull her up on it. He didn't speak to her at all.

It was only she and Alistair again at dinner that night. Alistair told her that she should eat or she'd become unpleasantly skinny. He said she should invite Mildred to call, he'd been to see her at the Grays' that afternoon, she was upset by Olivia not having come to meet her at the ship, feeling slighted. Olivia said she'd rather stick pins in her eyes than speak to Mildred, and Alistair smiled as though he thought it an intriguing idea.

Edward was on the stairs as she went to bed. Her skirt brushed his trousers. He swivelled his legs. She caught her breath.

The next morning, she waited in her bedroom until he left. He turned his horse, tipped his hat. And so it went on.

Edward was worried about her. He could think of little else as he galloped across the desert on yet another morning's hunt for her older sister. She'd turned so pale, so melancholy. She never went out, Fadil had told him. Ada said she'd stopped swimming too. She rarely talked, and every time Edward felt he might speak to her, say something that meant *something*, there was Alistair, hovering, watching. He had a new steeliness to his eye, like he had started to work things out. Edward cursed, thinking about it. He wasn't concerned for himself, he didn't give a damn for Alistair's good opinion, but he worried for Olly. Little as she'd done – and God knew she was still innocent of any adultery – Edward wouldn't put it past Alistair to punish her for a feeling. There was every chance Alistair would keep Olly locked in their marriage, make her life ever more miserable that way. But what if he went a step further, cast her out? The scandal would be colossal. She'd already borne so many years of cold shoulders, Edward didn't want another day of them forced upon her.

If she left Alistair, braved the inevitable condemnation, it *had* to be her choice.

But would she do it?

It had shaken Edward, the other night at the parade ground, how baffled she had looked when he'd finally raised the possibility of them running. Her words were imprinted on his mind. *I can't leave, you know that.* Then the way she'd fled from him on the rocks, so shocked by what they'd nearly done. He'd moved too fast, asked too much. *She had to be the first to cross that line.* Her reaction had forced him to stop, remember afresh how much she'd be giving up by throwing her lot in with him, pursuing a divorce. It wasn't just the life she'd have to leave behind here. She'd have no friends anywhere, no social life to speak of; just a small house in an army cantonment – if he didn't get dismissed – and him.

Was it enough?

He was desperate to ask her outright. But her grief, her malaise, made it impossible. He could burden her with nothing more until they found Clara.

If they found her.

He brought his horse around and narrowed his eyes through the muslin wraps he used to shield himself from the sun. He scoured the sand, yellow and brown waves that blurred into the burning sky; a wide expanse of nothing.

Clara had been gone five days now. *Five*. He had spent count-less hours combing these dunes for her; his men had searched every street, every farm. They had the Egyptian police watching the harbour and railway stations. But Clara's captors had left not a whisper, not a trace. With so little to go on, Edward had resorted to asking the Bedouin woman at Alistair's gate if she'd heard anything that might help. 'It's a bad season,' was all she had said. 'A sad one. Too many are being taken.' Edward had asked her what she meant, but she'd just clenched her lips and shaken her head, as though she'd already spoken too freely. He'd enquired then what had brought her to Ramleh, but again, she'd refused to answer. 'Where are you from?' he'd asked, trying a different tack. When she'd replied, 'Montazah,' Edward, remem-bering the strained atmosphere at the hut Jeremy had sent him to up there, had got that warning tingling in his spine. He'd gone back to Montazah, thinking to find the girl, Nailah, and question her more – discover what had made her so afraid that day. But the place had been deserted; the hut looked as if it hadn't been lived in for weeks.

Jeremy told him he was being paranoid, that all of that had nothing to do with anything, *old man*, and happy as he was to keep funding Babu's medical care *on the quiet*, he couldn't pay the ransom money, of course he couldn't. *Not possible.* He hadn't managed to hold Edward's eye as he said it, his face had been grim with anxiety. He was hiding something.

There was too much Edward didn't know. He needed to press Jeremy again. He had to track his man, Garai, down in the Turkish Quarter too. They'd left him alone long enough, he must have something by now.

First, though, he would try once more to find Wilkins at the police headquarters. Every time he called in to see that ransom note, Wilkins was elsewhere. Tom was having the same challenge. Enough was enough.

Edward set off across the dunes, sand skidding beneath his stallion's hooves, towards the haze-cloaked city on the horizon. His wraps flapped around him, his face burned, his mouth was parched. He squinted out at the miles upon miles of cresting sand. *Where are you, Clara? Where are they keeping you?*

The forecourt of the police headquarters thronged with Egyptian police at the end of morning shifts, smoking in the sunshine on lunchtime breaks. A cluster stood beneath a palm talking, others squatted on the stairs eating flatbreads and kebabs. The bulk of the force was made up of native men, it was only at the most senior levels that the British got involved. It was the way the Protectorate worked: influence and education from the top. Give the Egyptians jobs, badges, mould them in the image of the Empire, and there you have it: a happy enough race behaving just the way old Victoria wants them to. The army was the same. British companies such as Edward's were scattered around the country, just enough of a presence to be felt, then hundreds of officers had been seconded into the local army to train the troops, keep them in check. Manipulative as the system was, Edward couldn't deny it worked. For every local who resented the heavy hand of the Empire, there were three more too glad of their jobs and wages to protest.

One such man came running to Edward now, a stable hand eager to relieve the sayed of his horse. Edward handed his stallion over, requesting fresh water for him, a brush down, then ran up the stone steps of the headquarters, two at a time, and on towards Wilkins' office.

One of Wilkins' deputies tried to intercept him at the doorway, but Edward ignored him, striding into Wilkins' office without knocking. He stopped short at the sight of not only the commissioner, but Alistair and Jeremy within.

Wilkins sat, hands on belly, behind his desk. Alistair lounged, legs folded, in one of the armchairs. Jeremy stood by the window, facing away from them both. He was the only one to turn and greet Edward.

His face was even gaunter than it had been the last time Edward saw him, two days prior. His normally strong frame appeared diminished beneath his three-piece. He'd aged a decade in mere days, closer now to Alistair's fifty years than the forty he was. If anything, Alistair, relaxed in his chair, looked the younger man.

But then Alistair hadn't lost his wife. Only the woman who had turned him down. And since he was a cold bastard, he probably relished that on some level.

Edward couldn't think why Jeremy tolerated him.

He had asked him once what had ever led him into business with Alistair in the first place.

'He convinced me,' Jeremy had said. 'I wasn't much over one and twenty at the time. I knew him through our school's old boys' club. I had some family money, he talked me into investing it in Sheldon-Gray Limited.' He'd laughed, good-naturedly enough. 'Sheldon first, naturally.'

'Naturally,' Edward had replied, not smiling.

'Ah, he wasn't so difficult in those days,' Jeremy said. 'He was a more carefree man. It was in the early seventies, years before ... well, before that season in London when we were introduced to

Clara. He lured me in with stories of money to be made in the cotton fields of this land of the pharaohs. I was like a young pup being offered his first bone. I'd just come down from studying classics at Cambridge, I did my dissertation on theories behind the burning of the great Alexandria library . . . ' Jeremy shrugged helplessly. 'I was fascinated by it. I still am. I couldn't resist the opportunity to come out here, make my mark. The rest,' he sighed, 'is history.'

It was his wistful tone; Edward hadn't been able to help himself asking, 'Do you regret it? Wish you'd done something else?'

'No,' Jeremy had said, 'no, no. Not at all.'

Edward hadn't had the heart to press him. But now, as Jeremy looked at him despairingly from across Wilkins' office, he knew without asking that, given the option, Jeremy would go back in a heartbeat to that old boys' dinner. He'd tell Alistair to stuff his land of the pharaohs. He'd never have come here in the first place.

'What can we do for you, old man?' Jeremy asked.

'Yes,' said Wilkins. He sat up straighter in his chair, placed both hands on his desk, as though to remind everyone it was *his* office. He looked so smug, so bloody delighted with his own sense of importance. 'Can *I* help you with something?'

'I suspect he's here to see the note,' said Alistair.

'Ah,' said Wilkins, 'of course.' He patted his waistcoat pocket, dug around for a key, then opened his top drawer. He pulled out a piece of paper and slid it across the desk with a fat finger. He had a signet ring on, it cut into his flesh. 'Here it is,' he said.

Edward made to take it. Wilkins pressed his finger down, as though to resist.

'Let's not,' said Edward, pulling it from him. He scanned the typewritten words. It was exactly as Carter had related at the parade ground the other night: Clara was safe, she would remain so as long as the money was wired to the nominated account; it was time the British paid for something.

'We've checked with the bank,' said Wilkins. 'They have no information about who set the account up.'

'There's a surprise,' said Edward, eyes still on the note. 'Strange there's no timeframe.'

'What's that?'

'There's no deadline for the money.'

'What's wrong with that?' asked Alistair coolly.

'It's odd.' Edward frowned down at the paper in his hand. There was something else nettling him. But he couldn't think what. He looked from Alistair's pale stare to Wilkins' piggy eyes. Did he imagine the heat creeping through Wilkins' cheeks?

'Why odd?' asked Wilkins, his voice oh so level.

Edward ground his teeth, thinking. He could feel the eyes of the other men on him, waiting. 'A ransom note normally would,' he said at length. He smiled coldly, deciding to press the matter no more for now. Not until he'd done some digging. 'The men who wrote this are obviously amateurs.'

'Who's an amateur?' came a woman's voice from behind Edward.

He started at the raspy tone. He was hit by a smack of mothballs. Wilkins' face visibly dropped. Jeremy muttered, 'Jesus,' from the window. Alistair stood and said, 'Ah, Mildred,' and Edward felt a twist in his gut.

He turned to see her: Olly and Clara's grandmother. She even looked like a witch, dressed as she was in an old-fashioned grey crinoline, her bones angular beneath papery skin. She had clouded blue eyes. Her white hair was scraped back beneath a black silk bonnet.

'I thought we agreed you'd stay at home from now on,' said Jeremy. 'We *talked* about this, Mildred.'

'Did we? I can't remember. I was in town to buy something to help with the flies. I thought there'd be no harm in calling in again.'

'I'm afraid,' said Wilkins wearily, 'that we have no more news for you today than we did yesterday, Mrs Price.'

'How very disappointing,' she said, 'although no less than I'm learning to expect. Do I need to say again that I'm leaving next week?'

'You don't,' said Jeremy.

'The passage is booked. I chose it carefully to get us back in good

171

time for the start of Ralph's term. There's not another one from Alexandria for a fortnight after that. We can't miss it, it will throw everything out. It simply won't do. You have to find her.'

'For reasons beyond your travel plans, of course,' said Edward.

She turned to him, tilting her head back to peer down her nose. 'And who are you?' she asked. 'I don't know you.'

'Nor are you ever likely to,' he replied shortly. He felt sick, just breathing the same air as her. He couldn't be in the same room a moment longer. Knowing he was being rude, and relishing it, he told them all he'd leave them to it. 'I've wasted enough time here.'

Jeremy caught up with him as he reached the bottom of the headquarters' stairs. Squinting in the bright sun, he asked whether there was any news, anything at all.

'Nothing.' Edward ran his hand down his face, sand grating against his stubble. 'Just pay the ransom, Gray, for God's sake.'

'I can't.'

'You can.'

'Bertram, if I give in, they might come after the boys for more, target someone ...'

'Else? Yes, I know all that. But you see, I have this odd feeling there's another reason you're not paying the money.'

Jeremy hesitated.

The pause said it all. Edward felt a bitter beat of satisfaction. He said, 'You have to tell me what's gone on.'

'I don't know what you mean.'

'Yes, you do.'

'I don't.'

'Gray ...'

'I don't.'

'Come *on*.'

'I *can't*.' Jeremy shouted it. He pulled out a kerchief, wiped sweat from his brow. 'I don't.'

'For Christ's sake.' Edward wanted to throttle him. 'This is Clara we're talking about. *Clara*. Your *wife*, the mother of your sons.' As he spoke, he was hit by an image of her, not as she'd been the last time he saw her, face tense and sad, but smiling, rosy cheeks dimpled as Gus gurgled on her lap. He shook his head, thinking of the hours and hours he'd spent with her over the years, talking of Cairo, reassuring her that all the places she remembered were still there. *I can't go to visit, myself,* she would say, *it's too hard.* The way she'd lose herself in stories of her childhood, of Olly, picnics in Giza, the Egyptian murals their mother had stencilled on their nursery wall. *I tried to do the same for Ralphy, but I don't have her touch. We painted over them in the end.*

'You have to give me something,' Edward said to Jeremy now. 'I'm running blind. Surely you still care enough to want to get her back.'

'Of course I do,' Jeremy snapped. 'I love her, damn it. I realise *that* now.'

'Then help me. There was something strange about that ransom note, but I can't place what.'

'Just concentrate on finding her, Bertram. Please. Whilst we still know she's alive.'

'As easy as that.' Edward sighed in frustration. Seeing Jeremy wasn't to be moved, he turned to go.

'How's Livvy?' Jeremy asked as he went.

'Not exactly fine.'

'I'm worried Sheldon's bad for her. The way he talks about her.'

'I'd rather not know.'

'Clara's always loathed him. It's only recently I've understood—'

'I don't want to hear it,' said Edward, cutting him off. He'd had his fill of them all for one day.

Jeremy shook his head. 'Clara was so worried for Livvy whilst we were in Constantinople. She kept writing; most of the letters she tore up. She used up reams of paper. I saw her at it, day after day. I didn't know what she was struggling to get out. But she felt responsible, I think, for him going after her. Now I do. I could help Livvy. I need to work out how. Clara would have wanted that.'

'Don't talk about her in the past tense,' said Edward shortly. 'And

173

Clara needs you to help her.' He raised his fingers to his mouth, whistled for the boy to bring his horse. 'When you decide you're ready to tell me whatever it is you're hiding, you know where to find me.'

THE EIGHTH DAY

Chapter Sixteen

The morning that marked the week since Clara had been taken dawned bright and hot, and much against Olivia's will. It seemed stubborn, unfeeling of the seventh night to have rolled into the eighth morning. If Olivia could have, she would have stopped the sun before it rose, kept it beneath the horizon until they found Clara. *She hasn't been gone a week.* She had been holding on to that.

Ada came to help her dress. As she laced her corset, she muttered that Olivia was looking ever so peaky. Olivia said she was fine, could Ada please do her corset up properly, her gown wouldn't close with it like that.

'I'm not pullin' it any tighter,' said Ada. Then, with a pained sigh, 'I can't do it to you, Mrs Sheldon.'

Olivia looked at her in surprise. They never *talked* about it, her and Ada.

'Here,' said Alistair, his voice startling Olivia from the doorway, 'allow me.'

He crossed the room and pushed Ada aside. Ada, so short she barely reached Alistair's broad chest, raised her chin and gave him *A Look* (tense cheeks, hard eyes) that made Olivia think she mightn't like him very much after all.

She was still trying to make it out when Alistair tugged on her corset, hard, then quickly again. She nearly choked on the splintering in her skin, the blunt agony of her burns weeping. Tug. TUG. She clutched the bedpost, her eyes nearly bursting with the effort of containing her tears. Tug. She shook her head, biting her lip. Ada said she'd do it, she wanted to do it, it was her job. Alistair replied that she should watch, learn.

'Imogen Carter's sent word she'll call later,' he said with another tug. 'She says she has something she wants to discuss. Whatever that can be.'

'You read her message?'

'Of course. You can tell me about her call later. Mildred's coming too. I've invited her for morning tea. There,' he said, standing back, appraising Olivia's hourglass form. He ran his hand around her, inhaled. Ada, who was blushing fuchsia, averted her eyes. 'Perfect,' Alistair said.

Olivia took several long breaths. Slowly, she drew back from the bedpost. She didn't put her hand to her waist, she refused to give him the satisfaction of seeing her pain. She swallowed it. 'Why did you invite Mildred?' she asked, voice tight with control.

'I'm tired of you holding this grudge. How's it meant to make *me* feel?' He cocked his head, pomaded hair staying precisely in position. 'A suspicious man might think you haven't learnt to be happy. Even with everything you have.'

Learn to be happy. It's what Mildred had advised Olivia to do that January morning she'd visited Olivia at Beatrice's aunt's and first told her of the things she would do if Olivia didn't accept the elegant, eminently eligible, Alistair Sheldon's hand. *Why are you resisting so? He's sought you out, young lady, come all this way to find you. Be grateful. I can't think what's wrong with you. So wilful. Just like your mother.*

Alistair had said he was mortified when Olivia told him of Mildred's threats, that he'd never intended any of it. Olivia had tried to believe him. She hadn't hated him then. That had only started when he'd refused to talk Mildred round and insisted on the wedding going ahead. He'd revealed the truth – that it was he, not Mildred, who had come up with the idea of blackmailing Olivia into marriage – on their wedding night. Then he'd flipped her over and made love to her resistant body to *seal the deal*. Olivia had despised herself too, then, for being such a coward as to let Alistair get away with it, and Mildred most of all for cooperating with him with such malicious energy.

'Has it ever occurred to you,' she said to Alistair now, 'that I loathed Mildred even before you came along? She never visited me at school, she kept everyone away. I was a child, no older than Ralph.' Her voice, to her fury, shook. 'She told no one where I lived in London, *you're* the only one she let near me. She's a selfish, mean woman. I have no interest in speaking to her ever again.'

'Get your gown on,' Alistair said. 'She'll be here within the hour.'

He left. Olivia stared after him. Ada helped her dress silently, first loosening her laces even though she hadn't asked her to. Olivia exhaled as the battered, cracked flesh of her torso eased and flexed, and for the second time in years, she wept.

Mildred arrived in the Grays' carriage, dressed in taffeta, batting the air with a new-looking fly swatter, her skin defiantly pale against the angry morning heat. She made no move to embrace Olivia, and Olivia remained silent as Alistair, apparently in no rush to go out that morning, greeted Mildred with a genial smile and showed her through to the drawing room.

Olivia followed them, her muscles tense, taut with hate. She was determined to keep herself under control, not let either Mildred or Alistair have the satisfaction of seeing her break. *Don't look at her, don't speak to her. You can get through this.* Her mouth was dry, bitter. Alistair, looking over his shoulder as he ushered Mildred through to the drawing room door, arched an eyebrow at her. The smirk playing on his lips was unmistakable.

Olivia knew he did it to provoke her, but even so, she couldn't help the rage rising in her. She clenched her teeth, trying to contain it, but as his smirk spread, she feared she might just scream. It was then that she glimpsed Edward, leaning against the far wall of the drawing room, jaw set, arms crossed. *There.* His eyes flickered warmth at her. He gave her a small nod, and a breath of relief shuddered from her. *Not alone, not any more.* For the next half-hour, in spite of all her doubts, she kept her gaze on him: a ballast in the sea of Mildred's outrage over Clara's disappearance, her despair ('She's all I have, you know, the only family I count. What were you thinking, Olivia, leaving it so many hours before you sent for the police? You should have given word the instant you knew Clara was gone, it could have made all the difference. Imbecile gel.'), her dislike of Egypt, the foul smells, the dirty natives, the pungent food ('I'm eating only boiled broth and taking milk of magnesia every night, I hope you do the same.').

Olivia spoke not once. Neither did Edward. Sharing the silence made it so much easier. And with him there, Olivia could almost numb herself to Mildred's grating voice, the venom in her words. Almost.

It was as Mildred was leaving that she turned to Edward. 'You're very quiet today, young man.' She narrowed her eyes. 'Jeremy's told me you're working hard to find Clara. So,' she held out her knobbly hand, 'I'm glad to make your acquaintance. I'm told Clara thought very highly of you.'

Edward looked down at her fingers. He reached into his pocket for his cigarettes. He ran his tongue around his lips, placed a cigarette in his mouth, struck a match, and inhaled.

Mildred opened her mouth as though to speak, but nothing came out. It was the most discomfited Olivia had ever seen her. In other circumstances, it might have made her smile.

Alistair stared. His blood throbbed blue-green beneath skin taut with supressed rage. He said he would show Mildred to her carriage.

As they left, Edward took a final draw on his cigarette and flicked it out of the window. 'Are you all right, Olly?'

'Not really,' she said, since she couldn't lie. 'But thank you, for being here. It meant . . . ' She paused, struggling for the words. 'Well, it meant a lot.'

He shook his head. 'You never need to thank me.'

Olivia shifted on her feet. Edward held her eye. She only realised she was holding her breath when it burst out of her in a short rush.

'Olly,' he began, 'I—'

Alistair returned, cutting him off. 'You were both very rude,' he said, voice dangerously quiet. 'I'd have expected more of you, Bertram. As for you,' he turned to Olivia, 'we'll talk about how you behaved later.'

'I can't think what you have to talk about,' said Edward.

'Stay out of it,' said Alistair.

Edward drew himself up, tall and tough, a sudden hardness in his eyes. Olivia thought he might have had his fill of Alistair telling him what to do.

And Alistair, who stared at Edward, a flush spreading up his neck, clearly saw it too.

Olivia couldn't help but feel a stab of satisfaction when he was the first to turn and sweep from the room.

After the two of them left the house, though, she couldn't settle. She sat down at the piano, played a few chords, then stood again. She tried to read. Her nerves were still jumping when Imogen arrived in a cloud of French scent, just before lunch.

'I finally have news,' she said as she removed her hat and tucked a black tendril into place. 'I'm afraid Clara was definitely having an affair.'

'Wonderful.' Olivia dropped down into one of the drawing-room chairs with a thud.

'I wish she'd said something to me.' Imogen frowned. 'I can't think why she didn't feel able to confide. She must have known I'd be on her side.' She sighed. 'Anyway, I went up to Benjy's yesterday. As I said, I had a hunch someone there might know something.'

'I hope Amélie doesn't know what Clara was up to?' All Amélie ever seemed to do was gossip in her thick French accent. Friend or no, Olivia didn't think Clara's secret would be sacred for long with her.

'She made no mention of it,' said Imogen, 'so let's assume not.'

'Thank God.'

'She's very upset actually. She said she'd like to see you, will you call?'

'Fine,' said Olivia. 'But if Amélie doesn't know, how have you found out about Clara?'

'I had a little chat with Amélie's staff. One of her maids, a girl called Elia, told me how, just over a month ago, the night of my brother's ball, she went out with Amélie's old lady's maid, Nailah. Amélie went to bed early, a migraine, they were at a loose end.'

Olivia vaguely recalled Amélie mentioning her headache the next night, at the Sporting Club's party. Now she was thinking, she remembered Amélie talking about a Nailah too. *She just left, first zing zis morning, not a word as to where.*

'So,' said Imogen, drawing Olivia's attention back, 'Elia and Nailah went to visit Nailah's aunt, at her hut in Montazah. On their way back, they saw Clara heading down to the beach. It was after midnight, we'd have all gone home, but Clara was out, walking into the dunes with a tall, dark man.' Imogen sat back in her chair, raising her eyebrows as though to say, *Now what do you make of that?*

Olivia stared. 'Edward's tall and dark.'

'Yes, my darling, he is. But Elia knows who he is, he's hard to mistake, of course. And although she wasn't sure who Clara's man was, she said it wasn't him.'

'You asked?'

'I asked.'

'She's certain?'

'Almost certain.' Imogen's brow creased. 'She refused to swear her life on it.'

'So who is it?'

'Elia doesn't know. But she thinks Nailah does. Apparently, even though they were far away, Nailah jumped as though she knew who the man with Clara was. Although she claimed after that she did not.'

'Where's Nailah now?'

'That's the question. Apparently her aunt died and she had to leave to look after the children. Elia hasn't a clue where she's gone, and nor does Amélie, which is *ridiculous* since one should always know everything about one's servants. I've asked her to look into it.'

Olivia pinched the arch of her nose. 'What does this all mean?'

'That Clara's affair wasn't with Edward. And given all we're hearing about ransom notes, and how worried everyone is for you, it probably has nothing to do with her being taken. A red snapper . . .'

'Herring.'

'Exactly.' Imogen settled herself in the armchair facing Olivia. 'I still want to know who Clara's man was though, whether it was him that took that letter. *If* anyone took that letter. I'm starting to think Sofia might have jumped to conclusions there, sent us on a wild duck chase.'

'Goose.'

'What?'

'Never mind.'

'Is this an English sponge?' Imogen leant forward, the folds of her peach day dress rustling around her as she peered over the Victoria sandwich, lips pursed. 'May I take some? I'm so hungry at the moment. The worry.'

Olivia nodded. She flicked her fingers against her thumbs as Imogen lifted the fly net and served herself; she felt jumpy, pent up after the past days indoors.

Imogen held up a slice of sponge, jam oozing stickily between its yellow layers. 'I'd like you to eat some too. Please.'

'I think she must really be dead,' said Olivia, without realising she was even thinking it. The words dropped like stones. Imogen sat poised at the edge of her chair, holding out the plate. 'It's been so long.' Olivia's voice cracked. 'I can't even imagine what's been happening to her. How she's been killed. It's too awful.'

Imogen set the plate down on the table, a dull clink of crockery on wood. She walked over, crouched in front of Olivia, and took hold of her forearms, moving her head this way and that until Olivia relented and met her gaze. Up close, she saw how tired Imogen's eyes were. There were bruised pockets beneath her lids. For all her activity, her busy talk, she was exhausted with fear too. It brought no comfort to Olivia.

'I won't let you give in to this despair,' Imogen said. 'I *won't*. It's doing you no good. We need to keep going, find out what's happened. Clara might yet be alive. Perhaps we should go back to her house, see if we can find any more clues.'

'Perhaps,' said Olivia noncommittally. She couldn't face being at the Gray house, not at the moment: Clara's absence felt too real within its walls, and besides, she had by now imagined so many variations of clandestine meetings between Clara and Edward there, that even with this new information, she couldn't think of its winding corridors and nooks without wanting to retch.

'You need to snap out of this stupor,' said Imogen. 'I hate seeing you like this. What about the polo tomorrow afternoon?'

'What polo?'

'The semi-finals, the British Officers' League.'

'They're *playing*?'

'Tom says they can't cancel, he'd call it off if he could. Why don't you come, darling?'

'How can I go to watch polo with my sister almost certainly dead? *Why* would I?'

'Because it's doing you no good staying here. Everyone will be there. Edward, he's the captain of the team, Tom.'

'I'm not going to the polo.'

'Then go and visit Amélie, find out about this Nailah, work out who Clara's man is. Do *something*, darling.'

'I hear you have a polo match tomorrow,' Olivia said to Edward as she passed him on the stairs that night.

His forehead creased. 'I'd forgotten all about that.'

'But you'll play?'

'I don't know if I can get out of it.' He looked up at her, eyes reflecting the light of the candelabra on the window sill. She could smell his familiar scent, that something warm she had never been able to identify. 'I'll still have men hunting though, Olly. No one's giving up.'

The unspoken *Not yet* hovered in the air.

'I'm going to visit Ralph and Gus in the morning,' Olivia said.

'I owe it to Clara. I thought I might take them for a ride, get them out of the house.'

'Where to?'

'Amélie Pasha's asked me to call. We'll go there, they can play with her boys.' Imogen was right, she couldn't just sit at home. And Amélie might well have discovered Nailah's whereabouts by now. Olivia hoped so, she was increasingly desperate to know who Nailah had seen Clara with in the dunes. She felt a morbid curiosity to visit the bay herself. 'We'll go to the beach after,' she said impulsively. She looked at Edward, hard. There was a part of her that still needed to test him. 'It's been a while since I went to Montazah.'

He didn't even flinch. She felt a beat of relief.

'Fine,' he said, 'I'll come with you. The polo's not until three. I did have some business in town in the morning, a man I need to meet, but I'll send Fadil instead.'

She shrugged with forced nonchalance, then made to carry on up to bed. He caught her arm. She turned to face him and nearly doubled over at the intensity in his gaze. She stood motionless, her thoughts alive with the night's looming pain, the complete unbearableness of life as it stood. Edward shook his head, as though he knew at least some of what was running through her mind.

'I miss you, Olly.'

'You've never had me,' she said, reminding them both. 'Not yet.'

THE NINTH DAY

Chapter Seventeen

Nailah's mother was back from touring with her band of singers and dancers. She had come the night before, just as Nailah returned from the harbour with Kafele. Nailah met him there every evening now. She lived for the hours they spent together, her head on his shoulder, watching the fishing boats bob in the shadows of the city's buildings: Alexandria's stone heart. They would talk of a hundred small things, the two of them, just as often saying nothing at all. She had still been light with his kiss, undressing for bed, when her mother's deep show-woman's voice had vibrated through the rickety floorboards, announcing her arrival as though she were stepping on stage. 'My dear heart, my darling love,' Isa had called. 'I am here at last, your umi has arrived.' Nailah had gone running downstairs to hush her before she woke the children or the men in the house. She had made her wait until after breakfast to bring out her gifts, the usual trinkets: cloying scent, cheap rings and bracelets.

'I should have bought this one some herbs,' said Isa, frowning at Babu in Nailah's arms. She held out her hand to his forehead. 'He's feverish.'

'He'll be all right,' said Nailah, even though she was worried herself. After six days of blessed health, he had taken a turn overnight. He was refusing to eat, his skin was clammy with sweat. She knew she should take him back to Socrates, but she was reluctant to go again so soon. She didn't want Captain Bertram to think they were taking advantage. She didn't want to remind him of their existence at all.

She held Babu closer. She felt Isa watching her.

'I saw Jahi last night,' Isa said. 'I caught him as he was leaving that grand house of his. We didn't talk long, he had an errand, although he wouldn't tell me what. But I hear he has plans for you. Plans I don't much like the sound of.'

'Sending me away?'

'What else? What business does he have deciding what's what for you? *My* daughter.' Isa shook her head. 'I told him he was going too far . . .'

'Was he very scared, Umi?'

Isa sighed. For all her posturing, she knew as well as Nailah did that she'd never have the nerve to stand against Jahi, not when it came down to it. Throughout Nailah's childhood, she'd watched her mother tell Jahi to mind his own business, only to fold at a look, a word, then toss her head, go to pack her bags for a tour, leaving Nailah to be scolded for any number of sins: staying out in the street too late, not scrubbing the floors, speaking too freely with the stallholders at the market. (*You must mind your izzat, Nailah, your honour, it's all you have.*)

The only person Nailah had ever seen Jahi bend to was Tabia. He'd always listened to her. It was she who'd convinced him to let Nailah apply for her job at the Pashas'. ('I knew from Isa how you wanted it,' she'd told Nailah, 'so I talked to Jahi. He can be a stubborn man, my brother, but he came around in the end.' She'd hugged Nailah. 'I did it as much for me as you, habibi, for now I have you close by. And,' she smiled sadly, 'I won't have to worry about you alone in the slums any more.') Jahi had often been at Tabia's when Nailah visited, calling in on his breaks from work. His face would soften when Tabia spoke; there were times when he'd even laugh. Nailah closed her eyes, seeing them all together. *Before.*

'He feels responsible for you,' came Isa's voice, pulling Nailah back to the present, 'he always has. For your cousins too. Like a father.'

'A father?' Nailah shook her head. 'What do any of us know of such a thing?'

'He's coming tonight anyway, after he's finished work.' Nailah felt a slither of dread. 'He says he needs to keep an eye on you. Why, Nailah? What's he so worried about?'

'I don't know what Jahi's thinking at all.' Nailah set Babu down on his mat, pulled a bowl of dirty potatoes towards her, and began scrubbing them. Bracing herself, she asked, 'Did he mention if he's decided where to send me?'

'I don't want him to do it.'

Nailah jumped at Cleo's voice. She was staring at them, coiling her hair round and round her finger. Nailah could have pinched herself for speaking so carelessly. Cleo had been so quiet that she had all but forgotten she was there.

'I want us all to stay here,' said Cleo.

'Hush,' said Isa. 'None of you are going anywhere, and nor am I for the time being.'

'You're not?' Nailah was surprised. Isa's visits were usually so fleeting: a day, maybe two. She felt relieved that she was staying longer, although she wasn't sure why. It wasn't as though Isa ever did anything other than sleep and preen when home. Perhaps some part of her still wanted to believe she could depend on her mother. 'How long will you be here?'

Isa shrugged her turquoise-clad shoulders, silver beadwork tingling. 'We'll see.'

Silence filled the room. The scraping of Nailah's knife on the potatoes formed a steady rhythm against Babu's disjointed breaths and the click of Cleo's nails on her teeth.

Cleo got up and walked to the window, standing on tiptoes to peer out. 'Can I go for a walk?' she asked.

'Babu's too ill to be taken out,' said Nailah. 'I don't want you going alone.'

Cleo stuck out her bottom lip. 'Umi always used to let me when we lived at the beach.'

Nailah shook her head, mouth pressed tight, thinking of the police and soldiers who might yet be roaming the neighbourhood.

'Go with her,' said Isa. 'I can watch Babu.'

'I need to finish these potatoes, then there's the sheets, the floors.'

'I don't want you to come with me anyway,' said Cleo in the dangerously shaky voice she got when tears were close by. 'I want to be by myself.'

'We all want to be by ourselves,' Nailah snapped. She nearly reached out to belt Cleo. She stopped herself just in time. She was too tired, that was the problem; it was the late nights with Kafele, this worry over Babu's new bout of sickness, money, the laundry, all the rest of it. Cleo's sulking felt like ingratitude.

'Why does everyone want to be alone?' Isa asked. 'Company is such a pleasure.'

'I just do.' Cleo raised brimming eyes to Nailah.

Nailah threw up her hands, a shred of potato peel fell from her knife, plopped into the bowl, flicking her with earthy water. 'Go then,' she said.

Cleo picked up the small bag she carried everywhere and ran from the room. Her hair flew behind her, her sandals made a tap-a-tap on the stairs. Nailah, remembering the happy way she had used to trot off from Tabia's hut, felt sick with shame at her quick temper.

'Follow her,' said Isa. 'But if you want my advice, don't let her see you.' She frowned uncertainly at the rumpled mattresses, the breakfast things still strewn on the table. 'I'll help with the chores if I can.'

'Just keep an eye on Babu,' said Nailah, then hurried away.

She trailed Cleo's footsteps at some distance, watching her weaving at waist height around the street vendors, the carts of vegetables and livestock, increasingly puzzled as to where she could be going. They turned into a quieter passage, passing a small café where bearded men sat bent over backgammon, glasses of mint tea in hand. A hookah shop was next door, a carpet stall. They turned again, past a house, another house. Nailah let the distance between her and Cleo grow, instinct as well as Isa's advice warning her to allow Cleo privacy for whatever this errand of hers was.

Cleo turned a corner, then another, and abruptly Nailah realised where she was headed. *Oh, little one.*

She came to a halt at the entrance to a stone courtyard, empty of people, of mess, of anything except a trickling fountain. Tabia had used to bring her here as a treat, all the way from their hut up the coast. Nailah had come with them once, just after she'd started at the Pashas'. Tabia had handed Cleo a coin fashioned out of foil, she had whispered that Cleo should throw it in the fountain, just as Tabia had as a child, and wish for whatever she wanted. *The good spirits are listening.*

Nailah watched now as Cleo knelt in front of the fountain, as Tabia had shown her. She reached down into her bag and brought out Tabia's shawl, pressing it to her face. Nailah's throat swelled at her hunched shoulders, the way she held herself so still. After a moment, Cleo set the shawl down on the wall and reached into the bag again. This time it was Tabia's chipped cup that she brought out, one which Nailah had been looking for. Cleo pressed her lips to the rim, her back rising, falling, as though she were breathing deep, drawing Tabia's touch in. She set the cup down with a clink on the wall. The final item she brought from the bag was a tarnished chain. This she placed around her own neck. Then she did nothing. She just knelt, hands clasped together.

She had no coin with her. She threw nothing in the water.

Nailah held her breath, waiting for her to reach into her bag and fetch one.

But she didn't. The minutes passed. Cleo made no wish.

Eventually, she repacked her bag. Not knowing whether she was doing the right or the wrong thing but feeling there was little else she could do, Nailah hid in her corner, waiting for Cleo's padded footsteps to pass, and then trailed her home. She cut through a side street as they neared the house so that she could be there when Cleo arrived.

'You've been so long,' Isa said the instant Nailah opened the door. She had Babu in her arms, her elegant robes were covered with vomit, and her face was wild with anxiety. 'He's been puking and shitting since you left, he's like an iron he's so hot now. You need to take this boy to a doctor. He's sicker than I've ever seen a babe who has a life yet to live. Although,' Isa held up Socrates' bag of half-finished medicine in the hand not grasping Babu, 'tell me, daughter, where did you find the money to pay for care such as this?'

Nailah shook her head impatiently and walked breathlessly into the room. 'Sit down,' she said, 'I want everything to look normal when Cleo gets here.'

'Is she all right?' asked Isa, medicine still raised in her hand.

'Full of grief. I haven't paid her enough attention. She's a child too, just a child. I've let Tabia down.'

'It's too much, you taking all this on.'

'Who's to do it if not me? You?'

'I do my best.'

'You haven't been here. You're never here.'

'I send money.'

'Never enough.'

'Everything I earn, Nailah.'

'But it's not *you*. I've wanted *you*.'

Heat filled Isa's face.

Nailah took a deep breath, steadying herself.

At length, Isa asked, 'What are we going to do about this child? Are you going to take him to this doctor, or am I?'

'Just wait. We'll try and cool him. I'd rather get him better here.'

By noon, though, Babu was refusing to wake and the poky room stank with his streaming faeces and vomit. Cleo, who had spoken little since returning, hugged her knees as Isa and Nailah wrapped Babu in sacking, the only clean cloth they had left.

'Stay with Cleo,' Nailah said to Isa. 'She's scared. Tell her one of your stories. You've always been good at those.'

'How far away is the surgery?'

'Far enough.'

'Is there anyone who could take you? A neighbour?'

'Perhaps,' said Nailah, wondering if Kafele might be close by.

She decided to try the dockside warehouses. Kafele kept rooms there, as did most of his big suppliers; if he was anywhere in the quarter, he was most likely there. She ran straight for the cavernous stone buildings. She felt a rush of warmth on her waist as Babu soiled himself again, but she didn't stop, not until she reached the first alleyway behind the storerooms. Then she froze. Because there on the cobbles, amidst the crates and strewn rubbish, was a soldier in baggy trousers. He had a bald head, sun-withered skin, and bright, alert eyes. Nailah remembered him as the same man she had seen with the captain at Tabia's hut. *Fadil*. He was head to head with another Egyptian in workmen's overalls. There was no one else around. Instinct told Nailah the man in overalls was the informant Kafele had mentioned. Garai.

She edged closer, straining to hear what Garai said. ('I only had it confirmed yesterday, I didn't want to waste your time until I knew.') She shifted her weight, rubbed the stitch in her side. She kept silent, she didn't want Garai or Fadil to see her eavesdropping.

But then, out of nowhere, Sana appeared, carrying a basket, apparently heading for the docks. Nailah cursed, realising she must be taking lunch to her fisherman husband.

Sana called, 'What are you doing here, Miss Hoity-toity?'

Both men turned.

Fadil frowned. 'Nailah?'

'You remember me?' she asked.

'You know her?' said Sana at the same time.

Babu croaked and puked phlegm.

'What's wrong with your cousin?' asked Sana.

Nailah winced. In the same second, Fadil said, 'Cousin?'

Nailah felt herself pale. She managed to say something about going to a doctor.

'I'll take you,' said Fadil. His black horse snorted behind him. It dipped its head, chomped on the metal in its mouth, eyes glinting. Monster's eyes in a monstrously sized head.

Had the horse who'd stomped over Tabia been so full of muscle?

'I'd rather go alone,' Nailah croaked.

Fadil said no, he'd take her and her *cousin* himself.

The man, Garai, stared, obviously bemused. Sana's eyes had become slits through her veil.

'Come,' said Fadil.

Seeing she had no choice, Nailah did what every instinct in her body fought against.

She let Fadil lift her onto his horse.

Chapter Eighteen

Edward was waiting for Olivia when she came into the driveway in her riding habit. He wasn't in uniform, just a white shirt that accentuated his tan, polo trousers and long boots. Neither of them spoke as Alistair came from the house too, then looked them up and down. Under his scrutiny, Olivia instinctively took a step sideways, lengthening the distance between her and Edward. Alistair's eyes twitched. Her stomach turned. *No*, she thought, *surely not. He'll kill me if he's guessed.* She held his gaze, told herself she was imagining it.

'Are you to the office, Sheldon?' Edward's voice was measured.

'Yes,' Alistair said slowly, 'some of us have to work. But I won't be long, I'll call for you at the Pashas'.' He turned for the stables. 'Make sure you wait for me there.'

Olivia waited until he was far enough away not to hear, and, pushing his cold stare from her mind, said, 'Let's not.'

A smile spread across Edward's face.

And for the first time in a week, in spite of everything, Olivia felt her own cheeks lift in response.

She talked, something about having sent word ahead for Jeremy to have the boys ready; she wasn't sure exactly what she said. Edward was looking at her in a way that made her pulse pump. She could concentrate on nothing else.

Alistair trotted past them, back ramrod straight, tails arranged perfectly over his hunter's rear; a distinguished picture that was somewhat undermined when his horse lifted its tail and dropped a train of steaming dung by the garden gate.

Edward laughed. 'Ready?' he asked.

Olivia widened her arms. 'As you see.'

He led the way to the stables. He had his stallion tacked up in less than a minute. Olivia's fumbling fingers took rather longer. She tangled the reins as she pulled them over Bea's ears, then made a mess of buckling up the girth. She dug her elbow into Bea's soft belly, trying to force the metal prong through the eye of the strap. Flushing with the effort, she snatched a look at Edward.

He leant against the doorframe, one leather boot crossed in front of the other, watching. 'Do you need help?'

'I'm almost there.' She blew a loose curl from her forehead and, giving up, slotted the buckle closed on the next hole down. 'There.'

'You'll slip off if you leave it that loose.'

'It won't go any tighter.'

He clicked his tongue, appearing to ruminate. 'You know of course that it will, that it has done many times before?' He was laughing at her.

And for some reason, even though nothing was particularly funny, she laughed back.

He ambled over, looked down at her, and, with frustrating ease, flicked the buckle into place. 'Now your bottom can stay just where it should be.'

'How kind.'

Edward grinned. A light danced in his features, the one which had been so conspicuously absent recently, and she thought, *This place deadens him*, then, *Oh God, do I do that too?*

They led their horses outside. Edward crouched at Olivia's feet, hands cupped, just as he had done so many times before. She placed her heel in his palms, feeling the swift push of his lift, and grasped the saddle as she swung into it, one leg either side, just the way he had taught her. She straightened her habit's skirts, *proper*, waited for Edward to come alongside her, then walked Bea on. Edward matched his stallion's pace to Bea's as they left the driveway. He looked Olivia up and down, assessing her. She dipped her heels, shortened her reins, *feel the bit in the mouth*, and arched an eyebrow at him.

His eyes sparked. 'Good, that's good.'

They stopped whilst he talked to the Bedouin at the gate. Olivia had sent a basket of vegetables out to them the night before, and the mother was shelling the beans, shawl draped loosely over her head, whilst her boys gathered sticks. Edward's tone as he spoke was soft, kind, and theirs in response was friendly. Olivia asked what they were saying, and Edward told her that he had been asking if they were all right. The mother was a widow, he worried about her. 'She won't tell me what brought her here. I'm hoping if I keep talking to her like this, she'll come round.'

'You don't think she's had anything to do with Clara?'

'No, no. But there's something odd about her bringing her boys here. They only lived a few miles away before, in Montazah actually. Why make the move? To the house of a man they detest?' He shook his head. 'I can't work it out.'

Olivia frowned. Put like that, it didn't make much sense to her either.

She waited whilst Edward said something else to the mother. He told Olivia they should go. The boys patted their horses' silky skin, then hooted as Edward kicked off into a canter. When Olivia turned and looked, they were running after them in the sunshine, cropped trousers flapping around skinny calves.

She and Edward broke onto the coast road, Olivia breathed deep on the salt air, basked in the wind on her cheeks, threw her head back and her eyes to the blue heavens. God, but it was good to be outside. Her chest expanded, pressing against the bone bars of her grief, her skin rippled under the speed and the air and the hot, hot sun in the piercing sky. She brought her gaze back down and fixed it on the strength of Edward's back, certain of only one thing: that this day held something within it.

Jeremy was in the bougainvillea-covered porch when they got there, a typically enraged Gus lopsided in his arms, watching as Hassan and El Masri saddled up the carriage horses. Hassan waved at Olivia, El Masri simply nodded. She flicked a look at the front door.

She could almost feel Clara's shadowy form lurking within, just out of sight. *How splendid. What fun.*

Ralph, dressed for the heat in knickerbockers, waistcoat, tie, long socks and starched shirt (poor child), stood beside Hassan, trailing what looked like a lasso on the ground. He came running the moment he glimpsed Olivia and Edward.

'Are you a cowboy now?' asked Edward.

'Can I ride with you, please?' Ralph squinted up, freckled nose wrinkling beneath his straw boater. 'I don't want to go in the carriage like a baby. The Pasha boys will make fun.'

'Tell them they'll have to deal with me if they do,' said Jeremy, joining them. He shifted Gus's position so that he was facing outward, plump legs stretched taut as he wailed, and gave Olivia and Edward a strained smile. 'It's good of you to come like this,' he said. 'Thank you. Ralph's been excited.'

Edward dropped down to the ground. He took Ralph under the arms and hoisted him up into the saddle. 'We need to see about some lessons for you,' he said.

'Wilkins is coming to call,' said Jeremy, 'he wants to talk about progress.'

Edward gave a short, humourless laugh.

'He's asked for Sheldon to be here,' said Jeremy.

'He's already gone to the office,' said Olivia.

Jeremy nodded, he didn't seem particularly put out. 'Mildred's gone into town too,' he said. 'She left after breakfast, off to pester Wilkins, no doubt. I didn't stop her, or tell her Wilkins was coming here. I didn't say you were either, Livvy. I thought you'd be glad to miss her.'

'You were right,' said Olivia, taken aback by his thoughtfulness. 'Thank you.'

'Don't mention it.' He held out Gus. 'Do you mind taking him in the carriage? He's too young to ride, and Sofia's having the morning off. She's gone to see her family. I'll get someone to take your horse back.'

'Of course.' Olivia dismounted. As she took Gus in her arms, his crying eased and he gave her what might have been a small smile.

'Look at that,' said Jeremy, taking Bea's reins, 'he knows you.'

'Do you think so?' Olivia patted his bottom. She found herself examining his features, needing to check for a resemblance after all. But his skin was creamy olive to Edward's golden tan, his pretty face showed no hint of Edward's definition. His brown eyes were darker, almost black, and his hair was blacker too, no light flecks; not the same, no, not at all.

'Are you all right?' asked Edward.

'Fine,' she said. She turned for the carriage, the one she hadn't ridden in since the day they lost Clara. She tightened her hold on Gus with each passing step.

Jeremy walked with her, leading Bea on. 'Which beach are you off to after the Pashas'?' he asked.

'Montazah,' she replied, and wondered if she imagined the flash of alarm in his eyes. It was gone in the instant.

He said, 'I want to apologise, Livvy. I was shamefully behaved the last time I saw you here, that day after Clara went. Like a common drunkard. I absolutely crossed the line. It won't happen again. I . . .' he sighed, 'well, I let myself down, Clara down, by falling apart like that.'

'Clara said you were being awful, you know,' said Olivia, 'before she disappeared.'

'She was right. I was.'

Olivia looked at him askance. She hadn't expected him to admit it. 'Why did you take her away?'

'I'm not sure it matters any more,' he said. 'Just that I brought her back.' He hooked his free hand beneath her elbow, helping her into the carriage. Her thick riding skirts formed a cushion for Gus. 'Now we need to find her.'

'If we can.'

'We must.'

'You won't consider going to the papers? Giles Morton at *The Times* wrote. He asked if he could talk to me.'

'Best not for now.'

'Why? What is all this secrecy, Jeremy?'

Jeremy gave her a long look. 'If I told you that you don't want to know, would you believe me?'

'Probably. But I'm still going to ask you to tell me.'

'No.' He closed the carriage door, signalled for Hassan to get into his seat. 'That's one thing I can do for you at least.'

Olivia stewed on Jeremy's strange words, his look of panic when she mentioned Montazah, all the way to the Pashas'. She sat facing away from the horses to keep Gus from the glare of the sun; the only thing to distract her from what on earth Jeremy could have meant was El Masri's brooding face bobbing up and down on the rear step.

She narrowed her eyes at him.

He stared blankly back.

'You're not very genial, are you?' she said. 'I don't think you like me very much.'

He made no reply.

'You can tell me, and be honest. Please. I can't stand any more lies.'

'I don't dislike you, Ma'am Sheldon.'

'Yes you do.'

'I dislike your situation. That's an entirely different thing.'

'Because I'm British?'

He tilted his head sideways.

She frowned. 'Is that a yes or a no?'

Another one of those head tilts.

'Did you fight against the British, back in '82?'

'I'm employed by a British man, Ma'am Sheldon.'

'That's not answering my question.'

He breathed in, out. He said nothing.

He was too closed, too controlled. Olivia didn't like it. And she didn't trust the way he'd been looking at her ever since Clara had been taken. Had he had something to do with it? He'd been right there in the square, after all – he'd even stayed behind to wait for Clara after Olivia returned to Ramleh with Hassan. Olivia was sorely tempted to question him now, ask him outright if he was involved. She bit her tongue. What use would it be? He was hardly likely to admit it, for goodness' sake.

But oh, to have been a lizard on the wall when the police had interviewed *him*.

Benjamin greeted them alongside Amélie when they arrived at the Pashas'. He was as handsome as Imogen was beautiful, with the same coffee-coloured skin and slanting eyes; but there was an aloofness in his expression that Olivia had never seen on Imogen's face. He nodded stiffly at Olivia as she descended from the carriage, and although he was polite enough as he asked after her health, the children's too, his eyes were distant, detached. He made no mention of Clara. Olivia supposed he didn't know what to say.

Amélie had tea ready on the terrace and (seeming to know just what to say) did most of the talking, barely pausing for breath as she bemoaned Clara's fate, her disbelief that no one had found anything out yet, alternating between French and English the greater her anguish grew. 'Benjy, 'e is so worried too.'

'Is he?' Olivia looked dubiously over at the lawn where he was standing stiffly beside Edward, just next to his sugar-drinking roses, watching as his sons played tennis with Ralph. He and Edward appeared to be speaking not at all. 'He doesn't seem especially so.'

'Ah, he is,' said Amélie. 'Poor Clara.'

As she talked on, Olivia rocked a sleeping Gus in the Pashas' old cradle and tried to work out how to raise the subject of Nailah. Whilst she waited for an opportunity, she watched Edward. He held Ralph's hand on the racquet, guided his other with the ball. The Pasha boys ribbed Ralph, claiming he'd miss. Benjamin snapped at them to be quiet. Edward said something in Ralph's ear. Ralph's shoulders rose and fell. He threw the ball high, lifted his racquet, Olivia held her breath. String thwacked rubber, the ball sliced through the air. A smile of triumph warmed Ralph's chubby face, and Olivia wondered how Clara might feel if she could only see her little man now.

She ran her hand over her eyes, fighting the sudden waft of grief, and, with new impatience, interrupted whatever Amélie was saying to ask about Nailah.

'Ah, *oui*.' Amélie stirred lemon absently into her tea, her tone subdued. Now Olivia was looking, Amélie's entire person was. There was a greyness to her normally rosy complexion; her brown hair had a look of grease about it. Imogen was right, she was obviously badly upset. But then, she and Clara had been close; Clara was always calling on Amélie after visiting Olivia, chatting to her at parties and so on. Their tightness had been all the more notable for how few friends Clara kept. Even Imogen had said how she'd pushed her away. And as for Jeremy . . . well, of course there'd been something there once.

'I was so young when we met,' Clara had said one night, more than a few glasses of Chablis into a dinner. 'It was one of the first balls of the season. An older woman introduced me to Alistair and Jeremy, she told me about their cotton business, how rich they both were. Eligible, you know. But all I could see was how handsome Jeremy was. I didn't care about the money, I really didn't. And the way he talked to me, listened.' She had smiled wistfully. 'I used to be so happy when he called at Grandmama's to see me. And so fed up if Alistair came instead. Alistair tried to tell Jeremy to give me up, that if he was a true friend he would . . . ' She frowned, sucked in a breath. 'Sorry, Livvy. I won't go on about that.'

'It's all right,' Olivia had said. 'I really don't mind.'

Clara sighed. 'Anyway, it was like a dream, being with Jeremy. And moving here, to Alex . . . I thought I could find a home again.' She widened her eyes sorrowfully. 'But you weren't here, Livvy, our parents weren't. It wasn't the same. I don't know what happened to Jeremy and me after that, how we lost it all. Horribly careless, really.'

'I'm told Nailah might have gone to ze city,' said Amélie, drawing Olivia's attention back. 'No one knows ze address, although I expect eet would be somewhere in ze Turkish Quarter . . . 'er aunt was killed and she had to take care of ze enfants. An 'orrible business, a peasant's 'orse . . . 'ave you 'eard?'

'No.' Olivia looked around her. It was clear Amélie's uncertain rambling was going nowhere. A maid dusting in the drawing room beyond caught her attention. Could she be the Elia whom Imogen had spoken with?

'I 'adn't either until I enquired downstairs.' Amélie paused, sighed. 'Eet's bad of me, I should have pressed Nailah to tell me what was wrong when she left, offered to 'elp. She was such a sweet girl, a local of course,' Amélie held up the flats of her hands on the caveat, 'but good. I 'ope she's coping.'

'Yes,' said Olivia absently. She was finding it rather difficult to care about the misfortune of a girl she had never met. 'Would you mind watching Gus if I just run inside?'

'Non,' Amélie picked at a thread on her gown, 'make yourself at 'ome. Your sister loved eet 'ere, you know. Clara, ah Clara . . .'

Olivia smiled tightly. 'I won't be long.'

The maid in the drawing room wasn't Elia, but, doubtless broken by Imogen's inquisition, offered to take Olivia straight to her. She was upstairs, making the boys' twin beds. Olivia, not inclined to beat around the bush, asked her quite baldly if she was sure it wasn't Edward she'd seen with Clara.

'I am sure,' Elia said in a plain-speaking way Olivia liked and instinctively trusted. 'The captain, he is taller, and he has that way about him.'

'That way?'

Elia flushed. 'The man with your sister was different, ma'am. His clothes, they weren't fine, and his skin, it was dark.' She rubbed her exposed forearm. 'My kind of dark.'

Olivia leant against the doorframe. *Not him, for certain. Thank God.*

'Nailah's face when she saw them,' Elia shook her head, 'she was so shocked. And now she's vanished herself, like a puff of air. Although someone must know where she is, it can't be so hard to discover.'

'I don't know,' said Olivia, more to herself than Elia. 'Finding a lone woman in this city seems just about the hardest thing to do.' With that, she thanked Elia and left.

Back in the garden, she told Edward she wanted to get to the beach. Alistair hadn't yet arrived, if they were lucky, they'd be away before he came. She knew he'd be angry with her for not waiting, but she couldn't have him there; she needed to be where Clara had trodden without him crowding her.

She patted Gus absently as the carriage drove away, her mind a mass of questions, the loudest being: Who was this man of Clara's? Was he even important, or simply the 'red snapper' Imogen suggested?

By the time the horses drew up beside the sun-baked foliage fringing the slope down to the bay, Olivia's head was turning somersaults, cartwheels, of Clara. She barely saw where she was stepping as she set off behind Edward and Ralph, feet unsteady on the undulating sand. She thought, *Is this the same path Clara walked?*

'Be careful,' said Hassan as she nearly stepped headlong into a ditch; there was a sapling palm beside it, she made to reach out for it to steady herself, but Hassan caught her arm first. She thanked him. He gave her a sad kind of half-smile.

He accompanied her down to the shore. Wild pigeons stared out from the foliage around them, Olivia looked over her shoulder at El Masil waiting with the carriage, and remarked that he didn't look too happy at being left behind.

'He has little enough to be happy about, Ma'am Sheldon.'

'Does he have any family?' Olivia asked, curious suddenly to know more about him. 'A wife?'

'No, just sisters. Or one sister, actually,' he frowned, 'and her child. Neither of us have wives, Ma'am Sheldon. The cost ...' Hassan tailed off.

Olivia coloured, painfully conscious of her leather gloves and tailored riding robes.

Hassan, staring at his sandals, appeared not to notice her discomfort. He said, 'I had been planning to marry, saving.' He paused. Then, in a low voice, speaking more to himself, Olivia felt, than her, said, 'Such plans I have had.'

Olivia waited for him to tell her more. But he remained silent. Not wanting to pry, she didn't push him.

She invited him to sit with her on the beach, though, choosing a spot close to the shore. It was high tide, the waves rolled just shy of them. Hassan perched on his haunches, flicking a string of worry beads. Gus, propped between Olivia's skirts, ate sand, for once content. Ralph and Edward climbed on the rocks and skimmed stones into the sea. Every now and then, Edward caught Olivia's eye.

She looked sideways at Hassan. His dark face was contemplative. His beads caught the sun. Some of them had Arabic characters inscribed on them. Olivia had been learning the alphabet, and she studied them, trying to make them out. It appeared to be an endearment . . .

Hassan noticed her looking. He gathered them into his hand.

'A gift?' she asked.

'Yes,' he said, in such a heavy way, Olivia thought perhaps they'd come from the woman he'd been saving to marry.

The sun dipped behind a scudding cloud. Olivia pulled Gus's hand from his mouth. He dipped his fingers straight into the sand. 'Hassan,' she said, 'can I ask you about El Masri? I don't trust him, you see.'

'No?' A muscle twitched in Hassan's cheek.

'Was he really with you all the time you were waiting for me and Clara that day?'

'Most of it. He went to fetch water for the horses, then to buy tea.'

'Tea?'

'An errand for cook. He wasn't gone long.'

'Do the police know?'

'Yes.'

There was a short silence.

'Was my sister . . . close . . . to El Masri?' Olivia asked.

Hassan turned, frowning as though trying to make out her meaning. She raised her eyebrows. His puddle-like eyes widened, fit to burst. 'He's a *footman*, Ma'am Sheldon. Why do you even ask such a thing?'

A movement of Edward's caught Olivia's eye, preventing her from answering. He was looking over at the distant sandbanks, squinting.

She turned, resigned to seeing Alistair there. She could have been knocked over with a feather when she saw Fadil with him. 'What d'you suppose . . . ?'

She set Gus down on his tummy and stood as Edward climbed down from the rocks and jogged in Fadil and Alistair's direction. There was a loud plop in the sea.

'Don't use such large stones, little sir,' Hassan called. 'Come closer in.'

'It was a good one,' Ralph said. 'I'm going to find another, see how far I can throw it.'

Olivia watched Edward and Fadil talking. Edward looked over, expression widening in alarm, and shouted something. His words were obscured by the wind. Gus grunted, trying to turn himself. A gust lifted Olivia's skirt around her. Edward broke into a run towards her. A wave crashed, much louder than the others.

When Olivia turned, she could see no sign of Ralph. She too ran now, picking up her petticoats, and waded towards the rocks he'd been standing on. She gasped as the cold water swirled around her, pulling at her legs. She took a deep breath and plunged under, salt stinging her eyes as she scanned the murky water. Shorts, socks in sandals, perhaps ten yards away. Olivia came up for air, but couldn't see Ralph's head on the surface. She launched herself forward; the lesions on her ribs burned, her dress and stays dragged on her body. She submerged herself again, straining to see. A pain like a red hot poker lashed through her silk stocking. A jellyfish, Ada had warned her endlessly about them. She gasped, choking on the salt water, disoriented, and was dragged down and forward out of her depth.

It was an effort to break the surface again. She had no footing, and her clothes were like dead weights. 'Ralph!' she screamed. She went under again, and more from instinct than sight reached forward. Something solid came between her arms, still kicking. Thank God.

Ralph choked as she propelled them both to the surface, snorting and staring blindly in panic. 'I have you,' she said, even as Ralph pelted her in the stomach with his foot. They went under again, and the water rushed into her nose, her eyes. Her arms shook around Ralph's thrashing form. Her leg was agony, she didn't want to kick it any more. She did, though, and breathed air again. 'I have you,' she said, 'stop kicking, stop struggling.'

Finally Ralph's eyes locked on her salt-stung ones. His pale face was drenched and blurred before her. It took a moment, but the fear in his stare eased, and he relaxed in her arms. Trust. So easy.

The swell knocked around them. They went under. Then Fadil was there, olive face taut with purpose. He took Ralph's weight and dragged him up and away, cradling him close, like a baby. 'Come, little sayed.' He said it with such tenderness, it reminded Olivia he'd been a father once, before those rebels gave his children their blazing grave.

Edward's arms came around her, he pressed her to his chest. She felt his battering heart through his wet shirt. 'I have you,' he said, unknowingly echoing her own words to Ralph, 'I have you.'

He scooped her up, just like Fadil had Ralph.

'Why has Fadil come?' she managed to stutter.

'He needs to tell me something. I don't know what it is yet.'

'But why did he come with Alistair?'

'He didn't.' Edward sounded aggrieved, his breath came deep and rapid as he waded to the shore. 'They just arrived at the same time.'

Olivia was about to ask more, but then she caught sight of Alistair, dry as a bone, his arms folded as he stared at her cocooned in Edward's hold. He hadn't come to help her. He hadn't even tried.

And this time there was no doubting the suspicion in his gaze.

It turned her cold.

Chapter Nineteen

As they clambered back onto the beach, Alistair barked orders, insisting that someone, anyone, pick up that screaming, godforsaken baby, everyone else back to the horses, into the carriage. There'd been enough fun for one morning.

Olivia rode with a shivering Ralph as well as Gus pressed to her. And although Edward stayed close, so near she could easily have talked with him, Alistair was there too, so she remained silent. Alistair ordered Hassan to take the carriage to their house first, everyone else could go to the Graws' without them.

They pulled up. Olivia's stomach turned liquid at the narrow-eyed look Alistair gave her. Her heels stuck to the carriage steps as she climbed down, her whole body pulled back.

Edward dismounted and took her trembling arm. His damp hair was ruffled, his shirt and trousers sodden. He told her he'd be home as soon as he could, he had things he needed to see to for now, then the bloody polo. 'You can stop shaking,' he said, 'it's over. You're safe.'

'Safe?' she said with a glance at Alistair, heading down the driveway.

Edward frowned in confusion.

She shook her head and managed a wobbly smile. 'I'll see you later,' she said.

'Olly,' he called after her.

She didn't turn back, much as she wanted to. Alistair had reached the porch, she was caught in his frigid stare. He tethered his horse, ushered her in. Her mouth ran dry. She barely saw Alistair's manservant hovering inside, Alistair's case in one hand, a message in the other. It was only when Alistair began reading the note, frowned, looked at her, back at the paper, and then at her again, that she caught her breath with hope.

'I need to go away,' Alistair said. 'Something urgent has come up at,' he paused, then said, 'one of our mills.' He shot his manservant a look. The man gave a small nod.

Olivia didn't know why Alistair bothered with the lie. She didn't give a damn whether he was going to a mill or to hell. Only that he was going.

He told her that he had to catch the express to Cairo. She was to stay at home whilst he was away, he'd be asking Ada for a full report. He'd be gone a couple of days at least.

Her bones shuddered with relief.

And although Alistair's parting words – that he'd look forward to seeing her soon – felt horribly ominous, 'soon' was at least a night or two without pain.

She took her time in the bath. Her muscles eased as she slowly acclimatised to the barely believable respite of Alistair's absence. He was gone, not here. Gone. She imagined him on the train, speeding away from her, one pristinely creased trouser leg crossed over the other, a perfect gentleman in all but soul. She pictured the others too: Ralph back in his nursery, chubby and calm in the starched cushion of Sofia's hold; Sofia tsking as she rocked him back and forth, ruffling his tawny hair with one hand, holding a cigarette in the other; Gus, exhausted and napping in his crib, round (quite possibly sun-scorched) cheeks smooth beneath his curls.

She felt Edward's hold, his strong arms around her, heard his heart. *I have you.*

She decided she would go to the polo after all. She couldn't quite admit to herself why she dressed with such care, choosing her finest stockings, her favourite gown: a cap-sleeved, full-skirted frock that had a dipping bodice and pearl-buttoned back.

Whilst Ada pinned her hair, she fingered a silver butterfly comb of her mama's that Clara had given her. She sighed at its intricate beauty, and then for the first time slid it slowly, reverentially into her waves. She caught her reflection, and from somewhere in the depths of her mind, an image spun. It nearly choked her, so vividly and so rapidly did it surface.

She saw her. For the first time in fifteen years, she was there. Her mama.

Her *mama*.

It was as though she had never been gone. She was sitting at a dressing table, just like the one Olivia was at now, in a lace crinoline. *Mama*. She was laughing, eyes playful in the looking-glass. *You'd like to come tonight, my little Livvy? What fun that would be.* Her voice, the love, it came like a mist.

There was someone else there too, just beyond the shadows. Olivia thought it might be Clara. She closed her eyes, desperate to see. But the figure remained coy, hiding. All she could grasp was her mama. She reached her fingers out, as though it were possible to touch her face, trace the echo of her smile. She felt the chambers of her heart fill with the same strange heat of belonging she had experienced when Imogen had held her in her driveway the other morning.

And this time, even when she opened her eyes, none of it went away.

Fadil returned in time to take her to the Sporting Club. As he drove the carriage, she questioned him on what had brought him to the beach. He told her she should ask the sayed, it wasn't his place to say. His dark eyes were apologetic. Olivia felt his sympathy, his regret.

The polo was in full, thundering swing when they arrived. Imogen was on the pavilion, in the self-same spot Olivia had caught Edward and Clara talking, all those weeks ago. Olivia tried not to dwell on it as she filled Imogen in on all that had passed at Montazah. And she kept what she had seen of her mama to herself, just for now. She still felt dizzy, light with wonder, to have remembered; she was greedy for more to come back, to know her mama better, see her papa . . . Clara. She was hovering on the edge of a dome, and the filmy barriers keeping her out were wavering, fit to fall. As she stood beside Imogen on the terrace, watching the horses gallop, she played the memory of her mama laughing in the looking-glass again, and again. She *held* it. It was as though a part of her had been slotted into place; one gap fewer in the puzzle of her missing pieces.

The crowd on the terrace clapped at a goal. Edward and Tom were both on the pitch, whacking up the score in the late afternoon sunshine. As Olivia watched them, her damp curls rose and fell on her neck, running to frizz in the humidity. A brooding wind had blown up, hot with sand. It streaked through air abuzz with chatter and the clink of glasses, and brushed the animated faces of Alexandria's high society: red-faced men in top hats, ladies in bonnets, whispering behind frantically batting fans.

Olivia leant against the railing; gingerly, she shifted on her stung leg. Ada had poured vinegar on it (literal as opposed to the figurative kind), it seemed to be getting better. She raised her gloved hands to her brow like pseudo-binoculars, and followed Edward as he propelled the ball forward with a knock and pulled his horse around. He didn't know Alistair had gone away, not yet. Olivia hadn't spoken to him. She'd barely let herself think about what the coming hours might hold. But she felt a shiver of nervous anticipation, just thinking about them.

'They're winning,' said Imogen beside her. Her hair, in contrast to Olivia's fly-away waves, was as glossy as jet beneath her cream hat. 'It will be over soon, we can talk to Tom and Edward, find out what Fadil wanted.'

There was guffawing from a table at the periphery of the crowd. Olivia recognised the men there as policemen, all British, part of Wilkins' staff. They wore stiff-collared shirts and tightly buttoned jackets that had the cut and sheen of budget tailors. They lounged with an awkward forced ease. They often came to the club, admitted but never really belonging, which must have got under their skin. A bit like how Olivia had used to feel around the relatives of her school friends. Everyone would be nice to her, polite, but there was always that hint of confusion as to what place in the world she occupied.

213

She wanted to go over and tell the police to go home, not to bother. *None of this means a thing, none of it's real.*

'I wonder where Wilkins is,' said Imogen, following her gaze. 'Dining out? Dining in?'

Olivia laughed shortly. 'He was calling on Jeremy earlier,' she said. 'Maybe he's still there.'

'I'll go and ask them,' said Imogen, and, in a flurry of petticoats, a flash of satin slippers, she was off.

The men cowered at her approach, apparently as intimidated by her silk skirts and parasol as they'd surely be in the face of the hardiest criminals. Imogen's stance was imperious as she fired questions at them. Suddenly, her brow creased in confusion. Olivia heard her say, 'I don't understand this at all,' her lilting vowels weighted with a gravitas worthy of Queen Victoria.

Olivia was about to go and ask what was wrong, when Imogen crossed back over to her.

'Apparently Wilkins has gone out of town to investigate a lead,' she said.

Olivia's spine lengthened. 'Has someone seen something?'

'I don't know, *they* didn't seem to. And since Tom hasn't mentioned it, I don't think he knows about it either. You said Alistair's left too. He wouldn't have gone with Wilkins, would he?'

'He told me he was going to a mill.' Olivia thought back to the warning look he'd fired at his manservant. 'I'm not sure if he has though . . .'

'We'll ask Tom. It all feels very odd.'

Tom and Edward came onto the pitch together from the changing rooms, both in uniform, their tunics slung over their shoulders. Olivia followed Imogen out to meet them. As she jogged to keep up, her heels sank in the horse-softened grass.

'I don't know about any lead from Wilkins,' said Tom, once Imogen had finished filling them both in. He frowned. 'It could be the same one we've had.'

'What one's that?' asked Olivia and Imogen at the same time.

Tom didn't answer. He turned to Edward, expression preoccupied. 'I take it Gray mentioned nothing when you dropped the children home earlier?'

'I didn't speak to him,' Edward said, 'he was out.'

Tom breathed deep, trimmed moustache moving up and down. 'Let's go and find him after we've been to the ground. He'll be home by now. He should know whether Sheldon's really gone to that mill, if he'll be honest about it.'

'I think it's time we made him be,' said Edward.

'Indeed.' Tom turned to Imogen. 'We won't be too long, Immy. Can you get the house ready whilst we're gone? We're having some victory drinks.'

'No we're not,' said Imogen. 'How appalling. How can you even suggest it with Clara gone?'

'We can't search for her after nightfall, much as I'd like to.' Tom gave her a pained look. 'I'm the colonel, I owe my men a break, darling. We could all do with some light relief. You too.'

Imogen sighed in irritation, and turned for the pavilion.

Tom grimaced at Edward and Olivia and followed her.

Edward offered Olivia his arm. She took it, fingers resting on his tensed muscles. As they walked, Edward asked her if she was all right, she'd seemed very unsettled when he left her with Alistair earlier.

Olivia told him she was fine, whatever fine meant these days.

Edward frowned.

She swallowed. She said she was glad Alistair was gone. Very glad.

'Good.' Still he frowned. 'That's good.'

'What did Fadil want at the beach earlier?' she asked. 'What's this lead you've got?'

He hesitated, as though deciding whether to give in to her change of subject, then sighed and said, 'Someone's seen something they think might be useful, someone else has lied to us and we don't know why.' He shook his head. 'I'll tell you if it comes to anything, I promise.'

She was about to press him to tell her now when he said, 'Can I ask you to do something for me tonight, a favour?' He stopped walking, and looked down at her. He was so close she could see her reflection in his hazel eyes. 'After I've been to Jeremy's, I'll have to go to the Carters' drinks.' He paused, took a breath. 'Can you come, Olly? And when we're there can we try and forget everything? Put *all* of it aside. Just be?'

She didn't answer straight away. She studied his tanned, handsome face, the tension in his muscles as he waited for her reply. She knew they were both remembering how she'd run from him the other night in the garden. In the silence that followed, she couldn't help but think too of his secret words with Clara, on the terrace just in front of them, and of the doubts which had haunted her all week, gone now, but with bruises in their wake.

He said nothing. He didn't rush her for an answer. He'd understand if she said no. He wouldn't resist. He couldn't hurt her. Not him.

'Just being,' she said. 'I'd like that, I think.'

He tilted his head to one side, and smiled; a lingering tilt of his lips akin to a caress.

She felt her heart; a trip, a jump beneath the battered casing of her ribs. The night opened up before her and for once the darkness didn't fill her with dread. For the first time in a very long time she wasn't scared of it.

Quite the opposite, in fact.

Chapter Twenty

Edward saw the light come into her face. She didn't realise, but her fingers tightened on his arm. He felt the weight of her lean deeper onto him, and he wanted to say, *Keep doing that. Do that for ever.* With those five simple words, she'd made him happier than he could ever remember being.

'I'd like that, I think.'

He felt charged with possibility, his blood pumped with it. She did that to him. No one had before. No coquettish smile at a Cairo soirée, no touch to his shoulder, nor artfully arched brow, had even come close. Flawed, meaningless flirtations, they had been nothing but a waiting game.

He looked down at the cautious happiness in her features; it made her at once more beautiful and more vulnerable than she could know. He wanted to stay by her side, never let her go. Every instinct compelled him to do it, tell Tom to go on alone to the parade ground, the Grays', keep Olly close whilst he had her there to keep safe. He wasn't sure how far the night would take them, he only knew that after the past week's strange silence, she had come back to him. He had seen it in her smile that morning, the way she had rested her head against him when he carried her from the sea.

God, but the way she had turned so rigid when she saw Alistair staring from the shore.

The foreboding in her shoulders as she followed the bastard into the house.

It had disturbed him, how afraid she'd looked. It had turned him sick to the stomach. If it hadn't been for all Fadil had discovered, the children waiting under the care of Hassan and El Masri in the carriage, he'd have gone after her. For the first time it had occurred to him that Alistair might be guilty of more than just coldness. He could barely acknowledge the thought. Surely Olly would have said if he was actually ... No, Alistair couldn't be. Olly would have told him. She *would* have.

Wouldn't she?

The question, the day, the way she was looking at him now ... Edward's doubts over whether he should ask her to leave, go with him when he left for India, disappeared. This night was his chance, a God-given unexpected gift, to set things between them to rights. He told himself, *Don't waste it. Do not mess this up.*

'You're thinking,' Olly said, 'it makes you forget to talk.'

He smiled. 'Said the Duchess to Alice?'

'You've read it?'

'Hundreds of times, when I was home on leave last year. It's one of my niece's favourites.'

'I'd like to meet her.'

'I'd like you to, too.'

She smiled. She flicked a look at the pavilion. Tom was standing there, waiting. 'You'd better go,' she said.

Edward sighed, acknowledging it. 'I'll be as quick as I can.'

Her smile dropped. 'Make Jeremy talk,' she said. 'He's hiding something, I'm certain.'

Fadil had Edward and Tom's horses ready in the stables. He had told Edward on the way back from the beach what their informant, Garai, had said in the Turkish Quarter: that it was an Egyptian man who'd abducted Clara. It was why Edward had taken Hassan and El Masri to the ground for questioning, as soon as they'd dropped Ralph and Gus home. He didn't care that both men had alibis – Hassan because he'd never left the square, El Masri because he had a docket for the shopping he'd done in the short time he was absent – he had a hunch one of them was hiding something. Wilkins had interviewed them before; that arsehole couldn't interrogate a gnat.

He'd left one of his lieutenants, Stevens, an ambitious young subaltern with a strong nerve and a bad polo swing, in charge of the questioning all afternoon. Now Edward was on his way back to him, he was impatient to discover what Stevens had found out. He climbed into his saddle, told Fadil he'd see him later. He didn't need to ask him to watch over Olly, Fadil already knew to do that. Instead, he thanked him for all his work that day.

'Yes, you've done a good job,' said Tom, who was up to speed with all Fadil had discovered, Nailah eavesdropping in the alley-way included. Tom was as disturbed as Edward by Nailah's strange fear at being revealed as the sick child, Babu's, cousin, and not the minder she'd claimed to be when Edward first met her in Montazah, well over a month ago now, on the same May day that Jeremy had received those first threats.

Edward frowned. Why had Nailah lied? What made her so afraid of being associated with Tabia?

And what did the Bedouin at Sheldon's gate have to do with it all? Edward was becoming increasingly sure they were involved on some level, and that they'd left Montazah because of it. His sense that something very bad had happened at that secluded bay was deepening by the hour. He hardly wanted to know what it was, yet he knew he had no choice but to find out.

'Ha,' he said, and kicked his stallion into a canter.

Tom thundered by his side.

Dusk had fallen when they reached the ground. Oil lamps had been lit at the guard posts, within the huts. The horses were blanketed for sleep. Stevens, the man who'd been interrogating Hassan and El Masri all afternoon, jogged out into the dusty forecourt, saluting Edward and Tom as they dismounted. His brow was wet with sweat, his tunic was stained with it. The air was so damned close.

He told Edward he was sorry, but neither Hassan nor El Masri had given anything away.

Edward cursed. He'd been banking on something, anything. He'd been sure one of them held a key. It wasn't often he was wrong.

'You're certain?' he asked.

'Yes,' said Stevens. 'El Masri's a piece of work, but I don't believe he's a criminal. I must have asked him the same questions twenty times: what he was doing that day, when he did it, what he thinks of Egypt, Britain, Mr Gray, Mrs Gray. Any financial motives he might have for taking her. But there was nothing to cause any alarm. I'm sure he was being honest. He's too bloody rude to be trying to pull the wool over.' Stevens reached up, smacked a mosquito against his ruddy neck. 'As for Hassan, he seems a good man. You'll see that if you talk to him.'

Tom suggested that he and Edward do just that. They went to find Hassan and El Masri in the lantern-lit office they'd been kept in, but discovered nothing different to what Stevens had.

'I'm sorry not to have been more helpful,' said El Masri, his dead-pan face anything but contrite. 'It seems the search is foundering, if I am what it has come to.'

'The search is very much on,' said Tom

El Masri looked him over, Edward too. His eyes moved from their open tunics to their hair, still wet from bathing. 'I hope you enjoyed your sport today,' he said.

In spite of everything, Edward nearly laughed at his gall. Tom lay a calming hand on his shoulder, then said both men could go. He told Edward they better had too, to talk to Jeremy. Time was getting on and they had precious little to waste.

'I have no idea what bloody mill Sheldon thinks he's going to,' said Jeremy. 'I went to the office myself this afternoon. No one's mentioned it to me.'

'What about this lead of Wilkins'?' asked Edward. 'What's all that about?'

'I don't know. Wilkins just said that he's had word from one of his men in the provinces; apparently there's a peasant farmer in a village, Lixori it's called, who might have seen something.'

'What?' asked Edward. 'What have they seen?'

'I don't know, but Wilkins has gone to look into it. He was catching the express to Cairo this afternoon, then getting a guide to take him to Lixori in the morning.'

'And he didn't think to tell us first?' said Tom.

'I sent him to find you.' Jeremy pressed the heel of his hand to his forehead. He went to stand by the study window. 'Why the hell would he have gone to Alistair instead?'

'If he has,' said Tom.

Jeremy frowned. There appeared to be little doubt in his mind.

'We'll go to Lixori,' said Tom, 'speak to this farmer ourselves and find out what he's seen. There's a strange wind tonight, it's too dangerous to travel in the dark, but we'll make good time at sun-up. We can cut across the dunes, try and catch them there.'

'All right,' said Jeremy, then, 'You have to find her. She has to be found.'

'We've been trying,' said Edward.

Jeremy said, 'You've told me she went off with an Egyptian man . . .'

'And what a spectacular lead that is,' said Edward, 'there being so few of them.'

'But you took El Masri,' said Jeremy, 'Hassan.'

'We've let them go,' said Edward irritably.

Tom filled Jeremy in on what had passed at the ground.

When he had finished, Jeremy sighed. He turned to Edward. 'What about your man, then? Fadil?'

'What about him?' asked Edward.

'Well,' said Jeremy, 'he was there in the street that day.'

'Don't,' said Edward, voice low with warning. 'Just don't.'

'I know you think he's a good man—'

'He's a great man,' said Edward, 'but do you know who's not? Do you?'

'I have a rough idea,' said Jeremy, 'and I suspect you're about to confirm it.'

'You're a fucking bastard, Gray. You're hiding things, I know it.'

Jeremy didn't defend himself.

Edward told him of Nailah's presence in the alleyway, her fibs.

Jeremy blanched. 'Where is she now?'

'Fadil left her at the doctor's, the child was sick.'

'You have to find her, get her to tell you why she lied.' Jeremy grew paler as he spoke, obviously badly shocked. 'There might be other relatives Nailah hasn't told you about too. Speak to her, do that even before you go to Lixori.'

'We'll be the judge of what we do and when we do it,' said Edward. 'First you need to start talking. What do you care for Nailah's relations?'

Jeremy made no answer. He turned away, staring sightlessly through the window.

Edward and Tom exchanged a look.

'I'm reminded,' said Tom, taking a step towards Jeremy, 'that we never saw that first letter you received, back at the end of May. The blackmail attempt that had you hightailing off to Constantinople.'

'The letter was real,' said Jeremy.

'Why let Sheldon tear it up?'

Again, Jeremy gave no answer.

'All this fuss,' said Tom, 'about you and Sheldon, and no one else in Alexandria has received so much as a whisper of a threat.'

Still, Jeremy said nothing. His face was rigid with composure. Was that sweat on his forehead? Edward narrowed his eyes, certain that it was, that Jeremy was almost ready to talk.

Tom must have seen it too, because he took another step towards him. 'Then,' he said, 'you tried to keep that ransom note from us. Bertram and I must have tried to see it ten times between us.'

Edward frowned, thinking of the unease he'd experienced back in Wilkins' office, when Wilkins had finally shown it to him. He pictured Wilkins' podgy finger on the crisp typewritten paper. There was something so odd about it . . . It hit him. 'Jesus Christ,' he said. 'Gray, you bloody fool.'

'What's this?' asked Tom.

Edward kept his stare fixed on Jeremy. 'Next time you ask

Wilkins to fake a correspondence,' he said, 'you might tell him to have a care to fold the paper. Make it at least look as if it has been put in an envelope.'

Jeremy closed his eyes. He let go of a deep, shuddering sigh. It might almost have been relief. The tension went out of him; his shoulders dropped, his head did too.

Edward felt a grim stab of satisfaction, seeing it. *At last.* They finally had the bastard.

'Would someone tell me what is going on?' asked Tom.

Edward didn't lift his eyes from Jeremy. 'Gray here is about to,' he said. 'Aren't you, Gray?'

Slowly, as though he had any choice, Jeremy nodded.

'Was there ever even a note?' Edward asked.

'Yes,' Jeremy said, 'there was.'

'But that wasn't it,' said Edward.

'No.'

Tom's eyes widened in disbelief. 'You hid it? Why?'

'There were things,' said Jeremy, 'things we couldn't have getting out.'

Edward clenched his fists. It took every ounce of his self-restraint to stop himself landing one of them in Jeremy's ashen face. '*Fuck.*'

'I've wanted to tell you,' said Jeremy. 'God, how I've wanted to. Sheldon said there was no point. He's threatened to ruin me, leave the boys with nothing . . .'

'Well he's not here now,' said Edward. 'And we are. It's time to tell us what the hell has been going on.'

Chapter Twenty-One

Nailah blinked in the evening light as she came down the steps of the sanatorium. She was so tired that she thought she must be hallucinating when she saw Kafele standing there, jacket unbuttoned, foot tapping in just the way she remembered from the Pashas' garden. But then he ran towards her and the click of his shoes and the musty scent of his day's exertion were real enough.

She asked how he'd known to come. He said that he'd seen her mother in the street with Cleo. 'She told me you'd gone to Socrates, Socrates sent me on here.'

'How long have you been waiting?'

'An hour, maybe two.' He shook his head. 'It doesn't matter how long. I wanted to go in and see you but was afraid of making you feel awkward. How's Babu?'

'Alone.' Nailah frowned. 'I hated leaving him.'

'Why didn't you stay?'

'They wouldn't let me. They say they never do. But there were plenty of other women with plump faces and fine dresses who didn't seem in a rush to leave.'

'Do you want me to speak to the nurses? Ask them to let you back in?'

'No.' Nailah brushed the shoulder of his jacket, faded from the laundry brush. 'It won't work.' She smiled sadly. 'You smell too much like spices.'

'Since when is that a crime?' He frowned, but he didn't press the matter. He knew she was right, it was why he was fighting so hard to climb to somewhere else in the world. 'Will Babu mend?' he asked.

'Yes, Socrates says it's just dysentery, not cholera.' The relief of the pronouncement still fluttered within her, softening the edges of her anxiety; not that greedy sickness then, come to steal Babu with its crevice-burning claws, not yet. 'I'd say God is good,' she shrugged, 'but if He is then why was Tabia taken, and why isn't Babu running around with a head people only stare at for love?'

'Ah, Nailah, you're tired. Let's go home.' Kafele held out his arm. She looked at it, not moving. 'What's wrong?' he asked.

'I'm afraid.'

'Why?'

'Jahi's coming tonight,' she said, naming one of her fears. '*Tonight.*' The thought of it, and all he held over her, had been plaguing her all day, pouncing on her whenever her other terrors allowed room. 'I'm scared of him . . .'

'And this Fadil too?'

She caught her breath. 'How did you . . . ?'

'Sana's been telling the whole neighbourhood about you riding off with a soldier. What did he want with you?'

'Nothing.'

'I don't believe you.' Kafele pulled her hands into his, pressing them between his warm palms. 'I'm worried you've got yourself into some kind of trouble . . .'

'I haven't.' Nailah widened her eyes, entreating him to believe her.

'You swear?'

'I swear.'

'But you've not been yourself . . .'

'Because I'm worried about Jahi.'

'You don't need to be.' Kafele's frown was perplexed. 'You know I'll never let him take you away. I'd never let anyone hurt you.' He stared across at her. 'I would lay my life down for you, Nailah, do you understand that? There's nothing I wouldn't do. You are mine, I am yours, remember?'

She nodded.

'I'll look after you, Nailah, the children too. And if Jahi tries to make you leave, run, get to my house, we'll marry. It'll be sooner than we planned, but we'll manage. You're going nowhere you don't want to. Please believe that.'

She nodded again.

'Say it,' said Kafele, 'say you believe it.'

'I believe it.' She wanted to, at least.

They said very little on the journey home. Occasionally Nailah glanced sideways at Kafele's slender face, the slant of his bones, trying to warm herself with his presence. But she felt cold, so cold.

It was dark by the time they reached the first peeling streets of the Turkish Quarter. The air was ripe with sewage, rotting rubbish, and the scent of the night's cooking: onions and garlic, frying meat. Pans clanged through open windows, chattering voices carried.

'I'll leave you to go on now,' Kafele said.

She gave a wobbly attempt at a smile, then made to leave.

'Nailah,' he called after her.

She stopped.

'I love you,' he said.

Her whole body went still. Even her heart seemed to pause, hold its beat. He'd never told her that before. *I love you*. It echoed within her, and the stench, the filth, it all disappeared.

Slowly, she turned to face him.

He stared back at her.

'I,' she began, 'I . . . ' She couldn't seem to speak. She took a breath, tried again. 'I love you too, Kafele. I always have.'

His eyes shone.

Neither of them spoke for a moment after that.

Kafele took a step forward, touched her lightly on the arm. 'I'm glad we've said that.'

She lowered her gaze to his fingers, feeling her skin burn. 'So am I.'

'Remember,' he stooped, searching her eyes out once more, 'you'll always be safe whilst I'm here.'

Nailah didn't disagree. Not this time. She didn't want to. It was so much nicer to believe in the fiction.

'You'd better go,' he said softly.

Nailah nodded, and knowing if she didn't move now, she never would, she turned again and walked away, her feet carrying her back into the world she would run from, with him, if she only could.

Lost in thought as she was, her head dizzy with what had just passed, she didn't see Isa's muslin-clad form in front of her until she was almost upon her. Isa folded her arms, bangles clinking, her eyes glistened beneath the arches of her kohled brows. Nailah's heart, trying so hard to be happy a moment ago, leapt with nerves at the grave expression on her face.

Isa asked after Babu. Nailah answered that he was safe in hospital.

'Good,' said Isa. She tilted her head to one side. 'Jahi's waiting, he's as mad as I've ever seen him. He arrived just before two British officers came knocking, a captain and his colonel, Jahi said. He paid one of the boarders to tell them we were out and would be gone for the rest of the night, then made us hide in the dark until the officers had left.'

'How did they find our address?'

'Why have they come at all?'

'I don't know,' Nailah said.

Isa frowned. 'Jahi wanted to come and find you himself. Lucky for you I convinced him to send me instead.' Isa craned her neck, peering in the direction of where Nailah had left Kafele. 'We'd better go. Jahi's not in the mood to be kept waiting.'

'Welcome home,' said Jahi as Nailah and Isa returned. His long, muscular legs were crossed in front of him, he held his fingers in a pyramid beneath his nose. Cleo sat in the far corner, her hair a curtain over her face. A single candle burned in a saucer, all they could afford. Jahi rubbed his thumbs back and forth along the bristles of his cropped beard, the scraping a morbid accompaniment to the crackle of the flame.

'Babu's well, I trust,' he said, 'under the care of his grand doctor?

227

I'm curious, Nailah. Where did you hear of Socrates' skills? I'm sure you told me the other day, that you wouldn't have hidden it . . . ' He smiled tightly. 'Yet it seems to have slipped my mind.'

Knowing Jahi's skill for smelling a lie, Nailah didn't attempt one. 'I didn't tell you,' she said.

'Did a lady recommend him to you?'

'No.'

'A man then.' He nodded slowly, as though piecing it all together in his mind. 'Was it the kind Fadil who took you on his horse earlier?'

'Sana told . . . ?'

'Or Captain Bertram perhaps?'

Nailah swallowed.

'Nailah, was it him?'

'Yes.' The word croaked from her.

Jahi stared at her blackly. He tapped the floor next to him. 'Sit. I want to hear more about your day, these friends of yours.'

Nailah hung back.

'Nailah.' Jahi frowned 'Sit.'

'Brother,' came Isa's warning voice.

Jahi held up his hand. 'I just want to talk to her.' Nailah edged across the room and perched on her haunches next to him. 'Be comfortable,' he said with a sigh. 'Sit properly. This is your home.'

Isa snorted. 'For how much longer?' There was a jangle of ankle chains as she too crossed the room and sat down, squeezing Nailah's hand in hers.

Nailah tried to draw comfort from the pressure, but she knew that when it came to it there was nothing her mother could do to protect her. There was nothing anyone could do, certainly not Kafele, whose assurances in the street turned as fragile as a feather in Nailah's mind. Sitting face to face with Jahi, so close she could all but hear his heart, she was reminded that her future was not hers to control; not any more.

'Jahi,' said Isa, 'answer me. When exactly do you plan to steal my daughter away?'

'I'm not stealing her. I'm trying to take care of her. She clearly can't be trusted . . .'

'Sweet Mother.' Isa shook her head. 'All she did was let some soldiers help her. I'm sure the captain and his colonel were just calling to see if she was all right.'

'You're not sure about anything.'

'So arrogant, my brother, so certain you know what's what—'

'Stop.' Jahi's voice, taut with control, filled the room.

Isa's hand tightened around Nailah's.

Jahi looked down at his knees. He inhaled deeply, as though trying to keep his emotions within. 'I've had a bad day,' he said at last. 'A bad, bad day.' He turned to Nailah. 'Let's go outside, I want to tell you about it.'

'Stay here,' said Isa.

But Jahi was already on his feet, he pulled Nailah with him across the room. Isa called for him to stop, but he waved his hand. 'She'll be back in a minute.'

Isa stared after them helplessly, but she let them go.

The landing was dusty, the air stale with male sweat. As Jahi shut the door on the family's candlelit room, Nailah saw Isa shuffling over, ready to eavesdrop. Jahi must have seen her too, because he beckoned Nailah to follow him into the hallway below.

What did he want with her? What was he going to do?

As Nailah joined him at the bottom of the stairs, he appraised her, biting his lip, crooked tooth glistening in the grey light. Nailah held her breath, waiting.

He told her, voice low, of how he'd ridden into the desert the night before. 'I didn't want to, but I was told I must. Sometimes we have to put our own wishes second. It's a valuable life lesson to learn.'

'I know the lesson, Uncle.'

'Do you?' Another step. 'I'm not sure you do. Anyway, off we went, across the godforsaken dunes, to that spot where the twin palms grow.' Nailah caught her breath. 'And do you know what we found when we got there? I'll tell you, shall I? We found nothing.'

'What do you mean?' It came out as a whisper.

As he told her exactly what he meant, panic sprung in her chest. 'Are you sure?'

'Oh yes,' said Jahi, 'believe me, we checked. It was dawn by the time we got back, and what a day it's been.' Nailah stood mute as he went on, relentlessly. He'd been in trouble, he was angry, he told her how angry, she wanted to scream at him to stop, but she didn't, he didn't. 'And now,' he said, 'this news of you riding around with soldiers, British officers coming to call.' He bent down so their faces were almost touching. His eyes were black in the dim light. Nailah thought, *This is it, this is where he finally strikes me.* 'You have no place with Fadil, with Captain Bertram and his colonel. No business. Not after what's happened with Tabia. Especially not now. Do I really need to tell you that?'

She dropped her head. 'No, Uncle.'

He inhaled, took a step back. She breathed. 'Stay away from them, Nailah, I mean it. They're dangerous men. You try and play in their world and they will chew you up and spit you out, the rest of us with you.'

'Yes, Uncle.'

He gave her one last look, and nodded. 'I have to get back to work. Answer the door to no one.'

Nailah swallowed, held her hand to her chest. It was shaking. She summoned up her courage. 'I don't want to go away, Uncle.'

'You have very little choice.' He opened the door. 'Say goodbye to your mother and Cleo for me. I'll be back again soon.'

Nailah steadied herself against the wall as he left, blood pumping to the rhythm of his footsteps hastening down the street.

It was only much later, after Cleo was asleep and Nailah was lying in her own sack, that Isa rolled over and asked her, 'Are you in any danger, my love?'

'No.'

'I think you're fibbing,' said Isa. 'You've never been very good at it.'

'Umi . . .'

'Is that why Jahi wants to send you away? Is Captain Bertram threatening you, those other men?'

'No, Umi.'

'What do they want with you then? Why would such men bother with my Nailah?'

'I don't know,' said Nailah quietly.

There was a short silence. Nailah knew Isa was taking the measure of her. She was too exhausted to do anything but let her. And it was easier, so much simpler, to close her eyes and say nothing, than to attempt any more lies.

For lies were all she had to give. The truth, always terrifying, had never felt more impossible than now, in the wake of Jahi's visit. And his words about what he'd found, or failed to find, at the oasis where the twin palms grow.

Chapter Twenty-Two

'Are your ears burning, Edward?' Imogen asked as she tripped across the lawn, a glug of gin spilling from her precariously held glass. 'Tom's just been talking about you. He's as drunk as a skunk, he's hitting it very hard.'

'It's been a hard kind of day,' said Edward.

'So Tom's said. Will *you* tell me what happened at Jeremy's?'

'He won't,' said Olivia. She had tried herself to get it out of him. (He, in an eerie echo of Jeremy's words, had said, 'Would you believe me if I told you that you don't want to know?')

Imogen said, 'Tom says you need to question a local girl, that you're off to find her in the morning. I didn't catch her name.'

'No?' said Edward.

'No,' said Imogen. 'He said you were looking for her earlier, it's why you were so late here.'

'Well, I was just telling Olly that I'm going to fetch her a fresh glass of champagne.' His fingers rested lightly on Olivia's shoulder. 'I'll be back in a moment.'

Olivia watched through tilting eyes as he loped through the revelry. There was a burst of music from the piano on the terrace and a handful of couples stood to dance. There were close to a hundred people thronging in the garden, eating platters of couscous and richly scented meat, smoking in the candlelight. Just as earlier, when Olivia had felt Clara's presence in the Grays' driveway, she sensed her again now; a whisper of blonde curls hidden behind the shadows of the Carters' trees. *How splendid. What fun.* Olivia placed her hand

232

to her chest, pressing against the pain. The night felt obscene, it was as though they were all dancing on Clara's increasingly certain grave. She had said as much to Edward when he finally arrived. ('Drink through it,' he'd replied, downing the first of his brandies. 'I intend to.')

'We're going to go too,' said Imogen.

'What?'

'Pay attention, darling. Tomorrow, we're going to follow Edward and Tom, find out who this girl is that they're going to see, what they want with her. We can lurk in the street until they're finished and then get in to see her. I'll be waiting outside your house at seven sharp, just be ready to ride out.'

Olivia shook her dizzy head. 'Is that really necessary?'

'Don't be ridiculous. I'll see you at seven.' Imogen wandered away across the lawn.

Olivia sighed resignedly.

'Come,' said Edward. She jumped, she hadn't heard him return. He slipped a glass into her hand. 'Let's go for a walk.'

The two of them kept several feet apart as they made their way to the bottom of the garden. They picked up speed the further their legs took them, a silent agreement to hasten from view.

They passed through a leafy screen of palms and on towards the sea. Olivia let her arm brush Edward's, she felt his skim hers. Fingers in fingers, a tightness in her stomach. She forgot to breathe.

They sat down. The night was balmy, filled with the scent of ripe citrus and jasmine, the tang of the sea, the dust of the desert. Olivia dropped her head on Edward's shoulder, staring at the rippling water. She hiccupped. He raised her hand to his mouth and kissed it, soft, warm. For a second she thought about Alistair, how his face would look if he saw them now, whether there was a chance he'd ever agree to set her free. And knowing there was no chance, and exactly how his face would look, she pushed him from her mind too, determined to keep him away until he returned and she was forced to think of him again. She didn't want to think. She liked it, the not thinking. The booze-sopped evening had cast an enchantment on her. Imogen's plans for the morrow felt like an irrelevance, a happening that would feature in some other life.

Time swam by. Olivia wasn't sure what she and Edward talked about, only that they did, and that there was no agenda to their words. Just voices, a dip, a rise, a melody of trust.

He asked her to dance.

She gripped his fingers and rose unsteadily, head swimming as he pulled her up. He let go of her hands and ran his fingers around her silken waist. She could feel the pressure of him through her stays, but this time it didn't hurt. Not really. (The alcohol, perhaps.) She dropped against him, breathed in his scent: smoke, brandy, that something else. He held her tighter. He was drunk, she knew, but his arms were sure and his steps steady as he turned her to the lilt of the distant piano.

'I was terrified today, when you went into the water like that.' His words were quiet, murmured, that northern burr stroking her ear. 'You terrify me. Did you know that? No one has ever scared me before.'

'Imogen says we break her heart.' Olivia said, head thrown back, looking up at him. She could feel the warmth of his breath on her face.

'Let's go home,' he said.

She went ahead, climbing the lawn towards the candlelight and music ahead. She waited in the shadows of the drawing room. He came in, he ran his hand around her back as they walked through the house. Their footsteps echoed in the foyer, clicked on the porch steps, crunched on the gravel driveway. He held her in front of him as they rode home, his breath on her neck. She leant back into him, absorbing the strength of him against her. A silent, barely admissible question whispered in her mind: *Are we really going to do this?*

He lifted her down from the saddle in the driveway. They stood, looking at one another, almost unable to believe the other was there. His eyes glinted down at her in the darkness. He ran his hand around her face, drew a deep breath. She placed her own hand over his, turned it and kissed his palm. With a sideways glance, she saw him close his eyes.

He took his stallion into the stables; she watched silently in the doorway as he tethered him. Her body tensed, alive with anticipation. He came back to her, took her hand, and they went inside. He followed her up the stairs, his arms around her, unbuttoning her bodice, easing the straps of her dress down. Her heart was racing. Her fingers, as she opened the door to her bedroom, shook.

She backed into the room, he was half lifting her, his mouth on hers, pushing her onto the bed. He knelt, coaxed her stockings from her legs, around the still smarting jellyfish sting; he dropped his lips onto her thighs, her calves, as he slid them free. 'Olly,' he said, 'my Olly.'

She ran her hands around his neck, and let herself fall back. He leant over her, staring down at her. In that moment, all she knew was that he was there, and she was with him, and there was nowhere else she ever wanted to be. And all she saw, in his bottomless eyes, was a perfect, blissful reflection of everything she felt.

He unlaced her stays. She realised too late. She held his hand. 'No,' she said.

'Why?' he asked.

'Just don't.'

He looked at her askance, then shook his head. His fingers moved quickly, she couldn't deny expertly. She stared at the ceiling, biting her lip as she felt her corset come free.

He went still. 'No.' His eyes widened in horror and pain. 'No. Why haven't you . . . ? Was this why you ran, the other night . . . ? I'll kill him, I'm going to kill him.'

'Please.' She held his face, forced him to meet her eye. 'Just be with me, please.' His eyes flicked back to her body. She followed his stare, then looked away. It was distorted and ripped and not her own, not hers. 'Please,' she said, 'don't think about it.'

'I'm scared to touch you,' he said. 'I feel as though I'll break you.'

'You can't.' She pulled him to her, kissing him. 'Not you.'

His breath shuddered. Slowly, he kissed her back. Their eyelashes touched. His lips moved, kissing her ear, her neck, faster, more intense, as though he understood her need, skimming the salty, sweaty dampness of her collarbone. He ran his hand around her, tracing her skin, barely touching. He moved against her, softly, taking so much time. There was no pain. 'I won't let you live like this, darling Olly,' he said. 'I won't leave you here.'

'Just be with me now,' she said.

He held her afterwards, a cocoon, a tender cocoon. *Safe*. She closed her eyes in the warmth of his arms, the support of his firm shoulder.

'You're my world,' he said. 'You're everything. I can't let anything else happen to you. I don't think I could live.'

'Nothing's going to happen to me,' she said.

He pressed his lips to her head.

THE TENTH DAY

Chapter Twenty-Three

'Wake up, Nailah, come, open your eyes.'

'What? What's happened?' Nailah bolted upright, heart pounding at the wrench from sleep. The room was dark around her, Cleo was snoring, but Isa, crouched beside her, was already up and dressed in her turquoise robe. Her cheeks, for once clean of any rouge, had a glow of exertion about them. 'Has someone come?' Nailah asked. 'Who is it?'

'No one,' said Isa. 'It's me that's been out, to see Kafele.'

'Kafele?' Nailah rubbed her eyes. 'What time is it, Umi?'

'Early. I couldn't sleep for worrying. I told Kafele we need to get you away, today, before Jahi tries to, or those men come back. Come, get up. You need to fetch Babu. Kafele's going to take you to stay with friends of his in Port Said.'

'Port Said?'

'Yes, you can disappear there. Kafele says that once he's made arrangements for the business, he'll return to fetch you, marry you. He loves you so.' She sighed. 'I realised as much last night.'

'You move quickly, Umi.' Nailah looked around the grimy room, at Cleo's slumbering body, Babu's stained mattress, the stale half-eaten loaf on the table. 'I don't want to ask this of him though. It's not his plan.'

'Plans are for fools and rich men.'

'That must make you a fool then, Umi, for planning that I should escape.'

'Whatever I am, here is what you're going to do. Go to the hospital, make the nurses give you Babu's medicines, whatever he needs.

Take him to Kafele's rooms at the warehouses. I'll pack, have Cleo waiting for you.'

'As easy as that?' asked Nailah.

Isa nodded quickly. 'So easy.'

Nailah wasn't sure who she was trying hardest to convince.

'Why aren't you in your riding things?' Imogen asked, frowning at Olivia's cream day-dress as Olivia joined her in the early morning sun, just minutes after Edward had left. 'You're going to ruin that lovely gown.'

'There's not much I can do about that. If I'd got into my riding habit Edward would have smelt a rat.' He'd still been in bed beside Olivia when she woke, his fingers resting on her thigh. She'd watched the way his lips moved in a smile. And she'd come close, so close, to telling him all she and Imogen were planning for the morning, but the sweetness of the silence had held her short. He'd said nothing about what he was up to either. Secrecy was a compelling kind of habit.

He'd helped her dress. He'd kissed her neck as he wrapped her waist in muslin and fastened the clasps of her bodice, the intimacy so much more intense in the light of dawn.

'You're blushing,' said Imogen.

'No I'm not,' said Olivia, the burn in her cheeks intensifying.

Imogen's lips twitched. 'Let's get on. Edward's picking Tom up at the house, we can wait for them on the road into Alex.'

Olivia looked over her shoulder. 'I think Fadil spotted me leaving just now, he'll probably follow.'

'Let's ride via Clara's then,' said Imogen, 'and make him think we're going there. We have time.'

'All right.'

'How's your head?'

'Sore.'

'Like the rest of us. Ah well, nothing like a good gallop to brush the cobwebs away. Ready?'

'Ready.'

*

240

Olivia decided that since they were at Clara's, she'd check how Ralph was.

'The poor lamb's still asleep,' said Sofia in a whisper as she joined Olivia outside the nursery. 'The littly too, and sunburnt to boot. I could give you a smacked bottom, Mrs Livvy, for letting all that happen. I only wanted a few hours off, I didn't expect you to nearly kill Ralphy.'

'It was me that saved him.' Olivia's voice was indignant, she felt like a naughty child.

'What was he doing in the sea in the first place?'

'That's an excellent question.' This from Mildred, her dispassionate voice coming from just behind Olivia.

Slowly, Olivia turned to face her. Mildred was dressed in her usual grey taffeta, her hair scraped back beneath an old-fashioned cap. Her eyes glinted with something indiscernible, Olivia assumed disdain.

Seeing she had no choice but to speak to her, Olivia said, 'You're up early,' her tone leaving no room for doubt about how displeased the fact made her.

Mildred raised her eyebrows. 'Ralph's a child,' she said. 'How could you have let it happen? I'm disappointed, but sadly most unsurprised.'

'How unfortunate,' said Olivia, affecting a carelessness she didn't really feel. Her defences were down after last night, for once Mildred's poison had penetrated, and it hurt. It made her angry how painful Mildred's dislike of her was. She needed to leave before she let Mildred see.

She turned to go.

'Your poor sister,' said Mildred, her taunting tone a brake on Olivia's feet. 'Was it resentment that made you wait so long to call the police that day, were you getting your own back for all she'd had and you lost?'

'What?' Olivia's mouth gaped. How had such a thought even *occurred* to Mildred?

'Perhaps it was simple neglect,' said Mildred.

'Neglect?' The word, half-shouted, was out before Olivia could swallow it. '*Neglect?*' She sucked in her breath, recalling all those last days of terms, watching from her window as everyone but she was collected. 'Don't cry,' Sister Catherine would say, 'you mustn't cry. You know what Sister Agnes does to girls who do.' The questions from the other girls: 'What did you do to your sister and grandmama? Why don't they want you? Why can't you remember?'

She pushed the heel of her hand to her aching head. 'I was happy living with Beatrice in London,' she said to Mildred, 'I was truly happy again. And you ruined that too.'

'Stop feeling so sorry for yourself. Look at all you've got. Fine clothes, a beautiful house,' Mildred's lips turned, 'a good husband.'

Olivia clenched her fists. Sofia took her arm, she might have said something placatory but Olivia didn't hear her. All she heard was herself saying, 'I hate you. I hate you so much. Father did too, I think. He never mentioned you, not ever. And you know who told me that, who said she understood why? Clara, your precious, darling Clara.'

'That's quite enough.' Mildred turned on her heel. 'Cheeky madam. Just like your—'

'Mother? Is that what you were going to say?'

Mildred stormed away. As she disappeared from view, Olivia's anger dissipated, a grand deflating. It left her feeling strangely defiled, a bitter knot in her stomach.

'You shouldn't lose your temper with her,' said Sofia, 'trust me. She's the kind who likes to get a rise out of people, especially those she's wronged. It makes her feel better about herself.'

Olivia took several deep breaths. Sofia squeezed her arm. Her fingers were thick, scrubbed, her nails short and square; honest hands, kind hands. Olivia saw them, then she saw them again. On another arm. She blinked. They were still there. So was she: chubbier, wearing a pinafore, in a nursery with hieroglyphic murals on the walls and a plate of stew before her. *Hold your forks and knives like this*, agapi mou. The memory lingered, it stayed.

But Clara wasn't there. Still. Why wouldn't she come?

Sofia was staring at her, brow furrowed beneath her caterpillar hair. 'What's wrong?' she asked.

'Nothing,' said Olivia. 'I'm fine.' She glanced around the empty hallway. The house felt strangely quiet. 'Is everything else all right?' she asked.

'I wouldn't say that. Mr Teddy took Hassan and El Masri away yesterday.'

'What? Why?'

'I don't know, but they're both back now.' Sofia's bottom lip turned. 'Such a mess. All of it. To think of Mrs Clara . . . ' She caught her breath. 'It's killing me,' she patted her chest, 'in here. I want her home, that's all. Home and safe.'

'I know,' said Olivia.

Sofia sighed. 'Do you want to have breakfast whilst you wait for the boys to wake up?'

'No,' said Olivia, mind moving to Imogen outside, 'thank you. I have to go. I'll drop by again later.'

'I'll tell Ralph, he'll like that.'

Olivia nodded, and, conscious of the time, bade Sofia a quick goodbye and ran down the stairs, trailing her fingers along the polished banister, and out up the driveway.

Imogen called for her to hurry. 'Fadil came. I told him we were staying here for the morning, but I don't think he believed me.'

'Perhaps because you're sitting on a horse.'

Imogen held out Bea's reins. 'Come.' She nodded down the dusty road. 'He's lurking that way. We're going to veer off the road, there's a shortcut we can take. If we go fast, we should shake him off.'

'All right,' said Olivia. Shelving Sofia's news about El Masri and Hassan for later, she pulled herself into the saddle.

'Keep up,' Imogen called, and then she was off, haring away in a cloud of sand. She rode as if she meant business, and Olivia, struggling to follow, suspected Fadil, with his lagged start, was long lost. As Imogen broke off over the sandbanks and into the undergrowth, Olivia felt her saddle, fastened on the looser setting in her haste to get away after Edward, slip. She ducked as Imogen led them beneath the crackling branches of a tree, ripping her skirt, and then lost her balance as Bea jolted. She tumbled to the ground, instinctively shielding her body with her arms, and hit her cheek on a stone.

She stared at the sky, head hammering in earnest now, reorienting herself. She raised her fingers to her cut cheekbone, her chest bursting with exhilaration.

Imogen dismounted and jogged towards her. Her face, as she peered down, was creased in concern. 'Are you all right?'

'I think so.'

Imogen looked uncertain.

'Really, Imogen, I am.' Olivia pulled herself up, taking Imogen's hand.

Imogen bit her lip. 'You're going to draw quite a lot of attention, I'm afraid. You can see your petticoats through your skirt.'

Olivia shrugged. It wasn't as though they had time to do anything about it. 'Can you help me tighten Bea's girth?'

'I think I better had.'

They were off again within the minute. They arrived back on the main road just in time to see Edward and Tom's departing backs going towards the city.

'How serendipitous,' said Olivia.

'Keep back,' said Imogen.

They played cat and mouse all the way to the city, holding off as Edward and Tom disappeared from view, then edging forward to catch them before they vanished entirely. They wound their way through the harbour streets, full of vendors setting up for market, stalls laden with peaches and apples, fish salty from the Mediterranean. The scent of fruit mixed with the sea and spices, wafting in the air. They carried on further; the air soured, the streets narrowed and grew darker, until, finally, they reached a maze of ramshackle alleyways reminiscent of an exotic Dickens. Olivia caught her breath on the acrid stench of sewage, livestock and heat.

She batted at air thick with flies. Last night's champagne strained her gullet.

'Is this the Turkish Quarter?' she asked Imogen, thinking of Amélie's words yesterday.

Imogen confirmed it was.

'What if they're here to see Nailah?'

'Time will tell,' said Imogen. 'Tom certainly wouldn't last night. Come, we'll go the rest of the way on foot.' She dismounted and caught the shirt of an urchin with a shaved head and a belly that ballooned above his trousers. She gestured at the horses, speaking in rapid Arabic, and produced a coin. The boy's face shone in a toothy grin.

Imogen strode away. Olivia followed, frowning as she looked back at the skinny child holding their well-fed horses, grubby hands stroking silky skin.

With every step she took further into the quarter, it was as if the sun, so free to shine in the open spaces up the coast, became grimy: sickly shards of light that beat on the slumped, limbless lepers, and dingy laundry-covered windows, deadening the desultory eyes of the dark-skinned men and veiled women. God, just to think of the decadence on the Carters' lawn last night, and all the while these people had been existing like this. These Egyptians.

'They must hate us,' she said to Imogen.

Imogen opened her mouth to reply, but then stopped short and pulled Olivia backwards behind a stack of crates. 'Look,' she said, pointing as Edward and Tom drew to a halt.

Olivia crouched, silk skirts billowing in the rank mud. Edward and Tom led their horses to a poky house that might once have been blue but was now speckled with nothing but scabs of paint. She watched through the slats as Edward knocked on the door. Imogen clutched her arm. They waited. Edward knocked again.

No one came.

'Damn,' said Imogen.

Edward and Tom tethered their horses and sat down on a nearby doorstep, lighting cigarettes.

'We'd better get comfortable too,' said Imogen. She settled herself on a crumbling wall and produced a package of pastries from her bag.

'A picnic, Imogen? Really?'

'We have to eat, darling. Here, have one.'

'No, I couldn't.' Olivia felt as if a jug of soured wine was swilling in her stomach, bubbling with her nerves. She sat down beside Imogen, and watched Edward. It felt strange being so close and yet not talking to him. It hurt, this deception. 'Why do you think they're here?' she asked Imogen.

'I don't know. All Tom said was that they were coming, that I didn't want to know the rest.'

'Do you think it has to do with Clara's man?'

She shook her head. 'I've been fishing and I'm not sure Tom even knows Clara was having an affair. I've been tempted to tell him, but I don't want to betray Clara unnecessarily. The scandal . . .' She frowned. 'If Edward's keeping it secret it must mean he doesn't think it's important.'

'*If* he's keeping it secret,' said Olivia, the possibility that he wasn't dawning on her as she spoke. 'We still don't know that's what he and Clara were talking about, not for certain. He might have no idea Clara was having an affair. I should ask him, make sure.' Now she knew it wasn't Edward Clara had been involved with, she wasn't afraid of doing it. 'Shall I go and talk to him now?' She half rose as she said it.

Imogen pulled her back down. 'Let's see who they're waiting for first. Patience, darling. Speak to Edward later. I agree you should. This mystery man could be important.'

'Not a red snapper then?'

Imogen sighed. 'Maybe not.'

They fell into silence.

Edward said something to Tom. Tom shook his head wryly.

Olivia wished she could have heard what Edward had said.

'Where are you off to with that half-dead child?' Sana called from across the street. Her children were at her feet, playing with pebbles. One had snot streaming into his mouth. Sana nodded in the direction of Nailah's house. 'Have you forgotten, your hole lies that way?'

'I was on my way to the docks. My mother's taken Cleo there.'

'How good your mother is, so caring these days. Who would have foretold it?'

'Not you, I know that.'

'Ha, no, not me indeed.' Sana kicked and hissed as her boy tried to stuff a pebble into his mouth. 'In any case, I saw her with Cleo going back to your house. They were with your uncle.'

'My uncle?'

Sana's eyes smiled from within her veil. 'You sound surprised. There are other surprises waiting for you when you get back too.'

'What do you mean?'

'Such grand friends you keep these days, Miss Hoity-toity.' Sana fanned herself with the henna swirls of her hand, lengthening the moment, clearly enjoying herself. 'What fine soldiers.'

Nailah's heart dropped. 'Soldiers?'

Sana laughed humourlessly. 'You disgust me, you know that? Playing so loose with your honour. Although I shouldn't be surprised, the apple never falls too far from the tree, or so we're told.'

Nailah shifted Babu's weight. 'Why do you hate me so much?'

'I don't hate you.' Sana shrugged. 'I don't trust you. I don't think you can be trusted. Come, I'll see you home. Save your uncle the trouble of fetching you.'

The hairs on the back of Olivia's neck stood on end as the young woman appeared at the end of the street. She was swathed in a dusty robe, holding a child in her arms, like a frightened girl with an oversized teddy bear. He seemed too long to be carried, he must be four at least, perhaps five. There was something awry too in the way he was lolling in the girl's arms, distorted head bowed.

Edward and Tom both stood as the girl approached, hands

247

behind their backs, officers' poses. A veiled woman watched them all from behind the corner of the furthest building.

'I want to go and tell them to leave her alone,' said Olivia. 'She doesn't look equal to an interrogation.'

'Don't be fooled,' said Imogen, 'she'll be stronger than she seems. It's Nailah anyway, I saw her with Amélie once; I recognise her face.'

Even though Sana had braced her for it, Nailah faltered at the sight of the officers waiting for her. Why had they had to come, and so soon? Why had Jahi? Nailah had known the idea of escape was nothing but fantasy, but she had been hoping, desperately, to be proven wrong.

Since she had nowhere else to go, she carried on towards the house. Her tread was slow and heavy. She looked up at the window of the family's room, imagining Jahi's eyes locked on her, the scraping of his finger against his stubble. The glint of his crooked tooth.

'Good morning,' said Captain Bertram as she drew near. 'As-salaam.'

'As-salaam,' she echoed, her eyes darting from him to his colonel.

'How is Babu?' the captain asked. 'Are you sure he shouldn't still be in hospital?' He peered down at him. 'I hope you're not worrying about the cost.'

'No, I didn't take him out because of that.'

The captain sighed, then brought his eyes back to meet Nailah's. 'We need to ask you some questions, Colonel Carter and I.'

Nailah's arms burnt beneath Babu's slumbering weight. 'I know nothing that can help you.'

'And how do you know what can help us?' asked the colonel.

'I don't.' She glanced up at the window. 'I just don't know any-thing at all.'

The colonel followed her eye. 'Are you scared of something, Nailah?'

'No.'

'Are you sure?' he asked. 'You hid who you were from us.'

She swallowed. 'Around here you learn to keep your business to yourself.'

The colonel arched his brow.

'Please,' said Nailah, 'won't you leave me? I could get into a lot of trouble for talking to you. Women in these parts, we can't just speak to strange men.'

'We know that,' the captain said kindly, 'and we don't want to cause any upset. But, Nailah, we think you have some information that could be of interest.'

'What information?'

The captain hesitated, eyes appraising her, then said, 'What do you know of your aunt's death?'

'It was an accident,' she said. 'Just an accident. Nothing else, I swear to you.'

'I didn't say it was anything else.' The captain's forehead creased, his strong face grew perplexed. Sweat broke out in Nailah's armpits.

The colonel said, 'Nailah, why would you think he had?'

'I don't know.'

'Are you sure?' the colonel asked. 'Take a moment, think if you have forgotten anything.'

'I haven't,' Nailah looked again at the window, 'really.'

For the next minute or so, the captain and the colonel asked her about her relatives, her mother, her father, Tabia's husband. They were especially interested in Tabia's husband, why he'd gone, where he was. Not knowing if it was the right or the wrong thing, or perhaps a balance of both, Nailah told them that the last she'd heard he was living in the village of Hasr.

'He's still there,' asked the colonel, 'this Mahmood?'

'I think so.' Nailah glanced up at the window, distracted by Jahi's invisible presence. 'I have to go now,' she said, backing onto the front step. 'My cousin, I need to put him down.'

'Before you disappear,' said the captain, 'please, think hard about whether there's anything else you want to tell us.'

'There's nothing,' she said, even though there was, so much.

Perhaps if Jahi hadn't been upstairs, she might yet have found the courage to let it out.

She liked to think she would have.

She felt for the door handle. The captain frowned down at her, the colonel too. Babu moaned, snuffled into her collarbone. 'I really must go,' she said and, before they could stop her, she opened the door and darted inside.

She leant against the peeling entrance wall, chest tight, listening to the captain's exasperated sigh, the colonel's words that they might as well go, get on. 'We'll track down this Mahmood, see if he knows anything. First we'd better get to Lixori, find out what Sheldon and Wilkins are up to with that farmer, what he's seen. We'll need to ride like the wind if we've any hope of intercepting them there.'

'We should take Nailah in first,' said the captain. 'She's obviously lying. We should question her more.'

There was a pause. Nailah held her breath.

'No,' said the colonel at last, 'not yet. It would ruin her. She looks like she's been through enough.' Another silence. Nailah pictured the captain shaking his head. 'Come on,' said the colonel, 'we need to move.'

'I want to see Olly before we go,' said the captain. 'She needs to know to stay at home, be on her guard. She keeps haring off.'

'You're not thinking of telling her what's happened? We agreed last night.'

'I think she has a right to know.'

'Bertram, what good will it do?'

The captain didn't reply.

'Let it be,' said the colonel, not unkindly. 'And her too. She's married, man, there's nothing—'

'Please,' said the captain, 'can we not?' There were footsteps. When the captain spoke again, his voice was further away. 'God, but Nailah's face just then, when I mentioned Tabia's death . . .'

Nailah closed her eyes. She waited for the clip-clop of hooves leaving, and then exhaled, blowing hot air over her clammy face.

She held Babu tightly as she climbed the stairs to the family's room and let herself in. Jahi stared darkly from the window. Isa, who had Cleo cradled in her arms in the far corner, shook her head despondently.

'What did they want?' asked Jahi.

'I'm not sure,' said Nailah weakly.

Jahi opened his mouth to speak again. A knock at the door cut him off. He looked down through the window. His eyes widened in disbelief. Impulsively, Nailah moved to his side, looking too. Her knees jolted at the sight of Ma'am Sheldon below, her hair in disarray, a rip in her skirt. Was that Benjamin Pasha's terrifying sister with her?

'Nailah,' said Jahi slowly, 'what are they doing here?'

'I don't know.'

'I hope to God that's the truth.'

Before Nailah could swear it was, Babu woke and puked medicine-stained vomit all down her front. In the same second, more liquid streamed from his rear.

'Oh, Sweet Mother.' This from Isa, who was on her feet in an instant, mopping them both up with a dishcloth.

'That child needs to be in a hospital,' said Jahi. 'What in God's name were you thinking, Nailah, bringing him back here?'

'I thought he was mending,' said Nailah. She looked down at Babu, unconscious again but making odd noises, the whites of his eyes visible through half-opened lids. Why *had* she taken him out? The nurses had told her she was a fool. Tabia would have listened to them.

How upset she'd be if she could see him, see all of them, now.

'I suggest you get rid of your callers,' said Jahi, 'and then return Babu to the care he needs.'

There was another knock at the door.

'Go,' said Jahi. 'I'll ask Sana to watch Cleo until you return.'

'Keep her hostage more like,' said Isa, 'to make sure Nailah doesn't try and run away.'

Jahi said nothing.

'I don't want to go to Sana's,' said Cleo quietly. 'She pinches.'

'You won't go alone,' said Isa with a brave attempt at a smile. 'I won't leave your side.'

More knocking.

Nailah searched her mother's face, desperate to see something there that promised another plan to get them all away, today, now. But Isa stared back at her hopelessly. *What can we do?*

Chapter Twenty-Four

As Nailah descended the stairs, her nose creased at the stink of Babu's excrement, her own stale sweat. She tripped over her feet in her haste to somehow get past Ma'am Sheldon and Ma'am Carter – whatever it was they wanted – and then on to the hospital, its airy rooms, medicine, and space, silence, to think. 'My little one, my little one.' She knew Babu couldn't hear her, she spoke to calm her own rippling breaths, not his.

Steeling herself, she eased the door open and met the stares of the women before her. Ma'am Sheldon's eyes took her by surprise; she had never seen them so close before. A strange sea-like colour, they flitted from Nailah to Babu and then back to Nailah again.

'I know you,' said Ma'am Carter in crisp Arabic.

'What's this?' asked Ma'am Sheldon.

'I was just telling her we know who she is,' said Ma'am Carter, in English this time.

'Ah,' said Ma'am Sheldon, then, 'We've been looking for you, Nailah.'

The words landed a glancing blow to Nailah's stomach. She barely wanted to ask, but, 'Why? What do you want with me?'

'We need your help,' said Ma'am Sheldon.

'What did my husband and Captain Bertram want with you just now?' asked Ma'am Carter.

Nailah said she didn't know.

Ma'am Carter stared, her steely gaze penetrating. 'You were talking for rather a long time.'

Nailah squeezed Babu tighter.

Still, Ma'am Carter stared.

Nailah's scalp prickled with foreboding. She needed to be away, before either of them asked her anything more. Her mind was a mess of confusion, her fears spinning with truths and half-truths, so fast she could no longer tell one from the other. Until she'd worked out what these women wanted of her, and how safe it was to tell them, surely it would be best to say and do nothing at all.

She mumbled that she needed to get Babu to the hospital.

'How can you afford a hospital?' asked Ma'am Carter.

'I'm not sure that matters,' said Ma'am Sheldon with an awkward frown.

Ma'am Carter glared at Nailah as though she thought it mattered a great deal.

Nailah made to leave, desperate now to be away. She thought of Jahi upstairs at the window. *Walk*, she could hear him ordering her, *now*.

'Before you go,' said Ma'am Sheldon, 'just one question. We've come all this way.'

'I'm sorry,' said Nailah. 'I really am, but I don't have time.'

'Then let us take you to the hospital. We have horses. You can't walk. This heat.' Ma'am Sheldon held out her hands, like a supplication to Nailah to accept. For the first time Nailah registered the livid cut on her cheek, and wondered what had happened to her. She thought that if the captain could see her, he'd be upset, want to look after her. She remembered the way he'd used to watch her at the Pashas' parties, as though he couldn't help himself. Nailah had struggled to understand his adoration at the time. She'd always imagined it would take someone exceptional to steal his interest and Ma'am Sheldon had seemed too much like all the others – beautiful, yes, with those impish cheekbones that made Nailah feel so ordinary, but an empty doll in ruffles and ribbons all the same. Nailah just hadn't been looking at her properly, she saw that now. She wondered what it would be like to inhabit Ma'am

Sheldon's cream skin, feel that beating pulse, the blood within her, wear those sculpted features and strange eyes. To know you were married to Sir Sheldon, but loved, truly loved, by a man such as the captain?

Painful, probably. And then to lose her sister too.

Gone. Vanished.

Nailah studied Ma'am Sheldon's dust-smudged face, similar and yet entirely different to Ma'am Gray's, and felt an almost over-whelming desire to tell her to run, leave, there's nothing but badness here. 'I'll walk,' she said. 'Thank you though.'

'Don't be proud,' said Ma'am Carter. 'Let us take you, we'll talk more on the way.'

'Really, I'm very grateful, but I can't trouble you.' Before they tried to insist, she was off.

She was halfway up the street when Ma'am Sheldon called out, 'Which hospital?'

Nailah halted in her tracks, scanning her mind for the name of an alternative establishment to the one she was going to. 'St Aloysius',' she said at last, giving up and telling the truth.

'St Aloysius',' Ma'am Sheldon echoed. 'I'll see you soon.'

'St Aloysius' is a rather fine establishment,' said Imogen as Nailah hurried away. 'Someone else *must* be paying for it.' She narrowed her eyes at Nailah's retreating back. 'She has much to tell, our Nailah.'

'What do you suppose Edward and Tom wanted with her?' asked Olivia.

'I don't know. We'll have to get it out of them.' Imogen shook her head, still staring after Nailah. 'She's guilty as hell about something, the way her eyes kept scooting around. And terrified to boot.'

'She reminded me of a lost child.'

Imogen laughed sardonically. 'Perhaps not so innocent. When do you want to go and see her?'

'Soon, I'll go soon.'

'I?'

'I think she's frightened of you.'

Imogen rolled her eyes.

'I'll tell Edward about it,' said Olivia, 'I've kept enough from him. But I'll see Nailah by myself. I'll get more out of her that way.'

'Fine. Don't leave it too long though.' Imogen frowned. 'I have the oddest sense that we're running out of time.'

Chapter Twenty-Five

Olivia and Imogen's ride home was a muted affair. The late-morning sun was fierce in the sky, and Olivia's hangover firing in earnest. She felt a near-overwhelming desire to roll onto the dusty road, crawl into a shady patch beneath the palms, and vomit. The only thing that kept her from giving into it was the thought that when she got home she could relieve herself in private.

Imogen told her she should eat, and reached into her saddlebag for the remains of the pastries. Olivia gagged at their sickly sweet smell. A fly was feeding on the crumbs. *For goodness' sake.*

'Your mother could never take her champagne either,' said Imogen. 'I'll tell you what I used to tell her. Stick to the gin.'

Olivia thanked her for the sage advice.

She exhaled in relief when they finally arrived back at her gate. As Imogen left her, she rode down the deserted driveway, eyes fixed on the open shutters of her bedroom window, fantasising about the coolness within, guiltily (she hadn't forgotten the beggars, not quite, not yet), but wholeheartedly.

She led Bea down the side of the house, into the musty stables. Her heart jumped when she saw Fadil's stallion there. She pulled off her glove and held her hand to the horse's hot, damp belly. Just back, then.

Gingerly, she let herself into the house. Ada, crossing the hall-way with a pile of pressed linen, turned; her face paled in horror as she took in Olivia's bruised face and torn skirts. 'Lord above.' She

257

placed the lavender-scented laundry on the floor and came to peer into Olivia's face. 'What's 'appened?'

'I fell. Where's . . . ?'

'Fadil?' Ada asked, as though inside her mind (which Olivia was far from putting past her). ''E's in the kitchen, fretting about you.'

Olivia set off to find him.

The kitchen was at the back of the house, an echoing stone room with an open fire in one corner, and tiled counters lining the walls. In the centre was a large scrubbed table, its legs in saucers of water to keep the ants away. Cook and his kitchen hands surrounded it, chattering to one another as they chopped heaps of freshly washed vegetables and herbs. They all stopped, silent, as Olivia walked in; their eyes widened collectively as they absorbed the state of her.

She asked them where Fadil was.

'I am here,' he said, coming through the garden door. 'Who did this to you?'

'Me,' said Olivia.

Fadil's gaze moved to the ceiling, like he was seeking strength. His skin was like scrunched paper, waxy with sweat at the temples. He looked gaunt, tired.

'I'm sorry,' Olivia said. 'We shouldn't have ridden off like that. But I don't like it, you following me around.'

'I'm trying to keep you safe.' His soft voice was baffled. 'You cannot know the dangers of this land, the things people do.'

Olivia, thinking of his wife and children, winced. She felt suddenly very guilty at having taken him on the dance she had, a *heel*. She apologised again.

He nodded, expression set. She wasn't at all sure she had been forgiven.

She asked him where Edward was.

'I don't know, Ma'am Sheldon. I haven't spoken to him since yesterday.'

'I need to find him.' She frowned, remembering her earlier

promise to Sofia that she'd call on the boys. They'd be waiting for her. 'I need to go to my sister's too.'

'Then let me take you there,' said Fadil. 'I'll fetch Sayed Bertram for you after.'

'All right,' said Olivia, breathing a little easier, 'good. There's so much we need to discuss, you see.'

Ada insisted Olivia change her gown and bathe her cheek before going, there was nothing like the heat to set an open wound to festering. Olivia twitched impatiently whilst Ada rubbed ointment on the cut (her aunt's husband's mother's recipe, so she said; Olivia asked her if she wouldn't be more suited to life as an apothecary than a lady's maid, and Ada actually laughed. She had a surprisingly pleasant laugh).

On the way to Clara's, Olivia studied Fadil's olive face, the silent way he kept his gaze fixed on the road ahead. She found herself wanting to know more of him, this quiet, watchful man. Her uninvited bodyguard. Tentatively, she asked about his family. He told her that his parents were long dead, his brothers and sisters had very little to do with him. 'They don't like how I work for your army. We come from a small village near Sudan, they remember how you tried to steal land there when you first arrived. They think you're greedy.'

'And you don't?'

'I respect Sayed Bertram and Sayed Carter,' he said. Then, quietly, 'They were good men when I needed to know goodness.'

Olivia hesitated, she asked, 'How old were they, Fadil, your children?'

'Little,' he said. 'The youngest, she was just a few weeks old. My wife, I cannot tell you how much she loved them all. The other soldiers, the men who killed her, I talked about her with them at the barracks. I was proud.' He stared at the road ahead. 'It would have tortured my wife, more than anything else, to watch our little ones go. Like that.'

Olivia closed her eyes, seeing it.

Fadil took a deep breath. 'It means something to me, Ma'am Sheldon, to make your sister safe.' He turned to face her. There was such pain in his gaze it was all she could do not to look away. 'There has been enough hurt.'

The policemen were at Clara's gates when they got there. They tipped their hats at Olivia as the carriage rolled past.

Fadil pulled the horses to a halt and helped her down from her seat. He asked her not to go anywhere until he returned with Edward. She promised she wouldn't. She meant it. After their exchange just now, she didn't think she could ever try to trick him again.

Clara's butler took her through the house to the terrace. Ralph was eating lunch alone, face pensive as he chewed his flatbread and tomato, staring out at the lawn in the direction of some croquet hoops. A large fountain spilled water just beyond, so cool and fresh-looking it made Olivia feel her own sore head, her gritty mouth, all the more. The gardener weeded the bright flower beds, spine bent beneath his white tunic. Olivia studied him and found herself thinking of Hassan and El Masri. She frowned, remembering she still didn't know why they'd been taken for questioning.

'You've got a bruise on your cheek, Aunt Livvy.'

Olivia started at Ralph's voice. 'I fell from Bea,' she said.

'Naughty Bea.'

'Naughty me for not doing her saddle up properly. Where is everyone?' She sat down and took a piece of Ralph's bread. She studied it uncertainly, then bit into it. Tomato juice flooded her mouth, a hidden layer of goat's cheese hit her throat, sour from the desert weeds the goats grazed on. She reached for water and took a mouthful, swallowing on the urge to choke everything back up.

'Sofia's with Gus, as always,' said Ralph, oblivious to her discomfort, 'and Father's gone to work. He says he'll come home early though. He always does now. He reads me stories before bed.' Ralph frowned. 'He doesn't do voices like Mama though.'

He took another bite and chomped. He stared at the croquet hoops.

'Do you want to play?' Olivia asked half-heartedly.

He shook his head. 'Great-Grandmama told me to take it all down, but I don't want to. Mama helped me set it up before she went. We were going to play. I hope she gets back before I have to leave for England next week.' Ralph set his bread down, pinched his nose. 'I don't want to go, Aunt Livvy.'

'I know you don't,' said Olivia. 'I don't want you to either.'

'Do you think Mama's dead?'

'Oh, Ralph. I haven't given up on her.'

Sofia arrived, bottom swaying beneath her skirts as she backed into the sunshine with a sleeping Gus in his perambulator. 'Hello, you two,' she said, 'not planning any more outings, I hope.'

'I wouldn't mind,' said Ralph, then got up and wandered down to the lawn.

Sofia lowered herself into a seat. Her stays creaked as she arched her back and reached into her pocket for her cigarettes. She flicked a match, inhaled, looked down at Gus, back in the direction of Mildred's window, then shook her head wearily.

'You have my sympathy,' said Olivia.

'She's been telling me I have the nursery all wrong,' said Sofia, 'and that I should let Gus cry more, not cuddle him so much.' She took another drag and picked tobacco from her tongue. 'I know now why your poor papa would have nothing to do with her. Why Mrs Clara never went back to visit.'

'She didn't stop Mildred coming here though, for Ralph.' Olivia looked down at the miserable way he was kicking at the grass, still struggling to understand Clara entertaining the idea of letting Mildred take him.

'She was all over the place,' said Sofia, 'that was the problem, so worried, like I told you. I dare say she wasn't thinking straight. I'm not sure she'd have been able to send him off when it came to it.'

Ralph, apparently in hearing distance, said, 'Maybe she'll come back and save me.'

Sofia smiled. 'Maybe indeed.' She tapped his plate. 'Now come back here and munch up your bread. You know what happens to littlies that don't eat their lunches? Their hair falls out.'

Ralph looked at Olivia questioningly. She shook her head and mouthed, *Not true.* He gave her a small smile.

'I might leave you to it,' she said, thinking she'd go to the stables, have a chat with Hassan and El Masri, hear from the horse's mouth (so to speak) what they were suspected of.

Hassan was alone in the stables, leaning against a hay bale with a newspaper over his face, string of worry beads loose in his hand. Olivia paused, watching him sleep. As though sensing her presence, he woke.

'Ma'am Sheldon,' he said, sitting up. He rolled his shoulders, put his paper to one side. 'Is your leg better?'

'My leg?' It took a moment for Olivia to realise he meant the jellyfish. With everything that had been happening, she'd forgotten about it. 'It's fine. Actually, I fell off my horse earlier. I'm sore from that now.' She laughed, even though it wasn't particularly funny. It wasn't really funny at all. God, she was tired.

Hassan patted the floor. 'Come, rest.'

'All right.' She drew up her skirts and knelt, straw crackling beneath her. She breathed in the earthy air, rich with hay and horse sweat, then asked Hassan why he and El Masri had been taken for questioning.

Hassan told her it was because of the man Clara had been seen talking to outside Draycott's, then walking away with.

Olivia started, shocked. 'Clara went of her own accord?'

Hassan looked at her askance. 'No one's told you?'

'Obviously not.' Olivia's brow creased as she tried to make sense of it. 'Why would she have gone off with someone like that? She was meant to be waiting for me in the restaurant.'

Hassan shrugged.

'Who was he?' she asked. 'This man?'

Hassan shook his head. 'No one knows. Just that he was Egyptian.'

'An Egyptian?' Olivia's frown deepened. 'But why would Captain Bertram think it was you? What would you want with Clara?'

Hassan shrugged again, his dark eyes full of sorrow. He bit into his apple, crunched and swallowed. 'That Egyptian soldier you were looking for,' he said, 'when Ma'am Gray went . . .'

'Fadil? It wasn't *him*. For goodness' sake.'

'No,' Hassan's forehead pinched, 'of course. I'm sorry.'

They sat in silence. Hassan threw the remains of his apple for a horse to munch, flicked his worry beads. Olivia's mind worked, trying to slot everything together. What if the man Clara had left with was *her man*. The more Olivia thought about it, the likelier it seemed. And there was every chance that Edward and Tom still knew nothing of her affair – or indeed of what Nailah had witnessed at Montazah Bay. They could have been questioning her about something else entirely. Why hadn't Olivia just bloody well told Edward everything? She had to get word to him, now, send him back to Nailah, force the identity of Clara's lover from her if need be.

She stood so quickly that the room tilted. She held her hand to the wall, steadying herself.

'Are you all right?'

'I will be. Thank you, Hassan.'

She ran back to the now empty terrace, snatched up her purse and parasol, and then hurried back into the house, down the corridor, and blindly into Sofia and Fadil.

'What on earth's wrong with you, Mrs Livvy, running around like a flibbertigibbet?'

Olivia shook her head impatiently. She turned to Fadil and asked him where Edward was.

'He's gone, Ma'am Sheldon, the colonel too. To visit some villages.'

'What?' He couldn't have gone. Not again. Not yet. 'When will he be back?'

'The men at the ground said in no more than two days. They told me he was going to the house first, but when I got there, he'd already left for the desert.'

A shiver of foreboding shot down Olivia's spine. It wrong-footed her, literally, she had to grip Fadil's arm for balance. She'd felt something like it before, a different trip, the same desert.

Fadil asked her if she was all right. Sofia pulled out one of the hallway seats, told her to sit. 'What's come over you?' she asked.

'I don't know,' said Olivia, 'I feel as if something bad is waiting.'

'They'll be safe,' said Fadil. 'They know the sands.'

'But the storms. My parents . . .'

'Weren't seasoned soldiers,' said Sofia, patting her shoulder.

Fadil held out a sealed envelope. 'The sayed left you this.'

Olivia opened it with trembling fingers.

Darling Olly, Ada's told me you're out with Fadil. I've had no choice but to go myself. I'll be back as soon as possible. Fadil knows to keep you safe, help him do that, please. Stay in the house. If you leave, have him with you at all times. If Alistair returns before I do, just get away. Do not let him near you again. I love you. E.

She let the paper fall. He was gone, really gone.

Without her telling him anything. For two days, with every hour that passed perhaps the last that Clara had.

She asked Fadil if he could go after them.

He said he couldn't, that they hadn't left the names of the villages they were heading to. Besides, he wasn't willing to leave Olivia alone.

Olivia pressed her hand to her head, trying and failing to think of who else she could go to with all she knew. She could hardly tell Jeremy that she suspected Clara had disappeared off from the street with her lover.

She trusted the police not at all.

She thought about telling Fadil, then decided she'd better talk to Imogen first. She at least might have had a chance to speak to Tom.

But when Olivia and Fadil called at her house, Imogen was out.

Seeing there was nothing else for it, Olivia told Fadil they'd better call it a day. 'I want to go out tomorrow morning though.'

'It's better that you stay at home.'

'I'm going whatever you say, Fadil. I'd like it if you took me.'

He sighed. 'Where do you want to go?'

'St Aloysius',' she said.

THE ELEVENTH DAY

THE ELEVENTH DAY

Chapter Twenty-Six

Olivia struggled to sleep that night. It was the thought of Edward's empty bedroom downstairs, the pregnant plumpness of Alistair's pillow beside her, the intermittently visible moon through the billowing curtains: a glinting sliver that Clara might or might not be alive to see.

Questions taunted her, the old and tired (the naughtiness, Clara's missing letter) alongside the new (what did Nailah know? Why had Olivia concealed so much from Edward?). She kept seeing Clara in her mind's eye: the slow way she had of smiling, those dimples in her cheeks; that day they'd both laughed until Clara nearly cried. *Me, Livvy? I'm top-drawer.* Olivia pressed her fists to her eyes. *Where are you, Clara? Won't you please, please come back?* Her heart felt as though it were gasping rather than beating, sore punches in her chest.

She fell asleep at some point. She must have, because she woke to a golden dawn. Early as it was, the air was already stiff with heat. She lay still, waiting to see if everything felt miraculously better in the brightness of God's new day (a favourite maxim of the nuns).

It didn't.

Ada came in with a cup of tea, half of which had spilt onto the silver tray and was lapping around a plate of shortbread.

'Tell me again where you got your training?' Olivia asked, more out of habit than curiosity.

'At Lady Fitz-Darton's, Mrs Sheldon.'

'I have no idea who that is.'

'That bruise 'as come up, it looks nasty.'

Olivia pressed her cheekbone gingerly. 'You'll have to cover it with powder.'

'I'm not sure I can.'

'Try, please.'

The ride into town passed uneventfully, and before Olivia felt fully ready she and Fadil had reached St Aloysius'. With its sweeping marble staircase and cream stuccoed façade it had the look of a school or museum of some sort; it seemed too beautiful a place to house disease. Imogen was right: this was not an establishment for the impoverished.

Her conviction on the matter grew when she told a Greek nurse in the entrance hall that she was there to visit a young local woman and boy, and the nurse immediately answered that they were on ward twelve, as though the two of them were the only locals there.

Olivia's heels echoed as she followed the nurse's starched hood down the corridors. She looked through the windows of the ward doors. Neat beds, lots of light, flowers. Olivia had once spent a week in hospital in Hampshire having her tonsils out, back when she was ten. The air there had been filled with smoke from open peat fires, the hacking coughs of other patients. Nothing like this.

'Here we are,' said the nurse as they reached a door marked with an italicised '12'. 'This is Mrs Sheldon,' she said to three uniformed women congregated at the front desk, 'for Babu.'

'It's so kind of you to come,' smiled one of the women, a neatly proportioned lady with olive skin, classical features, and dark hair scraped back beneath her tented cap. She stepped forward and introduced herself as Sister Rosis.

Olivia looked around the room. There were ten beds, all filled with white children watched by bonneted women. In the far corner of the ward a set of screens had been set up, concealing whoever lay within. She pointed at it, confirming Babu was there. 'Why have you hidden him away like that? Is it because he's poor?'

'No, Mrs Sheldon,' the nurses chorused.

Olivia raised a disbelieving eyebrow.

'He's in a very grave condition,' said Sister Rosis. 'He's dehydrated and not rallying as we'd like. He slept poorly last night and can't keep down his medicine. His cousin took him out yesterday against our advice, and brought him back much worse than he was.' Sister Rosis' tone made her disapproval clear.

'Why did Nailah take Babu out?'

'She said they had to go away somewhere. She seemed very anxious.'

Olivia wondered if she'd been trying to escape talking to Edward and Tom. She thought the answer was probably yes, and became instantly more curious as to what they'd wanted with her.

However, as she followed Sister Rosis across the ward and peeked into Babu's makeshift cubicle, absorbing the tableau of Nailah's hunched shoulders, Babu's horribly thin form, his flickering eyes beneath his bulging forehead, she realised how difficult broaching the subject was going to be. It felt insensitive, to say the least, to consider jumping straight into it. *I'm awfully sorry to bother you, Nailah. I'll only be a tick. I think you know who my sister was having an affair with. Would you mind terribly passing the information on? While you're at it, could you share what business those officers had with you yesterday? As soon as you tell me everything I'll leave you to keep your vigil in peace.*

Sister Rosis pulled back the screens. The metal stands scraped the floor. Nailah started. She flushed as she met Olivia's eye.

Nailah was struck momentarily dumb by Ma'am Sheldon having come so soon. She took her in (yellowish-green bruise ill-hidden by powder, fine cream jacket, matching hat, lilac silk skirts), gathering her thoughts.

Ma'am Sheldon asked her if she'd been there all night.

Nailah said she hadn't.

In fact, she'd left at the end of evening visiting hours. Kafele had been waiting for her again. 'I'm so sorry,' he'd said, running towards her. 'I should have done something before, when you first told me what Jahi was planning, got you away. I'll find a way yet, Nailah.'

'I'm not sure you can any more. Not now.' She'd kept her eyes locked on her worn sandals as she spoke, the dusty pavement, unable to meet Kafele's gaze. For once it hurt more than it helped to see his determined face, floppy hair; the love in his amber eyes. 'You should forget about this,' she'd said, 'forget about me. Get on with your life.'

'How can you say it?'

She'd felt tears rising, and nearly choked with the effort of swallowing them down. 'It's for the best.'

'Of course it's not.' He'd grasped her hands, forced her to look at him. 'A life with you, Nailah, it's the only kind I want.'

'I'm so afraid it won't be possible.'

'It will, Nailah. It *will*.'

They'd walked home in near-silence after that. Nailah had tried to make herself feel better with the thought of Isa waiting there, telling herself that she might yet have come up with a plan for what to do next. But when Nailah got there, there was no Isa, no Cleo – they were both at Sana's – Nailah had been quite alone with Jahi, nothing to distract her from his words. *I don't know what to do, do you understand me? So out of control.* It was close to ten before he left. Nailah had finally let herself cry when he'd gone, wept herself to sleep, scared of so much, so very much.

'I would have stayed with Babu if I could,' she said to Ma'am Sheldon now, 'but it's not allowed.'

Ma'am Sheldon turned to Sister Rosis. 'Surely you can make an exception?'

'It's not hospital protocol.'

'But it would be a kindness.' Ma'am Sheldon took a seat on the other side of the bed, and smiled at Sister Rosis, head to one side. Nailah wondered if it was the same expression she had used to get her way as a child. Nailah could see her as a lively, curly-haired girl with pigtails and a nursery full of dolls. A beautiful mother, a rich father.

A beloved older sister.

'Just for a day or two?' Ma'am Sheldon said.

Sister Rosis sighed and agreed. As easy as that. She took her leave, advising Ma'am Sheldon that the gong would ring for the end of morning visiting shortly.

When she was gone, Nailah thanked Ma'am Sheldon.

She shook her head as though it were nothing. 'Babu should have you here,' she said. 'I was remembering earlier how I went into hospital as a child, not long after my parents died.'

'Your parents are dead?'

'Yes, when I was small.'

The news shocked Nailah. The picture in her mind of the laughing, pigtailed child evaporated immediately.

'I had no one with me,' said Ma'am Sheldon. 'Not even my teachers visited. One of the nurses told me if I kept crying she'd tell my headmistress I was causing trouble.' She shook her head. 'What a horror. But, Nailah, I'm sure Babu's mama would be grateful you're here. I can't help thinking mine would have wanted me to have someone like you.'

Nailah ran her forefinger over Babu's damp brow. She thought, *I'm not so sure about that.* She didn't know why Ma'am Sheldon had told her the story. Was she being deliberately kind, trying to win her trust? *Why is she here? What does she want?*

'I'm sorry about your aunt passing,' said Ma'am Sheldon, then frowned. 'I've always hated people saying that about my parents. "Passing" is such an ill-fitting word.' She grimaced apologetically. 'I feel for you, if that helps.' She gave a short, unhappy laugh. 'Which I'm sure it doesn't.'

Nailah didn't know what to say.

Ma'am Sheldon looked down at her lap. The rim of her hat shadowed her swollen face. Nailah thought perhaps she was thinking of her sister, so in a ploy to distract her she asked, 'Do you remember them, your parents?'

Ma'am Sheldon closed her eyes; it was as though the question upset her.

She didn't open them again for what felt like a long time.

Nailah shifted in her seat.

'I'm starting to,' Ma'am Sheldon said at last, breaking the silence.

'Just now, there was something. A morning, back in our garden.' Her brow creased. 'I must have been about seven. I had climbed a tree. Mama was standing at the bottom of it. I can see exactly what she looked like,' she tapped her head, 'here. I can hear her voice.' Ma'am Sheldon's own tone seemed full of wonder. 'Mama said, "Shall I fetch your lunch and you can eat it up there? A picnic in the sky, how splendid."' A smiling sadness lifted Ma'am Sheldon's lips. 'Isn't that lovely?' she said. 'Such a nice idea for a little girl's lunch.' She took a deep breath. 'I remember.' She ran a finger absent-mindedly over her cracked cheek. 'It can't have been long after that my parents died, and Clara and I were separated.' She took a breath, her expression became less dreamy, resolve snapped into her sea-sprite eyes. 'She's why I'm here, Nailah. I think you can help me find her.'

Nailah felt like she'd swallowed her heart.

'I know you know things ... ' The bell rang. Ma'am Sheldon talked over it. 'Things you might not feel comfortable talking about, but I have to ask you to do just that.'

Sister Rosis was walking over. She was almost upon them.

'Nailah,' said Ma'am Sheldon,

'Mrs Sheldon,' said Sister Rosis, 'time to go, I'm afraid.'

Nailah exhaled, so hard she nearly choked.

Ma'am Sheldon sighed, pushed herself to standing, and bade Nailah goodbye. 'I'll call again later,' she said.

Nailah nodded mutely.

She watched Ma'am Sheldon disappear from the ward, trying and failing to work out how much she suspected. *Stay out of this*, she told her silently, *ask no more, for you have no wish to know any of it*. She sank her head into her hands, wishing Babu would rally so that she could take him, force Sana to give her Cleo, and then flee with Kafele, as far from this place and Ma'am Sheldon's bubbling curiosity as it was possible to go.

Before anyone else got hurt.

Chapter Twenty-Seven

Imogen was waiting at the foot of St Aloysius' stairs when Olivia stepped outside, her carriage parked next to Olivia's beneath the jacaranda trees. She ran forward, meeting Olivia halfway up the steps, apologising for not having been in yesterday evening, she'd gone to call at Benjy's. Unfortunately Tom had left for the desert by the time she got back, she hadn't talked to him. Had Olivia spoken to Edward?

Olivia said she had not.

'You look very pale,' said Imogen. 'Are you all right?'

Olivia filled her cheeks with air, not at all sure that she was.

'Olivia . . . ?'

'I keep seeing her,' Olivia said, 'my mama.'

Imogen's eyes widened. 'Oh, darling.'

'At first it was just this one memory, of her dressing for a ball, but now there's more.' Even as Olivia had told Nailah of that Cairo garden, she'd felt those memories nudging at her, unremarkable, other than in their being: Mama talking over her shoulder as she helped Olivia lace her boots; her frown of concentration as she pored over a book in a library; an exclamation as she let a glass slip, fragments smashing on the tiles. 'I'm scared they're not real,' Olivia said. 'I have no idea if I'm making them up, because I want to see her so much. And I've got no one to ask.'

'You can ask me.'

'But I want to ask Clara.' Olivia heard the crack in her own voice. Imogen's beautiful face melted. 'I can't see her, back then,' Olivia

275

said, 'not at all. It's as if she never existed to me, and I hate it. I hate *me* for it.'

Imogen shook her head. 'I wish there were something I could say.'

Olivia let go of a long breath. 'I wish there was too.'

Imogen smiled sadly. At length she asked, 'How did you get on with Naïlah?'

'Badly. I'm going to go back later. I thought I might go to the shops first, fetch some fruit, soap, things to read.'

'Butter her up.' Imogen nodded. 'It's a good idea.'

'That's not why I'm doing it.' Olivia frowned, thinking about Naïlah's stained dress, the worry lines on her skinny face. 'I felt awful for her. She's got nothing.'

Imogen sighed. 'Any clue about who's paying for the hospital?'

'No.'

'I thought it might be Benjy, it's why I went to see him, but he said he's had nothing to do with it. He didn't even know Naïlah had left to look after her aunt's children until I told him. Apparently Amélie hadn't seen fit to mention it. He had some rather interesting things to say on the matter. Come, I'll take you to lunch, we can talk more there. There's no point in you going all the way home, we can pick up Naïlah's bits and pieces on the Cherif Pasha.'

'I don't know.' Olivia shuddered. 'I'm not sure I could stand going there.'

'I'll be with you. You'll have your bodyguard over there.' Imogen nodded in the direction of Fadil in the carriage. 'We'll go to Draycott's, it might do you good to go back there, face up to it.'

'Absolutely not.'

'I think it would help.'

'Think away, I'm not going.'

The marble foyer of Draycott's was exactly the same as it had been last time Olivia was there: cavernous, polished, clicking with the expensive shoes of officers and gentlemen. 'Welcome back, Mrs Sheldon. Good day, Mrs Carter.' The maître d' had the same obsequious bow (although the wary look he gave Olivia was new). 'I'll show you to your table.'

'You booked?' Olivia asked Imogen. 'Did you have this all planned?'

'No, no.' Imogen floated away after the maître d'. Her scent mixed with his fragrant pomade, leaving a perfumed wake. 'I always have a table here.'

Olivia suspected she was lying. Nonetheless, she followed her into the dining room. Her skirt brushed the tablecloths, she could see the parakeet's cage on the terrace beyond. She took a breath, feeling an echo of her panic eleven days ago creeping through her. Her pursuit of Fadil jumped into her mind. She heard Hassan's words in the stable yesterday, his question just after Clara was taken, too: *Did you manage to speak to the soldier you were looking for?* Something wasn't right about it. Olivia touched her fingers to her forehead, trying to work it out.

She sat down. A waiter arrived and took them through the menu. He recommended a particularly fine mullet baked with saffron and almonds. Olivia looked around, catching furtive glances directed at her, hands raised to whispering mouths. *What do you suppose she's doing here?* Lunch and a show, weren't they all lucky? Giles Morton from *The Times* was there – he raised enquiring eyebrows at Olivia, reminding her she still hadn't replied to his letter. She averted her eyes; she couldn't think how to respond to his digging now.

Instead she familiarised Imogen with all Hassan had said, and her suspicion that, since Clara had apparently left from outside Draycott's willingly, the Egyptian she'd gone off with was the same man she'd been having the affair with. 'I wish I'd told Edward. I asked Fadil if there was any way to get a message to him, but he says no. I don't know what to do. Should I just tell Fadil everything?'

'There's no point,' said Imogen, 'he wouldn't be able to do anything. He doesn't have the stripes.'

'What about someone else, one of the lieutenants? Or the police?'

'And have our Clara's business spread all over Alex by sundown? No, we can't do that to her, to the children.' Imogen clicked her tongue. 'Let me go to the ground, see if I can't get word to Tom. Meanwhile, you concentrate on getting this man's name from Nailah.' She frowned. 'There's something awry about her hiding so much. I keep wondering what it was Edward and Tom were trying to get out of her.'

'Whatever it was, they didn't get it,' said Olivia, thinking of their faces when they left her. 'They were ... *Put. Out.*'.

Imogen took a sip of water. 'Then there's the way Nailah left Amélie's service without telling Amélie or Benjy why she was going. It seems the other servants only got to hear about her aunt's death through gossip. Yet Tabia died right there, in Montazah. The man who killed her came to Benjy to confess. Why didn't Nailah tell anyone she was related to her?'

'Privacy?'

'It seems more like secrecy to me. And another thing, why did the peasant whose horse trampled Tabia confess at all? Tabia was mown down in the dead of night, the man could have got away with it if he'd said nothing.'

Olivia shrugged. 'Maybe he felt guilty.'

'That's what Benjy said. He claims the man burned the body on the beach, then panicked, turned himself in.'

'There you go then.'

Imogen shook her head. 'You should have seen Benjy's face, darling. He looked *just* as he did when he'd got into trouble as a small boy. There's more to it than he's telling me. He got rather cross when I pushed him.'

'It's odd,' Olivia conceded, 'but still, what could it have to do with Clara?'

'I don't know. Maybe nothing, perhaps everything.'

The waiter arrived with their lemon-scented platter of fish. As he served up delicate portions of couscous, beans, a citrus dressing, Olivia's mind ticked over all she knew.

When, at last, the waiter was finished, she sat forward in her chair. 'When did Tabia die?'

'At the end of May, the night of Benjy's ball.'

'That's when Elia said she and Nailah saw Clara heading into the dunes at Montazah.'

'You're right.'

'A coincidence?'

Imogen narrowed her eyes. 'I don't know. Ask Nailah about it. It's all tied together somehow, I'm sure she knows how.'

Chapter Twenty-Eight

Nailah hid in the window bay as Ma'am Sheldon approached ward twelve, skirts swishing on the floor, one gloved hand absent-mindedly skimming the bruise on her cheek. As soon as she had gone in, Nailah hastened towards the staircase, her footsteps echoing conspicuously in the long hallway. She held her breath, sure that at any moment she would hear that purring voice. *Nailah? Where are you going?* It didn't come. Nailah realised it wasn't going to. She had bought herself another night. And even though she felt sick at leaving Babu, even for a couple of hours, her pulse leapt with relief.

Behind her she could hear Ma'am Sheldon saying, 'What do you mean she's not here?' Her exasperated words bounced from the ward, off the whitewashed walls, splashes of colour in the air. 'She's running away from me, you know.' Nailah's skin burnt at the accuracy of the observation. 'I'll stay anyway,' said Ma'am Sheldon, 'sit with Babu. He shouldn't be left by himself.'

The kindness surprised Nailah, and didn't, all at the same time. As she ran down the stairs, she breathed easier thinking of Ma'am Sheldon's elfin eyes on her little cousin. Perhaps they would work a spell of health on him.

Nailah hoped so, she needed to get away, the children with her. She couldn't dance this jig of avoidance for ever. As sure as rock broke glass, Ma'am Sheldon wasn't going to let her. And nor was the captain. *We should take Nailah in. She's obviously lying.* He'd do it as soon as he came back from the desert, she was sure. She frowned, thinking of him out there with his colonel.

She wondered, *Have they spoken to Mahmood yet?*

Edward squinted down at his compass, up at the cresting dunes, then across at the ordnance Tom had spread across the flank of his horse. The green and red lines of the grid blurred in the heat. Flies buzzed everywhere, around Edward and Tom's muslin-wrapped heads, their sand-coated uniforms, the mouths and eyes of their horses; their hum grated the air, the only noise other than the frisking wind on the sand.

Edward clicked his compass shut. It was another three miles due west to Mahmood's village. 'We'll make it by sundown.'

'We'll bunk down again after that,' said Tom. 'Ride hard for the city in the morning.'

Edward nodded, loath as he was to accept it. Alistair would be well on his way home by now.

They'd missed him in Lixori. All Edward and Tom had found when they arrived in that hamlet of mud dwellings, late yesterday afternoon, was some half-starved camels, a patch of barely arable land, and desert folk who'd studied them with wary eyes and told them that they weren't the first white men to come: two more had been and gone, one fat, the other aloof, taking a villager away with them.

Edward, certain that the villager was the peasant farmer Jeremy had spoken of, asked what business Alistair and Wilkins had had with him. All he got in response was shaken heads, sealed lips, and furtive gazes that refused to meet his. He persisted, Tom did too. 'Where did the white men take him?' They asked it countless times. 'What did they say?'

Still, no one answered. The women pulled their children to them, as though afraid.

Eventually, Edward and Tom had given up and set off on the long ride they were now almost at the end of, stopping only to sleep.

'I feel sick,' said Tom, as he folded away the maps, 'wondering

281

what the hell Sheldon and Wilkins are about with that villager. I want to think they've taken him back to Alex for questioning, but I'm worried they're trying to hide him, and whatever it is he's seen.'

Edward frowned. He said the same fear had crossed his mind.

Tom ground his teeth, moustache twitching. 'It's Sheldon I don't trust. I'm not sure he's ever wanted Clara safely back, not with all she must know by now.' He shook his head. 'Too dangerous for him. He'd sell his mother's soul before he'd let what's been going on get out. Manipulative son of a bitch.'

'One of a kind,' said Edward, thinking of Olly's livid scars. If he could, he'd scratch the memory of them from his mind, make them never have existed; for her more than anyone. But he couldn't. And he was here, hours away from Alex, instead of where he should be: next to her.

He'd spoken to Ada before he left, cast caution to the wind and told her what he knew, asked her to help Olly. She'd told him that she wanted to, that she'd been trying. *Try harder*, he'd said. He could only hope it would be enough.

He sucked his breath through his teeth. 'Let's go. This Mahmood had better be worth the trip.'

The street outside Sana's house was full when Nailah reached it. A gaggle of children were playing in the shadows of the tenements with Cleo. Kafele was there too, even though he should have been working. He had his jacket off, the sleeves of his shirt rolled up beneath his waistcoat, and his thick hair was scruffy. He was smiling, that face-cracking grin he'd used to give Nailah so freely.

They were deep in a game involving a leather football and much screaming. Isa sat on the pavement, swathed in purple silk and silver beads, bruises of tiredness on her face. Like a tarnished ornament. For the first time, Nailah saw how lined her once ageless skin had become, the grudging sag of her cheeks. How old was she? Nailah didn't know, Isa considered age a dirty subject, but looking at her now, Nailah would bet money on her being older than most on stage. Was that why she was still here, not off on another tour? Nailah barely needed to ask. Much as she wanted to believe Isa was staying purely out of concern, love, she knew in her heart it was just as likely that Isa's career ending was making her behave like a mother for the first time in her life.

Nailah watched her laugh and clap. Kafele tossed the ball up and down in the air, eyes so bright they might burst. He was acting too. Nailah saw it with a sickening thud. Only the children had been duped into believing the show was real.

'Catch, Cleo, catch!' yelled a small boy as Kafele cannoned the ball in Cleo's direction.

Her eyes opened wide. She held out her hands, grabbing the ball before it hit her. Kafele swivelled, threw his head back and covered his face with his hands, feigning despair. Cleo burst out laughing, jumping around in a way that Nailah had all but forgotten she was capable of. 'I got it, I got it. You're out. My turn to throw.'

Nailah didn't call out, she didn't wave for anyone's attention. A fiction it all might be, but she hadn't the heart to ruin it. Instead she leant against the wall, and watched. Her eyes lingered on Kafele. For a second she let herself wonder what it would be like if the two of them were really married, about to go home to an evening meal, a soft mattress. What if it was their children scooting around the cobbles now, boys and girls with Kafele's dancing face? Nailah pictured them all, she painted her children in. She saw chubby arms, strong legs. She heard their voices. She gave them everything that was Kafele: his kindness, smart mind, whole soul. She granted them nothing of her. None of it came close to compare.

The image sat like a gossamer sheet over the real-life bodies in front of her. Nailah half-closed her eyes, struggling to hold on to it as Kafele caught Cleo in his arms and threw her into the air, making her dark hair fly. *Clown.*

Isa laughed, a deep peal that was almost believable, and then, as though sensing Nailah's presence, turned. 'Nailah,' she called.

Nailah started, her children evaporated. Gone.

Cleo dropped the ball. It fell with a desultory bounce, then another, rolling along the ground. Everyone looked at Nailah as though she were a storm that had arrived unexpectedly on a sunny day, ruining everything. End of show. Grubby curtain down.

Cleo ran over, locking Nailah with eyes that were at once hopeful and scared. And as she asked, 'Is he getting better? Is he mending?' Nailah wondered if anything could ever be better or mended again.

She stayed in the street long enough to be assured that Isa was managing the household's breakfast, with help from Cleo, and to learn that Jahi had called at lunchtime. 'I've never seen him so het up,' said Isa. 'He has Sana locking us in at night, says he doesn't want us in the house in case the soldiers come back, or you trying to run off with Cleo, but he won't tell me why.' She shook her head, brow creasing.

Nailah felt her heart soften. Whatever Isa's reasons for staying home, she really did seem to care now. Impulsively, she leant forward and hugged her mother, sinking her head onto her shoulder. She felt as though she could fall asleep standing.

'What is this mess you're in?' Isa whispered. 'What's happening?'

'I don't know,' said Nailah. 'I really don't know any more.'

Kafele walked her back to St Aloysius'. They held hands as they joined the wide avenues of the city centre. The roads teemed with carts and carriages, and men, so many men, hastening home, at the end of their day.

'When you're ready,' said Kafele, 'you'll tell me everything about this trouble you're in. You'll tell me, and I'll know how to help you.'

'I'm not sure you can.'

'Of course I can. This is a season of sadness, nothing more.'

'It might be a long season.'

'Then we'll share it. I'll always be here, remember that. I'd do anything for you, I would lay my life—'

'Don't say it. Please don't.'

She simply couldn't stand to hear him offering his life for hers again.

Babu was alone and asleep when she got back to him. His cheeks were flushed, but his breathing seemed steadier. His head was cooler too.

Ma'am Sheldon had left a pile of gifts at the foot of his bed: a clean robe, soap, a packet of cardamom biscuits, peaches, a book. Nailah thumbed the robe, a pale blue of the softest cotton she had ever owned, and looked down at the book. *Alice's Adventures in Wonderland.* She'd never heard of it. She turned back the cover and saw a short note folded inside.

I thought perhaps you could read this to your cousin. It's a story that has been much on my mind in recent weeks. I'm sorry to have missed you today, I shall return tomorrow. If you are not here, I will come and find you at home. I simply cannot wait any longer.

I hope you manage to get some rest tonight, and that Babu rallies. He woke for a few minutes whilst you were gone and smiled. A good sign perhaps? I shall see you in the morning.

Nailah rested her cheek on Babu's mattress, she took his soft hand in hers. 'What shall l do, habibi?' she asked his sleeping form. 'I wish you could tell me what to do.'

Over in Ramleh, Olivia followed Fadil into the house. As she dropped her hat by the stand, a movement caught her eye in the drawing room: fingers drumming an armrest. Her lips stiffened, her throat constricted. Alistair's head peered around from behind the chair.

'Where have you been all day?' he asked.

Olivia's voice as she said, 'With Imogen,' came out strained, taut, like it belonged to someone else. She swallowed. 'I didn't expect you back.'

Alistair folded his newspaper and crossed over to her. She stayed rooted to the spot. He took her chin between his thumb and forefinger. With his other hand he touched his fingers to her cheekbone. 'This looks ugly,' he said. 'I don't like it on your face.'

Olivia stared at him, heart walloping within her. He stared down at her. His pale blue eyes twitched. It scared her in a way it hadn't before. Had he somehow found out what she and Edward had done? Was that why he had come back, to punish her?

His expression, passive beneath his translucent skin, gave nothing away.

She knew she should ask him why he'd even gone off in the first place. Yet in the moment of her finding herself so very alone with him, she could think of nothing but getting away.

She looked to the stairs.

Alistair smiled, cocked his head to one side. 'You should take a bath,' he said. 'I'll come up. I like watching you.'

'I'm rather tired.'

'What do you have to do but lie there?' He pressed his lips to her forehead. 'It's nice just being the two of us again, isn't it?'

'Not really,' she said. Alistair smirked, as though her standing up for herself amused him. It made her angry that it should be a joke. Her anger gave her strength. She pulled away from him, took two steps back. 'I'd much rather you'd stayed away,' she said, her voice stronger with each word. 'I wish you were anywhere but here. I wish you were . . .'

'Dead?'

Olivia coloured.

Alistair laughed, a brittle chuckle. 'Dead in the desert? I suppose it wouldn't be the strangest end.' He paused, still smiling. 'Plenty go that way, of course.'

Olivia suspected he said it to be cruel about her parents, but it turned her cold for another reason, reminding her of her earlier foreboding about Edward's going off, her sense of something bad waiting in the dunes.

She wished she could find something to say to Alistair, a dismissal to put him down, trivialise her own fears, but she had no words. All she could do was stare.

'Run along,' said Alistair. 'Time for that bath.'

*

286

Ada was in the bedroom when Olivia got there. Olivia dropped down on the edge of the bed to steady her shaking legs. She pulled at her jacket, fingers fumbling on the buttons. Ada came over and silently pushed her hands away; her skin was cool, her touch calm. She removed Olivia's jacket. Olivia pressed her palms to her neck. It was covered in sweat.

'You need to wash,' said Ada.

Olivia looked up at her. 'I'm afraid to,' she admitted, and then started shaking even more. She'd never said it out loud before.

'Course you are.' Ada patted her on the shoulder and went off to draw the bath.

Olivia heard the taps spluttering, the clank of copper pipes as the downstairs geyser fired into action and pumped hot water upwards. She stayed exactly where she was until Ada fetched her. She followed in Ada's brown stuff-skirted wake, each step deliberate, heels then toes, heels then toes. She walked so as not to tumble. She was behaving like an invalid, she felt like one, disoriented by her own physical inadequacy, the menacing presence of Alistair downstairs. She had no idea why, having put up with his attentions for so long, they should suddenly feel so terrifying. Maybe the night with Edward had made her vulnerable, his tenderness had exposed her. Or perhaps it was the look Alistair had given her just now, like it was all about to get a lot worse. *Run along.* She couldn't bear it any more, the hovering flames above her stomach, the teeth on her skin, the semen-soaked cloths in her mouth ... She really thought it might kill her.

'Let's do this quickly,' she said to Ada as she stepped into the soapy tub. 'I just want to be quick.' She didn't want to be naked when he came.

Ada set to work scrubbing the heat of the day from her hair and skin, moving fast, methodically. She was almost finished when the door handle turned. Olivia tensed.

'I ain't leaving you,' Ada whispered.

Olivia looked up at her. Ada gave her a tight smile.

'How can you not?' Olivia asked.

'Just watch. You'll see.'

Ada was true to her word. She stood her ground, all five feet of her, batting away Alistair's attempts to take the soap, telling him he wasn't to worry, she was more than capable, best leave them to it, why not go downstairs and read the papers. As it became clear that she wasn't going to be moved, Alistair ceased trying to force the matter. He was angry, Olivia could tell, it was that tick in his glare. But it seemed he was too much of a coward to confront Ada outright. He didn't want to know that she was defending Olivia, not for certain, nor think about what that meant she'd seen. For him violence was a private pleasure, something to be kept within the sanctity of the marriage bed. Just the two of them.

A wife's privilege.

'He might just fire you for that,' Olivia said to Ada as he left.

'I was 'ired to do a job,' said Ada. 'I'm afraid I ain't been doing it properly.'

'You're not really a lady's maid, are you, Ada?'

Ada poured shampoo into her hand and said nothing.

'Why are you here, in Egypt?'

'I've been 'ere a while,' Ada said. 'I ... well, I help watch over people. The way I grew up, I learnt a bit 'bout looking out for myself. I did try for a while to work in service, but I wasn't best suited to it. It wasn't long before I fell into this work instead, keeping an eye out for others.' She rubbed the shampoo into Olivia's head. 'There's always a man somewhere who's got on the wrong side of another. They feel better knowing someone a bit savvy is watching their family, ready to raise a flag if anything untoward looks like occurring.' She lathered up the soap. 'I don't normally 'ave to be so secretive 'bout what I'm doing, of course. Mr Sheldon wrote I must though, back when 'e asked me to come and keep an eye on things, on you ...'

'When was that?'

'Right at the end of May. I came directly.'

Olivia, thinking of her conversation with Imogen at lunch, frowned at the timing. 'Why didn't Clara get a bodyguard?' she asked.

'She got taken to Constantinople.'

'Do you know what it's all about, Ada?'

'No. I'd tell you now if I did, I swear it. I'm sorry I've not taken better care of you. I didn't know what to do, you see, when I realised what was what.' Ada sighed. 'You're trapped, I think, I can't see no way out for you, but I'll 'elp 'owever I can.'

'Ada, I don't know what to say. I've been so awful to you.'

'No,' Ada's pointy face flushed, 'not a bit of it.'

Olivia caught her hand. 'Thank you.' It was a stay of execution, nothing more, but in that moment it meant the world.

As the evening progressed, Olivia's nerves grew. Ada stayed close, but she could hardly remain with her all night, it wasn't as though she was going to clamber between the sheets with her and Alistair. Olivia would just have to endure the hours, minutes and agonising seconds between dusk and dawn as best she could.

But she didn't know how to. It made her ill in the stomach waiting for it. She had to keep rushing to the latrine.

Alistair went out before dinner. He didn't say where he was going, just barked up the stairs that he'd be back later. A note arrived from Imogen saying she hadn't managed to get a message to Tom; Fadil was right, no one at the ground knew where he'd be. *Hopefully they'll come back tomorrow. I'm staying at Benjy's tonight. I want to see what else I can find out.*

Olivia undressed for bed shakily, bracing herself in the darkness. She remembered the words in Edward's note. *Get away.* She'd never thought of running before. Haring around seeking protection from your abusive husband was hardly the done thing. But she was so much closer to Imogen now – if she were home tonight she would have gone to her. She simply didn't know the Pashas well enough to involve them.

'What about your sister's house?' Ada asked dubiously. 'It'll be safe with the police there.' She didn't sound convinced. 'We could take Fadil.'

'Alistair would just come and find me.' Either that or Mildred would march her straight home.

'Somewhere else then?'

'There's nowhere else,' said Olivia. 'Isn't that pathetic? I have no one else.'

She went to the window. The Bedouins' lantern formed a puddle of light on the driveway. The mother and her boys would be settling down for the night. Safe.

Safe.

'Ada,' she said, 'I've had an idea.'

She heard Alistair returning much later that night. His horse cantered past, hooves on gravel, the noise startlingly loud through the fabric of the tent. She saw him in her mind's eye, discovering their empty bed, opening the doors of each of the spare rooms, peering through the keyhole of the locked one at the mound of a body within. Pillows lined up in just the way Sofia had said Clara used to. He might knock the door down, Olivia hoped he wouldn't, not on this, the first night of her making an escape – she willed him to content himself with the promise that he'd *speak to her* about it on the morrow instead – but he might. It was why Olivia had come here. He would never look for her amongst peasants, especially ones who despised him; he was too arrogant to even think of it. And if he did alert the police to her absence, well, it would be dawn before they came. Another day. One in which Edward might return.

She knew she was snatching hours, segments of safety. It was no way to live, not in the long term, but it was the only life she could manage for now.

She blew a slow breath through her lips. A hand touched her shoulder. It wasn't Ada's, she was fast asleep. It wasn't the Bedouin boys, they were too, curled up at Olivia's feet. It was the mother, her sad face shadowy in the near-moonless night. The woman who had asked no questions when Olivia and Ada appeared at her door, just beckoned them in, made room.

'No you worry,' she said to Olivia, touching her fingertips to her heart, then to Olivia's cheek. 'No you cry.'

'I'm not crying,' Olivia whispered back. 'I really never do.'

The woman shook her head.

She took Olivia's hand and laid it on her damp, tear-sopped face.

At dawn, Olivia and Ada crept back to the house. Fadil was already up and sitting at the front door, gun in lap. He could well have been there all night.

'Can you be ready to leave at eight?' Olivia asked him. 'We have to go back to St Aloysius'.'

'Will you tell me why?' he asked. 'What you want with that girl?'

'I won't for now.' Imogen was right, there was no point. Fadil couldn't arrest Nailah, and Olivia didn't want anyone knowing about Clara's affair unnecessarily. Once Olivia found out the identity of her lover, *then* she'd go to Fadil, get his help taking the man in. If Edward wasn't back by then.

Today, she thought, *it all happens today*.

THE FINAL DAY

Chapter Twenty-Nine

Olivia skipped breakfast, so avoiding Alistair, but also food. She'd barely touched her dinner, she was famished. The sunlight, the renewed distance of nightfall: it made things like eating possible again. She asked Fadil to stop at a bakery on the outskirts of town, a squat stone hut that smelt of flour and cinnamon and was bustling with wide-elbowed matrons. Fadil cleared a space for Olivia by the display of sugared pastries; he made her smile by reprimanding the owner for charging her too much.

'I don't mind,' she said.

'I do,' he replied.

When Olivia arrived on the ward, she was relieved to see Nailah's battered sandals beneath Babu's screens. No need to gird her loins for a return to the Turkish Quarter after all. She crossed the room. Babu was awake, and Nailah bent over him, stroking his cheek as he smiled. She wore the robe Olivia had brought her. Olivia wondered if it was a good sign, an indication that she was prepared to give in and start talking, or simply that her other dress was dirty and not as nice.

She held up her basket. 'I've brought breakfast.' Nailah thanked her. Olivia nodded down at Babu. 'He has some colour in him.'

'Yes. God is smiling.'

'Is he? I must say this is the first evidence I've seen of it in a while.' Olivia sat in the free chair, skirts spreading around her on the chemically scented floor. She hesitated before speaking, unsure which matter to raise first: Clara's lover or Tabia's demise? Feeling as though Tabia might (*might*) be the easier one to ease into, she said, 'Nailah, I want to talk to you about your aunt's death.'

Nailah's hand froze on Babu's cheek.

'Do you know what happened to her?'

Nailah blinked, then said, 'Everyone knows.'

'Do they?' Olivia gave Nailah a long look. 'I'm not so sure.' There was a short silence. 'I think there's more to it,' said Olivia. 'That it's got something to do with my sister disappearing.'

Nailah's expression didn't move. It registered no confusion. The connection, which still made no sense to Olivia, apparently held logic for her. Olivia leant forward, hands clasped on Babu's sheets. 'Nailah, what do you know that I don't?' Nailah's face remained immobile, as if it was stuck. 'Nailah.'

She swallowed. 'I don't know anything.'

'I think you do.'

'No.'

'Either you tell me what it is, or I'll fetch Captain Bertram to question you instead. He'll be back soon, or,' she bluffed, 'I'll get one of his men. Better me, surely?' Nailah shook her head mutely. 'You can trust me, Nailah.' Silence. Olivia decided to take a subtler tack. 'Your aunt lived in Montazah, didn't she?'

'Yes.'

'She was killed in the middle of the night. What was she doing out on the roads? Why wasn't she safe at home?'

Again, Nailah shook her head.

Olivia exclaimed in frustration: 'I'll go to the barracks, shall I? Or the police?' She made to stand. 'They'll take you in, you know, your cousin will be left all alone.'

'No, please.' Nailah reached out, face imploring.

'Why was Tabia out, Nailah? What was she doing?'

Silence.

Olivia turned to walk away.

'She was meeting someone.' Nailah's words came like a surrender. Her shoulders dropped. 'She might have been meeting someone.'

'Who?'

'Just a man.'

'A friend?'

Nailah's sallow cheeks flushed. 'A good friend.'

'Tabia was having a love affair?' Olivia needed it clarified; she was worried the activities of her own immediate circle were leading her to jump to the wrong conclusions.

Nailah's colour deepened. 'Are you shocked?'

'Probably not as much as I should be.'

'Tabia loved him. They were planning to marry, soon. She wasn't loose.'

'Who was he?' Olivia asked again.

Nailah cast her eyes down to the sheet, picking at it. 'Tabia called him Rohi,' she said quietly. 'My soul. A pet name.'

It was familiar somehow. Olivia frowned, trying to think where she'd heard it.

Nailah said, 'The night Tabia died, he took her to the beach.'

'The beach at Montazah?' Olivia stared, incredulous. What in God's name was it about that bay that made it such a den of iniquity? To think of it, Tabia and Clara, both there – perhaps even at the same time; Clara lifting her silk petticoats just out of sight from Tabia raising her roughened robes.

The idea settled like a rock within Olivia's abdomen.

'How did your aunt die, Nailah?' She forced the question out, she barely wanted to ask it; she'd become abruptly confident that wherever the answer took her it would be nowhere good.

Nailah stared across the ward. It was as though she hadn't heard.

Olivia asked her again.

Nothing.

'Nailah.'

'She was murdered.' Nailah's eyes widened the instant she spoke, as if she'd swallow the words back if she could. But the pronouncement was already shooting free; it bounced from Olivia's ear, chaotically off the scrubbed surfaces and crisp linen, filling the ward.

And there they were. Nowhere good.

'By whom?' Olivia asked, marvelling at how calm she sounded.

'The . . . that Bedouin man, his horse.' It was little more than a whisper.

'What happened to your aunt, Nailah?'

'I . . . I don't know. How could I know?'

'But you just said a Bedouin's horse killed her.'

'What?' Nailah frowned confusedly. 'Yes, it did.'

'You're lying.' Olivia raised her hand to her forehead. She looked around her, trying to anchor herself in the plain detail of the beds and vases of flowers, to think clearly. A trolley trundled metallically down the corridor outside, street noises floated through the open windows, a child in the far bed made his mother laugh. 'Did Clara know about this?'

'What?'

'Has she been taken by the man who killed Tabia to keep her quiet?' Olivia was struck by an image of Clara and Edward talking in the darkness on the Sporting Club terrace, the very night after Tabia's death and the Pashas' ball. Was Edward involved somehow? Had he been begging Clara not to say anything? Please not. Pleasenotpleasenotpleasenot. Olivia couldn't think it of him. She couldn't. 'Nailah, who murdered Tabia?'

'I can't . . . I don't know.'

'You do, I can see it in your face. You're involved somehow.'

'No.'

'Yes. And my sister was there, wasn't she, when it happened?'

'Wh— what do you mean?'

'I know you saw her that same night at the beach, with a man she shouldn't have been with.' Olivia reached across the bed, seizing Nailah's icy hands. 'I want you to tell me who that man was, Nailah. I have to find him. I think he's taken Clara.'

There, she'd said it. At last.

But the way Nailah was staring at her. There was no other word for it but *aghast*. Actually, that was quite wrong, there were several other words for it: *appalled, shocked, horrified*. Her face was the pictorial definition of terror.

298

'Nailah, is he threatening you, this man? To keep silent?'

Nailah's mouth formed a silent no.

'Tell me the truth, Nailah, there's nothing to be frightened of.'

Nailah shook her head as though there was a great deal to be frightened of. 'Ma'am Sheldon, please, leave this.'

'I can't,' said Olivia. 'Tell me, who was this man?'

'I can't. I . . . I don't . . . I never saw your sister with anyone.'

'Stop lying. You saw Clara with an Egyptian man at Montazah Bay. Clara was last seen with another such man outside Draycott's, before she went.'

'I don't know who that man was, I promise. And I swear to you, your sister knew nothing about Tabia's death.'

Olivia took a deep breath. Perhaps Nailah was telling the truth, about that at least. Now she had a moment's pause, she realised that if Clara had simply been taken to silence her, there'd be no reason for everyone's concern over her own safety. There'd be no police at the Grays' house, safeguarding the family. And whilst Clara had been far from herself the day she'd disappeared – and so guarded in her letters from Constantinople – she'd seemed saddened rather than traumatised. Certainly nothing like the kind of shocked one would expect from the witness of a murder. Besides, her melancholy moods had started long before Tabia's death.

But Imogen was right, everything was linked somehow. Olivia just couldn't see how. And she couldn't for the life of her think what part Clara's lover played in it all. Not to mention Tabia's. Olivia's shoulders sagged. She felt as though she were back to square one, the very worst place to be. 'I'll ask you one last time,' she said to Nailah. 'Who killed your aunt? And how do you even know about it? Did Tabia's lover tell you?'

'Ma'am Sheldon . . .'

'What's his real name, this Rohi?'

'I can't . . .'

'How's he involved?'

'Please . . .'

Olivia threw up her hands and got to her feet. She looked down at Babu staring amicably up at her, and then at Nailah. 'I felt sorry for you yesterday, I really did. But I don't any more. Clara could be dead, and you don't give a damn.'

'I do.' Nailah's eyes flooded. 'Oh, Ma'am Sheldon, I do. Please though, you must say nothing of this to anyone.'

Olivia gave a bitter laugh and turned to go.

'No, stop. Wait. Leave this alone.'

Olivia left. As she hastened past the nurses, Sister Rosis called out to her, saying she looked upset. 'I hope Nailah wasn't ungrateful, given all that's been done for her.'

Olivia stopped, caught by a thought. *Someone's paying for it.* She turned back to Sister Rosis. 'Is the account settled?' She kept her tone light. 'Do you need my help with it?'

'Don't worry, Mrs Sheldon, Socrates is forwarding all the bills direct to Captain Bertram. He's arranging payment with Babu's benefactor.'

'Lovely.' Olivia's smile felt like a knife slash on her face.

From across the ward, Nailah watched Ma'am Sheldon leave. She didn't deserve this pain. She wasn't a bad person; it was the people around her that were rotten, almost all of them.

Nailah included.

She felt like she'd been caught on a runaway spiral, carried off the day that he, Tabia's love, *Rohi*, had come to tell her of Tabia's death. Instead of leaping off, she'd stayed on, riding deeper and deeper . . .

She let her head fall onto Babu's sheets. Such a stupid snap about Tabia being murdered. Why had she said it? She should have kept her mouth shut, refused to tell Ma'am Sheldon anything, no matter her threats to go to the police, have her taken in. Selfish, *selfish*.

All she could hope for now was that Ma'am Sheldon would keep her suspicions to herself, and not just because Nailah needed time to get herself and the children away before anyone came to arrest her. She prayed Ma'am Sheldon would stay quiet for her own sake too.

For if *he* found out all Ma'am Sheldon had started to guess, there would be only one fate for her: the same one her sister had suffered.

Chapter Thirty

They were on their way home, thank Christ. They'd been riding since dawn, galloping hard, eyes locked on the endless dunes ahead as they willed away the distance.

Edward had been sure that Tabia's estranged husband would give them nothing. He'd been tempted not to bother speaking with him at all. As they'd approached his hut, and Mahmood had looked nervously up at them, shoulders stooped beneath his loose smock as he clutched a bucket of chicken feed, it had been obvious he was no abductor. He didn't even know of Tabia's death until they told him. He hadn't seen Tabia in years, nor the children. (*I was no good for them, you see. Then the sick boy arrived.*) He said he had no idea who might want to avenge Tabia's death. 'Have you spoken to Tabia's brother?' he'd asked.

Edward had felt his spine crackle. 'Tabia has a brother?'

'Yes. Jahi. He always visited, he used to work close by. He probably still does. He may know of something.'

'His second name?' Tom had asked.

Edward cursed now, thinking of Mahmood's reply. 'We need to arrest them all,' he called to Tom, voice raised above the sound of the wind, their hooves. 'They've all been lying. Nailah included.'

Tom didn't protest this time. 'We need to speak about India too,' he said. 'It can't wait. The ship, it leaves—'

'Not now,' said Edward, 'I can't think about that now.' He looked to the sun, already beginning its descent in the sky, the haze on the dunes. 'It can keep until tomorrow.'

*

Since Imogen was still at the Pashas' when she called, Olivia sent one of the servants to fetch her, telling them to bring her to Clara's, then asked Fadil to take her there. She couldn't go home, not with the chance that Alistair might be there, the sense of Edward in every room. She wanted to scream, lash out, rip at her own hair, anything to get rid of the confusion within her.

She wished she could see Edward. Against the growing weight of evidence, she refused to believe he'd played a part in Tabia's death, she simply couldn't think him capable of it. But she had to know what he knew, and why he'd kept it all from her. For the first time ever, she was angry at him, and she hated it.

The carriage jerked. Skinny goats stared with bored eyes. The acacia trees rustled in a lacklustre breeze. Olivia's fury grew, fanned by the stultifying heat, extending to everyone, herself included, for not being able to work it all out and see what everyone else apparently did.

The police were in Clara's front garden, smoking beneath the shade of her orange trees. Olivia cursed them silently as she climbed down from the carriage, hating them for all the lies they stood for, and for looking so relaxed, so dispassionately at ease, when they – and everyone else – had failed, so abysmally, to find Clara.

Fadil took the horses to the stables, she raised her fist to the front door. She held it in mid-air. She turned back to the police, looked up at the house.

Sometimes realisations took a while.

Had Jeremy killed Tabia? Was it *he* who had asked Edward to arrange payment for Babu's care, out of guilt? And were the police here now to protect the rest of the family because Clara had been taken as retribution? It would certainly explain the hush-hush investigation, all hands on deck to get to Clara, apprehend her kidnappers, bury it, bury them. No one would want it getting out that Jeremy, one half of Sheldon-Gray Limited, bastion of British commercial greatness, had murdered an impoverished local woman. Least of all Jeremy.

Or Alistair.

Was that why Alistair was helping with the search? Or did he have Tabia's death on his hands too? The more Olivia thought about it, the surer she was that he was involved. That was why her own safety was such a concern: she was next on the abduction list.

She could only assume that Edward was off now chasing a suspect. Tabia's lover? Did Edward even know she'd had one?

Quite possibly not.

Olivia took a long breath. It was *him* she needed to tell Edward about: Tabia's lover, not Clara's. He held the key to Clara's whereabouts, Olivia was certain of it. But where was he? *Who* was he? There was only one person who knew.

Resolve snapped through her. She set off to find Fadil in the stables, intent on sending him back to St Aloysius' to take Nailah in, sick cousin or no. She cursed herself for not doing it earlier; she'd been too shocked to think straight, that was the problem, wasted time. Enough. Nailah must be made to talk.

Fadil was brushing the carriage horses down. Hassan was there too, flicking his beads in a corner; El Masri leant against the wall, a piece of straw in his mouth. Olivia narrowed her eyes at him. He really was a good-looking man, even more so for his slight imperfections, that single crooked tooth. Could he have been Clara's lover after all? Or Tabia's?

She wasn't fool enough to ask.

She turned to Fadil and said she'd like a word outside.

She spoke to him in hushed tones, conscious that the other two, El Masri especially, could well be listening. She told Fadil as quickly as possible that he needed to have Nailah arrested, that she was certain the girl held the key to Clara's whereabouts. 'I can't say more now, just please, go and get her.'

'The hospital will never hand a girl over to me,' he said, 'even a local one.'

Olivia frowned. 'What if I came?'

'It needs to be an officer if we are to convince the doctors, and the lieutenants are all over the city looking for your sister.'

'Then what about the police in the garden?'

'They're Wilkins' men, Ma'am Sheldon. Sayed Bertram said not to trust them.'

'Fadil, we have to do something.'

He nodded, obviously thinking. At length, he said he'd take the carriage to the house to fetch his own horse, then go in search of the lieutenants. 'You wait here, Ma'am Sheldon. Don't leave until I'm back. You must promise me that. There is no one, no one at all, you should go anywhere with, but me.'

Nailah exhaled as she left the hospital. Sister Rosis let her go gladly this time. Babu was responding well to his medicine, he could finish it at home. Nailah supposed she was happy to be rid of them from her clean, white ward.

Nailah was certainly pleased to be gone.

On the way home, she banged on Sana's door, intent on fetching Cleo before she ran. She felt a fierce impulse to hug her, cradle her in just the way she was holding Babu. *You're not alone, little one; I'm sorry for how you must have felt you were.*

But Cleo wasn't at Sana's. Nor was Isa. 'Your uncle fetched them,' said Sana.

'He's back?' The words stuck like marbles in Nailah's throat.

'Yes, he looked as if he'd raced the whole way over from Ramleh.' Sana gave a short laugh. 'I've been so curious, you know, about what it is you're involved with that's got everyone running around like headless chickens. But, I'm not so sure I want to know any more. There's something else too, he had another—'

Nailah didn't stop to listen. She didn't have time for it. She hurried away.

'You're trouble,' Sana called after her. 'Nothing but trouble.'

Nailah let herself into the house. She climbed the stairs, hoisting Babu on her hip, and opened the door to their room, expecting Jahi.

But he wasn't there. It was another man who stared across at her from the window ledge, brown eyes fierce and panicked. In his hand he clutched the worry beads Tabia had given him, thumb moving over the central four, each one inscribed with a letter.

305

ROHI.

A gift from those days when Tabia had loved him so well. When he was a man who deserved to be loved.

Imogen arrived mid-afternoon, full of frustration at having found nothing more out at Benjamin's.

'Never mind that,' said Olivia, and proceeded to tell her of everything in motion.

'There's no point in Fadil going to the hospital,' said Imogen, once Olivia had finished. 'Nailah won't be hanging around there, not now she's let this out. She'll be planning to run, mark my words. We can't let her slip away.' She sucked in her breath. 'The secrets she's kept. I'll go to her house, take some servants with me. You stay here, darling. If Fadil comes back, send him to Nailah's. We might need his help.'

Nailah stood immobile under Hassan's gaze. In times before, he might have stepped forward, taken Babu from her arms, kissed him; this boy he'd said he wanted to be a father to. It was a mark of how far the past weeks had dragged him that he didn't give Babu a second glance. His only movement was to flick Tabia's beads, then pocket them. Nailah watched him, remembering how proud Tabia had been of the gift, wrapping it in fine layers of tissue, a ribbon. ('I've been saving for weeks,' she had said. 'I'll give it to him tonight. Perhaps we'll go for a walk first' – she'd bitten her lip in anticipation – 'Rohi.') Tabia had ever called him so. Cleo had used to make them laugh by following her lead, using the pet name too, back before she'd been afraid of him, in the old days when he would talk to her, tell her fine tales. Jahi, though, he had stuck to his true name. Hassan in turn had only ever called Jahi by his second name, El Masri, the one he went under at work. ('I'll call him Jahi when we're married,' Hassan would tell Tabia whenever she scolded him for being so formal. 'He'll never approve of me until then. He worries I'll let you down, I think. Like that coward, Mahmood. But I'll show him, I'll prove that I deserve you.')

'Where is everyone?' Nailah asked him now. Her voice sounded small to her own ears. 'My uncle?'

'He's taken your mother and Cleo away.'

'Why? Where have they gone?'

He didn't answer. Instead he asked, 'Why, Nailah? Why did you drag Ma'am Sheldon into it?'

'I never thought—'

'*Thought?*' He said it quietly, almost gently. 'If only you'd tried such a thing.'

'I didn't know what to do. She was going to go to the police, the army.'

'She's still going to go to them, and soon.' He frowned. 'Although I have bought some time for now.'

'What do you mean?'

He didn't answer. Instead he told her to tell him everything Ma'am Sheldon knew. *Everything.* As he fired question after question at her, she reluctantly recounted the sordid details.

'It's too much,' he said, 'she knows too much.'

'Not everything,' said Nailah miserably.

His eyes narrowed. 'You're certain she doesn't know it was me whom Tabia loved? She has no cause to distrust me?'

Nailah said no, no cause, then listened, horrified, as Hassan told her what must happen next.

'No.' She sank to her knees. 'No. You can't do this.'

It was exactly what she'd said to him that first morning after Tabia had died, when he'd come at dawn to fetch her away from the Pashas', telling her all that had happened to Tabia, what he intended.

'Tabia wouldn't want this,' she'd said. 'You don't need to do it.'

He had looked at her as though she baffled him. 'They trampled her, Nailah, burnt her. Sir Gray can't go unpunished. How could I let him? No, you must come with me. The children need you. Tell no one why you're going, or where.'

She'd gone along with him in a daze. At Tabia's, he'd handed her a paper and pen.

'We'll write a letter to Sir Gray, telling him that if he doesn't go to the police to confess, he'll pay. You write it, Nailah. No one will recognise your hand. Even if they do, they won't be able to find you. I've leased a room for you in the city.'

Nailah had tried to resist. But he'd said if she didn't do as she was told, he'd take the children from her right then, right there, far away to his own family's village. 'You'll never find them. I don't want to do it, but I'll stop at nothing to get justice. Write, now. Please.'

Cleo had tugged on Nailah's robe and said, 'I don't want him to take us away. I'm scared.'

Nailah had hesitated a moment more, and then written exactly what Hassan told her to.

He'd left her then, told her to pack, that he'd fetch her and the children later. She'd done her best to parcel up Tabia's belongings without tears, to be strong. But she'd been so afraid, especially when the captain and Fadil arrived and told her that strange story about Tabia being a cotton worker they wished to help. She hadn't been able to do anything but nod and tell her own lies in turn.

How could she have admitted the truth, when a letter in her own hand was already on its way to Sir Gray?

She had still been numb with terror when Hassan returned to fetch her and the children to the Turkish Quarter. Jahi was waiting for them there. Hassan told him, head high, what he'd had Nailah do, his plan to make Sir Gray pay. 'I will not let your sister down in this.'

Jahi stared. 'Sweet Mother,' he said, 'I could kill you.' He turned to Nailah. 'I could kill you both. What were you thinking, Nailah, letting him use you like this?'

Hassan said, 'I did it for Tabia.'

Jahi sneered. 'You did it for yourself. Let this be an end to it. God willing, you're never discovered.'

As he stormed from the room, Hassan called, 'Sir Gray will confess, just watch.'

If only Sir Gray had confessed. But he'd run away with the family to Turkey instead.

Hassan had come to visit Nailah the day after the Grays left. He'd told her that he'd spoken with a man, a great man, *my friend*. Hassan's friend was disgusted by what had been done to Tabia, he agreed Sir Gray shouldn't go unpunished. 'He says we can make Sir Gray take us seriously.' Nailah told him she didn't want to hear, to know, Hassan should leave. Hassan had given her a long, troubled look, then did as she asked. He never came again after that. Not once. Nailah had tried to convince herself that he was ashamed. She'd fought to believe, for the sake of Tabia's love for him, that grief alone had made him act so ill, that he regretted it. She'd sunk herself into the care of Cleo and Babu, her life back in the slums, ignoring the niggling voice warning her that something had grown in Hassan the moment Tabia was shot: a hatred that wouldn't let him rest. Eventually, she'd almost managed to forget about it.

And then that news had come that Ma'am Gray had been taken. She'd never forget the moment in the baths when she overheard the women talking, or Jahi arriving to confirm Hassan had done it. She could still smell that overripe watermelon.

'We'd better go inside,' Jahi had said. 'We have a deal to discuss, you and I.'

He'd asked Nailah if she'd known what Hassan was planning.

'No,' she'd said, 'but I must go to the police, tell them what he's done.'

'You can't,' Jahi had replied. 'Hassan says if either of us do, he'll tell them it was you who wrote that first letter to Sir Gray. You'll be arrested, Nailah, they'll match your hand.'

Nailah had run for the door blindly saying she didn't care, that they had to do something.

Jahi had seized her by her wrists, shaken her. 'Little fool, you do nothing.' Cleo, hunched in the corner, had started to sob. 'This isn't just about you,' Jahi had said. 'They'll take me in too, they'll never believe I wasn't involved. Think what would happen to your cousins then. You say nothing, Nailah. Do you understand me?'

Slowly, knowing how wrong it was, Nailah had nodded.

'The only path now,' Jahi said, 'is for me to help Hassan, make sure Ma'am Gray stays safe, and that you're neither of you found out. I must get you and the children away, find somewhere safe to hide you. It will take time. But hear me: if I get wind that you're planning to do anything stupid, or hear a whisper of you letting out what's happened, I'll take the children from you, long before the police can take us. I will not have them put at risk.'

Nailah had felt as though a trap was falling around her; she had tried to see a way out of it, breaths coming quicker and quicker at the impossibility of it, as panicked then as she felt now. Her terror had never lifted, not even for a moment, just intensified, reaching screaming pitch the night Jahi had told her that Ma'am Gray had done the impossible and run, escaped from that spot where the twin palms grow, even though there was nowhere but death for her to escape to in the miles of desert around. No water, no shelter: she'd have died within a day, maybe less.

'If they find us out now, Nailah, we'll hang. Stay quiet. You have no place with Fadil, with Captain Bertram and his colonel. No business.'

Nailah had tried to numb herself to Jahi's words, to close herself off from it all. She'd thought that it might be easier to live with herself that way.

But it wasn't. It never could be.

She loathed herself for not speaking out when the captain had come with his colonel to question her, telling them all whilst there was still a chance, however remote, that Ma'am Gray was alive. She'd failed Ma'am Gray. And now she was failing her sister too.

'This doesn't have to happen,' she said to Hassan now. 'It can all end here. I'll run, tell no one anything else. Please though, leave Ma'am Sheldon alone.'

'What are you talking about?'

Nailah started at Jahi's voice in the doorway behind her.

'What is going on?' Jahi asked again.

Hassan said, 'Ma'am Sheldon knows almost all. I told you I feared she did.'

'You are sure?' Jahi spoke through gritted teeth.

'Yes. She will have to be silenced.'

Jahi's face creased in pain. 'Surely as long as we get Nailah and the family away, hidden, it's safe. There'll be no one left to lead the police to you—'

'They'll work it out,' said Hassan, interrupting. 'You know that. If Ma'am Sheldon is allowed to talk, they'll question everyone – here, and in Montazah – they won't stop until they find out who I am, and' – he paused, gave Jahi a pointed look – 'who helped me. They'll track Isa and the children down, come after you. We'll all pay in the end.'

Jahi stared, then to Nailah's horror, closed his eyes and gave a short nod.

'No,' Nailah said, 'no. There has to be something else we can do.'

'There's nothing else,' Jahi said heavily. 'If there was, we'd do it.'

'No.' Nailah cast around in her mind for another way, something that might yet make it right. 'I could go to Ma'am Sheldon again,' she said, her mouth running dry at the prospect even as she spoke, 'explain. I would do that. I *would*. I can tell her everything, how we meant none of it. Maybe she'll help us.'

'Are you mad?' Hassan asked. His eyes widened, incredulous. 'You've explained enough. It is us who will fix this, not you.'

Nailah turned back to Jahi. Unlike Hassan, there was no energy in his face, no life. He looked beaten, exhausted.

'Please, Uncle,' she said. 'Please don't let this happen. I can see you don't want it.'

Jahi put his forefinger and thumb to his nose, thinking.

Nailah held her breath.

Hassan said, 'El Masri, we talked about this. You agreed that if she knew what we feared, this was the way it must be.'

Jahi waited a second more, then slowly inclined his head in assent.

'Uncle, no.'

'I can't put us at risk,' said Jahi, 'especially not you, Nailah. Not the children.'

'Nor me,' said Hassan.

'That is not what I care about.' Jahi didn't look at Hassan as he spoke. It was as though he couldn't. 'Nailah, it's time for you to go. I only came here to fetch you.'

'What? Where are you taking me?'

'You must go to my friend's,' said Hassan.

'Your friend's?' Nailah's eyes darted from him to Jahi. 'Where is that?'

'Somewhere you'll be safe,' said Jahi. 'We just need to keep you safe, out of the way.'

'No,' she said, 'please don't do this. I beg of you. And you must leave the boy alone too.'

Jahi winced. 'I have no part in Hassan's plans for the little sir.'

'You do,' said Nailah. 'By not stopping him, you do.' Fear pressed in her throat. She turned to Hassan. 'What would Tabia think?'

His eyes snapped. 'Don't bring her into it.'

'But she's what it's all about,' Nailah sobbed in dismay. 'Or have you forgotten that?'

'I have not forgotten.' Hassan took a deep breath. 'I do not forget.'

Nailah looked down at Babu, asleep and oblivious, a pink flush on his cheeks, 'What happens to him?' she asked. 'And where's my mother and Cleo?'

'I've taken them to the station,' Jahi said heavily. 'They'll get the train to Cairo once we drop Babu with them. I've given them money, all I have. Isa knows the city, she's been there often enough; I've told her to find them somewhere to stay. I thought to get them away in case the police try to question them, just for a few weeks.' His brow creased. 'Maybe they should stay there now.'

'Why can't I go with them?' Nailah asked.

'It's too dangerous,' said Jahi. 'We need you somewhere you can never be found. The captain and the colonel have already been after you, they'll want to find you more than ever once they discover Ma'am Sheldon visited you at the hospital.'

'And,' said Hassan, 'once they discover Ma'am Sheldon is dead. Bertram will raise hell when he finds that out. He loves her I think.' He shrugged. 'She's very loveable.'

Nailah let another sob go, this time full of disgust.

312

Hassan appeared not to hear it. 'He won't rest until he tracks you down,' he said. 'We need you to vanish, somewhere well away from Tabia's children.'

Nailah shook her head. How was this happening? How?

Hassan reached into his pocket for a pad and pencil, saying he had one final job for her. 'We'll ask Ma'am Sheldon to meet me on the outskirts. I'll do it at the oasis, I can have men collect her body, and no one will hear.'

'I don't want to know,' said Nailah, 'and I'm not writing that letter.'

'You must.'

'I *won't*.'

Jahi sighed and, in a voice as pained as Nailah had ever heard, said he would do it. His hand shook as he took the paper, but still, he wrote exactly what Hassan told him to, then handed the note over, not once looking at Hassan's face.

Nailah started to weep.

'Ah, Nailah,' said Hassan. 'This will all be over soon. And you'll wake tomorrow breathing.' He set his eyes on the door, made for it, and then paused, frowning briefly. He squeezed his beads in his pocket. For the first time, he looked unsure, nervous maybe at the night ahead. Nailah saw it through her tears and felt a stab of hope. But then Hassan gave a nod of resolve, and left, taking hope with him.

At length, Jahi said, 'We should go too.'

'No, please,' Nailah said. 'She doesn't deserve this, the child doesn't—'

'Come, Nailah.'

'I can't go.' Nailah sat down on the floor, gripping the boards with her toes. Now that the moment was here, she was overcome with panic. She'd never see the children again, she couldn't even say goodbye to Kafele, she would probably never find out what became of Ma'am Sheldon. 'It doesn't need to be this way.'

Jahi took her by the arm and pulled her, feet scraping, to the door. 'It's for the best,' he said grimly. 'It's too late for any other path.'

'It's not, Uncle, it's not. Please, you have to listen to me. Hassan's gone now, please stop and listen.'

But he didn't. He dragged her away, down the stairs, and out into the baking street.

It was as they turned the corner into the neighbouring alleyway that Nailah glimpsed Ma'am Carter and her servants approaching the house. Ma'am Carter hadn't seen them. Nailah opened her mouth to call out to her.

But then Jahi's hand tightened on her arm, and her voice wouldn't work.

To her shame, and despite all her protests inside, she said and did nothing at all.

Olivia sat out on the terrace with Sofia, running her finger around and around her water glass as she watched Ralph half-heartedly swing a croquet mallet. She was exhausted from the mess in her mind, her wonderings as to where everyone was, if Edward was on his way back.

She was sore from the weight of Mildred's shadowy presence in the drawing room.

'Don't slouch, Olivia,' Her papery voice sliced through the air from the chaise longue. 'And you should be wearing your hat, you'll get freckles. Your mother had them.'

Olivia closed her eyes. Sunlight ebbed through her lids; the high afternoon heat beat down, soaking through the stiff layers of her bodice, her shirt, her corset.

'The children have been out too long, Nanny,' said Mildred. 'Angus will get burnt again. Really it's most irresponsible.'

Where are you, Edward? Where are you?

Tom narrowed his eyes into the spout of his water flask. 'I'm out,' he said. 'You?'

'Same.'

'We won't make it back without water.' Tom nodded at a spot in the distance. Two palms formed a silhouette against the white heat of the sky. 'Let's go.'

It was a tiny patch of land. Barely an oasis at all. But there was a hut there. It had blankets within, a mound of ash outside. Edward sat down on his haunches and rubbed the flakes between his fingers.

'Nomads?' suggested Tom.

'I don't know.' All Edward's senses suggested otherwise. He frowned, trying to work out how far they were now from Lixori, that ramshackle cluster of dwellings from which Wilkins and Alistair had taken that farmer. A few hours' ride at least. Still, it was a fairly direct line from here to there. Had the farmer passed this place, spotted something? Was that why Wilkins had been so interested in him in the first place? It wasn't unthinkable: if the farmer had been travelling to Alex, perhaps to sell his crops, he might well have ridden by and seen . . . what?

Clara?

'I think she might have been here,' he said.

Tom looked around the small oasis. Edward followed his eyes. There was nothing but the hut, the palms, and a small water spring. No one but them.

'There's nothing we can do now,' said Tom at length. 'Come on. Let's get back to the city. We can still make it by nightfall.'

Imogen returned as dusk was falling. She told Olivia, in whispers in the hallway, how she'd failed to find Nailah. 'I'm going to the ground now to wait for Tom. Come with me?'

Olivia shook her head. 'I'll stay here, wait for Fadil. He can't be far away. I'll bring him on as soon as he gets here.'

Imogen frowned. 'I can't think why he's taken so long. I don't like it.'

'Nor do I,' admitted Olivia. It had been hours. She was worried about him. Had he been hurt, fallen from his horse?

Or had something worse happened?

Sofia bustled past with a pile of towels in one arm, Gus in the other, and Ralph in her wake. 'Bath time,' she announced unnecessarily. 'Mr Jeremy will be home soon for stories.'

Imogen smiled tightly and took her leave.

Olivia went back out to sit on the garden terrace. Mildred was still on the chaise longue. Her watchfulness, the crackle of her taffeta skirts, needled into Olivia's spine. Eventually, unable to bear it any longer, she decided to wait for Fadil in the front porch, and went to fetch her hat and bag from where she'd left them in the study.

The room was full of muted gold light. The air still. As Olivia lifted her things from the desk, she saw a note beneath them, and caught her breath.

It wasn't in a hand she recognised, although it was addressed to her; the thought that some stranger had put it there whilst she was outside made her skin crawl.

Meet me at the fork to the desert road at seven o'clock. I will explain everything. Come alone. Tell no one what you are doing. This is the only way you can be safe.

Chapter Thirty-One

If there was someone fool enough to go hightailing off to one of the remotest areas in Alexandria in this land where women went missing and were mown down by horses, it wasn't Olivia. There was no question of her not telling anyone about the note, no matter what idiocy her penfriend asked of her. In the ongoing absence of Fadil, and too jumpy to go anywhere alone, she decided to send word for Imogen to return. They could work out together what to do next.

She tried to find Hassan to fetch her. Since he wasn't in the stables, she asked an underservant to go in his stead. The boy spoke very poor English, but she managed to get her message through. With him dispatched, she tried to locate the police guarding the house, thinking to put them on high alert, ask if they'd seen anyone suspect who might have got in. Finding them nowhere (where the bloody hell was everyone?), she scribbled another note to be taken to the police headquarters, asking for two new, preferably competent, men to be sent. She handed it to the butler, who told her Hassan would take care of it; he'd returned from town not twenty minutes before.

'Fine,' she said, and went back outside to wait for Imogen.

It was about ten minutes later that the underservant returned. He told Olivia, in a mix of mime and broken words, that he'd gone to Imogen's house, but she wasn't there.

'Of course she wasn't. I told you she was at the parade ground.'

He smiled, nodded.

'Do you understand what I'm saying? I said the parade ground. The. Parade. Ground.'

Another smile.

She sighed irritably.

'Her servants, they say she go see you. I think, ah!' He raised his finger. 'She at Ma'am Sheldon's house.'

'My house? No.'

'No.' The boy grinned, nodded. 'Just Sir Sheldon. He say he come.'

'Right.'

'He need to . . . ' The boy mimed pulling on trousers.

'Change?'

He beamed.

Olivia sighed. The last thing she wanted was to be present when Alistair arrived. Since there was nothing else for it, she was going to have to go to the parade ground herself.

She dismissed the boy and went into the stables to tack up Clara's mare. Her hands trembled at the prospect of riding a horse other than Bea, the journey alone . . . never mind what came after. She eyed the mounting stand, struck by its morbid likeness to a gallows block.

She clambered into the saddle without it.

Just as she was about to kick off, Hassan arrived. He said the butler had given him her message for the police, but he'd just seen the two guards in the kitchen, they'd be back on duty soon. He asked Olivia where she was going.

She told him.

'It's almost dark,' he said. 'I'll take you.'

'No, really, that's too much to ask.'

'Ma'am Sheldon, please.'

'Thank you for doing this,' Olivia said to fill the silence as the two of them clopped their way along. Hassan held his reins in one hand, his beads in the other. The road around them was deserted. Cicadas burred, the dry shrubs on the sandbanks crackled. The wind had changed direction, it smelt of salt. On the horizon, the sun was bleeding into the Mediterranean, orange light seeping into the blue. Ahead to the right was the turning to the parade ground. *Not long.*

'Be still a moment,' said Hassan. 'Your saddle's loose.'

'Is it?' Olivia knew a loose saddle by now and it felt fine to her. Hassan leant over and took her reins, pulling her to a halt. His tarboosh was on an angle, his normally serene face appeared strained as he looked up at her. 'Are you all right?' she asked. He didn't respond, just stared back at her, twisting their reins together. 'Why are you doing that?' she asked. Was that sweat on his forehead? 'Hassan? You're worrying me. What is it?'

He glanced over her shoulder and frowned. Olivia followed his stare. Alistair was riding towards them. He looked smaller from this distance, but packed with force. The sight of him sent something loose in Olivia's stomach. And on edge as Hassan was making her feel, it was unfathomable to run towards him, her husband. The only plan that made any sense was galloping at all speed to the ground.

'I want to go now,' she said. 'Can you free my reins, Hassan?'

His eyes remained fixed on Alistair. Those puddle-like eyes. So sympathetic when Clara first disappeared. *Did you manage to speak to the soldier you were looking for?*

Oh God.

OhGodOhGodOhGod.

'I never told you that I was trying to find Fadil.' The words seemed to leave her slowly, it was as though time was stretching around her. 'You asked me, that day after Clara was taken, if I had. But I'd never told you I was looking for him in the first place.' She swallowed. 'Did you see me trying to find him, on the Cherif Pasha?'

Still Hassan watched Alistair; his face was fixed, intent.

She looked again at his beads, read the letters. 'You're Rohi,' she said.

His face didn't move.

'You are, aren't you?' Nothing. 'When you stopped me falling into that ditch on the way to the beach the other day, it was because you knew it was there. You've been there before. It's you. It's always been you.'

Alistair was coming closer, the steady tread of his horse not fifty feet away.

'Have you hurt Fadil, Hassan? Is that why he's not back yet? Did you follow him after he left the stables?'

Hassan reached into his saddle and drew out a single-shot pistol. Olivia's legs turned to water.

And time, which had been moving so slowly, suddenly sped up. Hassan freed her reins and whacked her horse on its rear. It jolted into motion. Olivia grabbed its mane, righting herself. In the same moment, Hassan yelled, 'Ha,' slapped the horse again, and she was off.

A gunshot sounded.

For a heartbeat Olivia thought it might have been Alistair that had fired. But when she looked over her shoulder, it was to see him keel backwards, bounce floppily in his saddle, then fall as his beast galloped off. She didn't have time to feel anything, be it shock, relief or fear, because Hassan was fully conscious, sitting upright in his saddle, and coming fast towards her.

She spurred Clara's horse on. She had no idea where she was going, only that she had to get away. Dust blew up around her. She kicked and hit and kicked again. She scanned the road for a sign of somebody, anybody, but it was empty.

She kept on, the ground rushed away beneath her. On and on. Hooves sounded behind her, striking a discordant rhythm with her own. *Give her the reins.* She could hear Edward's voice in her ear. *Let her go.* She loosened her grip and leant forward. 'Faster, faster.' She clutched her legs tight. She didn't look back at Hassan chasing her, but fixed her eyes straight ahead.

She realised too late that she had headed the wrong way. She was riding in the opposite direction to the ground, towards the deserted shores of the Aboukir Peninsula, away from people instead of closer to them. She risked a look behind her. Hassan was closer than she'd imagined, blocking her path back.

She rode on, on and on. *If I can just make it to the Pashas' house, any house.*

Clara's steady nut-brown mare slowed, exhausted. Olivia more felt than heard Hassan gaining on her.

'Come on,' she said, kicking again, 'come on.'

It was as they neared the cliff tops that Hassan caught up with her. She saw a flash of steel, felt pain in her face.

And then there was nothing.

Chapter Thirty-Two

Incense and sweet oils, it was all Nailah could smell. It filled the air, mingling with the tinkle of ankle chains and earrings, whispers and laughter. Nailah watched the women from behind her door, their heads tipped coquettishly, the slow smiles. A pair on the far side of the room were singing. One touched the other on the shoulder as she reached for the high note, flirting, even with one another, as though they couldn't help themselves.

She could barely believe Jahi had brought her here, to this fort in the desert, this, this harem. 'Hassan says you'll be kept safe,' he had told her as they rode, 'that is all that matters now.'

'It's not all that matters,' Nailah had said, tears starting again. 'If Tabia could only see what you and Hassan were planning, she would hate you both.'

Nailah ran her hands over her stomach, pushing against the churning concave there. She was still clothed in the same robe Ma'am Sheldon had given her. She was meant to be getting changed into her uniform, the same wide-legged trousers and silken top that all the maids here wore. She glanced at the garments waiting on her low mattress, the towels, soap and razor. A bossy lady had told her to use the blade on her armpits, her legs. 'No need for those red cheeks,' the lady had said, 'all the maids do it. He prefers things pretty. Rest tonight, we'll set you up with your duties tomorrow. Do your work well and you'll have a good life here. He'll watch over you.'

Nailah asked who *he* was. The lady told her it was Nassar Shahid, a man Nailah knew to be a peripheral star in the constellation of the Egyptian aristocracy, and as wealthy as Tut. Nailah had heard the rumours of his involvement in the uprisings of '82, his resentment of the British. She found she wasn't surprised that he was the *friend* who had helped Hassan steal Ma'am Gray, then told him where to keep her: that remote oasis with the small hut of provisions, a good water supply, and the shade of two palms.

She wondered why Shahid had done it, though. Was he saddened by Tabia's death, a charitable aristocrat with a good heart? Or an opportunist, a proud man on the lookout for a chance to stand up, make life hard for the British?

If Jahi was here, Nailah might have asked him. But he'd left already. He hadn't even seen Nailah in; he couldn't wait to be away from her. He'd simply hammered on the servants' door, bade her a hurried goodbye, then swung back onto his borrowed camel and ridden off. He hadn't told Nailah where for, only that he'd go to the oasis later, once he was sure it was all done, and help Hassan with Ma'am Sheldon's body. He had no stomach to witness the murder itself. Suddenly, the image of it filled Nailah's mind: Hassan taking aim in the darkness, Ma'am Sheldon folding over, sinking into her own silk skirts. It stole Nailah's breath. She held her hand to her chest, fighting for air, and her mind filled with other pictures: Babu cradled in Cleo's arms on the floor of the station, waiting for the train; Isa pacing the platform in her fading muslin, berating Jahi for stealing Nailah away, not letting them say goodbye. Kafele, amber eyes bewildered as he tried to find out where Nailah was.

She saw the captain, the pain distorting his handsome features when he discovered Ma'am Sheldon's disappearance, the wiping away of her smile.

Another smile.

Nailah went over to the mattress and picked up her new clothes. She ran the silk through her hands, as fine as any Ma'am Amélie had ever owned. She would wear them once – tonight. She would bathe, oil her hair, and let them all think she was happy to stay.

But then, somehow, she would escape. She was sickened at her own cowardice all these long weeks, for not calling out to Ma'am Carter earlier; she hoped she wouldn't be too late to help Ma'am Sheldon now. She didn't know how she was going to do it, only that she had to find a way. She had nothing left to lose. And she'd let so much that was evil happen.

It was time to make amends.

For all the luxury of the women's quarters, the embroidered cushions, gold-leaf mirrors and lamps, there was only one external door, and when Nailah drifted past it, trying the handle, she found it locked. She cursed, eyeing the women nearby to make sure they hadn't noticed her attempt to leave. They appeared oblivious, lost in their chatter, their fingers aflutter as they talked; birds all of them, fine in their feathers, but trapped in a gilded cage.

'Almost sleep time,' said one of them with a coy laugh.

Nailah's stomach flipped, half with disgust, half shameful curiosity. It was as though these women craved Shahid's attention. Nailah could feel his presence everywhere, unseen, unheard, yet alive in the air of expectation tightening minute by minute. She imagined an elegant man in his forties, assured and strong, with that streak of steel that enabled him to rebel and survive. What would it feel like to be looked after by such a man? To give yourself over to his protection, safe and blameless, a servant of his goddesses?

Nailah shook her head at the temptation, so hard that a couple of the women glanced at her strangely, said something to each other, and laughed.

Nailah ignored them. She looked around for another door, a hint of a way to escape. She pictured the vastness of the desert outside, the endless dirt track along which Jahi's camel had run to bring her here. Even if she got out of the compound, she could well die before she reached the city.

Like Ma'am Gray must have.

She returned to her room. She looked to her window, at the white muslin billowing in the breeze. She went to it and peered down at the gardens. Too far to jump. But the room just below had its shutters open. If she was careful she could balance on them before leaping.

She pushed the thought of the dunes aside; she'd deal with them when she got to them. If she got to them. She climbed onto the window ledge and leant out. Her silk trousers quivered in the wind. She turned, lowering herself.

Chapter Thirty-Three

Olivia heard the waves in her dreams before she connected consciously with the realisation that she was still alive. Groggily, she opened her eyes, wincing at the burn of her cheek, the sense of congealing blood. Hassan had struck her right on the same spot she'd hurt in her fall from Bea, fracturing the skin.

Moving her head as little as she could, she took in where they were. He hadn't brought her far, he probably didn't dare whilst it was still dusk. They were beneath a lighthouse, on the peninsula at Montazah bloody Bay. The lighthouse loomed above them in the grey twilight, its lamp black, no longer in use. The beach curved around to the left, some metres below. The horses were tethered beside them, too far from the road to be spotted. Not that anyone would think to look. Who came here at nightfall? No one but adulterers and murderers, it seemed.

How far were they from the Pashas' home, from the other scattered mansions and peasant dwellings in the area? Olivia had heard talk of plans to build a grand palace and gardens nearby for the royal family. She wished it had begun already, that there were a few hundred workers camping in the vicinity. As it was, there was no one close enough to hear her scream.

Why hadn't Hassan killed her already, if that was what he wanted to do?

He reached out, as though to touch her face. 'I've never hit a woman before today,' he said. 'I wish I didn't have to hurt you.'

He sounded sorry. She could almost be convinced that he was, if he hadn't hit her so bloody hard and didn't currently have the same gun he had blindsided her with dangling menacingly between his knees.

'Did you shoot Fadil?'

'Not shoot.' He leant against the fencing wall and shut his eyes. 'The gunshot would have alerted the house. I just helped him to have a rest. A long rest. He'll be sleeping yet in the cellar beneath your stables.'

'Oh my God. You battered him?' Olivia pictured Fadil tacking up his horse, weathered face set with purpose. Hassan creeping up from behind, not letting himself be seen. She caught her breath. As if Fadil hadn't been through enough.

Hassan's hair lifted in the breeze, his white robes rippled. Goose pimples prickled beneath Olivia's bodice. In contrast to the past nights' balminess, the air was growing cold. Edward had told her how freezing the nights could become in the open desert, how insignificant he felt amidst the rolling dunes.

Was he back yet? Trying to find her?

Had Imogen spoken to him?

'Here.' Hassan dribbled water into her mouth from a flask. She made to take it from him, but her hands stuck behind her, bound. She shifted her weight on her cramped arms and swallowed against the rising panic in her throat. 'Why are you doing this to me? Would Tabia have wanted it?'

'Please,' he said, 'don't say her name.'

She stared at him, wanting to hurt him. 'She died here, didn't she?'

His eyes moved to the distant horizon. He said nothing.

'Did Jeremy kill her?'

He nodded slowly.

Even though Olivia had guessed it, she felt a jolt of shock. Jeremy. *Jeremy.*

'It was as I was taking Tabia back to her hut,' said Hassan, 'close to dawn. We heard Sir Gray and your husband; they were shooting for wild pigeons, drunk, I think.'

327

Olivia remembered how they'd staggered from the Pashas' ball saying they were going to make a night of it. *Just like old times.* She'd been relieved, pleased Alistair wasn't going home with her.

'I was afraid of them seeing us,' said Hassan. 'I didn't want Sir Gray to ask questions about why I was there.'

'Had you brought my sister?'

'Much earlier, just as the party finished. I walked her down to the beach, I often used to take her there for her . . . Meetings.'

A picture of them together shot through Olivia's mind. What was it the maid, Elia, had said? *His clothes, they weren't fine, and his skin, it was very dark.* So it was Hassan whom Elia and Nailah had seen with Clara; Clara's driver, not her lover at all. Olivia cursed herself for a fool. It seemed so obvious now.

Hassan confirmed it was so. 'Nailah told me afterwards how she'd seen me with Ma'am Gray. She was shocked, worried I'd been untrue to Tabia.' He shook his head. 'I never could be.'

'No. You're quite the gentleman.'

'I was to Tabia,' he said sadly. 'After I left your sister on the beach, I would go to her hut. Your sister always made her own way home. That night Tabia died, we spent hours together, talking, walking. We were gone too long, it's how it was with us: never enough time. Tabia was rushing when we saw Sir Gray and Sir Sheldon shooting, we were a long way from her hut and she was anxious to get home before the children woke.' He took a deep breath. 'I hid in the undergrowth and let her go on alone. She wouldn't wait.'

He paused. Olivia held her breath, waiting.

Hassan said, 'As she drew near them, she tripped.'

'In that rut?'

'Yes. She screamed, Sir Gray turned. His gun went off.' Hassan closed his eyes. 'Her whole body slumped, her beautiful body. They ran to her. Sir Gray talked about fetching a doctor, but your husband told him it was already too late. They just let her die.' Hassan pressed his forearm to his eyes. 'They didn't even try to save her. They rode one of their horses over her body to pass her murder off as an accident, then burnt her anyway because of the bullet wound.

They fetched a peasant, they must have seen him in a nearby field, and blackmailed him into taking the blame. He had a wife, you see, children to protect.'

Olivia lay quite still. Slowly, sickeningly, Hassan's words seeped through her. Her stomach churned, her cheeks worked against the urge to gag. Even she, who knew too well the cruelty Alistair was capable of, felt numb at all he'd done. She could almost see the detached expression on his face as he stood over Tabia whilst she died; the barely concealed enjoyment as he led the horse over her bones.

The panic in Jeremy's eyes as he watched. Such a coward.

And then to drag that peasant man into it; to stand by whilst he was punished so horrifically. 'I suspect,' she said, voice cracking, 'that involving the peasant wasn't Jeremy's idea.' The coldness of it smacked of the inside of Alistair's mind.

'No,' said Hassan, 'I think not. The peasant's wife lives at your house now, her sons too. At your gates.'

'Oh my God.' It made awful sense. So *that's* why they hated Alistair so. Those poor people. That poor, kind woman. *No you cry*.

'I was going to speak to them,' said Hassan, 'about going to the police. But I thought the mother would be too afraid for her sons, and the police wouldn't have believed her anyway.'

'So you took Clara instead. An eye for an eye.'

'I told Sir Gray he'd get her back as soon as he confessed.'

'Why did you have to involve her at all?' Olivia's head throbbed at the needless malevolence of it. 'She's done nothing, *nothing*.' Rage bubbled up within her as she remembered Clara's face in the street that day, the concern in her round eyes as she left Olivia. *'Don't be long will you?'* She'd been so unsuspecting of what was waiting for her, so horribly naive. Thinking of it, Olivia wanted to lash out, wipe the conceited composure from Hassan's face, force him to see the pain he'd so selfishly inflicted. Her arms pulled uselessly against their binding. 'You didn't need to do it,' she said. 'Why not just go to the police yourself? You were a witness, for goodness' sake. You're a coward, nothing but a coward.'

Hassan's sickening calm didn't falter. 'I am not,' he said. 'You think the police would have taken my word against Sir Gray's?' He tapped his gun. 'No, the confession had to come from him.'

Olivia squeezed her eyes against rising tears of fury. 'Not Alistair?'

'It wasn't him that did it. Besides, I knew he'd be more difficult to ... bring round. He's a hard man.' Hassan looked at Olivia. 'I'm sure you know that.'

Olivia pictured Alistair's flopping body. She'd be relieved he was dead if she wasn't so afraid she was about to join him.

Hassan said, 'Once I take Ralph ...'

'Ralph?' Olivia's eyes snapped open. 'No. No. Not him. You couldn't.'

'I won't hurt him, I swear it.'

'You mustn't go near him.' Olivia nearly choked on the words. She thought of his chubby cheeks, the way he'd been swinging his croquet mallet so sadly all afternoon. His woollen socks crinkling beneath his knickerbockers. Ralph, poor little Ralph. 'He's a child. Just a child.'

'Stop,' said Hassan 'Please, stop. I will do what I have to.'

'They'll work out it's you,' said Olivia. 'They'll find out.'

'How? You won't tell them. Your husband can't. Fadil didn't see me.'

'Someone else, then.' There had to be someone left who knew something. 'Edward,' she said, 'Tom ...'

'They've already interrogated me and let me go.'

'There'll be others,' she said.

'No,' he smiled sadly, as if he pitied her, 'there is no one.'

'There *has* to be,' she said.

He shrugged.

And even as Olivia's mind still worked, trying to find someone, anyone – a clue hiding that might yet be found – the truth in Hassan's words landed like a thud. *Oh, Ralph.*

'Rest now,' said Hassan, as though she could. 'We have a while to go before we can move.'

'Are you taking me to where you took Clara?'

'Yes.' He frowned. 'I have to. We would be there by now if you'd met me on the desert road as I asked.'

'I'm sorry for inconveniencing you.'

He fixed her with sorrowful eyes. 'Of course you are not,' he said. 'And now we need to wait to cross the city, until everyone sleeps.' He leant his head back against the fence. 'You and your sister will be together soon.'

'I'll see her?' Olivia asked.

Hassan made no answer.

'Will I see her?' Olivia asked again.

'Ma'am Sheldon,' he said, 'rest.'

Neither of them spoke for a long time after that. Hassan brought out his beads, flicking them with one hand, the gun still in the other. Click-clack. The night grew darker, the first stars came out. Olivia stared up at the silver holes in the blackness, trying not to dwell on the unsettling way Hassan had looked at her when she'd asked to see Clara. *Find me, someone. Please, find me.*

'You don't seem angry.' Hassan's voice startled her. 'Your brother-in-law killed Tabia, made another man die for it. Doesn't it disgust you?'

'Amongst other things.'

'It disgusted your captain, his colonel too. I was there the other night, listening, when Sir Gray told them what he'd done. They'd just brought us back from the parade ground.'

'They didn't know about Tabia before then?'

'No.'

In spite of everything, Olivia was glad to know it, to have her anger, against Edward at least, ease.

'The captain told Sir Gray to confess, make amends, *fucking face up to it.*'

'Much good it did,' said Olivia.

Hassan sighed. 'Sir Gray said no one would take his confession anyway. Your husband, Ma'am Sheldon, he told Wilkins everything the night we took your sister. Wilkins told the consul-general.'

'And no one wants it getting out.'

Hassan nodded. 'Your captain said Sir Gray should insist. The colonel told him that he should go to the papers. But Sir Gray told them that Sheldon would just bribe them to keep quiet.' Hassan paused, eyes cast down to his gun. 'Money makes gods in this land of ours.'

Olivia rolled her head back, digesting the sordid web of deceit that had been unfolding all this time. Her cheek throbbed. She was shivering more and more. 'How did you even get Clara away?' Her curiosity was a numb kind; she both cared and didn't at the same time.

Hassan told her he'd had a man waiting in the street. He'd spoken to him whilst El Masri was buying his tea, pointed Clara and Olivia out, given him the note telling Clara to return to the carriage at all speed, word had come that Angus was ill. 'I knew she would do as I asked.' He shook his head sadly. 'She trusted me. I wanted my man to get her alone; we weren't sure how he was going to do it. You made it easy by going after Fadil.'

Olivia felt a stab of pain.

'My man made his move,' said Hassan. 'He took your sister on a shortcut back to the carriage. Unfortunately,' Hassan clicked his beads, 'they were attacked by some others I had waiting. They took her into a house, then down into the sewers until nightfall.'

The sewers? Oh God, *Clara*.

'Ma'am Gray never suspected I was involved,' said Hassan. 'I've never shown her my face in the desert, not once. We could have released her ...'

'I don't think you've ever intended to. I think you've wanted to punish her for taking you to that beach in the first place, for Tabia being there that night ...'

'You're wrong. And it could have worked, my plan. If Sir Gray had just confessed.'

Olivia clenched her jaw. 'Could have?'

'She ran, Ma'am Sheldon.' He turned his beads through his fingers, frowned. 'I cannot see how she could have survived in the desert. We left no water flasks, she had little food. I am sorry, so very sorry, that she did it.'

Olivia shut her eyes. 'Her body . . . ?'

'I couldn't find it. But I'm sure she's gone.'

'No,' said Olivia, 'I won't believe it.' But as she spoke, she felt herself shrivel inside. She had learned long ago, after all, that death didn't need a corpse to make it real. She was hit by images: Clara hugging Ralph, kissing Gus, blonde curls, that dimpling smile . . . A warm hand holding hers. She could almost feel her. She tried to picture her, again, as a child, her big sister. But she couldn't, she still couldn't, and now the only Clara she knew, all she had left, had been taken. Just as she'd got her back. It couldn't be real. It *couldn't*. The agony that it might be closed around her, an iron band. Her breaths came quick and shallow. She gulped, forcing herself under control. She needed to keep control if she was to have any hope of escape. She *had* to get away, for Ralph's sake if nothing else. 'Who helped you?' she managed to ask. 'Who were the men who took Clara?'

Hassan told her they were the servants of a man she'd never heard of. 'He was happy to support me,' Hassan said. 'The ending of an innocent woman's life is an awful thing.'

Olivia's stomach turned at the hypocrisy. 'Did El Masri help too?'

'He did not.'

It surprised her, but there it was. 'Please,' she said, 'leave Ralph alone. Jeremy will never go to jail now, you said yourself no one wants him to.'

'They might change their minds once Ralph is gone. Sir Gray has to be punished.' Hassan's voice rose, his eyes widened. 'He *has* to.' He took a breath, visibly gathering himself. When he spoke again, his tone shook with control. 'It might not come to it. I hope it doesn't. Once you're dead . . . ' Hassan tapped the gun. He said something else, about raising hell, but Olivia didn't hear it.

The 'dead' had deafened her.

'How are you going to do it?' Her lips trembled against her will. 'Are you going to roll me into the water? Are you going to shoot me? How's it going to be?'

'You mustn't be afraid. I won't let you feel any pain. This,' he raised the gun, 'is not working now. The catch, it's broken. I have

333

another hidden out in the desert, where we should have gone in the first place. I'll give you a clean death. I don't want to pound you. I won't unless I have to.'

'I suppose I should thank you for that?'

'Make no fuss and it will be easy.' He frowned regretfully. 'My friend, Shahid, he was upset your sister got lost. Very upset. He can send men for your body tomorrow.'

Olivia swallowed, hard. She didn't want to think about that. 'Why haven't you taken me already?'

'The roads around the city will be busy. I don't want anyone to see.'

'Then don't do it.' Olivia hated the pleading note in her voice. Why did it have to be so undignified, the simple act of begging for one's life? 'Let me go, won't you? Please.'

'Hush,' said Hassan, 'you're scared.'

'I certainly don't want to die. I beg of you, just let me live. I'll tell the world what happened to Tabia.'

'You say that now.'

'I will, I swear.'

Silence.

'You don't have to be this person, you don't need to kill me.'

Still he didn't speak.

She held her breath.

'Of course I do,' he said.

Another hour passed. Click-clack. Tick-tock.

'I need to go to the lavatory,' said Olivia. It was the truth. She'd been holding it as long as she could, but the pressure in her bladder was agonising, and the sound of the moving water below wasn't helping. She'd heard that men often soiled themselves before they were killed, she did not want that to be her. 'Will you let me go? I can't ride again until I have.'

Hassan tapped the gun on his knee. 'Fine,' he said, pocketing his damned beads, 'I'll help you.'

Olivia avoided his eye as he pulled her to her feet. Her legs buckled beneath her as he led her to the cliff edge. It was dark, the moon

334

was nothing but a segment of a segment, a swallowed smile. She had to strain her eyes to make out where the land ended and the drop to the sea began.

'Crouch,' he said.

'I can't get my drawers down.'

He moved towards her and drew her petticoats up. He averted his gaze. His hands skimmed her thigh; she felt the gun, cold and blunt on the exposed patch of skin above her stockings. She raised her eyes to the heavens as he pulled her underwear free. Was it possible that her parents were watching her? Clara? She drew breath, blinked. *Don't think like that . . . you'll fall apart if you do.*

Hassan backed away. Olivia heard her urine splash the dry earth. She considered attempting to push Hassan over the edge as he reclothed her. But they were too far away, she'd undoubtedly fail, and then he'd be on his guard for another attempt.

He led her back to her previous spot and pushed her until she knelt and then lay down.

'When are we going to go?' she asked.

'Soon.'

'Why are you still waiting? There's no one around now.' When he didn't answer, she thought, *He doesn't want to do it after all. He's delaying because he's lost his nerve.*

But then he said, 'You're wrong, there might be people still out. We have to wait,' and she realised that the only person struggling to believe it was really going to happen was her.

335

Chapter Thirty-Four

Nailah landed with a thud on the lawn. Her heart pounded as she combed the shadows of trees surrounding her, the statue-lined paths. She could hear the bass of male voices on the veranda, laughter. So at ease, so happy; yet they all must know another life was about to be ended.

She ran for the compound's boundary. She paused when she got there and glanced back at the light spilling from the house's arched windows, its thick clay walls built to keep the world out as well as the woman within. She felt one small, final stab of temptation to stay in this life of opulence, to forget the blood that lay, at least in part, on her hands, Cleo and Babu's needs, the impossible dreams she'd shared with her ambitious clown, and then turned, dug her nails into the bricks, grit slicing skin, and climbed, swinging one leg and then the other over the top of the wall. As she slid to the ground, her toes and palms grazed the rough brickwork. She turned to face the curves of the desert, and set off, feet sliding in the sand. She kept wide of the road until she was far enough from Shahid's gates not to be seen by his guards. As she rejoined the silver shadowed track towards Alexandria, she hummed breathlessly to herself, more to hear a sound, any sound, in the oppressive emptiness of the night, than anything else.

She had been walking less than half an hour when the clop of hooves alerted her to another's presence. The traveller was a cotton merchant heading into the city for the dawn markets. He agreed to take her with him. He didn't give her fine clothes a second glance;

if he found something odd about her being out alone in the darkness, he made no comment. He just chewed his tobacco and stared straight ahead as they covered the miles, minding his own business.

Perhaps he simply didn't care.

His silence gave Nailah plenty of time to think of what she should do next. She had no doubt Hassan would have Ma'am Sheldon by now, he wasn't going to let himself fail. They'd be well on their way to the oasis. Nailah had no idea how to find it, though. She had to get help.

The bells of St Mark's Cathedral tolled eleven when at last they reached the city. Nailah's driver dropped her at the cotton exchange. She thanked him and ran. Her feet slapped the deserted pavements, her mouth ran dry, a stitch spread painfully in her side. She fixed her thoughts on the warehouses where Kafele kept his rooms, intent on getting there at all speed; but when she passed her own house and saw candlelight burning in the window, she stopped short. She stood on the cobbles, staring at the flickering, and gathered her breath. Who was up there? Isa? Could it be possible she'd come back? Or was it Jahi? Nailah's blood raced, her silk clothes stuck to her sweating body in the cool night air. With quaking fingers, she let herself in, then made her way up to the family's room.

As she lifted the latch on the door, she let out a breath of relief. For not only was Isa in there, the children with her, both asleep in the corner, but also Kafele.

Before Nailah could say anything, Isa crossed the room and pulled her into a hug; a breath-constricting squeeze. 'I couldn't get on that train,' she said, voice lowered so as not to wake the children, 'not without knowing where you were. I fetched Kafele, he's been searching everywhere.' She pushed Nailah out to arm's length, studying her. The kohl around her lids was smudged, powder gathered in the creases of her skin. 'You're dressed like a whore,' she said. 'Are you hurt?'

Nailah shook her head. She turned to meet Kafele's anxious gaze. 'I need help,' she said, and without pausing to wonder if she

337

really had the nerve to do it, she told him everything, watching as his expression morphed from confusion to disbelief to grim acceptance.

When at last she was finished, she felt her shoulders sag.

'Sweet Mother,' said Isa, slumping to the floor. 'I don't understand how … How … ? Jahi, my own brother … You … ' She held out the flat of her jewelled hands as though to push it all from her, then spat once over her shoulder.

'Nailah,' said Kafele, 'why didn't you tell me?'

'I didn't want to put it on you,' said Nailah. 'I was scared.'

'Of what?' Kafele asked, his expression pained. 'Me? How many times have I told you that I want to help, that you can trust me?' He turned away, running his hands around the bare skin of his neck, gripping himself above his rough shirt.

'I'm sorry,' Nailah said to him. 'I'm so sorry.'

He took a deep breath. 'You could have saved Clara Gray, Nailah, if you'd just spoken up.'

'I never thought she'd get hurt. And I was scared, I didn't want to lose the children, be taken away.' She pressed her knuckles to her eyes, squeezing against the tears. *Don't make excuses*, she told herself, *there are none*. 'We might still be able to stop Hassan killing Ma'am Sheldon. I know where he's taken her, I can describe it, we have to go … '

'You can't,' said Isa. 'Everyone will assume you were involved from the start, hang you as accomplices.'

'But Kafele's done nothing.'

'It won't matter,' Isa said. 'One British woman dead, another about to be, both wives of the richest Englishmen in Egypt. There'll be no clemency in the settling of this score.'

'You don't mean we should do nothing?' said Nailah.

'Of course we'll do something,' said Kafele. 'I'm not about to let an innocent woman die.' He looked to the ceiling, a dent forming in his forehead. At length he said, 'We'll go to the parade ground, come clean. Tell them that you've only just found all this out. Hopefully they'll believe us. It will look better that we've gone to them.'

'It's so dangerous,' Isa said. 'Don't get dragged in, Kafele. It's not your affair.'

There was a hammering at the door.

'Nailah? Are you there?'

Nailah caught her breath. The captain's strong, deep voice, weighted with urgency, was unmistakable.

Kafele cursed.

Nailah opened her mouth to say she would face the captain alone. She was still forming the words when Kafele brushed past her into the stairwell, down the stairs.

'Stop,' Nailah called, going after him, 'wait.'

He paused, turning back; almond eyes on hers in the dusty darkness.

'Let me,' she said. 'My mother's right, it's too dangerous. I was wrong to come back for you.'

'You think I could leave you to this?' He tipped his head at the family's room, where Isa – for all her fine words of love and worry – lingered. 'I'm not her,' he said. 'You've always deserved better than that.'

There was more hammering. The front door moved on its hinges.

'I don't want you to get hurt,' Nailah said.

'I'll be fine,' said Kafele, 'and so will you.' With that, he opened the door.

The captain wasn't alone. He was surrounded by others in the darkness, more soldiers, the colonel and Fadil amongst them. Fadil's whole head was wrapped in blood-soaked bandages.

A woman's voice cut through the night air, the roll of vowels unmistakably Ma'am Carter's. 'So you're home at last.' She stepped out from behind the colonel. 'Where have you been?'

'We've been looking for you,' said the captain. His face, darkened by night, was strained with fear and fury.

'We were about to come to the ground,' said Kafele. Nailah winced at the sight of him, so slight against the captain's height, his lean strength, but squaring up to him, on her side in spite of everything. 'Nailah knows where Ma'am Sheldon is. She's only just worked things out.'

339

The captain turned to face Nailah. 'Where is she? Was it your uncle who beat Fadil, who shot Sheldon?'

Nailah's jaw dropped. 'He shot Sir Sheldon?'

'That's not an answer. Where. Is. SHE?'

'A small oasis, there are two palms . . .'

'Fuck,' the captain said, '*fuck.*'

'We know it,' said the colonel.

Nailah felt a brief easing of relief. 'But it's Hassan who has her.'

'Hassan?' The captain clenched his fists. 'The fucking coachman? I'm going to fucking kill him.' He turned to a soldier Nailah didn't recognise. 'Take them both to the ground, Stevens.'

Without another word he was gone, on his horse, thundering off in a cloud of black dust down the street, the colonel, Ma'am Carter, and Fadil behind him.

Chapter Thirty-Five

'We're almost there,' said Hassan.

His arm was tight around Olivia's waist where she sat in front of him, sideways in the saddle. The leather pressed painfully into her thigh. Her buttocks were numb, her back was cramped, and her stomach was liquid with terror. She eyed Clara's horse, trailing beside them, its reins tied to Hassan's stallion, saddle still on. If she could just get out of Hassan's reach for a second, she could try and make a break for it.

If.

She flexed her fingers, twisted her wrists, keeping her body as still as possible so Hassan wouldn't feel her movement. Ignoring the blistering of the rope on her skin, she caught her thumb in the knot, moving it back and forth like a piston.

'Look,' said Hassan, his breath hot on her neck, 'over there.'

Olivia saw the silhouette of two palms looming out of the darkness. The horizon was doing something strange beyond; it seemed to be moving. Hassan kicked the horse on. *Slow down*, Olivia screamed silently. Her thumb worked.

'It will be over soon,' said Hassan. Olivia thought he was talking as much to himself as to her. 'I won't hurt you,' he said. 'It will be quick. So quick.'

She pressed her lips together. Her breath caught in her throat, threatening to choke her. She told herself that she was going to fight: for herself, for Ralph. She would not let Hassan take him. She repeated it over and over, silently, a mantra. She tried to believe

341

the promise was making her stronger, but her legs wouldn't stop shaking.

Would she feel it when the bullet entered her? Where would he shoot her? Her head, or her heart? And would she die straight away, or would she have to wait, bleeding, for him to reload, take aim once more and end it?

'I need to go to the lavatory again,' she said.

'No,' he said, 'you don't.'

'I do, I really do.'

'It won't matter, not in a few more minutes. Whatever you feel now, it will be gone soon.'

What a strange and awful thought. Olivia struggled to make sense of it; she would no longer see, smell, *be*. Her cramps, the heat in her bloodied wrists, all of it would be gone. Where did it all go to? She'd learnt at school that Anne Boleyn had complained when her execution was delayed, anxious at the additional hours allotted to her, preferring to have it over and done with so that she might be past her pain. As though oblivion could be preferable to life and hope and the warmth of your own pulsing heart. Olivia couldn't see it, not even a little bit. She didn't want oblivion, she wasn't ready for it. She couldn't be so resigned.

Inevitably, and far too soon, they reached the palms. Nestled in their shadows was a small hut.

'Your sister stayed here,' said Hassan. 'It's almost like you're together again.'

'It's not like it at all.' Olivia's eyes strained as she stared out at the sands surrounding them. How far had Clara got? Was she really dead? Something in her fought it. It couldn't quite feel true. But then nor had it with their parents. How macabrely Shakespearean that these Egyptian dunes had laid claim to them all.

No. Enough. The desert might not have had Clara; it *would not* have her. *Don't give in, Olly, don't give up.*

Hassan got down and pulled her towards him. She arched away, her body rigid with fear. He pulled again and she reflexively kicked, catching his underarm with her boot. His dark eyes widened with

342

pain. He grabbed her wrists and yanked. She landed with a bump on the hardened earth of the oasis, her dress billowing around her.

She took a moment to catch her breath. She wriggled her hands; they still weren't quite free. She looked up at Hassan. His eyes were hard now, no trace of the warmth she had become used to back at Clara's. Silently, she asked, *Which version of you is real? The one I see now, or the man you were then?* Either way, it was clear he was bracing himself for what he was about to do. 'Please don't.' Her voice caught and at last her control slipped. Just at this moment of her needing her mind clear, it filled with pictures: her mother's smile beneath the tree in Cairo, Clara sobbing at those freezing London docks, the nuns, Beatrice's drawing room on Christmas Day, Edward teaching her to ride, Edward saluting her, his smile, the feel of his heart . . .

Hassan dragged her to the hut. The white fabric of his trousers quivered in the night air.

She couldn't think what to do. She was sobbing, snorting in terror. 'No,' she said, 'nononono.' She heard something, and didn't hear it, all at the same time. She couldn't make sense of it.

Hassan's head jerked sideways. He must have heard it too. His face creased in confusion. And El Masri was there, close, very close, with a gun of his own. Olivia didn't know whether to be relieved or even more scared, but before she knew what she was doing, her head darted forwards and she sank her teeth into Hassan's thigh, biting hard. She tasted blood. There was a high-pitched screaming. It took her a second to connect it with his pain. She didn't stop, she kept on biting, not letting up on the pressure until she felt the connecting blow of his broken pistol on her skull. Her vision swam, but she didn't lose consciousness this time.

Hassan reeled, as though striking her had taken the last of his energy, and grasped his leg. She rose unsteadily to her feet, spitting out the taste of him. Finally, with one last pull, she liberated her hands from the rope. She didn't pause to think, she didn't breathe to consider; she seized a stone from the floor and launched forward to strike Hassan over the head, then again and again. Somewhere in the back of her mind, the thought whispered, *El Masri hasn't shot me, he must be on my side.* She was no longer scared. It had been the doing nothing that had terrified her; there was nothing so frightening as surrender. Hassan tumbled to the ground and she whacked him again.

'Stop,' said El Masri, 'you can stop.'

She panted, staring down at Hassan. He lay at an awkward angle, a broken statue. His beads had fallen from his pocket.

El Masri knelt beside him. He took Hassan's wrist, gave Olivia a look, and then pointed his gun at Hassan's head and shot. The sound echoed hollowly into the dunes.

The stone fell from her hand. She backed away. 'Was he dead already?' she asked.

'You saw me shoot him,' said El Masri.

'Was he dead though? Did I kill him?'

'I killed him,' he said. Then, 'It's time for you to escape.'

She stared down at Hassan's lifeless form. A puddle of blood leached blackly into the sand. 'What about you?' she asked. 'What will you do?'

'It's time for me to disappear too. I am glad I did this first.'

'I don't know if I needed you to. I think I might have bitten him anyway, even if you hadn't been there.'

'You don't know that.'

'He's so dead.'

'And he was going to kill you. Now go. There's a storm coming.'

Olivia looked once more at the moving horizon. The stars were disappearing. She stumbled towards Clara's horse, still tethered to Hassan's, and unhooked the reins. She lifted her foot to the stirrup, but it was so high, her skirts were so full, and she was trembling too much.

She heard padding footsteps behind her and felt hands on her waist, a hoist. Propelled by El Masri's support, she pulled herself belly first onto the saddle and up to sitting. El Masri smacked Clara's horse on the rear, spurring them off. 'Ride fast and straight,' he called, 'don't stop until you reach the city. There's an ill wind coming.'

Olivia didn't need to be told twice. She urged Clara's horse on into a canter. She'd never ridden on undulating sand before and was unsteady in her seat, but she didn't slow. The faster she went, the greater the distance between her and the bloody stone she had clenched, the less frantic her heart. Her eyes flicked to the sky, she imagined her parents egging her on, her mother's voice, *She's going to live, how splendid.* Clara's came too, demanding to be heard. *Splendid, absolutely splendid.*

A sob broke from her, but she clenched her jaw against any more. She couldn't break down, not yet. For the wind was up, sweeping through her hair; the torn lace collar of her dress blew away. Her head and cheek throbbed. She cast a look behind her, absorbing the emptiness, the silver curvature of the sands. The stars had gone. Dust blew all around, an ill wind indeed.

Her eyes blurred, but not with tears. Tears didn't grate, they didn't burn. Tears weren't sand. And sand was suddenly everywhere, whipping her face, filling her nose.

Not splendid after all then.

Not bloody splendid at all.

AFTER

Chapter Thirty-Six

Nailah stared through the small window of the office she'd been locked in, and watched as the velvet sky turned grey, then white, and slowly by fractions to a yellow-tinged blue. The empty paddocks lost their night-time mystique of silhouettes, the huts and stables were thrown into bald relief.

A new day after all.

Wings battered as a flock of birds took off from the gateposts. A second later the colonel appeared, stiff as a rod in his saddle, but with a tension in him that looked as heavy as wet mud. His distinguished face was grim beneath his officer's cap.

Nailah stretched her eyes, searching, but try as she might, she could see no one else with him.

The captain wasn't there.

The colonel dismounted, tethered his horse, then disappeared into a hut marked 'Colonel Thomas Carter'. A minute or so later, he came out, slamming the door behind him, and made straight for the room next to Nailah's, the one Kafele was in. She rushed over and pressed her ear to the map-covered wall. All she could hear was the muffled staccato of the colonel's consonants followed by indistinct melodies in reply.

She watched the clock on the far wall. Five minutes passed, then six, then eight, then many more.

Hooves sounded outside. She returned to the window in time to see a big-bellied man dressed in an ill-fitting suit arrive with Sir Gray. The colonel must have seen them too, because he left the room next door, went to them, sent their horses off with a stable hand, then led Sir Gray and the fat man into his office.

Nothing happened for a while after that. More soldiers filled the ground. Nailah slumped on the floor.

Eventually the lock of her own door turned. She leapt up as the colonel entered.

'Is she dead?' Nailah couldn't wait another moment to ask.

'We think so.' His tone was distant, short. 'There was a storm, we couldn't get through, but we found her horse.' He fingered his neck. 'A lace collar.' His expression was cold. 'My wife's beside herself.' He paused. His jaw moved, as though it hurt him to hold it in place. 'We both are. Captain Bertram's still out there.'

'Is he all right?'

'No one is all right.' The colonel came further into the room. 'Clara had children, a baby less than a year old. He'll never know her. Poor Olivia's been on her own for years. They both had their whole lives ahead of them.' He took a deep, shuddering breath. 'They deserved their lives.'

A man barked orders outside. Nailah started as the door of the neighbouring room opened. There were voices, footsteps. Nailah glanced at the window, then back at the colonel. He nodded. She crossed the room, fingertips resting on the window ledge. Her throat tightened. Kafele was being loaded into a police cart by the fat man who'd arrived with Sir Gray.

'Where's he going?' She had to force the words out.

'Commissioner Wilkins is taking him to prison,' said the colonel.

'No.' The word nearly choked her. 'He's done nothing. I swear it. It was all Hassan. And me. I wrote that first letter to Sir Gray, you can check my hand.'

'We can't,' said the colonel, 'the letter was torn up long ago, as soon as you sent it.'

'What?' Nailah pressed the heel of her hand to her head, absorbing it. To think how scared she'd been of what that letter could do to her, and it had been gone all along. Destroyed.

'Kafele's offered to confess whatever Wilkins asks of him,' said the colonel, 'as long as you're left alone.'

'No,' she shook her head fiercely, 'no.' She turned again to the window, sinking her fingernails into the wooden frame as a policeman shoved Kafele forward, making him stumble, then slammed the barred door shut behind him. 'He can't confess,' she said, 'I won't let him.' She looked back at the colonel, a sob rising in her. 'Stop them,' she said, 'please.' She clasped her hands, entreating him. 'You have to let him go. Arrest me instead.'

'I can't,' said the colonel. An unspoken, *Much as I'd like to*, wisped through the air. 'Kafele's turned himself in; a confession's a confession, and Wilkins wants culprits. He'd rather have Kafele anyway.' His lips curled in a sickened smile. 'You're a woman, an Egyptian woman. Apparently we'd prefer not to go there.'

'Tabia was an Egyptian woman.' Her voice was high, panicked to her own ears.

'Yes, and as you well know what happened to her has been buried.'

'And you think that's right?'

'Of course I don't. But that doesn't mean I think the rest of it is either.'

'You can't let Commissioner Wilkins take Kafele.'

'What the hell do you think I can do?' The colonel shouted it. Nailah shrank in her skin. He stared at her, eyes shining as though they stung.

'He's innocent,' she said.

'So were Olivia and Clara. You could have saved them, if you'd just spoken up.'

'I came back for Ma'am Sheldon.'

'Not soon enough. And now they're both dead. *Dead* ... Alistair Sheldon's been shot. However reluctant your involvement, Nailah, you *were* part of it. You have to accept there will be a reckoning, even if it's not the one you want.' The colonel stared at the ceiling. A vein in his neck throbbed above his sand-crusted collar. 'Kafele ... he'll get decades of hard labour at the very least.'

Nailah held her stomach at the thought of him in chains, his face turning old and weary, or worse, puce in the hangman's noose. 'When?' she asked. It came out as a whisper. 'When will the trial be?'

'Soon.'

'He might not be found guilty.' A thin thread of hope spun within her, weaving between her ribs. It almost reached her heart. 'There'll be hearings, I'll speak for him, the truth must come out. About Tabia too.'

The colonel eyed her disdainfully. 'There'll be no hearings,' he said. 'The whole procedure will be nothing more than a tribunal. *Summary.* Wilkins is overseeing the evidence, conducting the *interviews*; he'll dress up what's happened to Clara and Olivia as acts of greedy violence, have it that they were taken for their husbands' money. *Bad* Egyptians, *wicked* Egyptians. Kafele will be punished, everyone else made happy. Believe me, Nailah, it's in Wilkins' interest to keep what happened to your aunt quiet. His pockets are so damned heavy with bribe money.' He shook his head. 'I doubt anyone would have let it out in the first place. It's all too ungentlemanly, too unseemly. Too dangerous.'

Nailah stared at her feet. It killed her to hear it stated so baldly: that Tabia had died so cruelly, with her murderers predestined to walk free.

'Is there really nothing you can do for Kafele?' she asked.

'The only hope is if we find Hassan or El Masri. *Good old Uncle Jahi.* If we can get them to stand trial, have them pledge to Wilkins that Kafele wasn't involved, then it should be enough to save him. Where are they, Nailah?'

'I don't know.'

The colonel looked at her disbelievingly.

'I don't, I swear it. I have no idea where they'd have gone.'

'Then who else has been helping Hassan? There must have been others.'

She told him about Nassar Shahid.

The colonel sighed. 'Nassar sodding Shahid.'

352

'Will you arrest him?' Nailah asked.

The colonel opened his mouth to answer, but then the door swung open, cutting him off.

Sir Gray was there, his face pale. 'I've seen Fadil coming,' he said, 'he has someone on his horse. I don't know who.'

The colonel went. Nailah followed him to the open doorway. As she looked into the courtyard, she felt her insides convulse. For Fadil was already there, dismounting not twenty feet away, his bloody bandages still wrapped around his head. The dusty body of a lady was draped stiffly over his horse's saddle.

Nailah watched as he lifted the lady into his arms.

He did it with such gentle tenderness it made her whole soul ache.

Chapter Thirty-Seven

Olivia bade Jahi goodbye on the road into Ramleh (she'd started calling him by his first name; 'El Masri' seemed too condescending for the man who'd appeared apparition-like through the swirling sands to rescue her). She unravelled the cloth he'd wrapped her face in, and patted his camel with shaking hand, *trusty steed*. She hated that she'd abandoned Clara's horse, but there'd been no choice. She hadn't been able to see, let alone follow, Jahi's frantic pace. 'Thank you,' she said to him, 'for coming after me.'

'Please, don't thank me.' Jahi looked anxiously at the lightening sky. 'Will you be all right to go the rest of the way alone?'

She nodded. 'You saved my life,' she said, stating the blindingly obvious.

'I should never have had to.' Another incontrovertible fact.

He turned to go, he was nearly gone. Two mounted soldiers rounded the corner of the road, their English voices clipped in the warm dawn air. Olivia told Jahi to leave, now, before they saw him. She heard the soldiers say something about arrests, Kafele, Nailah, and then Jahi did the unfathomable. He turned himself in.

Just like that.

Olivia protested against the soldiers taking him until she was blue in her battered face. It hurt to talk, her whole damn body stung, injured had somehow become her default state. She couldn't remember what it felt like not to ache in at least one part of her body, and it made her angry, it made her absolutely bloody furious. But no matter how loudly she shouted at the two lieutenants that they'd better just sod off, leave, go and play some polo or cricket or whatever it was they were qualified to do over here, for she was damned sure they were no bloody good as detectives, – Hassan had been living right under everyone's noses, *for goodness' sake* – they were having none of it. And nor was Jahi.

The three of them left, leaving Olivia standing like a fool in the empty road with only Jahi's camel and a stray cat for company. The cat rubbed against her skirt. Olivia looked around her. It was her first time alone and unobserved in weeks. She wished she'd asked the soldiers where Edward was, if he was safely back. She eyed the camel. It eyed her. She started shaking. Now it was all over, and she was doing nothing, fear ran loose within her, grief too. *Don't let it in. You don't know, not for sure. Not yet.* Even as she thought it, her body trembled; every part of her being vibrated with awful feeling. Since there was nothing else to do, she took the camel by its reins, picked up the cat, and set off for home. She was unclear what she was going to do with either animal when she got there, but she felt as though she'd abandoned enough helpless beasts for one day.

The Bedouin mother and her boys were peeling corn when she arrived back. The mother stood. She raised her fingers to Olivia's face. There were tears in her eyes. Olivia stared back at her. She wanted so much to tell her how sorry she was, but she didn't have the words.

Her arms ached. Her eyes were gritty.

Where was Edward?

The mother nodded. Olivia nodded back. She thought, *I don't know why I'm nodding*, and, *I want to go home, I don't want to be here any more*, and, *I don't have a home, not in England, not here. Please let Edward be safe. I need him. IneedhimIneedhimIneedhim.*

Ada's voice cut through the silence. 'Mrs Sheldon, you're alive.' She hastened down the driveway, brown skirts swinging, Fadil with her.

'Oh God,' said Olivia, taking in the state of Fadil, 'your head.'

'It's healing. Sayed Bertram found me in the cellar, he got me out. I am fine, Ma'am Sheldon.'

He clearly wasn't. He was haggard-looking; his skin was a sickly green colour, as if it had no blood beneath it.

He relieved her of the camel. Ada set the cat down and shooed it away. Together they walked her to the house. Fadil told Olivia that he had just returned from the ground. He paused, for a disconcerting length of time. His eyes shone with sadness.

'Oh.' Olivia held her hand to her stomach. 'Oh.'

'I'm so sorry,' he said.

'You found her?'

'She was exposed by the storms. About a mile or so from the oasis.' Fadil's cheeks worked. His face folded in on itself. 'I have failed, Ma'am Sheldon.' A single tear rolled down his papery cheek. 'I have failed again. I am so ashamed.'

Olivia wanted to say something, make him understand she didn't blame him, but she couldn't breathe. She clawed at the unforgiving bounds of her corset. She was gasping. Clara. *Clara.* It was abruptly far too real. Her sister ... The way she laughed, her voice ... *Top-drawer*; but not, *Not.* She couldn't stand it. It couldn't be ... She had been hoping, almost believing; it was only now she saw how much.

Fadil talked on. Edward was still out in the desert. He'd refused to give up looking for her. Olivia gasped again. He wasn't back? Fadil said no, he couldn't return. He was afraid, so terribly afraid, that she was gone too.

Unlike Alistair who, gut-wrenchingly, was still alive. Ada said that servants in a nearby house had gone to investigate when they heard the gunshot, then taken Alistair to the military hospital. He was unconscious but assuredly going to live. 'I'm so sorry, Mrs Sheldon,' said Ada. 'So very, very sorry.'

Olivia couldn't move. She barely seemed able to do anything. She ran her nails through her hair. Her scalp was thick with sand, it coated her. She could taste it, smell it, her tongue was parched and swollen. Like Clara's would have been. Until her very last breath. *I am rather gasping for a drink.* It hurt, God it hurt. Too, too much. She'd been alone. So very alone, with no clue as to how sorely she was missed. Olivia had never been able to tell her, nor how sorry

356

she was for the way their last hours together had been filled with such brooding distrust. Clara had died knowing only that Olivia doubted her, and that she'd forgotten almost every moment of their childhood.

A sob tore through Olivia's body. 'I want her back,' she heard herself saying, 'I just want her back.'

Edward saw her doubled over as he cantered into the driveway. Fadil and Ada stood awkwardly by her side. *Don't just stand there*, he nearly yelled at them, *comfort her, for Christ's sake.*

He pulled his stallion to a halt, and dropped to the ground. She turned to him, stared. One side of her face was swollen and covered in dried blood, her mouth too. Her hair was loose, and she was coated with dust. But she was there, real. He was dimly aware of Ada and Fadil leaving, he didn't turn to watch them go. Neither did she. It was a second of stillness, nothing more. Then they both moved, Edward scooped her into his arms. 'Thank God, Olly. My Olly.'

She touched his face. 'Alistair's not dead.' Her eyes overflowed. 'Clara is.'

'I know, Olly. I know.' It was he who had found her poor body hunched there in the sands. Alone, so broken. 'I'm sorry,' he kissed Olly, 'so very sorry. I can't tell you.'

'I don't know what to do, how to bear it.' Her eyes searched him out. 'Edward . . .'

'I'm here, Olly. I'm with you.' He never intended to leave her again. 'I came back for help.' His voice rasped. 'They have El Masri at the ground. They told me. I thought you were . . . I thought . . .' He pushed her to arm's length. 'Olly, look at you.' Her teeth chattered. Her whole body shook. He had seen fear like this before, even in seasoned soldiers, always after the danger had passed. 'I have you.' He held her tight to him.

She didn't mention Alistair again, neither did he; an unspoken pact to pretend he didn't exist. Just for a while.

He took her upstairs. He rolled up his sleeves and drew the bath.

She sat on the stool watching him. He didn't take his eyes off her. She didn't take hers off him. He helped her undress, slowly, so as not to hurt her, flinching afresh at her battered skin.

'Don't look,' she said. 'It's not me.'

'It is,' he said, 'but it won't be.'

She wrapped her arms around his neck. He lifted her into the water, then climbed in himself.

No one interrupted them. Only the distant murmur of voices in the kitchen betrayed there was anyone else at home.

Edward sponged her down, washing away the sand, the night.

The water became tepid around them.

She turned her head on his damp shoulder. She asked him how Clara had been when they found her. 'I need to know.'

'Olly, I'm not sure you do.'

'Please,' she said, 'I'm torturing myself anyway.'

He hesitated. 'She was bruised,' he said slowly, not at all sure he was doing the right thing. 'Quite badly. She had sun blisters, as if she'd been out for a long time ... Her arm was twisted, fractured we think.'

Olly said nothing. Had he told her too much? She kept her eyes cast down; her lashes shadowed her cheeks, her cream skin, that livid wound, a cloak to whatever she was feeling. He wanted to tell her to look at him, not shut him off, but he could see she needed time.

'Who beat her?' she asked eventually. 'Hassan told me he'd never hit a woman before.'

'Jesus.' His lip curled in disgust. 'How chivalrous.'

'But if it wasn't him ... ?'

'It could have been one of the other men who helped take her.' He paused, trying to decide whether to tell her of all he and Tom suspected of Alistair and his new right-hand man, Wilkins. What good would it do? It wasn't as though they could prove anything against them, after all.

Olly said, 'You're forgetting to speak.'

'I know.'

'So?'

Edward looked at her swollen face, the scars on her stomach, and thought of all she'd been through. He decided that little as he had to give her, he could offer honesty at least.

So he told her of his and Tom's trip to that small settlement in Lixori, their chase to track down Wilkins' lead: that villager who thought he *might* have seen something out in the desert. Edward told Olly how all they'd found when they got to Lixori was a cluster of wary fellahin who'd admitted only that Alistair and Wilkins had been and gone, taking a man with them.

'Wilkins' villager?' asked Olivia.

'We think so,' said Edward. 'Except Wilkins denies ever having found him. When he got back here, to Alex, he told Jeremy the villager had disappeared from Lixori before he and Alistair even got there.'

Olly frowned. 'Why would he lie?'

'I don't know,' said Edward, 'not for certain.'

'But what do you think?'

Edward looked to the ceiling tiles, turning it over in his mind for the umpteenth time. 'I don't know what to think.' His forehead creased. 'Alistair would have been afraid of Clara being found, of all she knew, and what she might say when she returned. Then . . . Well, you know better than anyone that he's never forgiven her for turning him down.' He drew a long breath. 'What if he convinced Wilkins that they should kill that villager, before he could tell any of us what he'd seen? Made *sure* Clara wasn't discovered.' Edward was far from putting it past him. He wasn't even sure that Alistair had stopped there. There was *another* possibility, almost too awful to voice. 'Clara's injuries,' he said, forcing the words out, 'what if Wilkins and Alistair found her alive? Wanted to be certain she never returned.'

There was a short silence.

Olly said nothing. But her face had paled in horror. In a wrenching movement, she pulled away from Edward, sat up. 'No, *no*. He couldn't. Even *he* couldn't do that.' She gripped the enamel edge of the bath, dropped her chin to her chest, breathing quick and sharp. 'I can't . . . I can't . . . ' She put her hand to her neck.

'Olly.' He reached out for her, alarmed. 'Breathe,' he said, 'just breathe. Slowly.'

'He couldn't do something so awful,' she said. 'Oh God, could he?'

'Maybe not.' He said it to comfort her. Her hand tightened on her neck. 'We don't know, Olly. Not for sure. It's suspicion, just suspicion.' He wrapped his arms around her, willing her to calm. 'Olly, please, look at me. Olly?'

She turned.

'We don't know,' he repeated.

'What about Jeremy?' Her eyes were glassy, full of pain. 'What does he think? Have you told him?'

He nodded. 'I spoke to him just now at the ground.'

'And?'

'He doesn't want to believe it, but I think he's starting to.' Edward had realised that from Jeremy's words as he left him. *Whatever the truth of it, he's finally got his way. He never wanted anyone else to have her. Now no one can.*

Olly closed her eyes. 'Alistair told me, when he came back the other evening, that plenty die in the desert. I thought he was being cruel about my parents. I was worried about you . . . But maybe he was talking about Clara.' She filled her lungs with a shuddering breath. 'There has to be a way to find out.'

'I don't see how we can. Even if the villagers could be convinced to speak up, *if* they even know anything, this is Wilkins and Alistair. They'll find a way out of it.'

Olly opened her mouth as though to protest, but then said nothing. Edward watched, pained, as her face folded and she saw the truth in what he'd said. Her shoulders dropped, her body slackened against him. 'I hate this place. I *hate* it.'

'I'm so sorry, Olly,' he said.

'I can't accept not knowing. I just can't.'

It felt too heartless to tell her again that she might have to.

Instead, he said, 'I wish that I could have found her for you. I wish so much I had brought her back.'

They were both silent for some moments after that, Olly lost in her thoughts, Edward trying to guess what she was thinking.

At length, she turned her gaze on him and asked, her voice flat with grief, what he'd been talking about with Clara, all those weeks ago on the terrace of the Sporting Club, in what felt like another life. 'Was it her affair?'

He shifted in the water. 'You know about that?'

'Not who it was with. Will you tell me now?'

Since there seemed no point in concealing it any more, he said, 'Benjamin Pasha.'

'Benjamin? But Amélie's Clara's best friend. Benjamin's Imogen's brother. He'd have known our mother ...'

'I know, believe me.'

'My God,' she said. Then, 'He was so ... stiff, that day we took Ralph and Gus to call at the Pashas'. I thought it was because he didn't care.' She raised her hand to her face, pinching the bridge of her nose. 'How did you even find out about it?'

Edward told her it had been a long time ago, well before Gus came along, at a winter party. 'I'd gone out for some air and caught them talking; it was the way they were standing ... Benjamin left as soon as he saw me looking. But Clara stayed. I wouldn't have pushed her to admit it to me, Olly, but she did. I think she wanted someone to talk to.'

'Clara. Poor Clara. She was so lonely, I think. Too, too lonely.'

He nodded, remembering how abashed she'd been the instant she let it all out, the raw shame in her tone. *I'm sorry, Teddy. What a slattern you must think me. And I've so enjoyed us being friends.*

'We never really spoke of it again,' he said. 'I tried to forget about it, actually. But then the morning of the Sporting Club's damned party, I saw her, at the beach ... She was so upset. She told me Benjamin had broken it off the night before, then taken her home. She'd walked back to where he'd done it though; she was still in her ball dress. She wanted to go to Amélie, tell her everything. I tried to talk her round. I took her home again myself, but she was beside herself.' He shook his head. 'When I saw her at the club, walking towards you both, I knew what she was about . . . It would have ruined her, ruined them all. I was too harsh with her. I told her she had no conscience, that she was being selfish.' He clenched his jaw. 'I could have been kinder to her, Olly. She needed me to be. But I wasn't.' He'd never forgive himself for that. 'She called me a hypocrite, you know, said she'd seen how I felt for you.'

'She knew?'

'She knew.'

'She never said.' Olly broke off. 'Or maybe she did. Before she was taken, in the street, she said the two of us weren't so different. I think she was trying to find the way to say it.' She closed her eyes. 'We were nearly there, Edward. We really were.'

'I'm so sorry,' he said, hating how inadequate it was. 'I should have told you all this before, but I wanted to get her back to you, Olly. Let her confide in you herself.'

'Did you talk to Benjamin though, ask him about who might have taken Clara?'

'Of course I did. More than once. He said he had no idea.'

'He didn't think to mention that Hassan used to bring Clara to meet him?'

'He said she used to come alone.'

'Maybe he thought she did.' She turned her head into his neck. He felt her tears on his skin. 'It's all too late now, anyway.'

Eventually, they went to bed. Olivia lay beside Edward, curled on one side. Edward's eyes traced the bruised contours of her face, memorising every inch.

'I saw you,' Olivia said, 'in my mind. When I thought it was the end. You were all I could see.'

'You're all I ever see. All I ever want to.'

She touched her fingers to his cheek, feeling the soft scratch of his stubble. 'I wish Alistair had died,' she said. 'Why didn't he die?'

Edward said nothing, just kept his eyes on her.

'I don't know how I can be with him again,' she said. 'I can't . . . Not now. Not with everything he's done, what he might have.'

Still, Edward didn't speak. But he drew her to him, holding her: life grasping life. All they had.

They fell asleep in one another's arms. Olivia had no idea how long they stayed that way, but the room was sultry with afternoon heat when a knock at the door roused her. She blinked. Her mouth was paper-dry. Edward had his eyes shut, but he pulled her closer, letting her know he was awake too.

Another knock.

Ada's voice called through the door that a message had come from Mr Gray: Clara's funeral was being held in St Mary's Church at four.

Edward sighed.

'Did Ada just say today?' asked Olivia groggily.

'Yes,' said Edward. 'Jeremy mentioned at the ground he wanted to do it before Ralph left. I barely listened, I was thinking about getting back here. Are you going to be all right to go?'

'I suppose I'll have to be.'

He kissed her, pushed a curl back from her cheek. 'We need to talk, you and I, afterwards. There are things we must discuss.'

Word came from the military hospital just as they were leaving. Alistair had been awake some hours, he would like to see his wife. Olivia did the only thing that felt possible: she pretended she hadn't received it.

The funeral was as awful as it was always going to be. Olivia sat beside Imogen in a side pew, battered face hidden beneath a large hat. She stared down at her black lap, up at the rays catching dust through the windows, across at the embroidered prayer cushions . . . anywhere but at the oak casket at the altar, the invisible shadow of Clara within.

Alone. So alone.

She wished she'd listened to Edward and Jeremy, that she hadn't

363

insisted on seeing Clara's body before the service. All she had left now in her mind were the lesions fracturing Clara's bloodless skin; they'd erased her laugh, her snub nose, gone as surely as her beating heart was gone.

Olivia's breath shuddered through her. Imogen squeezed her hand. Her own face was swollen from tears. Olivia turned to look at Amélie, in a pew near the front. She leant on Benjamin. His arm was stiff, his expression brooding.

'I can't look at him,' hissed Imogen, following Olivia's gaze. She had told Olivia before the service of how she'd spoken to him that morning; he'd known all along about Tabia's death.

'He has done ever since Alistair brought that poor Bedouin to him,' she'd said. 'Alistair didn't want to risk taking the man to the police himself, so he told Benjy that he had to help, that he knew about Benjy's affair with Clara, and would expose him if he didn't cooperate.'

Olivia thought Alistair had probably enjoyed it. He'd have hated Benjamin for knowing Clara in such a way. She wondered now if he'd had Benjamin pay the police to make sure the Bedouin died from his beating.

She asked Imogen as the minister read the eulogy. (*The senseless evil which robbed us of Clara is beyond our civilised understanding . . .*)

'Benjy claims not. Men do often perish after they've been thrashed. The heat, the disease . . . I don't know. I feel sick, even wondering, worse than sick. And to think of him, with Clara all this time. He was fifteen when she was born, Olivia. I once took him on a visit to your mama. He *saw* Clara as a baby.' She pressed her fingers to her mouth. 'And then to keep it all hidden like this. I'm so ashamed.'

Olivia looked at Benjamin's strained demeanour, his bowed head. She said, in a voice that was flat even to her own ears, that she thought perhaps he was too.

'I hope so,' said Imogen.

(*Let us hold a minute's silent reflection for Clara's life, ended tragically by greedy violence. Let us pray too for the recovery of our respected Alistair*

Sheldon, even now labouring under the wounds he suffered as he attempted to rescue his beloved wife . . .)

'I can't stand it,' said Olivia. She looked over her shoulder to where Edward was standing at the back. He shook his head grimly at her. She caught sight of the reporter, Giles Morton, busily scribbling away in the furthermost pew. It turned her insides out to think of the distortions he must be penning, the lies that would become the truth. 'Has that innocent man, Kafele, been freed?' she asked Imogen. 'Edward told me he should be, now Jahi's turned himself in.'

'Not a bit of it,' said Imogen. 'Tom's incandescent, but Wilkins is holding Kafele.'

'Why?'

'Who knows? But everything's in Wilkins' hands. He's arranging the charges, writing up the evidence, keeping why it all happened in the first place *hush-hush.*'

'Will they go after that other man, Nassar Shahid?'

'I doubt it. Not yet, anyway. He's so thick with the royal family. It would be risky, politically.' Imogen's lips turned, as though she was fighting the urge to sob. 'My father knew his father, you know. They were in the Egyptian army together. I used to see Nassar at parties as a child. I feel like I'm running mad . . .'

'He might yet go down.' Olivia said it without much hope.

'No,' Imogen said. 'Now Hassan's dead, there's no one to testify against him, or name the others who helped. Jahi knows nothing of his involvement. Even if Nailah could name names, I'd doubt they'd let her take the stand, not with all the other things she'd let out. She's been set free, by the way.'

Olivia turned in her seat. 'Really?'

'Yes.'

Olivia took a moment, trying to work out how she felt about it. She was surprised to find the news didn't entirely upset her. Enraged as she was at Nailah, there were others she hated far more. And she supposed she'd tried, in her own way.

'Wilkins has told her,' said Imogen, 'that if she breathes a whisper of what's gone on to anyone, he'll make her regret it, the rest of the family with her. He's been making noises about the Bedouin at your gate too, says they *must* have known what Hassan was up to.'

'Of course they didn't. The mother would have said something.'

'Would she?' Imogen sighed. 'Fear's a powerful thing. Anyway, there'll be a tribunal for Kafele and Jahi tomorrow at ten. If they're found guilty,' she raised an eyebrow, 'they won't waste time carrying out the punishments.'

'I'm going to speak to Morton,' said Olivia. 'Get the truth out about what Jeremy and Alistair did, all of it.' Her gaze moved, of its own volition, to Clara's coffin. 'I won't just do nothing.'

'I'm not sure you'll have much choice. I can't see the papers publishing anything, not now.' Imogen glanced over at Ralph, sweating in black pantaloons and jacket in the front pew, his hand in Jeremy's. 'Maybe it's for the best,' she said, eyes heavy on him. 'His papa's all he's got. Imagine what it would do to him to learn what Jeremy did.'

Olivia winced, thinking of it. But still, it didn't seem a good enough reason to keep it all hidden. Not even close.

She turned and looked again at Edward. He was still watching her. There was something in his expression that reminded her of the way he'd looked on the terrace the night Clara disappeared, back when he first spoke of going away. He'd said earlier that he needed to talk to her about things . . .

A coldness crept over her.

'How long does a transfer take to come through?' she asked.

Imogen grimaced. 'He's told you?'

'Not in so many words.'

'I didn't know how to. It's to Jaipur, a promotion too, to major. Tom's tried, but Edward has to go. His ship leaves tomorrow night.'

Olivia sat quite still. She couldn't take it in. A couple of hours ago they'd been in bed, yet this time tomorrow she would be about to lose him for ever. Like Clara. It was all too brutal, too soon. She couldn't bear it, wouldn't accept it. She'd never imagined it would be so immediate.

'He won't go,' she said.

'He has to,' said Imogen. 'I'm sorry, darling. He has absolutely no choice.'

Jeremy held a dinner after the service. There were seventeen of them, not including Mildred, who stayed inside pleading a headache or tiredness or grief or some such. Olivia had done her best not to hear her excuses. ('Cold gel,' Mildred had said as she stalked off.)

They sat at a table out on the lawn. The scent of Clara's orange trees carried in the air; her beautiful roses swayed in their beds. Olivia sat beside Edward. She eyed the lit nursery window upstairs, thinking of Ralph, due to set sail with Mildred in just two days. She hadn't spoken more than a few words to him; there hadn't been an opportunity. She hadn't spoken to Edward either. She didn't know what to say to him, or rather she knew what to say, just not if she could say it. Her eyes ached even thinking about it.

'There, there,' said a man whose name Olivia couldn't recall. He caught her eye with a gaze made veiny from years cigar-puffing around the clubs of the colonial circuit. 'Chin up, old girl.' He nudged his own indistinct jaw. 'You'll feel better once they're hanged. Take my word.'

'You have experience in such matters?' she asked.

'I have experience,' he said with a sympathetic smile.

'How fortunate for you.'

She felt Edward's leg press against hers.

A discussion ensued on whether hanging was or was not too good for the two men in captivity. Jeremy was assured he'd done the right thing, not giving into the threats. God only knew who'd have been next if he had. Bloody barbarians, ending an innocent woman's life . . .

Jeremy said nothing.

Olivia excused herself. She pushed her chair back on the lawn, shot Jeremy a look of sincere loathing (he had the good grace to colour), and walked away.

'Poor girl's overwrought,' said one of the men behind her.

'It's been hard on her,' said Jeremy.

There was a clinking of cutlery as knives and forks were once again taken in hand. Olivia made a silent pledge to herself to go to Giles Morton's office first thing. She heard someone say, 'She'll be happier when Sheldon's back,' as she climbed the terrace steps. 'A lady needs her husband . . .' She slid through the drawing room door. 'I'll say,' said another.

Edward told them all to fuck off. Or maybe he didn't. Perhaps Olivia just imagined he had. He was real enough, anyway, as he joined her inside and slammed the terrace door shut behind him.

He ran his hand behind her neck and pulled her towards him. She leant against him. If he let her go, she'd fall.

'Let's go home,' he said. 'It's time to go.'

'Yes,' she said, 'for you, to Jaipur.'

He frowned. 'Bloody Imogen. I was going to tell you.'

'Why didn't you?'

'I didn't know how to, with everything going on. I couldn't find the words to ask.'

'Ask?'

Edward placed his finger under her chin, tilted her face so she was looking at him. 'Come with me, Olly. Divorce Alistair, plead violence, get him to sue you for adultery for all I care . . .'

'He never will . . .'

'We'll make him. I'm not leaving you with him. I'll take care of you, I don't give a damn what anyone else thinks. Come.'

She didn't know what to say to that.

They went to bed together again that night. Olivia had no idea what Ada thought, she was sure the rest of the servants were appalled. She didn't care. If she could bring herself to let Edward go without her, stay behind to be an aunt to her nephews, she wanted to make the most of the time they had left. If she was going to go too, as she so badly wanted to, what did it matter anyway?

Could she do it to him, though? Subject him to the scandal? Wouldn't it be unspeakably selfish?

She agreed to nothing, but as she lay in his arms she thought of how it would be to leave this hellish wonderland with him, spend a lifetime feeling cherished, safe. *How splendid.*

'I'd ruin you,' she said. 'I'd be your scarlet woman.'

'I'd rather have you scarlet than not at all.' He leant on his elbow, staring down at her in the silver half-light. 'We'd get by, people forget, and even if they don't, sod them, sod them all, we'd be happy.'

'Would we?'

It was a pleasant fantasy.

The dark had the stillness of deep night when shouting in the garden awoke her. She rolled over to see if Edward had heard it, but he was no longer by her side.

She crossed to the window slowly, not at all sure that she wanted to see what was out there. She frowned as she pulled back the curtain and pushed the shutter wide, trying to make sense of the strange shadows before her.

The Bedouin mother was sobbing, Edward was in his trousers and shirt-tails shouting.

And the Bedouin brothers were being manhandled into a cart by two uniformed members of the Egyptian police.

Chapter Thirty-Eight

Nailah returned home when they released her from the barracks. Isa edged around her, barely speaking; Nailah wasn't sure whether it was guilt that made her act so – shame at the way she'd remained hidden whilst Nailah and Kafele were arrested – or anger at Nailah for all she'd done, her part in Jahi being in jail. Perhaps it was simply grief. Either way, for the first time in Nailah's living memory, her mother was speechless.

'I wish Hassan hadn't done it,' Cleo whispered to Nailah as they went to bed, 'but he can't have been really bad, can he? Not if Umi loved him. He did it for her, I think.'

Nailah tried for a smile. 'He shouldn't have, little one. It wasn't the way.'

'What *was* the way?'

'I'm not sure there ever was one. Maybe if Sir Gray was poor, lowly.' She shrugged. There was no point turning it all over again. What was done was done, the past was dead. And if she couldn't think of a way to stop it, so would Kafele and Jahi be. *I'll try the whole cause, and condemn you to death.* Out of all the strangeness in the whirling, winding book that Ma'am Sheldon had given Nailah, that was the sentence that had lodged in her memory, scaring her almost as much as Kafele's pledge of his life for hers.

'The trial's at ten,' said Isa when she returned from the market the next morning, shock apparently making her remember how to talk. 'Kafele's being sentenced alongside Jahi, the sons of that

Bedouin man they had flogged for Tabia's death too. Sweet Mother.'
Isa raised her hand to her head. She didn't have any rings on, no
bracelets, she must have forgotten to wear them. 'I feel as though
I'm rotting inside, just thinking about them all. They say Jahi wrote
a note to Ma'am Sheldon, they're using it to show he meant Ma'am
Sheldon mischief.' Nailah groaned, thinking of how she'd refused to
pen Hassan's note herself. 'That's not all,' said Isa, 'they've accused
him of murdering Hassan, as well as helping Hassan murder Ma'am
Gray. No matter what, Jahi hangs. And those white men walk free.'
Isa shook her head. 'It's already in the papers. The things they're
saying, that Jahi and all of them were after Sir Gray's money, Sir
Sheldon's too, common criminals who'd stop at nothing. Sir Sheldon
had worked it all out apparently, and was riding to your Ma'am
Sheldon's aid.'

'Is there any mention of Tabia?' Nailah asked it without any hope.

'Not a sniff,' said Isa, 'or of how Jahi brought Ma'am Sheldon
home.' She threw down her basket and slumped to the floor. She
sank her head against her knees. 'My heart is breaking, *breaking*. I
keep seeing him in his cell, in shackles. My brother. He's worked so
hard his whole life, been so proud.' Her voice shook. 'He's always
cared for you children, you know, in his way, passing his money to
me, to Tabia. And now he's in prison. And poor Kafele. Kafele who's
done nothing, *nothing*. I can picture him as a boy, running around
after you, Nailah. I dreamt of it last night.'

'Don't,' said Nailah, 'please.' It made her dizzy with pain, just
thinking about him. It was all wrong, so wrong. She felt as if the
ground had become the deck of a tilting boat and the sea was
moving to take the place of the sky. She couldn't just sit here, let it
all come to pass.

'Where are you going?' asked Isa as she made for the door.

'There's something I have to do.'

Olivia packed. Edward was out, although she didn't know where
he'd gone; she presumed the court. She kept thinking of the
Bedouin boys standing trial. That they'd even been taken made

her seethe. They were children, little older than Ralph. Her movements jerked as she folded her underclothes. Her newly acquired cat (she'd named her Dinah) sat on a cushion and watched her. (The camel was still in the stables; no one seemed to know what to do with it.)

Olivia wasn't sure why she packed. She hadn't decided to go to India, not fully, but she couldn't resolve not to, either; she supposed it was better to be prepared. As soon as she had news of the trial, she'd go to *The Times'* offices and see Morton about the story. She had a strong urge to visit Wilkins too; she couldn't face Alistair, but she had to at least try to force Wilkins to admit what he and Alistair had done with that villager in Lixori.

And whether it was them who had beaten Clara.

Just the thought of them touching her made Olivia want to retch; she shook, physically, thinking of it. She didn't know if Wilkins would ever confess – or what she could do if he did – she only knew that she couldn't stand not knowing.

A small voice told her she should stop, visit Clara's grave, not leave her alone. But she wasn't ready, and she couldn't let herself stop moving, pause to think. Her mind kept trying to drag her back to that coffin, those curls, that waxy skin, thoughts of what Clara's final moments had been like . . . She clenched her eyes shut. She was scared, too scared, of the sadness; the finality of it. She couldn't seem to accept it. Not for Clara. Not yet.

The hands of the carriage clock moved to time. Nine o'clock. Twelve minutes past. Half past . . . tick-tock.

At twenty-nine minutes to ten a tight-lipped Ada poked her head around the door. Nailah was waiting downstairs; no, Ada couldn't believe it either.

'You have some nerve coming here,' Olivia said as she joined Nailah in the hallway, Ada behind her. ('Don't try and dismiss me,' Ada had said upstairs, 'you'll have to knock me out before I leave you alone with 'er.' Olivia wasn't sure how Ada could leave her to do anything if she was unconscious, but she didn't press the matter.)

Nailah stared at them both, her mouth half-open, as though

waiting for words to come. She was back in her old robe, pulling at the frayed sleeve with nails bitten blunt.

'What do you want?' Olivia asked her.

'Your . . .' Her voice cracked. She coughed, tried again. 'Your help, Ma'am Sheldon.'

'My help?' Olivia was incredulous. 'What could you possibly want of me?'

'You have to save Kafele, Jahi.'

'How am I meant to do that?'

'Money. Get Sir Gray to bribe the police. I know he can.'

It wasn't the worst idea. Now Nailah had put it to her, Olivia suspected Wilkins might even be expecting it, that he'd enjoyed his recent rise in income and was looking to maintain it. Perhaps it was why he'd insisted on hanging on to Kafele, had the two Bedouin arrested: he'd guessed they would try to save them. 'All right,' she said, 'I'll ask.'

'Thank you.'

'I'm not doing it for you, Nailah. I'm doing it for them, there are some boys too who need help.'

'Please, just concentrate on Kafele and Jahi first.'

'I'm sure Jeremy's pocket can stretch.'

'At least he'll be paying,' said Nailah quietly, 'in a way.'

Olivia laughed unhappily. 'We've all of us paid,' she said. 'Just some more than others.'

Nailah flushed.

Olivia sighed. 'You'd better leave this with me. I'll go and see Jeremy now.'

Jeremy wasn't home. Accounts varied amongst the servants remaining as to whether he was at the police station, the courts, the club or the office.

Olivia looked anxiously at the clock. It was after ten already, the court would be in session, who knew if the powers that were would wait until dawn to carry out the punishments? Not she. She couldn't risk a delay hightailing around Alexandria. She'd have to go to Alistair at the hospital, get him to front the money. The idea of laying eyes on him, let alone asking for anything, sickened her, but there seemed little choice.

She went up to the nursery before she left. She paused at the door, eyeing the wooden duck; she found herself imagining Clara placing it there, fingers tracing the wood. Olivia's chest contracted; she took a deep breath, gathering herself, *not yet*, then went in. Sofia was feeding Gus from a glass bottle. She nodded in the direction of Ralph, hugging his knees in the window seat. *Poor little lamb.*

Olivia went to him. He raised desultory eyes. 'I only have one night left,' he said. 'We're packing. And Mama's dead. And I . . .' He clenched his chubby fists and stretched his lips back across his teeth. 'I . . . I . . .' Olivia pulled him into her arms. 'I wanted her to come home,' he sobbed into her shoulder. 'I thought she would be rescued.'

Olivia held him, pressing her lips to the crown of his head. 'I wanted her to come back too.' As she heard the hopelessness in her own words, for a moment her guard slipped, and before she could stop herself, she saw Clara dying, that moment when she must have given in, given up, and accepted that she'd never see her sons again, closed her eyes in crumpled agony on the sand . . . Such pain, all that pain, it made Olivia want to scream. It quickened her breath, tightened her arms around Ralph; the sheer, bloody pain of it.

Ralph made a noise. Olivia realised she was squeezing him too hard. She pushed her awful thoughts down, and him out to arm's length. His full eyes stared back at her. His cheeks were swollen and round, such a baby still. Olivia was reminded of how he'd looked that first night Clara was taken, asleep in his bed as Sofia spoke of Clara's letter in the bookshelves. The one that had so mysteriously disappeared. Had he heard? Taken it himself to protect his mama, afraid that Olivia wouldn't get to it in time?

Olivia brushed his hair from his sweaty forehead. She dropped her voice to a whisper, and asked. 'You can tell me, Ralph. I won't be cross.'

Slowly, he nodded. 'I . . . it . . .' He bit his lip. 'It was to Mr Pasha,

374

Aunt Livvy. I didn't want anyone to know.' His eyes welled again. 'She wanted him to meet her. She said she'd get Hassan to take her. If I'd just showed it to you, or Teddy.' His lip trembled. 'I should have showed it.'

'Oh, Ralph.' Olivia pulled him back to her. She held him for what felt like a long time. Too long, considering all she had to do. She refused to think about the implications of what he'd done, or not done. What was the use now?

At length, she kissed him. She said she was sorry but she really had to go. She went over to Gus, by now in a milk-sopped doze, and touched his cheek. Her nephew, Imogen's too. Clara's boy. Could she leave him, leave them? Didn't she owe Clara more than that?

'Can I speak to you, Mrs Livvy?' Sofia stood, gestured at the adjoining bedroom, and bustled towards it.

Olivia followed. She waited whilst Sofia laid Gus in his crib.

'You looked like you were saying your goodbyes just then,' said Sofia.

Olivia sighed.

'Tell me,' said Sofia. 'We need to warn Ralphy, *agapi mou*. He doesn't deserve to lose you just like that, too.'

Olivia opened her arms helplessly. 'I don't know if he will.'

'What do you mean?'

With one eye on the mantelpiece clock (five minutes to eleven), Olivia told Sofia what Edward had asked, how she hadn't decided what to do, and she really didn't know if she could leave Ralph and Gus, but before she did anything else she had to go and see Alistair, innocents were in trouble, relying on her, she mustn't delay. Sofia asked her if she was going to tell Alistair that she might or might not be India-bound. Olivia said no, of course not, he'd only stop her. And besides, what was the point when she wasn't definitely going? 'Apart from anything, I'm worried about Edward's career. He says it doesn't matter, but ... I don't know. Does it matter? I want to go, Sofia, so much. Alistair is ... cruel, so very cruel ... And I ... well, Edward, he ... I can't lose ...'

'You love him. I see it.' Sofia sighed. 'Oh, I've never liked it, you being married to that man. I can't help suspecting he's involved in what's happened to poor Mrs Clara.'

'Oh, Sofia, he was. In ways you can't imagine. If you knew what he's done, what else he might have. I'm going to go to the papers, tell them everything.'

Sofia held up the flats of her hands. 'I don't think I can stand hearing it.' She eased herself into her rocking chair. She didn't reach for her cigarettes. 'You have to leave, Mrs Livvy. Your mama would want you to. If only you could know how she'd want it, how she loved you and Mrs Clara.' Sofia tugged a handkerchief from beneath the shelf of her bosom and blew her nose noisily. 'She'd tell you to be happy now. There's nothing left for you here. Ralphy's off, and Mr Jeremy's making noises about sending me and Gus with him for a spell. I'll take care of them both. I can do that for you and your sister.' She blew her nose again. 'It's little enough.'

'I'll come and say goodbye.' Olivia spoke and made up her mind all in the same moment. Her heart lurched, even in spite of her grief. She was going to India. Away from here. They were going. They would be a 'they'. She and Edward, Edward and she. They'd have a home, one day they might have children, they'd wake together, sleep together, walk together, breathe. Always. *They*. 'I'll be back later.' She turned to leave, impatient now, so very impatient.

She glimpsed a movement beneath the corridor door. It stopped her short. She narrowed her eyes and pushed the door wide. A swish of grey taffeta disappeared down the stairs.

Had Mildred been listening?

Olivia didn't know why it should matter, but even so, the possibility sent her pumping blood cold.

Her sense of foreboding deepened when she discovered Mildred already at the hospital when she arrived there, sitting next to Alistair. Olivia touched her hand to her stomach, *calm*, and proceeded across the ward of sunburnt soldiers towards them. Mildred watched her, not moving. It was only as Olivia drew near that she rose and glided silently past her, taffeta skimming silk.

'What did she want?' Olivia managed to ask Alistair.

He smiled tightly. He was shockingly pale, even by his standards. Someone had combed his hair into a side parting rather than the slicked-back way he normally wore it. His torso was bare, covered with pristine bandages. He looked smaller. Pathetic.

Then he spoke, and he wasn't small or pathetic at all. He informed Olivia that he knew what she was planning, Mildred had told him. He'd received word from the tribunal, by the by, everyone had been found guilty, Hassan of Clara's death, Jahi of Hassan's, the rest of them of aiding and abetting. Jahi had been sentenced to hanging; Kafele and the Bedouin's sons were to receive fifty lashes that very afternoon. Quite a lot. *Men died from less.* There was nothing to be done for Jahi, his execution had been scheduled for a week's time. Besides, he was as guilty as all hell. Still, Alistair was happy to pay Wilkins to let the Bedouin boys and Kafele escape, if that was what Olivia wanted. He was as loath as the next man to see innocents suffer. He wasn't the criminal here. He'd write Olivia a letter to give Wilkins directly, naming a sum. Wilkins would do as required.

Alistair paused. He smiled.

He had conditions.

Of course.

If Olivia so much as set foot on the ship tonight, Alistair would ask Wilkins to round up the boys, and this time there'd be no mercy. They'd hang. If Bertram *didn't* get on that ship, there'd be no mercy. If Olivia breathed a whisper of Tabia's death to anyone, let alone the papers, there'd be no mercy. If Olivia in fact did anything but live in their house and behave as any reasonable man might expect his wife before God to behave, there'd be no mercy. 'Go if you like, ask for your divorce, tell the world all you believe Gray and I have done to that Tabia woman. Just bear in mind that as soon as you do, you sign three death sentences.'

'You can't do this.' Olivia spoke with more conviction than she felt. What she felt was nauseous, dizzy. 'I'll get Jeremy to pay for their release instead. He'll do it.'

'And I'll still pay Wilkins more to round them up.'

'Then,' she said, scrambling for another way, 'I'll go to the police, whoever I have to, I'll tell them about what you and Wilkins did with that villager in Lixori . . .'

'Did?' He arched an eyebrow.

'I know—' she began.

'You know nothing,' he said, cutting her off, 'because there is nothing to know.'

'I don't believe you.'

'That means very little to me, Olivia. Nor will it to anyone else.' He sneered. 'Have you forgotten who we are, that Wilkins *is* the police? That I am who I am.'

'I don't care—'

'You should. If you want my help for those boys, you should. It's over, Olivia. You've lost. Or won.' Alistair winced as he adjusted his weight. 'You get to stay married to me. Won't that be nice? Now, do you want me to write this letter?'

'Alistair . . .'

'Olivia,' his eyes sparked, 'say another word, about any of it, and I won't write a thing. Now, are you going to fetch me paper?'

What choice did she have?

She fetched a pad from the nurses, watched Alistair write. He paused midway through, looked up at her, back at the paper. His lips twitched.

'Is something amusing?' she asked.

'Not at all,' he said. And yet still he smiled.

It unnerved her, that smile.

He finished writing, signed his name with a flourish, and held the sealed envelope out. She tried to take it; he gripped it, stopping her. 'I hope you'll think hard,' he said, 'before trying to make a fool of me again.'

He let the letter go.

She must have left his side, because she found herself exiting the ward. She looked down at Wilkins' letter in her hand, fighting the impulse to open it, read it, tear it into fragments and shatter its

378

existence, all it meant. She didn't know how it could be real, how any of it could be happening.

She passed into the corridor. Mildred's voice calling her attention penetrated the air. Olivia turned to face her. The hate which surged through her body as she met her grandmother's gaze nearly made her stumble. Of all the things Mildred had done to her over the years, this felt like the worst.

'Why did you do it?' she asked her.

Mildred raised pointy eyebrows. 'I couldn't let you ruin yourself.'

'What does that matter to you?' Olivia's lips turned as she spoke; the urge to weep at all that was happening pulled on her cheeks. But she fought it, refusing to give into it. Not in front of Mildred. 'You've never cared for me.'

Mildred stared. 'It's true,' she said at length.

The admission made Olivia feel no better. 'Why couldn't you just let me go?'

Mildred shrugged. 'It would have affected me, Clara's boys. Word spreads. I couldn't allow it.'

'You couldn't allow me a chance to escape. That's what you couldn't allow. Do you know all Alistair's done? What he is?'

'I don't care,' Mildred snapped.

'How can you not?' It came out as a shout. 'What did I ever do to you?'

'You? Nothing.' Mildred gave a wrinkled pout. 'Your mother however . . . she was a horrible gel.' She looked Olivia squarely in the eye. 'She took my son, I took her children. She'd have hated you being separated. It would have killed her, if she'd been alive to see it.'

'You're the devil.' Olivia spat it. 'I can't stand that you're taking Ralph.'

'And yet, as with so much, there's nothing you can do to stop it.'

Olivia turned from her in disgust. She didn't want to spend another moment in Mildred's presence.

'You look like her, you know,' said Mildred to her back, 'much more than Clara did. Where are you going? Come back, I haven't finished.'

Olivia ignored her. She would take no more of her poison. There weren't many hours left in the day. She had to get to Wilkins, find Edward. There was so little time left to them now, and he didn't know.

He didn't know.

Somehow she had to let him get on that boat without her. It would be the cruellest thing she ever did, to both of them if no one else. But she had to do it.

Chapter Thirty-Nine

Wilkins ushered Olivia into his office as though she were the only person he would wish to see. He offered her tea, cool lime perhaps. Olivia wanted only one thing, Wilkins' jowls twitched as she told him what it was. 'I think I'd better take a look at Sheldon's letter,' he said.

Olivia gave it to him. He opened the envelope, his eyes moved across the paper. He looked up at her, back at the letter, then at her again. The sound of his nasal breaths filled the office.

He set the letter on the desk. Olivia tried to read it, but Alistair's upside down hand was illegible.

'It seems I'm to keep an eye on everyone.' There was a definite smile on Wilkins' florid face now, *that smirk*. 'Watch them in case we need to bring them back in. Plus we want to make sure they keep ... ' He mimed a key locking his lips, winked with one piggy eye.

Olivia fought the urge to reach for one of the pyramid paper-weights on the desk and strike him with it. 'You've done rather well out of this, haven't you?' she said. 'How much has Alistair been paying you for your cooperation?'

He laughed throatily. 'Enough. But I was glad to help.' Another wink, a cold kind of intimacy.

Olivia narrowed her eyes. 'How much, exactly, have you helped?'

He smiled. 'I've done everything in my power, of course.' He cocked his head to one side, appraising Olivia. 'You look a little ... off colour, Mrs Sheldon. Is everything all right?'

'Not really,' she said. 'Not at all. Nor is it for the innocent people who've had the misfortune to cross your path, the ones you have locked in your prison.'

'Innocent?' Wilkins laughed shortly. 'Jahi killed Hassan.'

'I killed Hassan.'

'What's that?' Wilkins hooked a fat finger behind his ear. 'I didn't hear you. Damned earholes get so clogged up. Don't repeat it, I'm sure it's unnecessary. No one else will be able to hear you either. Your voice is so soft, so female, so *British*.'

Olivia stared.

Wilkins said, 'Jahi El Masri knew what was going on and he didn't put a stop to it.'

'He didn't take Clara.'

'He didn't help her, either.'

'Nor, I think, did you.' She took a breath, ready to raise the matter of Lixori again.

Wilkins spoke, though, before she could. 'I'll help those two boys,' he said.

'What?' She frowned, confused. 'No, it's three.'

'Two, Mrs Sheldon.' He leant back in his chair, spread his legs out before him, and rested his hands on his straining waistcoat. 'Your husband's been quite specific, he said you are to choose which ones go free.' Wilkins frowned. 'You seem so shocked. It's strange, Sheldon said this should come as no surprise to you.'

'I ... I can't ... choose. How can I choose?'

'You must. Otherwise they'll all be punished.' Wilkins tutted sympathetically. 'So who's it to be? Chop chop, the lashings are scheduled for four.'

Nailah waited in a dingy room near the cells, a private wing, she'd been informed with a sneer, for especially dangerous criminals. The air was dirty with sweat, urine and fear. A low groaning was coming from somewhere, the drone broken only by the drip-drop of rusty liquid from a pipe in the corner.

Nailah tried to reassure herself that Ma'am Sheldon would set matters to rights, she'd be doing it even now. Kafele was going to be fine. They all were.

The groaning continued, the drip-drop.

Nailah stared at the peeling stone walls, watched the light move through the window. She tried to picture Kafele close by, see his face, hear his voice, feel his unruptured skin. She remembered his toes in the water next to hers that first night at Eastern Harbour.

Why had no one come to free him?

Hours seemed to pass.

It was taking Olivia too long to find Edward. Everywhere she went – the courts, the prison, the parade ground – she was told she'd just missed him, shouldn't she be at home (furtive glance at the cut on her cheekbone), she'd been through so much, after all. In the absence of any other idea, that was where she went; perhaps he was packing. He wasn't, but the Bedouin mother was. Fadil was with her, waiting in the shade of the fig tree. He told Olivia that he was taking the mother to a small village up the coast, her boys were being secreted there at nightfall, they weren't going to receive their lashes. Edward and Tom had spoken with Wilkins, Tom had fronted the money for their release, Kafele's too.

Olivia could have screamed. She need never have gone to see Alistair at all, all three of those boys would have been released instead of just two. She would have been leaving this tropical hell at nightfall. She looked down the silent driveway, bursting with rage at Nailah for involving her again, herself for letting her, and Alistair and Wilkins most of all. She had to find a way to beat them, she couldn't let them get away with this. 'Where's Edward and Tom?' she asked Fadil. 'I have to find one of them.'

Fadil said he didn't know about the colonel, but Edward had left about ten minutes ago. 'I don't know where he's gone.'

Cursing, Olivia resolved to ask Ada if she did. First she bade the Bedouin mother a hasty goodbye. Fadil translated as she told her how sorry she was for all she'd been through, that she wished her only the best. The mother kissed her own fingertips and placed the kiss on Olivia's forehead. 'Take you care,' she said. She pointed at the house. 'No more,' she said, 'no more.'

Olivia smiled tightly and set off inside.

Ada told her that Edward had seen Olivia's half-packed trunk and gone to the harbour to buy tickets. "'E's getting me one too. You'll need an ally for what you've planned.'

'We're not going anywhere at the moment,' said Olivia, and watched Ada's face fall as she told her why. 'I have to go,' Olivia said, 'but if Edward comes back, tell him what's happened, that he has to fix it.'

She rode for the harbour. With two ships in dock, one for India that night, the other for England on the morrow, the place pulsated in the sunshine: luggage trolleys being towed to the cargo holds, horses pulling carts of fruits, vegetables, sacks of flour and cotton, flies buzzing, vendors calling the prices of imitation sphinxes and pillars. Olivia pushed through it all, skin burning in the relentless heat, found a likely-looking boy to watch Bea, and made straight for the ticket office.

Edward wasn't there. He'd left half an hour ago. 'Are you one of the ladies accompanying him?' asked the clerk from behind his parchment and inkpot. 'You'll need to be aboard by nine, the ship sails at ten. It's close to three already.'

Olivia told him she was fully aware of the time.

Oh God. OhGodohGodohGod.

She went back outside, she stared at the crowds. Her hands were wet with sweat inside her gloves, her armpits and forehead were beaded with it. Unless she was granted a mammoth stroke of luck (not bloody likely), she wasn't going to find Edward within the next hour. She had to think of something else. *Fifty lashes*. What did that even do to a person? Would there even be anything left to whip?

What in God and bloody hell's name was she going to do?

At last a guard arrived in the waiting room. He told Nailah she could see Jahi. She said, 'But I want to see Kafele.'

He told her to shut up and be grateful.

She tried to think what she could say to Jahi as she followed the guard down the dripping corridor, smells so fetid they burned her throat. But her mind remained blank, numb. Her eyes darted from left to right, skimming the iron-barred cells, the dirty, slumped forms of prisoners within.

The guard came to a halt, and took out his keys. Opening the door, he ushered Nailah into a small stone room, turning the key behind her. Jahi was shackled against the damp brickwork, his face bruised and swollen.

'As-salaam,' he said. It sounded like a snake's hiss. Someone had knocked out his crooked front tooth.

'Who did this to you?' Nailah asked.

'A guard.'

'British?'

'Egyptian. Apparently it's scum like me that give our countrymen a bad name.'

Nailah clenched her hands. 'Are you scared?' she heard herself asking.

'A little.'

She told him what she'd asked of Ma'am Sheldon. 'You'll get out of here, you'll see.'

He gave her a sad smile, as though he felt sorry for her. 'I don't want you to come,' he said, 'when they hang me. I'm told they let it go on a long time. Don't come here again either. I have no wish for anyone I love to see me like this.'

'You . . . love me?'

He winced. 'You're my niece, Nailah. So much better than all of this . . . You ever have been.'

'I'm not sure you're right.'

'Of course I am.'

Nailah looked at the slimy stone floor. She felt as though she should say something else. She didn't know if she could leave him like this. Just as she was summoning the courage to tell him that she realised he'd only ever been trying to protect her, that she knew he was sorry, she was so very sorry too, the prison guard clanged on the bars and told her to get on and get out, he needed to take a piss.

'Livvy, I thought it was you.'

It was Jeremy, coming out of the ticket office behind Olivia. He squinted beneath his top hat. There were silver puddles of exhaustion beneath his eyes. Olivia wasn't sure why he was there. Buying Sofia and Gus's tickets perhaps? She wasn't about to ask; frankly, he was the last person she wanted to see. But whilst his presence felt like the polar opposite of luck, un-luck in fact, he was all she had.

'The scum,' he said, once she had finished telling him everything. 'Both of them. I already gave Wilkins the money to free those boys earlier.' He suggested they bribe Wilkins to tell Alistair that the lashes had been given when they hadn't been.

'A bribe to counter the counter-bribe,' said Olivia.

'Precisely. It's simplest if Sheldon doesn't find out. We'll fix it, Livvy.'

'You're sorry now, are you?'

'I've always been sorry. But yes,' he spoke heavily, 'I am. Never more than now.'

She gave him a cold stare. It was all too little, far, far too late.

'Come on,' he said, 'we don't have much time. Let's get to Wilkins' office.'

As the guard led Nailah back towards the waiting room, they passed a cluster of men, the fat man, Wilkins, amongst them. He seemed very angry; he was breathing loudly, shouting, gesticulating. He looked like Isa did when she was performing in one of her shows. 'Gone? Gone?' he asked. 'How can two boys have just disappeared? You,' he pointed at the other white man there, 'have the streets searched, leave no stone unturned.'

'Yes, sir, right away, sir,' said the man, and then failed to move.

Another guard arrived, he said something in Wilkins' ear. Wilkins' eyebrows shot up. 'I'll be down in a minute,' he said, 'I'm dealing with this outrage for now. *You.*' Nailah stepped back as he pointed at her. 'What do you want?'

'I . . . I just wanted to see Kafele.'

Wilkins' eyes rolled, his head wobbled. 'Hear that, my esteemed colleagues, Nailah here wants to see Kafele. Can we help her with that? Or have we arsing well lost him too?'

Nailah stared. Her heart hammered with confusion and dread. 'You haven't lost him?'

Wilkins frowned. 'Why would we have? He's down there,' he nodded towards another row of cells, 'getting ready to take his just deserts.' He turned back to the other guards. 'At least one of our prisoners is. We'll have to keep what's happened with the Bedouin boys quiet; God knows what will become of you all if it gets out they've escaped.'

Nailah barely heard. She ran in the direction Wilkins had nodded, panic pounding in her ears. A cell door opened at the end. Kafele was led out between two guards. He was stripped to the waist, his hands were bound.

Nailah must have called his name because he turned and saw her. His amber eyes sparked, his cheeks were sickly pale.

'No,' she said, shaking her head. 'No, no, no. I don't want this, I don't want it.'

Someone took her by the arm and pulled.

'Don't hurt her,' Kafele shouted, 'don't hurt her.'

'I'm sorry,' she sobbed, 'I'm so sorry.' She turned to the guard manhandling her. 'Stop, you have to stop.'

But he didn't. He lifted her away. She kicked, she screamed, 'No,' again and again.

But Kafele was still dragged from view.

Olivia and Jeremy heard the yelling from the side room they'd been shown into. Jeremy flicked open his pocket watch, he told Olivia it was gone four. The streets had been busy, it had taken them longer than it should have to get to the prison, and they'd wasted precious minutes trying to find Wilkins at the police offices.

387

The shouting ceased. The minutes stretched, all the longer for the speed of the hours that had just passed.

Eventually Wilkins arrived. He mopped his blotchy brow as he came into the room, wheezing, as if out of breath. Jeremy wasted no time in telling him what they wanted.

'It's a bit late,' said Wilkins, 'they're about to start.'

'Then stop them.'

'I'm not sure I can, or that I need to. This morning's been ... lucrative.' He raised a smug eyebrow, his evident enjoyment of his brief flight of power over Jeremy somewhat undermining the superiority he was taking such pains to assert.

Jeremy's left eye twitched, he drew himself up. He looked at Wilkins as though he might have been thinking of crushing him beneath his little toe. Wilkins lifted his chin defiantly, but took a step back nonetheless, then another as Jeremy asked him who the hell he thought he was, what games he was playing, what delusions he was labouring under that made him believe he could double-cross Jeremy in this manner? Olivia couldn't help but feel a bitter shot of satisfaction at seeing Wilkins' confidence falter, the wobble in his flabby cheeks, his sinking recognition that whatever temporary imbalance might have been struck in the universe, it was levelling now. Here stood *Jeremy Gray*; even though Olivia hated who that was, all Jeremy's status stood for, there was no denying that his rediscovery of his gravitas was timely.

'Here's what you're going to do,' said Jeremy, his voice low, controlled. Olivia could almost see the hairs on the back of Wilkins' neck standing on end. 'You're going to call off the lashings, you're going to lie to Sheldon and tell him they happened, pay whoever necessary to say the same thing, and then we're going to get Kafele the hell out of here.'

'If Sheldon finds out ...'

'He won't.'

'He might.' Wilkins shook his head, he was blustering now. 'I don't know what I can even do for Kafele. I got the others away without anyone seeing.'

Jeremy took a step forwards and seized Wilkins by the lapels, lithe with force against the man's lumbering mass, pushing him against the wall. 'Find a way.'

Wilkins swallowed; his Adam's apple looked as if it might choke him.

A wailing started up somewhere above.

Jeremy rammed Wilkins by the shoulders. 'Do it, Wilkins. Or so help me, I will tell the world about your trip with Sheldon to Lixori. That vanished peasant. Clara's bruises, her broken arm.'

'I told you this morning, I don't know what you're talking about . . .'

'I think you do.'

'You can't prove anything.'

'Maybe not, but I can make my suspicions known.'

'You wouldn't,' said Wilkins. 'Sheldon would drag you down too, we both would.'

'I really don't care.'

'You're bluffing,' said Wilkins.

Jeremy rammed him again. 'Try me.'

Wilkins hashed a stab at affecting calm, his nose wrinkled, chin so far back in his neck it became five – it was grimly unsuccessful. Seeing it, Olivia knew with a dull thud that it must be true: Wilkins and Alistair had concealed – perhaps murdered – the man who would have led them to Clara.

There was every chance they'd done more.

The realisation shuddered through her. It left her cold with hate, but not numb. Her body filled with rage. She would have gone for Wilkins then, let her fury, her grief, loose; it was only Kafele's screams that held her back.

Jeremy said they needed to go now. This time Wilkins didn't argue. Jeremy propelled him from the room. 'Move, man, run.'

What followed passed very quickly, not in a blur. The nightmare was clear, distinct. Wilkins led them down a peeling corridor, up sloping steps, and hammered on the door of the screaming room. No one answered, not for many screams. 'Open up, open up!'

Wilkins yelled. Thwack, thwack. The noise became a wet, dripping thing. 'Stop, for God's sake, stop,' Olivia and Jeremy shouted. Finally, it did. The heavy wooden door opened and was thrown wide. A sweating, panting man peered out. Olivia didn't look at his face, it was his rod of ropes that took her attention. She watched the way they oozed with blood and white matter.

The man said he hadn't heard them. He waved his rod at a pulpy mess tied to a pole in the corner, surrounded by a hungry cloud of flies. 'That one was making such a racket.'

Olivia stared. She didn't know what she was seeing. She felt a hand take her arm. It might have been Jeremy's. He told her to turn away, but she didn't. She heard steps coming up behind her. Everything swam. Exposed muscle, peeling flesh, buzzing flies feeding on the remains of a man, not a man, a boy's back.

His face was distorted, open eyes staring, wet with tears.

'I did this, I did this,' she said.

She felt arms pulling her, they felt strong like Edward's. Could he be here? 'Come away, come away.' It sounded like him.

'I only got to twenty-eight,' said the man with the ropes. 'We've still got a way to go.

Olivia heard someone say, 'No.' (It might have been her, it might have been the pulpy mess.)

'Let's call it a square fifty,' someone said. (Jeremy?)

'What the hell is going on?' (Edward? Could he be real? Had Ada sent him?) 'How could you let her see this, Gray?'

'Will he live?' (Olivia?) 'Will he live?'

'Probably not,' said the man with the whip. He turned and spat across the room.

The globule flew through the air. It landed on Kafele's dripping calf.

Chapter Forty

Olivia wasn't sure how she got outside. It must have been Edward who took her, because it was he who was kneeling beside her as she retched into the roots of a palm tree. He took her hand; she felt his fingers squeeze hers. Amidst the heat, the smell of blood, the hanging flesh and the screams, he had come for her. He'd known to be there, that she needed him. Her need was a force larger than she could consciously understand, yet in hours he was going to be gone.

She didn't know how it could be.

She ran her hand across her mouth. Edward gave her his handkerchief; she dropped it, her fingers were trembling too much. He picked it up, wiped her lips, then pulled her to her feet. She looked up at him. His eyes were dark with barely contained anger.

'Ada told you?' she asked.

He nodded. 'You have to come with me, Olly.'

'He'll kill them.'

'He'll kill you if you stay. We can have those boys protected. Tom will watch them.'

'It won't be enough.' If there'd ever been any doubt in her mind about Alistair's limitless capacity for cruelty, Wilkins' reaction to Jeremy's words about Lixori had eradicated it. 'He did it, Edward. He made sure Clara died. He won't stop at doing the same to them.'

Edward said, 'I won't let you lay your life down for theirs.'

Olivia thought of Kafele's face, his curled toes, those screams, and said nothing.

'Olly . . . ' Edward shook his head and pulled her towards him.

She rested her head on his chest, feeling his warmth, inhaling his smell, the smoke, the soap, that something else … Still there, still hers. She raised her eyes to his face, his clenched jaw, the pain in his gaze. If she could have, she would have sent him from her now, given him that part of her he loved to take with him; she didn't want to be this thief.

Jeremy arrived, a glass of murky water in hand. He held it out to Olivia; it was boiled, he'd checked. She looked at it dubiously, took a sip. It felt grainy in her mouth, but it eased the taste of vomit.

Edward asked Jeremy if he was proud of himself, Jeremy said not particularly. But he was taking Kafele home, he'd make arrangements for his care. Nailah was inside, Jeremy had spoken to her. It had turned his stomach to face that wretched girl, but he'd done it. She was going to come, help nurse Kafele at the house, and yes, he appreciated the irony of the situation.

He squinted at Olivia in the sunlight. 'I'm going to go and talk to Alistair. I'd kill him if I could, but I think it better I help you. God knows Clara would want me to.'

It was nearly dark by the time Nailah arrived at the Grays'. She'd gone to see Isa and the children before coming; she'd told them what was happening, and asked Isa to watch over things.

'All right,' Isa had said, 'for tonight. But can you come in the morning, I want us to visit Jahi. You can go back to Kafele afterwards.'

Nailah's stomach clenched in dread. 'Jahi doesn't want anyone there.'

'Want isn't need,' said Isa. 'And he'll need us now, for the time he has left. Tabia would want us to comfort him.' She looked to her toes. 'I can do that for her at least.'

Nailah hadn't had the energy to fight. Thinking of Jahi alone in his damp cell, the bruises on his face, she wasn't sure she wanted to.

Isa had sighed. 'There's some broth on the stove,' she said. 'I picked up some pomegranates at the market. Eat, you look like death. Then go.'

Nailah looked up now at the Grays' pale pink mansion; she breathed, swallowed, breathed again. She took her surroundings in. A plump Mediterranean woman stood up on the terrace with Ma'am Gray's angry baby in her arms. Beside her was an equally chubby nurse, just arrived, by the look of the case in her hand and the sweat on her brow. Their voices, as they spoke in rapid Greek, rang through the evening air. Sir Gray was on the lawn, holding Ralph's hand. He watched, expression grim, as an elderly lady in a crinoline clambered into a carriage. It was loaded with trunks, and manned by a nervous-looking servant in an oversized uniform.

The elderly lady's reedy voice carried above the Greeks'. She spoke of ingratitude, distrust, bad choices. She'd never felt so put upon, so used. She was most aggravated.

'For God's sake, Mildred,' said Sir Gray. 'I've told you I don't want you on the same ship as the boys, Ralph's been through enough. I'm putting you up in the best hotel in Cairo, and in a week's time, you'll be taken to Port Said for a passage to England. The voyage is quicker from there, you'll be back in no time. You have nothing to complain about, and you are *not having Ralph*. It's enough, it all ends here—' He broke off; he appeared to have spotted Nailah.

'More house guests?' asked the old lady.

Nailah coloured under the intensity of Sir Gray's stare. He pulled Ralph behind him. Did he think she would hurt him? Did he imagine she could?

He nodded towards the two women on the terrace. He told her the one with the baby was called Sofia, the nurse was her sister, Leila, they would show Nailah inside. Kafele was in the back room. 'I have to go out,' he said. 'I need to persuade my sister-in-law into something she's not going to much want to do.' He narrowed his eyes at Nailah. 'Perhaps I should get your uncle to send her another note.'

Nailah said nothing.

'How's your young cousin?' Sir Gray asked. 'Babu? Better, I hope.'

Nailah remained silent, the realisation that it was he who'd been paying for Babu's care dawning on her. She wished she didn't know, that he wasn't being kind now to Kafele; it felt selfish of him to complicate her hatred of him.

He sighed. 'You'd better go inside,' he said.

As she went, he called out to her to wait. She paused, turning.

He hesitated before speaking. 'I know how you must despise me,' he said. 'I,' he ran his hand down his pallid face, eyes moving from her, to Ralph, then back to her. He sighed again. 'I'm sorry, Nailah,' he said. 'I'm sorrier than I can ever tell you for what happened to your aunt.'

Nailah stood completely still. She'd never expected him to apologise.

'Please,' he said, 'whatever you might think of me, I'm trusting you to behave now in my house, with my children. Let's not let each other down any further.'

Kafele was in a large bedroom, unconscious and swathed in iced muslin. A trickle of blood dripped down his side, saliva seeped from his half-open mouth. The lady called Sofia bustled over to him, the babe still in her arms, and said something bossy to her sister. Leila tsked and replied in Greek, waggling a finger. She opened her bag and set to work cleaning off Kafele's blood, his lips. Despite her indignant manner, her fingers moved delicately, as careful as Nailah would have been. Sofia nodded in approval, evidently pleased too.

There were a few moments of silence. Only the baby's grizzling and the soft rustle of Leila's skirts interrupted it.

Nailah's throat felt dry and sore, parched by Kafele, her clown, in front of her.

'I'm here,' she said to him. 'I'm so sorry.'

He made no reply.

Nailah went to kneel by his side. She took in his torn body, his muttering lips. She raised her hand and, not knowing if she was right to move him, but unable to help herself, took hold of his.

She thought she felt him squeeze.

*

Olivia sat on Edward's bed, staring at his half-packed trunk. The air beyond the open window was black. The day had vanished. Olivia didn't know how it had happened.

She raised her eyes to Jeremy in the doorway. 'Alistair said I could go to England?' she said. 'With Ralph, Sofia and Gus? Tomorrow?'

Jeremy nodded.

'And he accepted that?'

'He didn't like it.'

'Did he admit anything?'

'What do you think?' Jeremy's laugh was short and bitter. 'He doesn't want me letting my suspicions out, though. Like Wilkins, he's had enough sense to believe I'll do it.' He stared at Olivia with bloodshot eyes. 'He wants you back here in six months. We'll work out how to get around that then.'

Olivia examined her hands, the band on her fourth finger, so loose it was uncomfortable. Even Alistair's jewellery hurt. 'I thought you were going to persuade him to divorce me.' She'd been hanging on to the possibility all afternoon. It was the only thing that had kept her calm whilst Edward insisted he was going to risk a court-martial and Alistair's vengeance and stay, he wouldn't leave her with him. 'I don't want to go to England,' she said, 'I want to go with Edward.'

'Alistair won't agree to it,' said Jeremy. 'You're his, he says. And besides, you know by now his abhorrence for scandal.' Jeremy looked from her to Edward. 'Have you two considered what it would do to you? That even if Alistair consented, it would take months, maybe years, for a divorce to be finalised?' He turned to Edward. 'You'd be ruined.'

'I really don't care.'

'Not now perhaps. But in time, when you're watching your children get shunned . . .' Jeremy sighed. 'It's a moot point anyway. If you attempt to go against Alistair, he'll round up those boys. You can't doubt he means it.'

A short silence followed.

'How can you stand to be near him?' Olivia asked Jeremy. 'How

395

can *you* stay? In that house, knowing what you've done, what he's done, thinking of Clara—'

'I can't,' said Jeremy, cutting her off. 'Of course I can't. As soon as I can make arrangements for my share of the business, I'll leave. But I want the boys away now.' He crossed the room. He made to take Olivia's hands, but she kept them firmly grasped in her lap. 'I loved your sister, Livvy,' he said. 'I know it didn't look much like it, but I did. I can never make any of this up to her, and she didn't deserve, she hardly deserved . . . ' He took a breath. 'Let me do this, Livvy. If not for you, then for Ralph and Gus, Clara's sons.' He hesitated. 'My sons. They've lost her, but they can have you.'

'Don't,' Olivia said, cheeks straining. 'Please don't play that card.'

'I'm not playing anything.' His voice was low, sincere. 'They need you, and you have to leave. It can't be with Bertram here . . . ' He tailed off.

Olivia turned her wedding band. She could feel Jeremy's eyes on her, Edward's. She heard Edward moving, she saw Jeremy step aside and Edward crouch in his place.

She gave her hands freely to him. She felt the warmth of his fingers, their strong, gentle hold.

She looked up at him.

He looked at her.

Neither of them spoke. There was nothing to say.

They both knew now how it was going to end.

Chapter Forty-One

Jeremy said he wouldn't come to the docks to see Edward off; he was anxious about leaving the boys alone with Nailah in residence, there'd been enough abductions for one year. Edward didn't push him. Grateful as he should be for all Jeremy was doing for Olly, he could barely look at him as they bade one another goodbye in the moonlit driveway.

'I shouldn't have kept so much from you,' said Jeremy, one hand on his horse's reins, 'I realise that.'

'I don't want to hear it.'

'No,' Jeremy looked at his boots, 'no. I don't expect you do.' He sighed. 'Good luck, Bertram. I hope you find a better life in India.'

Edward had little hope of it. The Empire had never seemed more rotten to him; the only thing that could have made working out the remaining years in his commission bearable was having Olly there, and now she'd be nowhere near him.

His eyes moved to the house. He saw her framed in the candle-light, still on his bed, stare locked on his trunk. He thought of all she had ahead of her: her grief, the long voyage with Clara's boys, months – possibly longer – in England, with only Ada and the nanny for support.

He didn't know how he could bring himself to leave her to it. He wished he could see another way.

Jeremy held out his hand.

After a pause, Edward shook it.

'I'm sorry, old man,' Jeremy said.

'Of course you are,' said Edward.

They were all so bloody sorry.

Tom and Imogen arrived as they were about to leave, Fadil too, back from delivering the Bedouin mother to her sons. He drove them all in the carriage to the harbour. They arrived as the last stragglers were boarding.

They stood in a cluster on the swarming quayside. Tom made to take Edward's hand, then, apparently thinking better, pulled him into a brief embrace. 'Take care,' he said, with a slap to Edward's back. 'I wish you happiness, Bertram, only happiness.'

Imogen stepped forwards. She stood on tiptoes to kiss Edward, and whispered something in his ear. Olivia had no idea what it was, only that it made Edward smile slowly and say, 'Thank you.'

Edward turned to Fadil. He spoke to him in Arabic. Fadil's eyes glinted beneath his bandages, bright in the darkness. Edward squeezed his shoulder, Fadil nodded. He looked horribly small, withered, and very, very sad.

He backed away. Everyone did. And Olivia and Edward were alone, silent, only inches from one another in the cool night air.

'Five minutes,' came a yell, 'that's five minutes left to board.'

Edward looked down at Olivia; she ran her hand around his cheek, her thumb down his jaw. There, still there, real and warm and hers. It seemed impossible that in less than a minute he no longer would be.

The sirens sounded, whistles blew.

'Go,' she said, 'please.'

More whistles. *Final call.*

'This is only for now,' he said. 'I'll come for you, I swear it.'

He kissed her, then he turned. He left.

By the time he reached the deck, the detail of his face was impossible to make out. Olivia could only imagine the bass of his voice. She raised her fingers, he raised his: a mock salute

Goodbye.

*

Imogen held her tight for the carriage ride home. Tom sat opposite them. They said very little. It was as they were approaching Ramleh that Imogen broke the silence and told Olivia she wanted to go with her to England. 'I don't think I can stand to be here, you see. And I watched you go away once, all those years ago ... ' She shook her head. 'I ... Well, I can't let you face anything more alone.'

'We neither of us want you to,' said Tom.

Imogen bit her lip. 'Is it all right, darling? Would you like it?'

Olivia didn't answer straight away. She thought of Imogen's whisper, Edward's smile. Tears of relief pressed in her throat. She looked from Imogen's anxious face to Tom's sad one. 'Of course I'd like it,' she said. 'Of course I would.'

The next morning, whilst Ada supervised the trunks being loaded into the carriage, Olivia went to the stables. The air was sweet and warm, dusty in the morning sun. She stroked the camel, thinking of Jahi in his hopeless cell, awaiting his hanging, condemned for so much. And she didn't know, she still couldn't say, whether she blamed him for any of it or not. She knew only that she didn't want him to die and that he was going to anyway because she couldn't save his life as he had saved hers.

She turned to Bea, pressing her lips to her neck. 'Goodbye, old friend,' she said. 'Fadil's going to look after you, the camel too. You're all moving to the Carters'. Tom will keep you safe and happy.' Dinah twirled around her legs, Olivia scooped her up, holding her warm, purring body tight, and rested her forehead against Bea. She closed her eyes, remembering again that day Edward had brought Bea home, the strength of him as he helped her into the saddle. Her legs, they'd shaken. 'Don't be afraid,' he'd said, smiling, 'it's such a waste of energy.'

Olivia took a deep breath.

There was one more thing she had to do before she left.

The cemetery was deserted. The mound of Clara's body was marked by a small wooden cross. Flowers lay all over it, Ralph's treasured book of Sherlock Holmes stories too, and a single pomegranate. Olivia couldn't think who would have put it there.

She cleared a space near the top of the grave, where she assumed Clara's face, her heart, must be. She placed on that space a cluster of white roses, and some oranges. *Try one, Livvy, they're positively bursting with sunshine.* Slowly, Olivia knelt and picked one up. She stared at it, then removed her gloves. Fingers shaking, she peeled the skin. She raised one juicy segment to her lips. The flavour flooded her mouth.

It transported her to another place, another time. She nearly choked as the force of the images hit her: a ship's cabin, herself sitting on a bottom bunk, a porthole to her left. She could smell coal, feel the sway of the waves. And there was a gangly girl kneeling before her, all dressed in black. She had yellow hair, round freckled cheeks, and an orange in her hand.

It was a glimpse, nothing more. But it *was* of Clara.

She held the orange out. 'I've taken off all the white bits. Eat, Livvy, please. I can't let you get sick, we're all each other's got now.' Her child's eyes widened, so like little Gus's, 'You mustn't be scared, Livvy. I'll look after you, I promise.'

Olivia heard her voice. She doubled over at the sound, and the pain of that stolen promise. A sob wrenched through her. Then another. The tears, at last, came very easily. She didn't even try to fight them.

They stood out on deck as the ship left dock. It was full of tourists waving goodbye to Pompey's pillar, the pyramids, and the distant swell of the sands. They pushed through them, Olivia holding Ralph's hand, Sofia pushing Gus's perambulator, and Ada and Imogen following, parasols over them all. They reached the back railings just as the ship pulled away.

'Look,' said Ralph, pointing at Jeremy on the cobbled quayside, 'Papa.' His arm pumped.

Jeremy's did too.

Ralph's chubby cheeks tried for a smile. Olivia pulled him close.

She kissed his head. She felt Imogen's arm come around her own healing waist.

The ship picked up steam, furry wake forming in the deep, dark Mediterranean. Olivia watched Jeremy become smaller and smaller, and the shoreline of Alexandria disappear from view. And she realised that she was glad, so very glad, that she was where she was. It broke her in two that Clara wasn't with them, but it was right that she had come. For Ralph and Gus would always be loved, they would never be alone. And in spite of everything, Olivia thought Clara would be jolly relieved about that.

You mustn't be scared, Clara. I'll look after them, I promise.

Epilogue

London, January 1893

The frigid air struck Olivia's throat as she let the door of 5 Dunlop Place swing shut behind her. She felt her nose turn red in the instant. She looked to the sky, white with winter, clouds cushioning the horizon.

She paused by Dinah's milk bowl on the front step, and looked back through the frosted panes of the drawing room window. A fire burned in the grate; the Christmas tree bowed beneath faux sugarcanes and sledges, wilted and ready to retire. Ada said they should have taken it down days before, that it was unlucky not to, but Ralph had wanted to leave it up.

Olivia smiled through the window at him, cross-legged beneath the tree, winding a jack-in-the-box for Gus. She never had been able to bring herself to send him off to board, but had enrolled him at a nearby prep school in Maida Vale instead. He looked up, as though sensing her gaze on him, and pulled Gus's chubby two-year-old arm into a wave, making Gus grin toothily.

With his round toddler's cheeks, Gus was looking more and more like Clara.

It hurt, just a little less with each day, to see that in him.

Olivia waved back, she turned to go. Her foot crunched on iced paper. It was the day's broadsheets, front page still dominated by the story that had shocked but not surprised her. That unsolved shooting at point-blank range of the illustrious businessman, Mr Alistair Sheldon, and the long-serving man of law, Commissioner Archibald Wilkins, on the steps of Draycott's restaurant, Alexandria, back in December. *Could it be*, pondered Giles Morton, *that these seemingly motiveless murders are tied to the yet ill-explained abductions and violence of July '91, that other Draycott's incident?*

Olivia thought it more than likely. Imogen, who had returned to Alex just before Christmas, did too. *I doubt we'll ever find out though*, she wrote. *Wilkins had protégés, there's many left to keep everything hush-hush, carry on in his image. It's business as usual here. I'm growing so tired of it. And I miss Clara, very much, I miss all of you. I've been talking to Tom about whether we might move too.*

Imogen's weren't the only letters Olivia received. Jeremy wrote often, asking to be updated on news of the boys. *I'll come and visit soon, it's proving much harder than I'd hoped to tie everything up with the business, although it might be easier now Alistair's share of it all has defaulted to you. Alistair had told me he'd planned to remove you from his will, when you stayed on in England. I suppose he never had the chance. Funny how things work out.* Nailah, for her own incomprehensible reasons, sent the occasional missive, words of her new village home, her marriage to Kafele: *We're trying to be happy, to forget, but he's angry, so angry,* the children, *healthy and growing, God smiles,* her mother, *she lives with us now, she tries to help.*

Post came from further east too, from Beatrice, married to a sergeant-major, and more often from Edward. Precious envelopes that took too long to arrive and bore the scent of spices.

It had been a month since he'd last written. There'd only been a wire since. That wire . . .

Olivia tucked her chin into the scarf Ada and Sofia had knitted her for Christmas, smiled into the wool, and set off towards Oxford Street. Her heels clicked on the frozen pavements as she hastened to the restaurant she normally frequented with the eldest of Edward's five sisters, Danielle. ('He's told me to watch over you,' Danielle had said the first afternoon they'd met, not long after Olivia and the boys had returned nearly eighteen months ago. 'Make sure you eat enough cake and so on.')

Olivia dodged a broken cobble. She stood back as a hansom cab passed, then crossed the road. Wind blew from rooftops, lifting the frost. She picked up her pace. It was as she approached the restaurant that the clouds bowed and the first snowflakes started to fall.

She looked to the sky, the flakes formed grey whispers in her eyes. She opened her mouth, breathed it in. Life, *life*. A sense of anticipation tightened in the pit of her stomach.

Slowly, she dropped her gaze. She turned to the restaurant porch. He was there, at last, right there, gazing directly at her . . .

. . . He could hardly stop himself looking.

Acknowledgements

There are so many people I want to thank for their help and support, it's hard to know where to begin. Let me start though with my fabulous agent, Becky Ritchie, for loving Olly and Edward as much I do, understanding the book I wanted to write, all the time spent helping me get there, and for being such a wonderful champion. Becky, I couldn't have done it without you! Thank you too to Melissa Pimentel, and everyone at Curtis Brown – I'm very grateful for all you do.

Huge thanks also to the team at Little, Brown, I feel incredibly lucky to be working with you. Manpreet Grewal, thank you for loving this story in the first place, your amazing editorial insight, and all you have done to help transform it from word document into an actual real-life book. Thank you too to Thalia Proctor for all your work on editing, to Liz Hatherell for brilliant copy editing, and to Emma Williams and Stephie Melrose for everything you do on PR and marketing.

I have some wonderful friends I want to thank too: Kerry Fisher, for all your wise words and friendship over the years – it has meant the world and I honestly don't know where I'd be without you; Iona Grey, for so much, but most of all for your unswerving belief and support when I needed it most; Amanda Jennings, for long lunches, literary quizzes and keeping it fun; Tracy Buchanan, for a great deal – not least our writerly chats over tea and cake with our children; Dinah Jefferies, for believing you would hold a book of mine in your hands one day (I am so very glad you were right);

Amanda Munden, for being a champion cheerleader from the word go; Chloe and Jon Coker, Nicole Nortmann, Hannah Clark, Tim Moore-Barton, Chloe Archard and Jane O'Connell, for being early readers and always being so supportive.

Finally, so many thanks go to my family. To my parents, who read endless drafts and re-drafts and never stopped believing I could do it – I can't tell you how grateful I am to have you. To my mother-in-law, Heather, for reading early versions and offering such great insight. To my sister, Chloe, for all the pickings up and dusting back offs again. To my husband, Matt, for being by my side in everything and never ceasing to *know* I could do this. And last, but never least, to my children, for so much more than I can put into words, and reminding me every day that if I'm going to practise what I preach, I had better never give up.

Did you love *Beneath A Burning Sky*?
Read on for an exclusive extract from Jenny Ashcroft's next novel
Island In The East

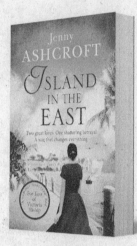

'*Island in the East* is that rare thing: a dual narrative novel in
which both strands of the story are as engaging and compelling
as each other ... it's impossible to put this book down'

Kate Riordan

Singapore, October 1897

The heat in the bedroom was solid, damp and close, trapped by the shutters. The windows hadn't been opened in days. Mae's skin was slick with sweat; the moisture coated her neck, itched her scalp. She could feel it running beneath her gown. Outside, cicadas screeched in the garden and in the jungle beyond; distant monkeys cawed. She listened mutely to the night-time cacophony, struggling with the thought that she'd never hear any of it again. It was only a matter of hours now, and she'd be gone – not as she'd hoped, not as she'd planned – but away, far from this place, this island. Her breaths quickened in the heavy air. *Not alone*, she reminded herself, and placed her hand on her stomach. *Not alone.*

It was almost time.

Her eyes darted to the shadow of her bureau, the stack of papers on top of it: travel documents, certificates ... bank notes too, from Alex's safe. She was terrified there wouldn't be enough. There had to be enough. Her damp brow creased in familiar panic that there mightn't be. It was too late though to do anything about it.

She wanted to go now. It was the waiting that was hard. But she had to see Harriet first. She'd finally worked out what it was that she must do. Her fingers curled in anxiety, gathering the bedsheets beneath her. *Just hang on. She'll come.*

She'll come.

An hour passed. She fretted about where David was, what he was thinking. She studied the door, and willed Harriet to come through it. *Come.*

Come.

And then, at last, a noise in the silent house. She'd have known it anywhere: Harriet's tread, creaking on the floorboards. She didn't lift her gaze from the door as she waited. She kept completely still. *Hang on.* The handle turned, and the door opened, bringing candlelight and her twin sister in.

She met Harriet's eyes, identical to hers in every way. She watched as they widened, filling with desperate alarm.

'Oh God,' she said. 'Oh, Mae.'

Chapter One

London, January 1940

Ivy paused outside the door to the surgery waiting room and took a slow breath. She dropped her eyes to her feet, her brogues on the hospital linoleum, the way her nylons crinkled at the ankle. *You can do this*. She straightened her naval uniform jacket and made her way in.

The waiting room was silent. There was an oak door on the far side with a brass plaque reading, DOCTOR MICHAEL GREGORY, MB CHB, MD, CCT, FRCPSYCH. Faded armchairs lined the other two walls, a desk the third. A receptionist, about the same age as Ivy – mid-twenties or thereabouts – sat at the desk. She had a battered copy of *Time* magazine spread out before her, a cigarette in her hand.

She smiled up at Ivy. 'Hello.'

'Hello. I'm Ivy Harcourt, here to see Doctor Gregory.'

'Yes, of course.' The woman waved her cigarette at the oak door. 'He won't be long, he's just finishing with a sailor back from the Med. Take a seat.'

Ivy lowered herself into the chair closest to her, feeling the springs creak. She crossed her legs, and then uncrossed them again.

The receptionist eyed her curiously. 'Cup of tea?'

'No, thank you,' said Ivy.

'Cocoa?'

'I'm fine, really.'

'Coffee, then? We've got Camp.'

Ivy shook her head. 'Thank you.' She couldn't imagine drinking anything.

The woman continued to appraise her. 'All right, are you?' she asked at length.

'Apparently not,' Ivy forced a laugh. It sounded horribly nervous. 'I suppose that's why I'm here.'

The woman opened her mouth, clearly ready to ask more, but then the oak door opened. A pale boy in sailors' whites slunk out, head bowed. Another man followed. Doctor Gregory, Ivy presumed, from his tweed suit and capable air. He wore spectacles, a bright red handkerchief in his pocket. Ivy wondered how often he offered it to his patients.

He turned to her. He had kind eyes.

'Officer Harcourt,' he said, 'do come in.'

The office was small, heated by a gas burner. It had a mahogany desk, two more armchairs, and a single window which was or so crossed with brown tape to protect it from bomb blasts. A rug covered the linoleum floor and a vase of plastic flowers stood on the desk. Someone had tried to make it homely.

Doctor Gregory settled Ivy into one of the armchairs then sat himself in the other. He reached across to his desk and pulled a file from it, a pipe too. He asked her if she minded him smoking. (She didn't.)

'So,' he said. 'You've rather been through it.'

Ivy cleared her throat. 'I'm ... ' her voice cracked. She tried again. 'I'm all right.'

'Your ribs aren't causing you any more pain?'

'No.'

'And no more breathing difficulties?' He made a show of checking his notes. Ivy thought it might be for her benefit, to make her feel less like he knew everything about her already. 'You had a nasty infection from the dust,' he said. 'You were buried for nine hours, I see.'

'I'm fine now.'

He gave her a troubled smile. 'But you've been referred to me.'

She swallowed, wishing she'd asked for a glass of water earlier. 'Yes.'

'Because the doctor who's been treating you since the accident,' another glance at the notes, 'Doctor Myer, he doesn't think you're fit for service.'

'No.'

'Do you think you're fit?'

'I want to go back to work.'

'Hmmm,' Doctor Gregory said. 'Doctor Myer is concerned about,' he flicked a page in the file, adjusted his spectacles, 'recurrent and acute attacks of claustrophobia coupled with severe shock.' He looked over at Ivy. 'Is that right?'

Ivy forced herself to hold his gaze. 'I'm fine.'

His eyes crinkled regretfully. 'He thinks not. And I'm told that you've requested a transfer from your old post in Camberwell. That you lodged the request from hospital?'

'That's right.'

'You were caught by that bomb very near the bunker you worked at, weren't you?'

'Yes.'

'And you'd been badly shocked at work, earlier that evening?'

'Yes.' She had to force the word out.

'You don't want to return there after all that happened that night?'

'Would you?'

'We're not here to talk about me.'

Ivy shifted in her seat. The room was so hot.

'Ivy,' Gregory said, 'I want you to tell me, in your own words, why you can't face returning to Camberwell.'

Sweat itched beneath her woollen uniform. She gestured at the heater. 'Do you mind if we turn that down?'

He set his pipe on his arm rest, got up and crossed the room to the heater. He looked back at Ivy as he knelt to turn the dial. 'I know this must be difficult for you,' he said. 'You don't want to be here. No one ever does. I try not to take it personally.' He smiled. It was a joke. Ivy tried to summon a smile too. 'But for me to help you heal,' he said, 'I need to ask you these questions. I want you to trust me, to talk to me about everything that's happened. This will all be much easier if you do. Does that sound all right?'

'Yes,' said Ivy, even though she wasn't sure it did.

'Good.' He reclaimed his seat, turned the pages of his file. 'Let's start with something a bit easier. When did you join the Naval Service?'

'At the start of the war.'

'Why the Navy?'

'My old tutor suggested it.'

'Because of your languages?'

'Yes. He knew they needed people who spoke German. He thought of me.'

'And you're a listener.' Gregory smiled enquiringly. 'What is that, exactly?'

Ivy looked at his file. 'You don't have it written down?'

'Humour me.'

Her back prickled. She heard Gregory's words again. *You'd been badly shocked, earlier that evening.* She knew where he was steering her. 'I'm not meant to talk about what I do,' she said. 'Walls have ears.'

His lips twitched. 'A valiant try, Ivy. But the only ears here are mine, and I've signed the Official Secrets Act. So . . . ' He nodded, indicating that she should go on.

'We eavesdrop,' she said guardedly, 'on radio signals.'

'Who's "we"?'

'WRENS, men from Naval Intelligence. There are some WAAFS at our station as well.'

'In Camberwell?'

'Yes.'

'And who do you eavesdrop on?'

'Ships, communications coming out of Germany . . .'

'Pilots mainly though, yes?'

'Yes,' said Ivy slowly. 'At our station.'

'British pilots?'

'We hear them sometimes. But we're mainly interested in what the Luftwaffe are saying.'

'Why?'

'They give things away when they talk,' she said. 'About where their ships are below. We send that to the admiralty. Then their flying course and altitude. It helps Fighter Command know where to send the spits to intercept them.'

'Very clever.' He sucked on his pipe. 'Is that all you hear? The co-ordinates and the targets?'

'No,' she said carefully.

'No?'

'No, the men talk about other things too.'

'Such as?'

'The moon,' she said, knowing it wasn't what he wanted from her, 'how beautiful it looks on the sea.'

'It must do, up there.'

'Yes.'

'What else do you hear?'

She felt like she was being circled, backed into a corner.

'The pilots talk to us,' she said, still evading him.

'Talk to you?'

'They've guessed we're listening.'

Gregory smiled. 'And what do they say, Ivy?'

'They say things like, *Guten Abend, meine Fräulein. Deutschland aufruf.* It means, *Germany calling.*'

'Yes, I speak some German myself.' He looked at his notes. 'You studied at Cambridge?'

'Yes.'

'Japanese too?'

'Yes.'

He glanced up at her. 'I love languages.'

She smiled tightly, tensed for his next question.

'And what do our boys say?' Gregory asked. 'In their spits.'

'Lots of things.'

'Give me an example.'

She took a breath. '*Tally-ho,*' she said. '*Watch your altitude, your wing. Bandits, ten-o'clock.*' She raised her shoulders. 'They say so much.'

'And,' his eyes became pained, 'occasionally you hear them die.'

Even though she'd been braced for it, she flinched.

'Ivy?'

'Yes,' she said.

'How do you feel, when you hear them die?'

'Upset of course. Very upset.'

'Anything else?'

'I think of the people they love, who love them. I wonder if they know what's happening.'

He grimaced sadly, like he understood.

There was a short silence. She wondered hopefully if he was going to leave it there.

But, 'You heard someone you care about die, didn't you?' he asked. 'The last time you were at the station, barely an hour before you were caught by that bomb.'

She stared.

'Ivy?'

'I don't want to talk about that,' she said.

'I think it will help you to do so.'

'I want to forget about it.'

'I know,' he said, 'but I don't think you can. Not until you face it.'

She said nothing.

'You can't run from things, Ivy, you'll be doing it your whole life otherwise.'

She looked at her brogues. There was a scuff on her right toe. She should polish it.

'Doctor Myer told me that in hospital you woke screaming Felix's name in the night, and that you needed to have a light to sleep. He wrote here,' Gregory tapped his file, 'that your claustrophobia after being buried was so bad that you never wanted to go to the shelter, you begged to be allowed to stay on the ward instead.'

Ivy felt her cheeks flame.

'No one's judging you,' said Gregory, 'except perhaps you.'

'I'm all right now,' she said. 'Really.'

'You don't need a light to sleep any more?'

Ivy's flush deepened.

'How are your nights now you're home, Ivy? How are you when you go to the shelter?'

She said nothing. But she pictured herself, trembling like a child in terror beneath the corrugated roof of her gran's Anderson, waiting for the next bomb that would find her.

'Why don't you want to return to Camberwell?' Gregory asked.

'I,' she began, 'I . . .'

'What worries you more?' Gregory asked gently. 'The idea of going back to where you were caught by that bomb, or to where you heard such a horrendous thing happen to your beau?'

'He wasn't my beau.'

'No?'

'No. He only used to be.'

'Perhaps,' Gregory said, 'that made it worse?'

Ivy pulled at her collar. 'That heater's still so warm.'

'I can't imagine how traumatic it must have been,' Gregory said, 'to hear something like that, I really can't. And then to nearly be killed yourself, the very same night.'

She turned towards the steamed-up window. It was getting dark. Four o'clock, and it was already almost night.

'Why are you so keen to go back to work, Ivy? What do you think you'll gain by taking another posting?'

'I'll be able to move on.'

'Fail,' Gregory said.

Startled, Ivy said, 'Excuse me?'

'You won't move on,' he said. 'You can't until you've processed what's happened.'

'I have processed it.'

'You won't even speak about it.'

She looked again at the window.

'What's bothering you outside, Ivy?'

'It's getting dark,' she said.

'And?'

'I don't like to go out in the dark any more.' The admission was out before she could stop it.

He sighed. 'Go on then, go home.'

That surprised her. 'You'll certify me fit, authorise my transfer?' It seemed too easy, too good to be true.

'Of course I won't,' Gregory said. 'I'll see you tomorrow. Come at one, we'll have more time that way.'

She was there by five to, determined to do better.

'Back again?' asked the receptionist.

'I'm afraid so,' said Ivy.

The woman looked at her, musing. 'Your hair's lovely and dark, isn't it?' She raised her magazine, eyes moving from a picture of Vivien Leigh to Ivy. She frowned. 'No,' she said, 'no. I thought there might be a likeness but ... ' She shook her head, disappointed.

Ivy found herself apologising.

The woman told her it was all right. 'Mind me asking what's wrong with you?'

'I'm fine.'

'Are you?'

'Yes.'

The receptionist sighed. 'They all say that.'

The fire was on low in Gregory's office that day. It had started raining since Ivy had arrived at the hospital; the drops slid down the windowpane.

'You're living with your grandmother at the moment,' Gregory said. 'Is that right?'

'Yes.'

'And before that?'

'I was in a billet with some of the other girls at the station, near Camberwell.'

'Do you miss them, the other girls?'

'They call on me quite often.'

'Oh yes?'

'Yes,' she said. 'They want to know when my convalescence is going to be up.'

'Do they?' He almost smiled. 'Do you ever go out with them, the girls?'

'For tea sometimes. They've asked me to go to a dance next week.'

'That sounds like a good idea.'

'Does it?' Ivy wasn't so sure.

Gregory studied her. 'Do you like it at your grandmother's?'

'Yes, of course.'

'She raised you, didn't she?'

'She did.'

'Are you comfortable talking about why?'

Ivy wasn't, but, 'My parents both died in the last war.'

'That's very sad.'

She wasn't going to let him shake her, not with this. 'It is,' she said.

'How did they die?'

'My father was killed in Mesopotamia. My mother caught influenza just after I was born. She was an Australian VAD.'

'She's buried here?'

'Yes.'

'Do you visit her grave?'

Ivy did, often. Her gran used to take her every month as a child; together they'd show her drawings Ivy had done at school, tell her about trips they'd made to the seaside.

'Ivy?'

'Yes, I visit her grave.'

'And your father's? Have you ever been to see that?'

'I'm not really sure why we're talking about this.'

Gregory said nothing.

Ivy sighed. 'We went once,' she said. 'We travelled out there.' It was the only time Ivy had ever seen her gran cry. *My boy,* she'd said as they'd stood over the simple wooden cross marked CAPTAIN BEAU ALEXANDER HARCOURT, ROYAL LONDON GUARDS. 1898–1918. *My boy.* 'There were so many graves there,' said Ivy, 'it was awful.'

'Did you think of your parents, Ivy, when you were buried by that bomb?'

Ivy winced. So that was why they were talking about this. 'No,' she said. 'I didn't.'

'Not at all?'

'I don't think so.'

'What did you think about? You were down there for a very long time.'

Her eyes flicked to the window. The rain was really coming down. She didn't have an umbrella.

'Nine hours is a long time to be trapped beneath a building,' Gregory said.

'It is,' said Ivy.

'You don't want to talk about it?'

'No,' she said, 'not really.'

'I'm going to ask you to anyway.'

'I had a feeling you might.'

'Ivy, would you look at me?'

Slowly, dragging her gaze from the raindrops, she did as he asked. He peered from behind his spectacles. He had a blue kerchief in his blazer today.

'You left your shift early,' Gregory began. He didn't check his notes. 'It was just after ten in the evening.' He sounded like he was reading the opening pages of a story. 'You'd just heard Felix get shot down.'

'Yes,' she said quietly.

'You'd been sent home.'

'Yes.'

'Because you were very upset.'

'Of course I was upset.'

'The All Clear had sounded?'

'That's right,' she said.

'It must have been very dark in the street.'

'Yes.'

'Describe it to me, Ivy.'

She adjusted her weight in the armchair. 'It was cold,' she said. 'Foggy. I didn't have my torch.'

'So you couldn't see.'

'Not clearly.' She'd stumbled, crab-like, against the building walls in the blackout. Had she been crying still? She couldn't recall. Probably.

'Where were you,' Gregory asked, 'when you heard the planes coming?'

'About halfway to the underground.'

'You weren't expecting them?'

'No. They'd snuck back over.'

'No siren?'

'Not until after they started bombing.'

'And they were bombing all around you?'

'Yes.'

'What was it like?'

She filled her cheeks with air and expelled it, remembering against her will: the blinding flashes, the cacophony and sudden heat of the flames; her terror as she ran through the fog.

'You must have been beside yourself,' Gregory said.

'I couldn't hear,' she said, 'I couldn't see.'

'You thought you were going to die?'

Ivy made a strange sound, halfway between a laugh and a sob. 'Yes,' she said, 'it felt likely.'

'What happened?'

'There was a man, he just appeared.' Her voice caught at the mention of him. 'I collided with him, nearly fell. Then, I don't know.' She closed her eyes, back there again. Why had Gregory forced her back there?

'What happened next?' he asked.

'I woke up. I was on my front. My face was pressed right down on stone. When I raised my hands,' she pulled them up a few inches to demonstrate, 'I touched stone.'

'Your ribs were broken, weren't they?'

'Yes. The man, he was called Stuart, he was on top of me. Everything was black.' *We find ourselves in a cocoon*, Stuart had whispered. *Now don't move an inch, let's not risk damaging it.* 'It never got light.' Ivy shuddered, recalling the relentless dark. 'No matter how hard I stared. It was just black.'

Gregory wrote something down.

'This man, Stuart,' he said, 'tell me about him.'

'He saved my life.' Again Ivy's voice broke.

'How?'

'He kept me calm, distracted me. He asked me so many questions, about,' she drew a deep breath, 'everything. He talked and talked, told me about his wife, his children. He stopped me breathing too fast and using all the air.'

'He did that until you were rescued?'

'No.'

'No?'

Ivy met his gaze. 'You know he didn't.'

Gregory looked back, unflinching. Ivy checked the wall clock. She'd been there more than an hour. Surely it was time to go?

Gregory said, 'How did you feel when you heard people coming to help you?'

'I thought I might be dreaming.'

'It took them a long time to get to you, didn't it?'

'Yes.'

'They nearly gave up. And you were running out of air, so it was hard to shout.'

Ivy nodded.

'Why didn't they give up, Ivy?'

'I scratched at the stones. A woman heard me.'

'Stuart didn't do anything?'

'No.'

'Why not?'

Ivy swallowed. 'You know why not.'

'What had happened to him, Ivy?'

She stared at her lap. She could feel the weight of him on her back, his head pressed into her neck. 'He'd died,' she said. 'He'd been bleeding.'

'So you were trapped in a tiny hole, with a dead man on top of you. A man who saved your life. And you'd just heard someone you cared about deeply being shot down.'

The rain pattered the windowpanes. The wall clock ticked.

'What a horrendous night that must have been, Ivy. What an awful, awful night.'

A Letter from Jenny

Firstly, I want to say a very big thank you for reading *Beneath a Burning Sky*. The characters and their stories – not to mention the setting of Alexandria itself – are so close to my heart, and it means the world that you've chosen to travel back to the 1890s and meet Olly and Edward, all the others too, and spend your time with them. I hope you enjoyed it!

If you did, I'd be so grateful if you could post a short review on Amazon or Goodreads. This will help others discover *Beneath a Burning Sky*, and, personally, I love nothing more than hearing from readers about what they thought of my book. To everyone who has already left a review – thank you, I can't tell you how much it means.

You can also contact me directly, on my Facebook page or via Twitter. I'd be so interested to know your thoughts on *Beneath a Burning Sky*. What did you make of Clara's disappearance? What did you think had happened to her? Did this change as the book progressed? And how did you feel about Olivia, and her fight to carry on in Alistair's house? How did you react to the ending? Please do get in touch!

For my next book, *Island in the East*, I've left Egypt and have travelled instead to colonial Singapore, for a story set in two eras: the Second World War, and the 1890s. I loved every minute of writing it, and hope very much you enjoy it too!

Jenny Ashcroft

Facebook: @jennyashcroftauthor

Twitter: @Jenny_Ashcroft

Dive into a breathtaking story of separation,
tragedy and fierce love . . .

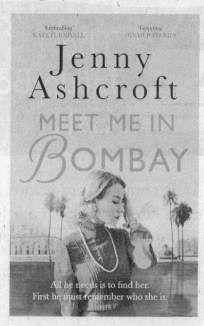

'Enthralling'
KATE FURNIVALL

'Gripping'
DINAH JEFFERIES

Jenny
Ashcroft

MEET ME IN
BOMBAY

All he needs is to find her.
First he must remember who she is.